neel

Praise for Janet Lynnford's
sweeping romances . . .

Lady Shadowhawk

"A provocative tale with intense characters and some heart-pounding twists that leave the reader wanting more."   —*Rendezvous*

"Breathtaking."   —Connie Reinhold

Lord of Lightning

"Rich in passion and intrigue. . . . A delightful romantic adventure."   —Teresa Medeiros

"Spirited. . . . An enjoyable romance with a heroine to admire."   —*Romantic Times*

Pirate's Rose

"A vivid tale of a jaded noble and an industrious young woman destined to find love."
          —Kat Martin

"Dynamic, spirited, richly detailed. . . . I expect great things from this author."
          —Linda Lael Miller

Also by Janet Lynnford

LADY SHADOWHAWK

LORD OF LIGHTNING

PIRATE'S ROSE

Firebrand Bride

Janet Lynnford

A TOPAZ BOOK

TOPAZ
Published by the Penguin Group
Penguin Putnam Inc., 375 Hudson Street,
New York, New York 10014, U.S.A.
Penguin Books Ltd, 27 Wrights Lane, London W8 5TZ, England
Penguin Books Australia Ltd, Ringwood, Victoria, Australia
Penguin Books Canada Ltd, 10 Alcorn Avenue,
Toronto, Ontario, Canada M4V 3B2
Penguin Books (N.Z.) Ltd, 182–190 Wairau Road,
Auckland 10, New Zealand

Penguin Books Ltd, Registered Offices:
Harmondsworth, Middlesex, England

First published by Topaz, an imprint of Dutton NAL,
a member of Penguin Putnam Inc.

First Printing, March, 1999
10 9 8 7 6 5 4 3 2 1

The ballad words that appear on pages 127–28 are from *The History and Poetry of the Scottish Border: Their Main Features and Relations* by John Veitch, L.L.D. Glasgow: James Maclehose, Publisher to the University, 1878, pp. 356–57.

 REGISTERED TRADEMARK—MARCA REGISTRADA

Printed in the United States of America

*This book is dedicated to
all of you
who believe in the power of love
to change the world.*

*And to Connie Rinehold,
also writing as Eve Byron,
a talented woman with a heart of gold.*

Chapter 1

Scotland, 1592

Lantern light flickered, casting grotesque shadows on the wall behind John Alexander Malcolm Graham as he knelt in the straw of the large box stall and soothed the exhausted mare lying on her side. Her swollen belly looked unnaturally bloated after her prolonged labor.

"Easy, now, Gellie. Your foal will be born soon, and all will be well." He stroked her nose gently as he forced the reassuring words from his lips. Despite the boiling desire to shout his fear and frustration, he confined his ministrations to rhythmic, soothing motions. But the mare's dark eyes, usually so bright and alert, remained unresponsive and dull with pain.

She must not die. Not his best breeding mare.

"Can't you do something for her, Robbie?" he growled at the young man sitting at her tail. "There's been no progress at all."

Robbie bowed his head, his expression twisted with anguish. "I-I dinna ken half the things the head stable man did, my lord," he stammered. "I canna see what's wrong."

"The foal should have come earlier, while Gellie was pushing. Something's holding it back," Graham muttered, angry to be reminded that his head stable man had been killed reiving two months ago. Reiving stole all the best men from his keep.

Determined to take matters into his own hands, he slid over to Gellie's hindquarters and studied the opening of the birth canal as he smoothed her velvety flank. Devil take

it, he'd never attended a problem foaling. All the ones he'd
witnessed had gone without flaw.

He probed gently with one finger and encountered something hard. Spreading the soft flesh, he discovered the tip
of a tiny hoof. That much was as it should be. Hind legs
came first.

He moved again, this time to palpitate her belly as he'd
seen old Willie do. With cautious fingertips he investigated
the outline of the foal's form. Here was the head, he
guessed, and here the creature's side. Blast it, but it seemed
perfectly normal to him.

Stymied, he sank back on his heels. Clearly, something
was gravely wrong, and if the foal wasn't born soon, the
pair would suffer through the night and mayhap into the
next day, their strength ebbing in an excruciatingly slow
death.

It bore a most unpleasant resemblance to his father's
death.

The memory flickered through Graham's mind—of his
father, Thrawn Jock Graham, stretched on the table in his
chamber, clutching his bloody side. Three years ago it had
happened, during a night of reiving when the fighting had
been particularly fierce. But the leader to all the Grahams
and their many kindred branches hadn't begged for comfort
as his end loomed near. Instead, he'd consoled his last living son.

" 'Tis the way I always intended to go, Alex. Fighting to
the last," his father had whispered as his life oozed between
his fingers and dripped to the floor.

Helpless, Graham had been sickened as his father's
strength drained away. As a youth, he'd never felt the
slightest twinge at spilling a rival's blood, but gradually the
years had changed him.

His youngest brother, Geordie, had died in a raid. How
he missed his brother's good humor and jests, even his
chasing anything in skirts. His two older brothers, jovial
and laughing, had fallen to family feuds as well, followed
by his mother, who had withered away after the death of
her three sons, as much a victim of Border violence as those
who fought. Uncles and cousins too numerous to count had
fallen, the result of what most considered no more than a

good night's work. Even Sarah Maxwell, his young bride . . .

He clenched his jaw and cut off the thought before it began. He would not think of her tonight. Her loss five years ago had been the final blow. At first he'd retaliated against the Maxwells, but his father's death two years later had shown him the futility.

To fight loss meant only more loss.

Upon becoming chief, he'd vowed to stamp out reiving. The practice had decimated his family, leaving him the last direct descendant of his line and without a son.

Now another senseless death reached with its bony white claw for his mare.

Devil take it, he would not give in so easily. He would fight for her life, in the same way he struggled for peace. Shifting position, Graham lifted the mare's chiseled head and settled it on his lap. He took up a cup and cloth, and dripped water into her mouth. No more would he accept what everyone else in his family took for granted. His father had considered it a gift to die at the hands of a rival rather than wait for old age and infirmities to carry him off.

Graham's fingers tightened on the cloth as the familiar fury bloated his veins. A gift? Or a damned waste of healthy human life?

As a lad, he'd longed to join his powerful father and grandsire on their dangerous, exciting raids. He'd labored to perfect his use of the claymore, panting for the day when he would wreak havoc on the enemy families, English or Scots alike. At fourteen, he'd proven his worth. His father had taken him reiving, and he'd served the Grahams well . . .

Until he finally understood that all he ever accomplished was death.

Not that he was afraid to fight when needed. Graham would face war for Scots honor as willingly as the next man. But daily toil should yield satisfaction and profit, not slaughter. Reiving as a profession reaped no rewards and cost more than it gained.

"Laddie, ye dinna ken the auld ways," his father had insisted as his strength waned. "Ye're not to fight the ways o' the family, ye're to uphold them. Ye're chief now. 'Tis yer place."

His place. Graham snorted in derision. He knew his place well enough. If other families insisted on violence, they would die by violence. But as a landed baron, he demanded peace of his men—the peace to cultivate fields to fruitful harvest, to raise sheep and cattle and the swift, long-legged horses so coveted in Scotland.

That had been his plan when he bred high-spirited Gellie with a fine Berber stud—to breed a colt that had his dam's endurance and his sire's speed.

In truth, the quickening of Gellie's foal had become a symbol to him—a sign of hope for life rising out of carnage, the chance to breed permanent change. But now, if he didn't do something to save the mare and foal, his dreams would crash to ruin.

Graham concentrated on drizzling the cool water into Gellie's mouth. With relief, he saw her neck muscles contract as she swallowed. As long as she could still take liquids, there was hope.

Putting aside the cup and cloth, he cradled Gellie's head in both hands and gazed into her eyes. His voice, as he spoke, was heartening and firm. "We've been through too much together, old girl. I've raised you from a filly. You can't give up now."

The gallant mare snorted softly through her nostrils in answer to his plea. Using the uncanny sixth sense he had with most horses, he heard her reply as if she'd actually spoken. And he knew she'd understood him as well.

Gently he lowered her head to the straw and rose. "Robbie, fetch me soap and a basin of very hot water. And make sure the basin is clean before you fill it."

Robbie scrambled to his feet. "What are ye gang tae do?"

Graham knelt at Gellie's tail and stroked her flank. Her flesh quivered, as if she knew his intent. "I'm going to reach inside and find out what's wrong."

Robbie eyed his chief with concern. "Yer hands are powerful big, Graham. Are ye sure ye should?"

"I won't stand by, doing nothing, and watch her die." His impotence infuriated him, as painful as a hot brand to the flesh, though it came from within, like the wound he carried from his wife's and father's death. The brown stains of his sire's life blood still marred the floor of the tower chamber, a permanent reminder of his violent end.

Graham had left the stains as a warning to his kin to keep the peace. He looked at them daily as he entered tallies into the home farm records or reviewed reports about their more distant land. He could have used his own chamber in the new wing of the castle, but he chose to occupy his father's most of the time.

None of his kin liked that part of the castle. They claimed the passage leading to the tower was haunted, though he'd never seen any signs of it.

At times he heartily wished he might see a ghost or two. The real thing would be far easier to ignore than the demons that dwelled within his own soul.

The door to the box stall creaked behind Graham, and his bailie, Arthur Johnstone, entered. "Cousin Will's at it again, Graham. I've word he's gone reiving near Carlisle."

Red-hot anger shot to Graham's brain. "By heaven, I'll kill him. When did he start out?"

"I'm no' sure. But if we hurry, we might catch him red-handed," Arthur said.

Graham swore beneath his breath with unaccustomed violence. His demented cousin had probably chosen tonight on purpose, disobeying orders when he knew Graham was busy with the mare.

Now Graham must choose . . . to leave the mare and salvage lives if he could. Or ignore Will and let the hard-won peace he'd achieved crash down on their heads.

Family duty prevailed—the nagging, insistent family that dragged him down daily into its quagmire of violence and death. No matter how he struggled, it seemed like fighting an out-of-control moorland fire, a hopeless task.

With a concerned look at Gellie and fury in his heart, he rose. He must see what he could save from the night's folly, but quickly, so he could return to the mare.

Anticipating his chief's intentions, Arthur drew a mighty claymore from its scabbard and offered the belt. "I took the liberty of asking Jasper to assemble a few men."

Graham reached for the belt and buckled it on. "My thanks. Who did Will lure into going this time?"

"The Langs, a few Mosleys, some broken men from the Debatable Land."

"Our men will be sorry when I'm finished with them. If they haven't been killed, that is." Graham hefted the claymore and fit it into the sheath on his back. He must take Will into custody swiftly before his cousin realized what was happening, he decided. "I'll be back," he whispered as he bent over the mare. "Hold on 'til then." Her ears twitched slightly in reply.

With a last caress of her soft muzzle, Graham straightened and assessed the stable lad. "Drip water into the corner of her mouth, the way you saw me do," he advised, then watched critically as Robbie emulated his earlier ministrations to the mare. "That's right. Keep it up. I'll be back as quick as ever I can." He met the young man's anxious gaze with a bracing nod of approval. Might as well give the lad some confidence, even if Graham felt none.

With the trustworthy Jasper at his heels, Graham clattered through the castle's gate. The six other men his captain had selected fell in behind.

Graham acknowledged them tersely as he drew in a lungful of night air. It smelled of sweet summer heather, reminding him that once, he would have spent such a night with his wife. Early spring was a time to worship renewal, for a man to spill his seed the way his heathen ancestors had. Instead, he must race hell-bent into the night in a mad attempt to stop a raid in progress. "Do you think he went to Devil's Gully?" he demanded of Jasper.

Jasper nodded. "What if we're too late?"

"I pray we're not." If they were, Graham knew he must order the stolen animals identified and corralled so they could be returned on the morrow. He must then negotiate settlement for the kin of those killed. He must fight for the return of peace. And he would lock up Will Mosley for a fortnight. Or mayhap for the rest of his life.

They were indeed too late. Graham found Will at Devil's Gully, the herd of stolen horses and cattle he had reived seething in the moonlight as their restless hooves churned the turf to mud. Neither the chill night nor the heavy rain earlier had daunted Will's incessant taste for reiving, Graham noted, as he halted on the granite outcropping that overlooked the cleft in the land.

From his superior vantage point, he surveyed the shadowy herd and was reminded that this fertile crescent had been vacant for months. How hard he had labored to maintain peace along the West Border March. Blast Will for destroying it again.

But Will would be punished. As the family head, Graham intended to see to it, though he must pretend only mild displeasure until they arrived back at Castle Graham. Then, when Will least expected it, he would overpower his cousin and lock him away.

Signaling his guard, he pointed out the clump of men below that had to include his cousin. "Bring him to me. Tell him we have no quarrel if he'll not start a fight."

"What o' the others? They've disobeyed orders as well," Jasper growled, clearly thinking the other reivers might spot their chief and slip away.

Graham snorted in deprecation. "They would never be here but for Will. One of you bring him. The rest stay out of sight."

Minutes later, as his flame-haired cousin pulled his horse to a halt beside him, Graham confronted him with a stern gaze. "What the devil do you think you're about, Will, reiving after I had expressly forbidden it? How many are dead?"

Will grinned broadly and avoided the final question. He looked feverish with the night's excitement, his eyes wild in the torchlight. "Ye never tried to stop me when yer faither was alive," he said. "Nor did ye refuse that mare I brought ye, the one ye're so powerful fond of."

"She wasn't taken in a raid, and you know it. She was compensation granted to us for a Maxwell raid," Graham growled.

" 'Tis all the same," Will taunted. "If I hadn't raided the Maxwells, they wouldna have raided back."

Graham longed to leap on his cousin and pummel him with both fists. They had fought often in their youth, settling their differences with split lips and blackened eyes. But he couldn't risk a show of choler yet. "How many are dead?" he demanded again.

"None ye'll miss." Will was uncaring and insolent.

Graham held his voice level. "I take that to mean you lost one or two Langs." He couldn't pretend to be sorry.

Most of the males in that particular family branch had persistently defied his orders to abandon reiving. "Any more?"

Will's grin widened, full of confidence this time. "Nay, coz. Tonight is all gain, and ye're to have the prize. A stallion fit for a god." He scanned the restless animals below, then pointed. "There."

Sorry to know men had died but relieved it wasn't more, Graham condescended to look. He would not be distracted from punishing Will, but he always spared a second to look over a prize animal, whether he intended to keep it or not.

At the edge of the herd, a magnificent stallion galloped, head flung up, mane streaming in the night wind. Like a shimmer of black smoke beneath the light of the moon, he raced flat out, legs a blur. All other movement whittled to nothing in comparison, as if only the stallion moved. The animal was incredible.

Amazed at the sight, Graham nudged his mount forward for a better view.

Behind the stallion loped one of Will's men, clearly intending to capture the beast when he tired or was cornered, whichever came first. Of course he couldn't escape the gully. Graham knew Will's men had blockaded the south end.

Scarcely acknowledging his pursuer's presence, the panicked stallion tossed his head and raced on, as if to say he would escape, despite their plans.

In that moment, Graham wanted that horse. Just as he'd wanted Sarah Maxwell to wife the day he'd first seen her. Just as he'd wanted to rebuild part of Castle Graham from the ground up after it was burned.

When he wanted something, he usually got it. Though Will's transgression tonight outraged him, though Graham would return all the beasts in the gully to their rightful owners, he craved the stallion. The magnificent creature dropped like a spark of interest into his dull life. The sizzle of flame sprang to life within him, a minute breath of warmth in his otherwise cold breast. How had another Borderer come to possess such a find? And how much gold would he require in exchange for the beast?

Before Graham could speculate on an answer, a sharp whistle rang through the gully. He squinted as another

horse appeared, racing after the stallion. Its rider brandished a flaming torch.

Will squinted also, craning his neck to see around Graham. "Who the devil is that?"

"Whoever it is, he's a damned fool to ride so fast," Graham said. The gully was riddled with holes that could break
a horse's leg, although that was undoubtedly the reason for
the torch.

The rider drew nearer their vantage point, then flashed
by, trailing light like a shooting star.

Graham glimpsed a slim, willowy female, skirts billowing
in the wind, a long braid streaming out behind.

Damnation. It was a lass.

A lass like a firebrand, as daring as the torch that roared
in her hand.

"What the hell is a woman doing here? Bring her to me
at once," he cursed aloud, incensed at the intrusion of a
female on a reiver's raid.

But before Will could move, the girl's mare gained on
Will's man and passed him, then worked on closing the gap
between her and the stallion.

Once more her piercing whistle reverberated off the gully
walls, startling and shrill. The stallion checked his pace in
mid-stride. Ears pricked forward, he allowed the gray horse
to overtake him until they ran side by side, their legs a blur
of motion by light of the moon.

Graham would have sworn the beast was green—young,
untrained, and still partially wild. But without question, the
frightened stallion had responded to the girl's signal. He
could never have been overtaken otherwise. The long legs
and deep chest, the perfectly chiseled head and muscular
shoulders, shouted his obvious capacity for speed.

Uncanny. And unsettling. The stallion's response to the
lass was both.

The two horses raced neck to neck now. With a swift
movement, the lass suddenly threw away her torch and
bundled up her skirts. What madness was this? Squinting
at the galloping trio, Graham saw her swing both legs to
the left side of her mount and balance. The two horses
matched strides, as if they knew what was expected. Could
she possibly intend to change steeds?

Graham grimaced at the insanity. She would fall and be

trampled beneath the pounding hooves. She must be more crazed than Cousin Will.

As if to defy his certainty, she leaped. She straddled the black and settled in place with unerring precision. Girl and stallion merged into one as she bent over his neck, her face hidden in the smoke of his mane. They raced toward the far end of the gully where, Graham realized with sudden concern, without reins or bit to guide him, the horse would surely swerve as he encountered the sheer rock wall. The lass would lose her seat.

Yet once again, she performed miracles. Apparently in response to her touch, the animal slowed to a collected canter, then turned and bore her back the way they had come.

Graham knew she was trouble. A lass like a firebrand. A lass as at home on a horse as on her own two feet.

Yet her stallion raised an interest in him that had been dead for five long years, ever since he had lost Sarah and nothing had mattered anymore.

Graham considered his next move as the lass recovered the dappled mare and halted the two lathered animals. They looked exhausted. The mare's head hung low. The splendid stallion's flanks heaved while his rider scanned the gully as if searching for a way out.

In a moment she would realize her escape was blocked, her horses too tired to attempt flight. She'd been mad to slip past Will's men and enter the gully, though plainly she'd dared it to recover her horse. He examined the gray's equipment, searching for clues of her origin but unable to decipher anything given the distance and lack of light.

If the woman was trouble, the stallion was an enigma. Where could she have gotten so magnificent an animal? How could she, a female, have trained him so well?

Will chuckled, as if he wondered the same thing and intended to learn the answer straight away. With a jangle of metal harness, he swung his horse's head toward the steep descent to the gully floor, a diabolical smile of anticipation on his lips.

"Stop where you are, Will. You'll not kidnap her," Graham ordered, recognizing that smile.

Will halted obediently. "Verra well, keep the honor to

yersel'." He bowed with mock deference as Graham
passed. "After ye, Graham," he taunted.

Graham smoldered and said nothing. His cousin, for all
his foibles, knew him too well. The wish to claim the prize
stallion was strong within him, though he would resist. He
would buy the horse instead. Without question, the lass
would sell him. Any reluctance he vowed to overcome.

But as he reined in his mount before the stallion, his
gaze was drawn inexplicably to the rider rather than the
horse. By the light of Jasper's torch, he saw she was older
than he'd had imagined, mayhap all of twenty some years.
She sat the stallion with regal posture, straight backed and
defiant, the lift of her head graceful and proud.

Was the prize the stallion or the lass?

Or both?

As if echoing his thoughts, Will leaned closer and whispered, "Ye might reconsider, coz. She would bring many
pounds sterling if ye negotiate ransom. 'Twould give ye
enough to buy that new seed wheat ye want for the south
fields."

"I told you, no," Graham grunted, amazed that Will even
remembered his plans for the south fields, though it didn't
warm his heart. He'd learned that Will collected information only to serve his own purposes, and those seldom ben-
efited the surname.

"Then dinna ransom her," Will's tone was flippant.
"Keep her *and* the horse. She'll no doubt make good bed
sport."

She was indeed bonny. Fine, heavy hair, glossy by torchlight, framed her face, except for the wayward strands that
floated loose, refusing to stay in her braid. She had a lush
mouth that hinted at sensuality, but he read stubbornness
there as well, as if she were used to getting her way.

He couldn't abide headstrong women and refused to tolerate them. It was difficult enough living with headstrong
men. He had more than his share of quarrels to control.

"Who are you?" he demanded. "Did you train this
horse yourself?"

She twitched slightly, as if startled by his unexpected interest in her horse yet trying to hide it. "Aye, I trained
him." She lifted her chin haughtily. "I saw him born and
worked with him from a colt. This is his dam."

Her accent immediately identified her as English. Without a trace of civility, he scrutinized her. "What are you doing in Border country alone?"

"I have inherited some land and intend to claim it. Not that it's any affair of yours." Her brusqueness equaled his.

So she had come to claim a piece of land. Fascinating. If he judged rightly, she would have difficulties, an Englishwoman trying to tame wild Border land. Intrigued that she offered this information but failed to give her name, he assessed her clothing. Good woolen cloth and a quality cut to her cloak and kirtle indicated a refined lady. So did the leather boots peeping from beneath her skirts. But no lady wore a full kirtle skirt to hide the fact that she rode astride. She spurned convention.

She also stared back at him, wide-eyed and defiant, despite his unquestionably rude perusal of her person. She would be unruly and impossible to control, like Will.

There the resemblance ended. She had a soft femininity that contrasted delightfully with her amazing control over the powerful stallion. Reed slim, she sat the massive horse, one dainty hand holding the reins of the dappled mare, the other twined in the stallion's black mane. His gaze locked on those delicate fingers, and he forgot her frailty as a new idea formed in his mind.

Small, delicate hands skilled at controlling a powerful stallion might be capable of other things . . . of reaching into tight spots . . .

He thought of Gellie and her fruitless labor. His gaze dropped to his own, large hands, then returned to assess hers. Would she be a help to him? Or would she bring him trouble, as he'd thought?

He wrestled with the dilemma. Was it wise? Or was it just an excuse to bring her under his power and coerce her into selling the coveted horse?

As he admitted the attraction of the latter, his body responded willingly to her feminine charms, his healthy male appetite clamoring for attention in his groin. He couldn't deny the attraction of bringing her under his power.

The reaction she evoked convinced him she was trouble. Yet her bond with the stallion proved she possessed the right temperament to help Gellie. She had the right size hands . . .

He made a decision. He would bring her along for the sake of the foal and mare. She would be his to command, at least for a night.

"She'll do. Bring her along," he barked. He motioned to his men, and they sprang forward from beyond the boundaries of Jasper's torch, surrounding her on every side.

"I'll do for what?" she cried, eyeing his men uneasily.

"You're coming with me to Castle Graham."

"You're kidnapping me?" she flared. "How dare you. 'Tis bad enough that your men stole my stallion and pack-horse, and all but killed my brother when he tried to stop them, but—"

"I am not kidnapping you," he interrupted, impatient to be on their way. "You will be my guest for one night at Castle Graham. On the morrow, you're free to go." He was unwilling to admit more in front of his men, that he needed a woman's help to bring the foal.

"I am staying with Sir Edward Kincaid at Carlisle Castle," she argued. "Now that I have my stallion back, I will return to my host." An obstinate expression settled on her face.

"You won't come quietly?" he asked, voice deceptively soft to hide his mounting anger. If she delayed too long, his mare might die.

"You have caused me enough trouble already," she hissed, seeming bent on delay. "Why should I wish to be your so-called 'guest.' "

Conscious of the moments ticking away, each of them bringing Gellie closer to her end, Graham's patience snapped. With a flick of his hand, he once more signaled his men.

"Sorry, mistress," Jasper murmured as he grasped her wrists and lashed them together. She struggled valiantly, but he worked quickly, binding her fast.

"Not so rough," Graham cautioned as another man, Hugh, twisted the mare's reins from her hand. Still another prepared to slip a halter over the stallion's head. The black shied, crashing into Jasper's mount and nearly unseating the lass.

"Calm him," Graham ordered her, "or he may be injured. You don't want that."

Her head whipped up, and she blasted him with a look

akin to cannon fire, but she did his biding. As she soothed
the stallion, their gazes locked. "Aren't you hospitable,"
she mocked furiously. "You force invitations on guests like
a jail sentence. A woman at Carlisle told me you once had
charm but had lost it of late. I quite agree."

He scowled back. He could charm a woman if he wanted
to, but this one put him out of temper, with her arguments
and delays. Why couldn't she just obey?

By the light of his torch, he saw she seethed with resentment. He also realized for the first time that her eyes, lined
with a lacy fringe of dark lashes, were the clear color of
violets nestled among leaves in early spring.

Refined lady or no, she would never be obedient. With
eyes like that, the lass had to be fey.

Chapter 2

Lucina Cavandish endured both her guards and bound hands with ill grace as they rode through the darkened Scots countryside. She had suffered tonight because of these Border rogues and longed to tell them so.

First they had stolen her beloved Orpheus and their two other horses, leaving her and her younger brother leagues away from Carlisle with only her mare. No sooner had they walked the exhausting distance to the castle of Sir Edward Kincaid, the English West Border March warden, than Roger had insisted on riding after the thieves.

"I know how much Orpheus means to you," he'd insisted. "And Sir Edward will be too busy fighting the reivers to the death. Dozens of people lost their herds tonight."

Lucina's horror revived at the thought of men caught between dying to recover their property or starving if they did not. She had been equally upset that her brother insisted on risking his life in a Border brawl. He'd already fought one battle when the reivers stole their mounts.

Now the leader of these frightening men was forcing her to be his "guest."

True, the one called Will seemed to have caused the trouble, not the Black Graham. Nor did the leader approve of what his cousin had done, according to a serving woman at Carlisle Castle.

"The Graham dinna allow reivin', but he canna stop his mad cousin." Cynicism had glittered in Maggie Johnstone's gray eyes as she advised Lucina not to follow her brother. "Will Mosley comes from good blood—he's second cousin to the Graham—but he acts like a devil incarnate. They'll kill each other one day."

Ironically enough, Lucina had felt a sudden optimism at Maggie's words. If the Graham and his cousin were busy quarreling, they wouldn't notice her. She could reclaim Orpheus without their ever knowing she'd been there.

That, however, had not proved the case. Lucina glanced at the guard on a rangy chestnut to her left. She had asked him a question earlier, but he'd refused to answer, sitting stiff in the saddle, his gaze trained straight ahead.

Never mind, she reassured herself, taking heart from the feel of Orpheus's sure, strong stride. She was glad to be reunited with him, glad to have Cygnus, his dam, cantering at her side, despite the fact that her rash decision to enter the gully *had* put her in this rogue's hands.

It wasn't the first time her choice had gotten her into trouble. Her brother's earlier words returned to her, spoken as a fierce gale had swept the wild grandeur of the Cumberland hills, warning them of the coming storm. "Yes, we're going to be drenched, and no, I don't blame you. I just should have insisted we stay in Penrith."

"And you're being a martyr about it, as usual, never once blaming me," Lucina had admitted as she'd surveyed the dangerous thunderclouds approaching. "But I couldn't sit another second in that stuffy inn while you and Tom searched for a coach horse to replace the lame one. It might have taken days, and I simply must—"

"Claim your land," Roger had teased, mimicking the impassioned statement she'd repeated so often since they'd left Dorset weeks ago. "How could I not know? You've talked of it incessantly since Lady Ashley willed it to you. I agree you deserve a reward after working your backside off caring for her, but could we speak of something else for once?"

Lucina twined her fingers tighter in Orpheus's mane as she remembered how old Lady Ashley, out of love, had nurtured her dreams as if they'd been her own. Though querulous since her widowhood, the woman had unbent once Lucina insisted on becoming her companion. During their three years together, they'd discovered a growing affection that had brightened both their days. In return for

Lucina's devotion, her friend had left her an inheritance meant to fulfill her wish for an independent life.

Perhaps she shouldn't have come to Scotland, as her elder sister Rozalinde had warned. Yet Orpheus's presence was warm and comforting beneath her, and with Cygnus only an arm's length away, she felt reassured. As long as she had her horses, she still had her dreams.

The magical image of her future hovered before her. On her own piece of land, she would build an equine dynasty of noble, loyal animals like Orpheus and Cygnus, who had no peers in endurance and speed.

Love has no law, she thought, silently repeating Lady Ashley's favorite saying to bolster her courage. Her friend had often said to follow her heart wherever it led, and Lucina's love for horses had brought her here. She would confront whatever lay ahead.

Heartened by memory of her ladyship's tenacious will, Lucina wondered what the Graham wanted. Why did he insist she be his guest for one night, then on the morrow be free to go?

He either lied or told the truth but was crazed, she decided as their party slowed to splash across a shallow ford. A moment of moonlight illuminated the Graham's face as he glanced back, reaffirming her belief that he wasn't crazed. His eyes reflected calm, the set of his jaw spoke of deliberate control, his urgency to reach their destination displayed purpose.

The flame-haired demon at his side was another tale. She had quaked with true fear as his gaze had briefly met hers, revealing a lack of rational hold on his thoughts and doings. He was the madman, not the Black Graham.

It struck her then, how certain she was of the Graham's identity, as if they'd been formally introduced. Quite simply, he looked like a leader, with his muscular, powerful body and the deadly sword strapped to his broad back. And his face fit his name. Though attractive, he wore a thundercloud for an expression, and his eyes reminded her of the darkened sky just before the earlier storm—full of dangerous passions about to break loose.

The others also treated him like their leader. He had only to raise his finger, and they leaped to obey. She would relish the chance to order others about like that. Being fifth in a family of loving but domineering siblings, she'd had her fill of having to jump when told.

But as her gaze settled again on the head man, his forbidding figure moving ahead of her on his horse, she reconsidered. Never would she trade affection for power like his. Mastery over others was a barrier to closeness, and she suspected that his life included neither love nor friendship. Why else would he be called the *Black* Graham?

The last thought brought her worries full circle to her first question. What did the man want?

Whatever it was, it couldn't be too terrible. What made her so sure, she couldn't explain. Yet his probing questions about her training of Orpheus had warmed her to him, as had the way he'd stared at her hands with undisguised interest. She guessed he knew exactly why she had come into the gully, despite the peril and the dark. Her impetuous decision destroyed any chance of concealing her heart from him.

Oddly enough, she didn't care, though she still didn't trust him. Having let him see her love for her horses, she'd given him a ready weapon to use against her. Yet in both his careful questions about Orpheus and the considerate way he handled his own horse, she read the possibility of a common passion. From experience, she knew that people who loved horses understood and had patience with those of like mind.

Still, she couldn't imagine a smile replacing his grim expression, or tenderness lighting up his eyes. He seemed too hardened.

With a sigh of frustration, Lucina captured the wayward bent of her thoughts and redirected them. She must be practical and talk her way out of her situation, not think herself into deeper involvement with this man.

Glaring at her self-appointed host, she cursed her ill luck at running into him. She would be a belligerent guest and hope he tossed her out the door. Anything rather than stay with him until dawn.

Their party slowed and rounded a hill. A stone tower suddenly appeared, looming over them like a dark predator. She ran a trembling hand over Orpheus's neck as her confidence drained away. The fortress looked cold and dismal, as if it held no comforts within. How fitting for a man called the Black Graham.

The Black Graham. The man who noticed everything.

Maggie Johnstone had cautioned that he was a formidable foe. She must be strongly girded, Lucina realized, for whatever lay ahead.

Whatever she had envisioned, it wasn't this, Lucina thought as the men guided her into a warm stable some moments later. She inhaled the reassuring odors of horses, hay, and grain. No odoriferous piles of manure lurked in corners. The hard-packed dirt floors were swept clean, and lanterns hung at intervals on the walls, lending a cheery light that dispelled the gloom.

The men dismounted and, at the Black Graham's curt dismissal, left their horses to stable men. The animals melted away with their attendants in one direction as their riders went in another.

Gripping Cygnus's reins and Orpheus's mane, Lucina thought longingly of the hot drinks and warm beds the men went to, while their steeds were given rubdowns and hot mash.

"Get down." The Graham's brusque order startled her. He reached up and untied her hands.

"Tell me what I'm to do here first." She clung stubbornly to Orpheus, determined not to be dislodged. She felt safer up here, looking down on his impatient, scowling face.

He shot her a look of disgust or frustration, she wasn't sure which, then turned and strode away. He entered a box stall nearby and disappeared.

A crooning drifted to her ears, the words addressed to someone named Gellie. The dramatic shift in his tone from cold command to tender caring astonished her. She hadn't imagined him capable of such concern.

"You bumbling codshead, your hands are dirty. Don't touch her!"

Lucina jumped at his sudden bark of anger, though it seemed more in character than the previous crooning. The stall door wrenched open, and a lad tumbled out, propelled by Graham, his expression still resembling the thundercloud. "Fetch very hot water," he ordered. "And wash your filthy hands first. With soap."

As the lad scuttled away, Lucina nudged Orpheus closer

for a better view, then froze in alarm as the Black Graham fixed an intent gaze on her. His face, so cold and stern before, suddenly pleaded for something, his blue eyes eloquent with fear.

His plea plucked at Lucina's heartstrings like skilled fingers at a lute. Without thinking, she slid from Orpheus's back and, keeping a firm hold on his mane, approached the stall.

The Graham stood aside, offering a clear view of what lay within.

A beautiful mare the color of a shiny copper coin lay on her side, her swollen belly and her unnatural position for foaling announcing her distress. A pair of fragile legs protruded from her hindquarters, further evidence that her foal refused to be born. Her condition was indeed grave.

"My God, why didn't you tell me sooner?" With a reassuring pat to Orpheus's neck and a word to Cygnus, Lucina approached the mare, taking care not to startle her, though the poor thing barely had the strength to notice her, let alone startle. Quick, shallow breathing marked the advanced stage of her deterioration. She must have been like this for some time. "Don't you know what's wrong?"

"That's what you're to find out."

"You want *me* to care for her?" she asked, incredulous as she spun around.

"Aye," he said gruffly, his face contorted with the difficulty of the admission.

To confess he needed a woman's help was, to most men, the same as admitting utter stupidity. Yet love for the mare clearly overshadowed his pride, and realizing that, Lucina knew why he'd studied her hands so intently when they first met, why he'd asked if she had trained Orpheus herself. He'd sought someone with hands smaller than his who wouldn't hurt the mare. Embarrassed to announce his need in the presence of his inferiors, he had demanded she accompany him without explanation.

The mare grunted, the sound like a plea. Lucina whirled back in time to see the limpid eyes roll with pain. She must set to work at once. "I'll need to wash," she announced, briskly turning up her sleeves. "Where is that boy with the water?"

The relief in his face startled her. Had he really imagined she might refuse?

But before she could wonder further, he pushed past her without a word of thanks and vanished in search of the lad. Left alone with the mare, Lucina hurriedly hung her cloak on a nail and knelt in the straw. Wanting to forget the chief and his lack of gratitude, she studied Gellie's bloated belly, trying to guess how the foal lay.

With gentle fingers, she cautiously probed the mare's taut flesh. Gellie quivered at her touch, radiating pain. "I am sorry to hurt you, my pretty one." Lucina drew back, aching for the beautiful creature. How Graham must ache for her as well. But if that were so, why must he be so arrogant, taking her captive when a courteous request would have served better by half.

Yet a strange pride suffused her as he returned with the lad in tow, bearing a steaming basin in outstretched hands. The chief had trusted her instinctively, as did Gellie, who now acknowledged her ministrations with a soft whicker.

"There, now, my beauty," Lucina whispered as the mare lifted her head, a questioning appeal in her eyes. "I'll see you right again. I swear I will."

She washed hastily, aware that Graham watched as she handled the soap and dried her hands on the towel.

"Would you be so kind as to care for my mare and stallion?" she asked the lad. "Orpheus could use a hot grain mash. Cygnus ate earlier, but she would appreciate some hay, and they both need water and a good rubdown."

The lad shot a questioning look to his chief, who granted permission with an arrogant nod of his head.

"I believe I have a coin or two if you are thorough," she added, irked that the boy seemed to require Graham's permission before he would obey.

"I'll be verra thorough, m'leddy," the lad assured her, his Scots accent so thick it could be cut like corn cake. He hurried away, leaving her alone with the mare and the Black Graham.

Ignoring the Graham's disapproving frown for her offer to pay his servant, Lucina knelt at the mare's hindquarters and forced herself to concentrate. Never had she dealt with such a problem alone, though she'd twice watched difficult births.

The Black Graham knelt beside her, looking as if he suspected her inexperience. "I wish the young fellow had chosen a better birth hour. 'Tis late."

" 'Tis a fine hour," she said shortly. "I was born at the first stroke of midnight myself." She thought he flinched at this news but couldn't imagine why.

"Do you know anything about foaling?" he demanded harshly.

"I know enough," Lucina snapped, determined to succeed despite his sudden skepticism. "Cygnus had difficulty when she foaled, and I watched a skilled friend deliver her safely. He explained everything as he went along, so I know what to do."

Taking a deep breath, she parted the mare's soft flesh and wedged her hand next to the tiny pair of hooves. Their appearance was a good sign, signaling that the foal faced the correct way. But at the same time, she must squeeze her hand past them, which could cause the mare new pain. Lucina hoped poor Gellie would be too spent to feel it. With a determined set of her jaw, she eased her hand into the dark realm where the foal lay.

Fear ground in her stomach. What if she couldn't fathom the problem? What if . . . ah, here were the foal's outstretched hind legs. She breathed again with relief to find something recognizable. And here were the hindquarters . . . and the body. New hope awakened as she continued her discovery of familiar parts, until she suddenly encountered something hard.

"This isn't right," she muttered, bracing on her left elbow as she explored with her right hand. "The front feet should come out last, but this feels like another hoof."

"Mayhap one leg is bent back," the Black Graham offered.

She looked up to question him further, but the words died in her throat as she met his gaze. Stripped of his role as commander, in his present role of helpless observer, the cold warrior who had taken her captive wore an unguarded expression that revealed his vast love for the mare. It burned in his eyes, showing him to be as vulnerable and capable of caring as her brother Roger.

But the instant she perceived his emotion, he flung up his cold exterior to hide it. Resentment at her intrusion into his privacy radiated from him as he stared, silently ordering her back to work.

Moisture stung Lucina's eyes as she quickly refocused on her task, remembering that people who had been hurt often hid their softer emotions. Her eldest brother Jonathan had taken years to recover from his ordeal as a war prisoner. Her older brother Charles had also endured pain during his dangerous time on the Spanish Main and had needed time to heal.

The thought that the Border lord's pain might equal that of her adored brothers redoubled her desire to save both mare and foal. Inching her hand forward, she called on heaven to guide her, for although Graham seemed to care little for people, she saw that he adored this horse. And having lost her father, she knew well enough how it felt to watch a loved one die.

Suddenly the mare struggled against her as the birth canal contracted. Crushing pain shot up Lucina's arm, robbing her of breath. Grimacing, she relaxed her muscles and waited, praying the contraction would pass. Instead, the mare's muscles squeezed even tighter than before.

Graham gripped her shoulder. "What's wrong?" he demanded, as if fury would pull the answer from her lips.

She couldn't bear to look at him, too terrified of seeing his naked fear for the mare. "A birth spasm," she gasped, hurrying to reassure him. " 'Twill pass, I'm sure." But she wasn't sure. What would happen to her arm if she were wrong?

"Bring out your hand," he ordered starkly.

Lucina shot him a startled glance. Wasn't he wholly intent on the mare, willing to sacrifice anything to meet her needs? Yet he commanded her to withdraw, as if he feared she would be harmed. She shook her head with vehemence, unwilling to give up. "Mayhap you should go to her head and soothe her," she urged. Anything to avoid his kneeling beside her, helpless agony written on his face.

He shifted position in silence and bent to croon to Gellie. As a stream of tender phrases flowed from his lips, as he called the horse his "wee filly" and his "old girl," Lucina gritted her teeth, struggling not to cry as pain radiated through her arm. If she so much as whimpered, he would order her to give up, and she refused to admit defeat. *Let it be over,* she prayed frantically, angling her body in a futile attempt to ease the pressure. She wasn't sure how much more she could bear. Her bones would be crushed.

As if in answer to her entreaty, the birthing muscles relaxed.

Quickly Lucina wiggled her fingers, feeling in the slippery darkness for the misplaced hoof. Her arm throbbed in agony, and for one heart-stopping moment, she feared her fingers had gone numb. Were they even moving in response to her commands?

Obey me, she ordered, working them with grim insistence. *Nothing is broken. You cannot fail me now.*

Ah, the hoof! With a gasp of relief, she found it and nudged it forward. Her back and neck shrieked in protest as she leaned forward, her unnatural position becoming even more unnatural as she strained to extend the foal's leg. She *must* succeed.

Sweat popped out on her forehead as she worked, wanting to shout at the frustration of working blind.

The leg moved in response to her continued pressure. She curled it forward until another contraction hit the mare.

Lucina moaned as the muscles clamped around her arm, squeezing relentlessly in their attempt to expel the foal. Her arm, immersed beyond the elbow, felt as if it were being crushed.

"Pull out." Graham was at her side instantly, ordering her to give up.

"Leave me alone," she cried, full of pain and frustration.

Abruptly, her arm was pushed backward and partially freed. Lucina stared down as a set of rounded hindquarters adorned by a limp, wet tail crowned at the opening of the birth canal. She had moved the leg, which had freed the body, allowing more of the foal to be expelled.

Gellie stirred and groaned, signaling another contraction. Yet this time Lucina endured the pain, spurred on by hope. If she could finish the task, all might still be well.

"We're making progress, my girl," Graham crowed to the mare as he moved back to stroke Gellie's muzzle and chant encouragement to her.

Lucina panted for breath, then steadied herself for another try as the contraction passed. She groped, found the leg she had lost, and uncurled it farther. "I know you like it in there, little one," she muttered beneath her breath, "but you're coming out *now*."

Graham studied the young woman who lay flat on her stomach, her entire arm up his mare's hindquarters, and fought off agonies of doubt. Did this unknown female have the stamina to continue? He wasn't especially superstitious, but common lore said people born at midnight were fey. Her violet eyes reinforced that likelihood. Would that trait in her save his mare and colt?

"Easy, now, Gellie. 'Twill all be over soon," he assured the mare, praying he was right. Gellie grunted and flailed her hind legs, barely missing the lassie with sharp hooves. Panicked, he dived to the rescue. "Steady, girl, she's only helping," he gasped, capturing both the mare's legs and holding them firmly. Concerned that the mare might have nicked the lass, he glanced at her to be sure. To his dismay, she was frozen in place, her mouth screwed into a tight bud of concern. "Trouble?" he demanded, assaulted by a new wave of fear.

"It's stuck," she puffed, her eyes glazed as she concentrated. "The leg seems pulled back, as if the foal were leaping to clear a hurdle. It probably grew in that position. I don't know if I can—"

"You've moved it some already," he rapped out. "Do it again."

"I'm trying, damn it." She scowled at the rafters and shifted position. "It won't budge."

"Push harder," he ordered, wrenched by dread.

She shot him a look of irritation. "You men think brute strength is always the answer. If I did it your way, I might break the leg."

"I'm not suggesting you mangle him," he shot back, equally irked, then stopped. A quarrel would hinder, not help her. "Your pardon," he forced out with an effort. He couldn't remember the last time he'd apologized to another, but the foal was everything. Swallowing his pride, he searched for words of encouragement. "You might try working it down instead of ahead."

"That could puncture the mare's womb."

"Go carefully."

"Easy for you to say," she grumbled, but fell silent as she continued her efforts.

His hope returned as movement rippled across the mare's belly. "Progress?" he rapped out.

She paused and panted for breath. "I'm straightening the leg downward," she explained, leaning forward again. "So far, there seems space enough. I do believe it's . . . oh!"

As he watched in anxiety, the tight bud of her mouth spread into a smile of triumph, then suddenly contorted with pain once more.

He inhaled sharply, recognizing the problem but helpless to change it. The only way he could help was to stop her, and he couldn't bring himself to give up. Not when they were so close . . .

With a surge, more of the foal appeared. Graham lunged to her side, eagerly cupping the foal's hindquarters in both hands. "I believe you've done it. Can you ease your arm out now?"

"Well, of course I've done it. I'm not a milksop, sir." She sank back in the straw and reached for the discarded towel to wipe her wet arm, her pain seemingly forgotten as the miracle of the foal emerged into his arms.

It was going to be a beauty, he thought with excitement. From his view of the glossy rump, wet against his hands, the colt would be russet like his sire and dam. Gellie snorted and shifted as, inch by interminable inch, the neck, then the classically formed head, slowly appeared, followed by the front legs. Each part was flawless in size and form.

Graham wanted to whoop with relief as he gathered the slick, warm body with stilt-like legs into his lap. Gellie might live and he would have a fine colt as well.

He took the towel from the lass and rubbed the tiny creature to stimulate blood flow. A renewed twinge of concern tugged at him as the newborn lay limp and lifeless, with no sign of breath. By heaven, what was wrong now?

"You must clear his nostrils," the lass directed. She leaned over his shoulder and pointed with authority. "Hurry. He needs to breathe on his own."

Chagrined to have forgotten, he manipulated the towel, attempting to cleanse mucus from the tiny muzzle, but his fingers were too large. Seeing his trouble, the lass whipped out a lace-bordered handkerchief and bent across him to clear the foal's air passages with deft swipes.

The pretty handkerchief was immediately ruined, but she appeared not to care, instead watching with awe as the little fellow gasped, sneezed, and sucked in a deep breath.

By God, his colt was going to live! Elation shifted to heat as the girl's breasts brushed against his arm. Alarmed by the force of sudden awareness, he sought her gaze. Absorbed in the newborn, she seemed unaware of their contact. Awe transformed her face from comeliness to beauty as she watched the colt raise his head and look around with wide eyes.

Both the violet eyes of the girl and the limpid gaze of the foal contained a unique quality of innocence, and as he recognized it, a pang pierced what was left of his heart. To look on the world with the guile of innocence . . . he would give anything to possess that gift once more. He'd seen too much that was ugly in his one and thirty years, too much that had left him jaded and immune to others' grief.

Disgusted by his useless welling of sentiment, he cut it off. Sniveling fool, he mocked himself, there was the afterbirth to deliver, and if it was done wrong, Gellie could still die. He'd best heed his tasks instead of dreaming of chasing selkies—fairies that couldn't be caught.

He waited patiently for the mare to expel the thick mass of flesh, and examined it thoroughly to ensure none remained behind. Then he reached for a roll of twine to tie off the colt's cord, only to find the lass had done it for him.

A reprimand sprang to his lips, but before it could pass, Gellie raised her head, an inquiring expression on her intelligent face, and he knew she wanted her offspring near. Hurriedly he gathered the mite in his arms and snuggled him next to Gellie, who began to groom her baby with her warm, raspy tongue. He placed a bucket of water within her easy reach so she could quench her thirst at will.

"My God, isn't he perfect?" The lass's awestruck whisper brushed his ear, warning him as he knelt by Gellie that she stood at his back. "And we helped bring him into the world. What shall we name him, do you think?"

Though her words mirrored his own triumph, he resented her claiming the privilege of the colt's naming. Turning to tell her so, he felt the graceful sway of her body as she

dropped to her knees at his side. A shock of warmth
crossed his neck as she draped her arm around him and
leaned so close, their cheeks almost touched.

Caught off guard, he stiffened, appalled by her audacity.
No one touched him, not even females, unless invited first.

Yet the lass seemed unaware she'd done anything forbidden, nor did she show fear, as did most people who knew
his short temper and cold, unfeeling ways. "I'll name him,"
he said rudely.

As tranquilly as if the point no longer mattered, she
leaned against him to gesture with one hand. "Look, aren't
they beautiful?" She seemed oblivious to the torment her
contact brought him. "We've seen a miracle tonight. No,
it's more than that." Caught in the fervor of the moment,
she turned and looked straight into his eyes. "We helped
start a new life."

Graham looked away quickly, smothered by his inability
to respond. His lungs refused to take in air, and a hard
lump tightened in his throat. His mind reeled from the deluge of emotions that had broken over him like a tidal
wave—the agony of believing he would lose Gellie and the
foal, rage with Will and his raid, the triumph of this unex-
pectedly successful birth, and now this . . .

If she'd just flung her damnably alluring body in his arms
and purposely kissed him, an open invitation, he might have
been comfortable. Things could have progressed normally,
and he could have bedded her right here with a minimum
of emotional involvement.

But no, she had to talk of miracles and new life, touching
his deepest yearnings, until awareness of all the things he
lacked shot through him, bringing new pain. Worse still,
she seemed unaware of how she aroused him. Her generous
mouth hovered within inches of his, her very innocence
tempting him to fling caution to the winds. It was too much.

"If you like to think it's a miracle, I won't stop you," he
grated, harshly reminding himself that for him, it was
merely the natural course of nature.

"But we helped them together," she insisted, pursuing
her wild fancies without an inkling of the ugly reality
haunting him. To his further astonishment, she gathered his
face in both hands and kissed him on the forehead. Her
lips brushed against his flesh, like flower petals opening in

spring. Then she wrapped both arms around him and hugged him fervently, causing heat to knife through his groin. "I'm so happy," she sighed, oblivious to his body's hardening. "Aren't you?"

He wasn't happy; he was driven to distraction. Despite her obvious inexperience, he would bed her on the spot if this nonsense continued. "You're exhausted," he stated, sure she would never behave this way otherwise.

As if to prove him correct, she swayed unsteadily. Responding instinctively, he closed his arms around her, and she nestled against him, her head on his shoulder, her breath warm against his neck. Her eyes drifted closed, and a small smile played across her lips.

Oddest thing. With the colt delivered, his mare alive, and this charming selkie in his arms, Graham felt a rush of protectiveness that was the closest thing to pleasure he'd felt in years.

Carefully shifting the exhausted girl, he lifted her and rose to his feet. "Ho, Robbie," he called softly, not wanting to rouse her, "come attend Gellie and her new colt."

As he pushed past the lad and strode from the stable, the lassie cushioned one hand between her cheek and his chest. "Forgive me, but I'm so tired. If you'll take me to Orpheus, I'll sleep in his stall. On the morrow I must return to my brother . . . and my land . . . I must find . . ."

"You'll sleep in a bed, as is proper," he snorted, indignant that she should think him willing to house a female guest in such an unseemly manner. He snorted again as he stalked across the courtyard, ignoring his men's astonished looks. He would do things correctly from here on out.

He would see she behaved as became a lady until she left his care. And for the sake of her own safety, that had better be soon.

Chapter 3

By first light of morning, Graham stood at the edge of the curtained alcove and brooded on the lassie who slumbered so peacefully in his narrow bed. Her petal soft cheek lay cupped against one palm. Her other hand rested on her breast, which rose and fell gently as she drew deep, even breaths.

She looked brushed by the breath of innocence, yet he knew she was potent magic. First she unsettled him with her uncanny skill at riding. Then she saved his mare and colt. But her unusual caresses after the birth had disturbed him most. Sensual yet innocent, she had kissed his forehead, touching memories deep within him. At that moment his youth had flashed before him, and he'd remembered that once his future had held a beckoning light of promise. Could it do so again?

A powerful urge to possess this female assailed him. Not her magnificent stallion, but her. Illogically, he wanted to bind her to him so she could never leave.

He must be as mad as Will.

Years ago he had reached for the things he'd wanted and expected to have them without thought to consequences, just as the lass had last night. But that time had passed. He'd learned that even miracles such as the safe delivery of Gellie's colt arrived accompanied by strife. His mind still reeled from yesterday's madness. He could only hope he would come to his senses once he'd had more sleep.

Thoughts of her had kept him awake last night. After a brief, unsatisfying doze, he'd ridden out while it was still dark to parley with the English families raided by his cousin. Only a few of his distant kin had been lost, but Will had cut down many on the other side. Probably enjoyed doing it, too, heedless of possible retribution, leaving Graham to heal the wounds.

He'd doled out money and promised to return cattle. He'd stood beside new widows as graves were dug, and his own grief had been real. He, too, was death's intimate. It whispered at his back, driving every commitment he made.

Yet throughout his dismal tour, he'd carried a scrap of hope within as images of the lass replayed in his head—of her galloping through the gully with her shooting star of a torch that flashed in the night, of her wondrous hands coaxing his hope for the future into the world.

Upon his return, a moment with the new colt, still unnamed, had recaptured the magic. The young fellow had nestled against Gellie, his stumpy tail twirling in contentment as he suckled his dam's milk. At the sight Graham had known an alien stab of joy. Hot and vivid, it reminded him of his desire for this fey maiden who stampeded into his life. Now the unusual pleasure of looking at her, juxtaposed against the strife of his world, struck him forcefully, prompting guilt. How could he take delight in anything when he'd just been comforting mourners? Yet he delighted in her.

A ray of sun angled through the closed shutters to play on the lassie's brown hair, sparking to life shimmers of gold. It was false treasure, he told himself, and as fragile as his false, foolish hopes that could so easily be crushed. The breached peace still gaped like a jagged wound across his life and his land. On top of that, his blasted cousin Will had kidnapped an English lad who was surely this lass's brother. She didn't know it yet, but she would soon.

Fingering his bristling chin, for he'd given up his chamber to her and hadn't shaved, he considered her story that she had come to claim inherited land. She'd mumbled about it again as he'd carried her to bed. Impossible. Every hectare of the Border was owned and jealously guarded by someone. She must be mistaken about her inheritance. Yet the idea pained him. She would be heartbroken if there was no land, having come so far and endured so much for its sake.

With effort, he set aside the concern. He had other matters to deal with and didn't need pity coupled with desire

to complicate matters. Since he owed her a favor and in-
tended to repay it, he would make time to assist her. Later.
Just now he must confer with two irate Border wardens,
Scots and English, in order to heal the broken peace.

'Twas time to leave, yet his body stood rooted to the
spot as she turned onto her right side and burrowed blissfully among the blankets, a rosy flush highlighting her por-
celain cheeks. He pictured the sleeping selkie coming
awake, opening her iris-colored eyes, and embracing him
as she had in the stable. The thought of her unexpected,
fervent clasp triggered a heady rush of interest in his loins.
It scrambled his thoughts and drove all notions of work
from his mind.

"Go ahead, since ye want her," a voice whispered. "Slip
into her bed."

The thoughts so exactly mirrored his own that for an
instant, Graham wondered if he'd spoken aloud . . . until
he sensed the presence at his elbow and knew exactly who
it was.

Spinning, he stared into Will's jaunty, confident face.
Choler consumed him, and he longed to be rid of this
cousin who was too much like him and knew it too well.
Curse the November day their mothers had borne them,
cousins giving birth at the same time lacking but an hour.

As usual, Will seemed to read his thoughts with ease.
"Ye think ye're different from me, Graham, but ye're not."
Will smirked, as if still buoyed by his accomplishments the
night before. "Ye want to swive her as much as I do. Go
on. I'll have her later, when ye're done."

Graham gritted his teeth, furious to be goaded. Will always seemed to know what he liked, in women and otherwise, and would dare him to take it. No one else knew
instinctively how he felt and what he wanted the way Will
did, including his basest desires.

"I've chosen a different path, Will." He straightened,
willing his refusal. "One you can't understand."

"Och, I ken yer ways. Ye always had to be different from
the rest," Will sneered. "You passed Thrawn Jock's test
and took to reiving younger than me. Ye brought the most
cattle across the Border in one raid. Ye bested two men in
a fight instead of one. Ye wed and bedded the most win-
some lassie to be had. Now ye've forbidden raiding." He

spat on the floor. " 'Tis no more than a new way to best me."

"I forbid it for a reason." A dust mote danced in the sunbeam, reminding Graham of the one way he failed to resemble Will, be it as small as this spot of dust. Their life's goals differed like water from wine. "Times are changing on the Border," he said. "We must change as well."

"Ye're the one who's changed," Will declared vehemently, puckering his mouth in derision. "Look at ye, squeamish as a woman over a little killing. The Grahams and their kin ha' always lived by reiving. 'Tis in the blood."

"There won't be any blood left, nor Grahams for it to flow in, if you keep at it." Graham moved away from the curtain, realizing their argument would wake the lass. "You'll have us dead and buried and this fortress given to someone else," he said, determined to confront Will with his trespasses. "They'll rename it Castle Dacre." He chose the name of an enemy English family and watched with perverse relish as a frown spread across Will's face. Shocking him was the best way to capture Will's attention. And what he intended to do next would shock him still more.

Lucina awoke abruptly to the bark of angry male voices close at hand. Startled by the rude awakening, disoriented by the unfamiliar surroundings that greeted her, she struggled to remember where she was.

A creamy-white blanket wrapped her in a cozy cocoon. A moss-green brocade curtain slashed by a welcome ray of sun surrounded the tiny sleeping alcove where she lay. Hazily, she recalled being borne here last night in the Black Graham's arms, while she wearily babbled about her land and her brother. Exhausted from her long day of riding, spent from fighting off the harrowing attack of the reivers, then rescuing Orpheus and delivering the miracle foal, she had let him put her where he would.

Memory of the tiny creature's first tottering steps gladdened her, and she knew they had gladdened the Graham as well. Surely she could trust him; she'd felt it instinctively. A man who loved his horses so wouldn't betray her. His strong arms had seemed reliable, the sway of his step solid as he bore her into the castle and up a seemingly unending flight of spiral stairs.

She had welcomed the warmth of the dim chamber they entered, lit only by the glow of a smoldering peat fire. The softness of an eiderdown bed had welcomed her; then the Black Graham had disappeared. As she'd drifted toward sleep, she had remembered his expression as he'd bent over his laboring mare. Who would have thought it? That the Black Graham, a fierce warrior with a reputation for violence and coldness, could look as he had—his face tender with an ardent, honest love.

"Where have you hidden him?" a man demanded, his voice hammering with concentrated fury at someone she couldn't see. "Tell me or I'll—"

The stark contrast of the voice to her memories of the past night snapped Lucina back to the present, reminding her that all was not well.

"You'll what?" the other taunted. "Ye'll nae harm me, yer own kin. I intend to collect a handsome sum for the lad. I'll even share it wi' ye if ye're more polite."

"He's her brother, damn it. I want him released."

Lucina sat bolt upright, terror squeezing her heart. Roger, a prisoner?

She peered around the edge of the curtain, needing to know the worst. One glimpse of the two men confirmed her fears. The Black Graham stood with his broad back to her, quarreling with the red-haired savage who had accompanied him last night. The twisted sneer on the lunatic's face sent a chill shooting through her blood. Could this mad barbarian truly have captured her brother? She imagined poor Roger, cold and hungry after their trials, a prisoner in a primitive shelter with no one to meet his needs. Dismayed, she sank back beneath the blankets as her brother's captor chortled, the sound malicious enough to put fear into braver souls than hers.

Maggie Johnstone had said the Graham chief and his cousin would probably kill each other one day. It might even happen now, within mere paces of her bed.

"So, cousin, the wench pleases ye more than ye let on," the mad one cackled, clearly pleased with his observation. "Ye've asked after her, and found she's a rich merchant's child."

"Her father's dead," Graham growled. "I'll not hold her for ransom, even if he were not."

His cousin's answering laugh ended on a wild, high-pitched note as he ridiculed Graham's claim. "Deny it if ye like, but 'tis clear ye want her. Take her. She's yers, just as the lad's mine."

"The lad is not yours." Graham's tone had the bite of steel. "Nor any of the cattle you reived last night. God, I ought to kill you, going against my direct orders and starting more strife when I'd just settled it. But no, you have to take a hostage that sets the Border wardens on us. I'll give you one more chance to tell me where you've hidden the lad."

A stubborn silence ensued, followed by the sound of determined footfalls stalking across the wood floor. A door latch rattled. "Arthur, see Will escorted to one of our special guest chambers," Graham barked. "And lock him in."

Will swore an ugly oath as the rattle of weapons and tramp of feet signaled several men entering the chamber. "What's the meaning o' this?" he shouted.

"I intend things to change, Will, starting with you," Graham snarled. "You'll be locked in until you tell me where the boy is. When you do, I'll consider letting you out."

A string of curses merged into a scuffle. Fists cracked against flesh, and men grunted as they fought for control.

Lucina gripped the blanket in horror as the curtain separating her from the quarrel rippled.

"Ye canna do this," Will shrieked, obviously getting the worst of the struggle.

"I'm head man here, Will, and I can. I'm locking you in until you repent. Until you're an old man, if required. If you try to escape, I'll flay your back raw."

Lucina shrank down, wishing she could be transported back to yesterday, before disaster had struck. If only things had turned out differently.

The door banged shut, and Will's furious shouts died away. Lucina's relief that he was gone vanished as heavy footfalls approached her alcove. Brass rings screamed on the rod as the curtain flew back and light flooded her bed. She stared at the Graham in alarm. He looked every bit the barbarous Scot this morning. His tousled hair stood on end, as if he'd already been for a reckless ride despite the early hour. Black netherstocks and canions defined his muscular thighs and calves. His shirt hung open to the waist, flaunting his highly developed chest. Sun illuminated the angular planes of his face and the snapping blue of his eyes. They seethed as he studied her, his attention most frightening.

He and his cousin were more alike than he knew. Both were calculating, determined to reach their ends regardless of the means. Both were ruthless when required. She was glad to have Graham's brute fortitude on her side, but just now she felt almost as frightened of him as of Will.

He offered no good morrow nor apology for waking her in such a distressing manner, only stood and observed her, as if waiting for her to begin.

"Your cousin has kidnapped my brother?" she blurted out.

"If your brother is Roger Cavandish, aye." He made no attempt to spare her sensibilities. Apparently after her performance last night, he expected her to have none.

She swallowed and willed away fear. "Have you any idea where he is?"

He sent her a derisive look, as if she ought to know he didn't, and moved toward the hearth. Sinking to one knee, he kindled the fire.

"Will you guide me to your cousin?" she demanded, anxious to take action at once. "Mayhap he'll tell me where Roger is."

The look he cast her over his shoulder strongly suggested she was mad to consider going within a hundred hectares of Will.

"I can be most convincing at times," she pleaded.

"Mistress Cavandish, you can be most stubborn at times." He faced her, a menacing figure with his jaw bristling a new black beard and the heavy poker brandished in one hand. "You proved that last night. But Will is worse."

"I must find my brother." Hopelessness yawned before her as tears pooled in her eyes.

"I can't abide sniveling women." He swung back to the fire, as if offended by her sorrow.

"I'm not sniveling," she cried, outraged by his lack of sympathy. "I want to know where my brother is, which is perfectly reasonable. I fear for his safety. For all I know, he's dead."

"He isn't dead," Graham muttered coldly. "My cousin

wants him alive for ransom. He'll be fed and kept reasonably dry and warm." He placed a block of peat on the embers and regarded it with a commanding air, as if the fire had best burn or else.

If he meant to be reassuring, his manner didn't suggest it. "If you really wished to stop your cousin, you would tell Sir Edward Kincaid not to send a ransom. You would tell your cousin his scheme won't work. But I suspect you intend to keep any gold that—"

"Don't tell me what I intend," he roared, his face terrible to behold.

Stung, Lucina lifted her chin. "Don't shout at me when 'tis Cousin Will who's done wrong. Pray remember, *I* saved your mare and the foal."

His scowl relaxed slightly, as if he were remembering the beauty of the spindly legged foal, wobbling in his first steps to his dam. "I thank you," he said, his manner stiff yet sincere.

"How are they this morning?" she asked more calmly, honestly wanting the news.

"Gellie's back on her feet, and the wee one is taking his mother's milk."

"I thought of a name for him," she ventured, enthused by the news and the softening of his manner. Mayhap talk of the foal would make him more reasonable about Roger. "We can call him Fortune. What do you think?"

The ghost of a smile that had played around his mouth dissolved. Baffled by his reaction, she opened her mouth to question him. Did he find the name a poor choice?

"Your stallion," he cut in before she could speak. "You say you raised him from a foal?"

Once again, the hard edge of doubt in his voice caused her to prickle like a threatened hedgehog. "You don't believe I did?"

"Women lack such skill."

"How do you know?" she demanded. Did he think all women were fools?

"I've never known one to have it," he said dryly.

She straightened her back despite the soft bed. "Well, now you do."

He looked utterly unconvinced, as if he had no plans to change anything he thought or did because of her. With another skeptical glance, he showed her his uncharitable back as he settled a second peat block on the first.

Determined not to let this opinionated tyrant get the better of her, Lucina pushed back the blankets and swung out of bed. She wouldn't be held captive. She was going to look for her brother as soon as she washed and broke her fast. Pulling up her sagging stockings, she realized she was bootless, though she'd been wearing footwear last night. The idea of Graham tampering with her person while she lay exhausted and vulnerable to his desires outraged her further.

The last thought triggered a rush of forbidden excitement that frightened her. She didn't like being vulnerable, nor did she like the idea that he desired her, as his cousin so blatantly said. But if he *did* wish to tamper with her, she admitted she might be tempted to let him, to see how it felt. Seeing his honest care for the mare and colt, she had been moved to embrace him, and had discovered an illicit pleasure in the feel of his body, warm and comforting against hers.

But that was last night. This morning she refused to cringe in bed all day, fulfilling what he appeared to expect of a female. Bounding to her feet, she searched beneath the bed for her boots and found them, along with a great deal of dust. Shaking them clean, she donned and laced them, her temper smoldering as she glanced around the tower room.

It was so cluttered with male belongings, the furniture was almost invisible. Odd pieces of clothing, fishing gear, horse furniture and harness lay scattered hither and yon. Against one wall, a court cupboard groaned under a collection of books stacked in bizarre, precarious positions. An old, quilted doublet hung from one of the cupboard's spindles, hooked with a motley collection of metal barbs and feathers that she guessed were fishing flies.

Documents on a huge table situated at a right angle to the hearth were heaped so high, the slightest breeze would topple them. Some had clearly suffered avalanches in the past, lying untouched where they had drifted to a stop. And before the hearth, a huge brown stain marred the wooden planks, as if a spill had been left to soak into the raw wood. She concluded that the Graham was a poor housekeeper, which was putting the case mildly. "My stars, you should let someone clean in here," she said, rising to her feet. "Or do you *like* living in a trash heap?"

He finished with the fire and swung around to face her, his expression grim. "Do *you* always do foolhardy things for the sake of a horse?" he shot back.

Though she had been ill-mannered to criticize her host, his derogatory tone left her unwilling to apologize. "I wasn't foolhardy to enter the gully," she informed him frostily. "I was loyal to one I love. In my place, would you have left him to be ruined by a new owner? Would you have let his mouth be cut by a vicious bit like the one your horrid cousin uses? Or his sides bloodied by spurs?" She scowled at the memory of Will's mount, bearing wounds on both flanks. That coupled with the bloodied foam from the cruel bit told her all she needed to know of Will. Despite Graham's assurances about her brother, she was sickened to imagine the thoughtless cruelty that might be inflicted on Roger by such a man.

Graham frowned at her accusation, but she didn't care. She knew well enough he was angry with his cousin. And she was more than angry—she hated the brute for kidnapping her brother. And she hated the Graham, too, for dragging her into this coil.

"I wish to wash," she informed him haughtily. "You'll have to retire."

He rose as if to obey and began gathering things to take with him. Despite the clutter, he seemed to find what he wanted—a book, a leather strap for a bridle, a clean shirt. But he didn't leave. "Hot water was brought up earlier. It's probably still warm." He bent down to test the temperature of a pottery pitcher standing by the hearth. "You may keep this chamber while you're here. I'll sleep elsewhere. A maid will bring you something to break your fast."

Lucina felt distinctly uncomfortable to have usurped his private space, but since she intended to leave Castle Graham the moment she found Roger, she didn't argue. "Are you going to search for my brother now?"

"I said I was." He spoke as if she were an unmannerly child who shouldn't have asked.

His continued rudeness maddened her. "I'm going with you."

He added a last book to his armload of belongings. "Clearly no one ever taught you a woman's place."

"And I've no intention of learning it from you."

"I thought you were here to claim your land."

"So I am. What does that have to do with knowing a woman's place?" Admittedly she was unsure of her chances of claiming and holding her land, but that was none of his affair. "I'll hardly be thinking of my land as long as my brother is in danger."

"Where's your proof of ownership?" he demanded.

"Still strapped to my packhorse," she snapped. "Which was stolen last night. Pray see it returned to me with all haste." By now she didn't care how rude her demand was. Being separated from the valuable deed worried her. She needed to have it safely back in her hands. "I also want paper and quill," she added aloud.

"What for?"

She sent him a venomous glare as she stepped toward the paper-strewn table. Since he didn't move, she picked up the quill balanced across an ink pot and sat down. Last night, she'd felt profound affection for him as they'd worked over Gellie. So profound, she'd embraced him, wanting to share her joy. What a miserable blunder. The trust and confidence she had felt for him, based solely on his devotion to his horses, now scattered to the four winds.

By the clarity of morning's light, she saw he used anger to mask his emotions, leaving his expression inscrutable. He made sure not the smallest drop of feeling leaked past the barrier he had erected to keep others out.

Why?

It was none of her affair. She didn't care, either, she insisted as she motioned him near. "I wish to write to Sir Edward Kincaid, the English West Border March warden," she said. "I'll expect one of your men to carry the letter when it's finished. I require paper. *Now* if you please."

Graham took a firm grip on his patience as the Englishwoman dipped her quill and wrote a message in a neat, flowing hand on the paper he provided. His female cousins had never been taught such a foolish thing as writing. They had tended to their needles, the kitchens, and the laundry, as they should. Last night he'd welcomed the firebrand's impropriety when she served his purpose, but by light of day, no more. She seemed to prefer flaunting her talents rather than following his helpful instructions, which tried his temper. Nor did she seem aware that as a lone female, she *must* have a male protector, which was him until her brother was found. It cost him time and trouble, but it couldn't be helped. Someone must save her from her own folly.

Resigned to his duty, he added some clean linen to his bundle and stalked toward the door.

She looked up from her writing, the quill poised primly over the vellum sheet. "My message will be finished momentarily. I wish it to go off straight away."

Her imperious tone irked him. He barked a last order for her to keep to the tower, then yanked the door shut and descended the twisting stair. His blasted cousin had given him problems to last him well into the new year, one of them being this infuriating female. He cursed again as he remembered he had meant to thank her more graciously for helping Gellie. But he'd been incapable of tendering more than terse thanks in the face of her haughty manner.

Worse still, he kept remembering the tenderness he'd seen in her eyes as she'd helped the new foal breathe. She had no qualms about openly pinning her feelings to her sleeve like favors for all to see.

Then there were the two horses she guarded so possessively. Both creatures displayed a blind devotion and instant obedience to her that could only be born of love.

He snorted derisively as he dumped his belongings in his own, unused chamber, then headed for the stables. He didn't like people who spilled feelings the way unplugged kegs spewed ale, though he had to admit she didn't exactly spew. Last night with Gellie, she'd been calm and competent . . . except when she'd kissed him, her face wreathed with joy.

The memory unsettled him. She reminded him too much of Sarah, who'd been given to husky whispers of devotion and impetuous embraces whenever she willed.

Desire twisted with the pain of loss, and he reminded himself that she wasn't Sarah. Mistress Cavandish said and did things that were unseemly for a woman, forcing him to reprimand her. In response, she erupted in a show of temper that his mild-natured Sarah would never have displayed, had she possessed such a thing.

As he led five men from the castle gate, mounted and set for a day of hard riding, Graham redirected his thoughts to practical matters. Still, he wondered if any of these men would be as loyal to him as the firebrand was to those she loved. They'd been loyal to his father, but half of these folk thought him mad for his odd ideas.

Disgruntled by the knowledge, he settled into the ride. Against his better judgment, and because of Mistress Cavandish's distress about her brother, he'd changed his plans to meet with the local sheriffs, sending Arthur in his stead. He would search the Forest of Ae today, one of the places where Will had harbored prisoners in the past.

"Graham, someane's a-followin' us." Jasper captured his attention before they were a league from their own gates. "Appears to be the English lassie."

"The devil." Graham twisted around and spied the firebrand, then cursed anew. He hadn't imagined she would openly defy him. How dare she do so in front of his men?

But they didn't know what he'd told her. Nor would they know the extent to which she defied him. A diabolical plan formed as he noted she rode her black steed bareback, with neither bit nor reins to lead the way. His stable men had obviously done their duty, refusing to provide saddle or bridle, though she seemed not to care. Yet a full day of riding without a saddle could cripple even the hardiest rider. If that was the medicine she wanted, he would give her a full dose.

With a show of disapproval, he pulled up and admitted her among them, despite the resentful and appraising stares of his men. Though they disliked a woman in their midst while riding, he could all but see the thoughts of having her in bed click through their minds.

"This is Mistress Cavandish." He purposely omitted their names from the introduction to discourage her from communicating with them. "She will accompany us on our search today. You will accord her all respect." Despite his attempt to control her, he wondered uneasily what outrageous event she would incite next.

He brushed the thought aside. There wasn't a female alive he couldn't control, if not with his anger, then with his charm. And this one he vowed to wear out with a day of hard riding. By the morrow she would be begging to rest her saddle-sore bottom at the castle, where it belonged.

Six hours of riding later, Lucina was discouraged and weary to the bone. Their search had yielded no sign of her brother. Nor had they found anything faintly resembling a place where he might have been held captive in the last day.

Disappointed, she agreed to Graham's order that they turn back, but her indignation grew as they retraced their path to the castle. At no time during the day had he conferred with her about the search, though she had expressed opinions several times. Yet whether she spoke or remained silent, he and the men ignored her so thoroughly, she had been forced to demand her right to aid in the hunt. Each time they had stopped, she had dismounted and examined caves along riverbanks or on high hillsides or the brush of overgrown gullies. Her reward had been nothing, either in clues to her brother's location or a solitary word of encouragement from Graham.

As she patted Orpheus's neck, she promised him a hearty supper when they arrived home. Yet all the while she cast Graham baleful glances. The splendid cut of his profile never hinted at his unreasonable nature. Yet he was as moody and unpleasant as the bad weather that had assaulted them yesterday.

Besides that, she had considered Graham's strategy of the day and found it lacking. She had cajoled Jasper during a private moment, guessing he was the nicest of the lot despite his mountain-crag features, and he had explained that numerous routes remained to explore. At this rate, finding Roger could take weeks.

Yet despite her concern for her brother and her frustration at the unprofitable day, she had reaped a small consolation. The richness of Scotland enthralled her. Orpheus had seemed to like it as well, and they had even shared an exhilarated race across a meadow dotted with bluebells and smelling of sweet grass, The warmth of the sun had heated their limbs as pleasure put wings to his heels and hope in her heart. On the meadow's far side, they had entered a shady glen, and she had spied silver water tumbling over mossy stones, the enchanted song loud in her ears. It all seemed magical, and if her own land were anywhere near as beautiful, she would count herself well blessed.

But her brother must be found first. And the caves they had searched left her little hope that Roger would be somewhere clean and dry.

The sun sank lower and lower in the western sky, and dusk cast a glow of gold over the land. Finally the flaming ball winked out entirely, and her spirits sank with it. She turned to Graham, wanting reassurance, though she doubted he would oblige.

"We will try again on the morrow," he said in response to her probing. "Many places remain to be searched. We can count on spending days."

"But we don't have days," she objected, sure now that he didn't believe they could find Roger. He should be forcing answers from his cousin, not roaming the countryside. "I must find my brother now."

"Is the company poor?" he asked with a bland, impenetrable stare.

She frowned at him, unwilling to be deflected from her purpose by commenting on the merit of the company. She had decided the men didn't dislike her entirely, for Jasper had unbent and talked to her, as had two of the others during stolen moments. But that was hardly the point. "I don't want my brother kept in some nasty hole," she countered. "He might fall ill."

"That is possible," he acknowledged, seeming, as always, insensitive to her fears.

His surly expression hinted that he would hardly alter his plans to accommodate her. He was just like her brother Matthew, who refused to listen to anyone and was uncomfortable in female company. Graham had been clearly unsettled when she'd kissed him last night. In better circumstances she would have been amused, but she was too worried about Roger. Besides, Graham needn't be troubled. She felt no inclination to touch him today.

"Who was that man we met by the river?" she demanded, remembering the stiff greeting Graham had grudgingly offered an older Scot and his retinue as she'd gone to tend her private needs in a thicket.

"None of your affair."

"It is my affair until I find my brother alive and well," she informed him crisply.

But he wouldn't tell her, and judging from the veiled tension in the air and the clipped speech the pair had exchanged, she could only guess it had been someone Graham hated.

Anxiously she mulled over these details as she crawled into the narrow bed after a quiet supper in the tower room. The linen had been changed, and she settled into it gratefully, inhaling the scent of fresh air and soap. Someone had cleared the room as well, though she noted that many loose items had been stuffed onto the shelves of the court cupboard. The trash heap had merely been consolidated into one place.

Silently cursing the Black Graham, she jerked the curtain into place to hide his clutter from view. He had purposely barred her from the company of the hall, shutting her in this isolated chamber, as if afraid she would give his people plague. It meant she had no further news of how settlements progressed or whether peace held.

But even as she considered Graham's secretive, callous attitude, she remembered his love for his mare, and her feelings about him wavered.

Quickly she reprimanded herself for her weakness. She must not trust him. He had his family's interests to protect, not hers, and she dared not rely on him.

He disdained females in the bargain. No matter that he had cast her a reluctant look of admiration when she had announced her intention to ride with him again on the morrow. Did he think her incapable of spending hours on horseback? How did he imagine she'd gotten here from Dorset? Carried in a hand litter by doting slaves?

She was on dangerous footing here, in a stranger's household, dependent on him for her safety and the rescue of her brother. She must move warily and guard her emotions lest they hinder her purpose. And she vowed never again to be swayed into touching the Black Graham. Not for the rest of her life.

Chapter 4

Though Lucina was weary from her day of riding, the mattress that had cushioned her so blissfully last night felt like a bed of jagged rocks tonight. She tossed and turned, unable to find a comfortable spot. Or was it her fear for Roger that gouged her? How she longed to be with her brother. His presence would calm her fears about this strange country with its cold men and their violent lives.

The last thought conjured the image of the Black Graham, his dark hair whipping in the breeze as he rode, as if he didn't know she was there and didn't care. Yet she had once looked up to find him studying her, and in his wary, sardonic gaze, she had seen full awareness of her presence and knew he watched every move with distrust.

She sat up wearily and rubbed her tired eyes, convinced she must try another way to find her brother. Combing the countryside could take weeks and still result in failure. Roger could be anywhere. Only the man who knew Roger's whereabouts could help her.

Tucking up her single long plait with hairpins, she donned her kirtle bodice and moved toward the chamber door. If the Graham chief refused to question his cousin further, she would not be so shy.

The stone staircase dizzied her with its endless downward spiral. A feeling of foreboding crept into her soul. The chilled stone walls seemed to grieve, as if sorrow lingered here.

Lucina dismissed the uncomfortable notion as fanciful. Stones didn't have personality. If anything, the occupants created the grim atmosphere.

At the bottom of the wheeling staircase, eerie darkness stretched before her like a black, impenetrable wall. How she longed for a candle to light her way, but there had been none in the tower room. Despite the warmth and comfort of the chamber above, its only light source was two unwieldy oil lamps on the table, much too heavy to carry on a midnight jaunt.

How would she ever find Mosley in this confusing labyrinth? The castle was old and, she guessed, added to many times. It seemed a veritable maze of corridors leading to additional wings and chambers. Feeling with both hands along the wall, Lucina ventured into the cold passage, deciding her best course lay in finding the great hall. She would start from there.

The silence of the great castle weighed heavily on her as she ventured forth. Maggie Johnstone, the serving woman at Carlisle Castle, had told her the place was haunted. She should know—her family had been intermarried with Grahams for generations, and she'd grown up here. Lucina agreed the grim castle seemed robbed of human cheer, even though numerous men were housed somewhere. Were they all as morose as the Graham?

How glad she would be to leave this place. The stones of the passage felt cold and unwelcoming as she touched them, but at least she could follow them to the hall. Seeing a light flicker ahead, she increased her pace.

"Alice, ye missed a spot," a female grumbled from the hall beyond the screens passage.

"Oh, aye, Grissel," another muttered, sounding resentful.

Lucina peered around the carved wooden partition into the drafty hall, then drew back. The three females scrubbing the trestle tables would see her if they looked up. Repositioning herself to ensure her cover, she took another cautious peek.

The maids attacked the wooden planks with brushes, dipping them periodically into buckets of water. At the far end of the hall, several men lounged around a crackling fire in the huge hearth. Lucina resented her relegation to the tower. Yet these females were the first she'd laid eyes on since arriving, and clearly they were servants. With no other females present, Lucina supposed she was safest in a private room.

"This water is clarty," declared the women called Grissel, apparently the senior among them. "Alice, fetch fresh from the scullery, and be sure 'tis hot."

"I'll no' fetch it alone. Ye wouldna ask that o' me." Alice sounded aghast.

"Fetch it however ye like, boot fetch it," Grissel snapped, "or we'll never see our beds."

"Why dinna ye tell *her* to go." Alice indicated the third female among them, who appeared far younger, mayhap not over twelve years.

The girl squeaked in alarm. "I canna go. Bonnie Mary's oot there."

"Bah," Grissel grumbled unsympathetically. "The ghostie hasna shown itself o' late."

Lucina thought Grissel's response far too rough, given how frightened many youngsters were of the dark. At eleven, she'd appointed herself Roger's protector, guarding him against the foul beasties he had imagined lurked in the night.

"Dinna make me go. I pray ye," the girl pleaded. Dropping her scrub brush, she sank onto the bench and burst into tears. "She's there, awaiting for me. I ken it, for I saw her last night. Bonnie Mary Maxwell hersel', wi' death in her eyes."

Lucina's irritation with Grissel increased. Didn't she know how much she'd frightened the child? She shifted her gaze from the girl back to the women, wondering if she dared intervene, only to find them staring at the girl, expressions of terror written on their faces. Could they possibly believe in the ghost as well?

A breath of air ruffled the back of Lucina's skirts and stirred her hair, warning her that someone approached. Instinctively she flattened herself against the screen and searched the dark passage behind her. Someone must have opened a door beyond. She braced herself, an excuse for her late-night wandering ready on her lips.

Seconds passed, but no one appeared. Puzzled, Lucina peered into the passage leading to the tower but spied no movement. Relieved, she turned back to the hall, sure the gust of air had blown from under a door somewhere. Still, the air around her seemed frigid, as if it seeped from the unforgiving stones of the castle itself.

She chided herself for her wayward thinking. People could be unforgiving, not stones.

But the three women in the hall also seemed to think the chill was more than mere cold.

"It can summon her, tae speak her name aloud, Annie." Alice sighed and reached for a bucket with one hand, a rush light with the other. Her gnarled hands shook. "But she only coomes to those alone, so we'll fetch the water together. Hasten, now."

Lucina slipped back into the dark passage as they approached the screens, confident she would not be seen. But instead of crossing to the kitchen door, the women stopped at the entry, as if checking for foul creatures that might lurk in the dark.

"Why dinna ye tell me afore aboot Bonnie Mary," Alice asked Annie in a low voice as they peered warily into the dark.

"How could I?" the young one whimpered. "His lordship swore tae punish the next one asayin' her name aloud. *He* never sees her, he claims."

" 'Tis no affair o' ours what he sees or dinna see," Alice admonished. "We ken what we ken. But did ye see her eyes, fer truth?"

"Weel, nay, not her eyes," the girl said. "She were a mere flutter o' white. But I felt the cold o' death."

She finished her testimony with a shiver, and they each gabbled through a prayer, finishing with breathy amens. As they scuttled through the door leading to the kitchens, Lucina stared after them in surprise. They had concluded with words suggesting Mary's ghost walked the castle because she had died a violent death by the hand of her lord.

Depressed by the possibility, Lucina rubbed her bare arms. The grim walls of Castle Graham had loomed dank and unwelcoming from the first, but now they seemed to tighten their cold grip on her. Not only were there few women in this horrid stone heap, but those who did live here were frightened halfway to idiocy every time the sun went down. Being practical-minded, Lucina didn't believe in ghosts, but she did believe people could die of imagined fear.

"Did you learn aught to help in your quest?"

The husky whisper near her left ear frightened Lucina

out of her wits. She whirled to find the Black Graham within a pace of her hiding place.

She almost wilted with embarrassment. Clapping one hand to her chest, she willed her racing heart to slow as she glared at him, wishing she could disappear as suddenly as he'd appeared.

"If 'tis useful information, tell me," he cajoled, as if to a fellow conspirator. "You've gone to such pains to listen in."

His sarcasm bit into her sensibilities and fired her temper. "I intend to find my brother," she said with all the contempt she could muster. "And will use any means necessary to do so."

"I'm chief here. I'll find him. Your part is to wait," he shot back.

"Wait?" She tested the word, not liking it. "I don't care to wait for others, especially when I can perform the task at hand better than those who stand in my way."

Graham gazed stonily at Mistress Cavandish, who had disobeyed him once today and apparently thought nothing of doing so again. Why hadn't the day's ride exhausted her? Why wasn't she groaning in bed from a sore backside? And why hadn't she covered herself in more than a smock and kirtle skirt? She chaffed her bare arms with both hands—a natural invitation for him to stare at the soft, exposed flesh. Interest knifed through his groin even as her words soured his mood. She had no inkling of the insurmountable problems he faced, hinting she could do better than he. From the first he'd feared his irrational wish to claim her would lead to trouble.

Sure enough, she marred his decisions. He'd wasted today solely to please her—a full day that should have been spent in negotiations—and he'd imagined nothing ill would come of his choice? "Go to your chamber," he growled. "Unpleasant things can happen to lasses who wander alone in this place."

"Like being frightened to death by a nonexistent ghost?" With that sally, she prepared to sail off, eyes flashing with angry disdain at his veiled threat.

"What do you mean?" He caught her by the wrist and jerked her back, furious at her mention of the ghost. The bones beneath her flesh felt fragile as he absorbed the distrust in her eyes.

"Your serving maids are so afraid of a ghost called Bonnie Mary, they can hardly do their work. Yet you forbid them to mention it."

He narrowed his eyes and kept his hold on her. "My grandam died and was buried years ago. There is no ghost. Talking about it only makes their gossip worse."

"You should *prove* to them there's no ghost so the gossip stops entirely," she snapped back. "But you won't do it because it's my idea, and you can't bear anyone else to have an idea, especially not a female."

Graham shook his head in disbelief at this impassioned speech. Only moments earlier he'd risen from his bed, tormented out of sleep by erotic images of this fey female. Over and over he'd relived the moment when she'd kissed him, her lips brushing his stubble-roughened cheeks. Her amazing skill with horses had jolted his feelings back to life, but he was far from happy about it.

She was a troublemaker, his rational side warned.

Torchbearer, his emotions proclaimed her. Harbinger of new hope.

He remembered the sight of her on Orpheus, her body gracefully moving as one with the galloping steed's. During one soaring ride across a meadow today, her face had been transformed by serenity, as if she and her horse used their motion to rise above the troubles of the world.

Moved by the image, he hung on the brink of acting out the wish that had left him sleepless. He was sure this refined female's innocent sensuality would staunch the darkness flowing through him. She could turn his painful thoughts and memories into a forgiving, forgetful haze.

On the verge of relenting, he cut off the impulse, replacing it with the stern litany that kept him going from dawn to dusk. His duty lay in controlling the fire and sword, in preserving his kin's blood. What he wanted mattered not a whit. More than that, he'd have hell to pay with the English if he touched this refined daughter of an English merchant, and he had problems enough as things stood. Beyond that, he'd been wed once and had no intention of entering the state again. The first time had torn him apart.

Disgusted that he had detained her so long, he abruptly released her. She backed against the wall, eyeing him warily, her lips quivering as she panted for air. Beneath the

fabric of her smock, the outline of her shapely breasts rose
and fell rapidly, revealing that she was as aroused as he.

"Go to your chamber and stay there," he barked, furious
with their obvious response to each other. "If you venture
out again tonight, I'll tie you to the bed." He spun on his
heel and slammed through the far door into the kitchens.
He *would* tie her to the bed if necessary and hoped he'd
frightened her by saying so. He'd put her in the tower room
and intended her to stay there rather than nosing into
things that weren't her affair, not to mention firing his
blood with a single look. He would set a guard on her
after this.

And he would find her brother and send her out of his
life forever, as fast as he could.

With her orders from the Black Graham insultingly clear,
Lucina hurried down the passage toward the tower, her
heart banging like a smith's hammer in her chest. Stars
above, but he was a scoundrel, creeping up on her like a
thief and shouting in her ear, then ordering her to leave
while holding her back. When he'd clamped his huge paw
on her wrist, his male interest all too apparent, she'd
thought to die on the spot. She might still if her heart didn't
slow down.

She stopped at the foot of the spiral stairs, knowing she
would never make it to the top without first recovering
her breath.

But try as she would, she couldn't regain her calm. The
women's distress over the ghost had unsettled her, as had
the cold, hungry look in Graham's eyes. Might he do as
Will had urged him and "have" her? He'd looked in the
mood.

How did she know that? she questioned. With her lack
of experience, she shouldn't have an inkling of what he
wanted. Yet she had felt the snap of energy between them
as he'd held her by the wrist, insolently studying her face,
then letting his gaze head south. Fire had curled through
her belly and down between her legs as his gaze lingered
on her body. She'd wanted to settle against his chest and
offer her lips to be kissed.

Instead, she'd used her argument about banishing the

ghost as a weapon to fight the knowledge that she had liked his interest, worse yet, wanted to respond to it.

But she wouldn't. She had no wish to be involved with a man, thus trading her newly found independence for the bondage of male possession. She had only recently escaped from her mother and four older siblings who, without realizing it, had pushed their decisions on her well after she was one and twenty.

Yet if the Black Graham used such fell arts to beguile her, he ought to be called "Black Magic" Graham. Working at his side over Gellie, she had felt the attraction between them dance through her blood, as dazzling as stars. He excited her unbearably. The white-hot thrill of pleasure had streaked through her when she touched him, just as it did when she raced Orpheus. With it had come the knowledge that his interest in her raced just as quickly through his blood.

Stars above, the ordeals she'd been through in the last twenty-four hours were enough to give a person gray hairs.

Gathering up her skirts, she raised her foot to the first step but halted as a flicker of white caught her eye. A moonbeam, she told herself. Nothing more.

It moved again, fluttering . . .

Cold settled in the pit of her stomach. Could it be that something waited for her in the dark . . . something with huge, hungry jaws that would . . .

An indistinct flutter of diaphanous white materialized at the far end of the pitch-dark passage, coming toward her, as silent as death.

Lucina spun around and raced up the stairs two at a time, too frightened to look back.

At the top of the stairs, she sprinted across the narrow landing and slammed the door shut. Spying a heavy bar on the wall, she swung it into place and leaned against it, panting. It couldn't be a ghost. She didn't believe in them. It must have been something else.

She was too tired to take any more tonight. She felt as if she would fly to pieces, torn apart by her fear for her brother, by her rage with the Black Graham for doing nothing to free him, for exciting her by merely being, even when he didn't touch her.

Diving into the bed, she pulled the blankets over her

head and prayed for the oblivion of sleep. Her worst night-
mares seemed to be coming to life, taking over the rational
life she had always led in Dorset and filling her days and
her nights with eerie specters and an inexplicable lust for
a man she'd only just met. She couldn't expect to see him
ever again once her brother was safe, nor did she want to.
The things he did to her were too frightening, things she
dared not admit she felt, dared not want to feel again.

Chapter 5

Early the next morning, Lucina drifted from sleep to waking, drawn across the rift by the uneasy sense that she was not alone. Something heavy hit the floor nearby, proving she did have a visitor. Yet she had barred the door from within last night, and that should have guaranteed privacy, if nothing else.

Somehow she knew it had to be "Black Magic" Graham.

Suddenly, the dreary fortress of Castle Graham seemed to tighten around her, ensnaring her in its web of secrets— Will with his hiding place for Roger, Graham with a mysterious past that had soured his life, this chamber that seemed to offer refuge but, in fact, did not. And she was the poor fly, forced into the impossible task of sorting out the sticky web spun by the spider, but instead getting caught in its coil.

Sitting up in bed, she strained to hear some movement but could make out nothing. Tweaking back the curtain, she spotted one of her saddlebags lying on the floor. Overjoyed to see it and forgetting all else, she scrambled from the bed and pounced on it. But before she could open it, she felt an intimidating presence.

Looking up, she found the Graham sitting at the table, going through the contents of her other bag piece by piece.

"Just what do you think you're doing, sir, violating my privacy?" she cried, aghast at his audacity. "And how did you come here when I purposely barred the door?"

"You might say you're the one who's violated my privacy," he said blandly. "This is my chamber, loaned to you to keep you safe."

"Am I safe if people come and go as they please?" she said stiffly, wishing she'd donned her bodice and skirt before confronting him. Her smock felt entirely too thin.

"Not all people come and go here at will. Only the master," he said with an annoying calm. "As for your safety . . ." He paused to sweep her body with his smoldering gaze. "You're the one who tempts a man to want more, Lucina Cavandish, flinging yourself in my arms and kissing me."

"I didn't fling myself. And I didn't kiss you in *that* way." Despite her denial, she felt her face flame with embarrassment. But she was suddenly distracted by a new issue. How had he learned her name?

As if divining her puzzlement, he waved a paper at her.

"My deed!" Leaping forward to claim the precious paper, she remembered too late her thin smock with its unlaced throat. Eager to escape his probing gaze that seemed to undress her, she snatched the paper from his hand, dashed behind the curtain, and yanked it into place.

With shaking fingers she examined her key to the future. Was the deed undamaged? Would it still support her claim? With relief she found it intact. Her dreams were safe.

Now impatient to oust Graham from the chamber, she pulled on her kirtle bodice and skirt and struggled to arrange her hair in some semblance of decorum. But as she reemerged, she found Graham thumbing through the old Bible given her by Lady Ashley just before her death.

"Be careful. The pages are brittle." She sprang forward to take it from him and cradled it to her chest. "It was a gift from a dear friend, and I don't like anyone touching it. I would like my saddlebags now. And privacy, so I might change into fresh clothes."

"You require a bath first." Graham closed the flap of her saddlebag and stood.

Lucina bristled at the personal nature of his order. "We don't have time for that. We must search for my brother. Where do we try today?"

"You're staying here today."

"I'm not," she insisted, dismayed by his sudden announcement. She was only a little stiff today, having proved yesterday that she could ride as fast and as hard as the men. Why shouldn't she go with them? The alternative—

staying in a room that clearly had a secret entry—unsettled her. Nor did she wish to listen to gossiping servants telling tales of a ghost. By light of day, she regretted her panic of last night. She should have confronted the thing she'd seen and proved it a sham.

Firebrand, Graham thought, fully aware that interest crackled between them like an out-of-control moorland fire. And to think that, without understanding the baseness of male nature, she desired him, too. Why else had she embraced and kissed him that first night, despite her claim that she hadn't meant it that way?

He imagined her lying naked on his bed beyond the curtain. Her thighs would be soft and ivory pale, like the gleaming flesh of her bare arms. So much in his life had been ugly and tragic, but she was not. Her unique freshness interested him more than was healthy, especially when he ought to be more interested in finding her brother. Yet sexual interest wasn't something a man could turn on or off like a stream of grain from a sack. She would be safer here for the day.

Besides, new developments forced him to keep her hidden. Last night he'd scarcely laid down to sleep before being roused again. English families had staged a return raid on the Mosley and Lang branches of his family. He'd reached their smoking cottages in time to drive off the attackers but failed to save lives.

In the face of his tenants' fury and outrage, despite his own agony, he'd spent hours convincing them that no good would come of pursuing the English reivers in a hot trod. Murder wouldn't bring back their loved ones, and another raid, even a legal one, would only heap more vengeance on their heads. Now he carried the burden of his promise—to obtain just recompense.

He'd been hard at work since. Recovering her packhorse had been an afterthought on his return trip to Castle Graham. He'd hoped to catch a few hours sleep, but had been unable to resist a few minutes with the alluring English lass.

He'd had the minutes, but he didn't feel better. His neck and shoulders ached with fatigue. His head throbbed like a military drum. And he'd seen something on her deed that worried him. He believed the location specified was in the

Debatable Land. She could never live there. "What do you
intend to do with your property?" he asked.

Her face lit up with innocent enthusiasm at the mention
of her future. "Do you know where it is? Is there good
pastureland? Are there likely places for a barn and house?
I do want to plant a crop or two, as well. Do you think
oats would grow there?"

Oats? Pasture? His mind reeled as the implications of
her words registered. "What do you intend to do with this
land?" he repeated impatiently. "Answer me straight."

"I intend to live there," she said with simple dignity. "I'll
build a house."

"If you can indeed manage such a thing," he said skeptically, "what then?"

"I'm going to breed horses. Orpheus will make a splendid stud, don't you agree?" She tilted her chin just high
enough to suggest defiance, should he contradict her.

He snorted and turned away, disliking the concern that
knifed through him. Why should her plans trouble him?
'Twas none of his affair if she lived in a place where murder
and mayhem thrived. Why should it pain him to imagine
her disappointment when her attempts met with defeat,
when her house was burned to the ground and her horses
stolen from beneath her nose?

It did pain him, though. It gouged him hard, as if he'd
sat on his own dirk and it had sliced his leg. He studied
her hopeful expression and found he couldn't tell her the
unsavory nature of her inheritance. It would hurt her, and
he had all the hurt people he could manage.

"Aren't you pleased to have someone else nearby who
shares your interest?" she persisted, her sweet face re-
proachful at his lack of answers. "We might work together,
you know. I helped with Gellie and your foal. You might
help me find a splendid mare to breed with Orpheus. The
result could be beyond our wildest dreams."

Graham flinched at her choice of words. His dreams had
all crashed to ruin years ago. And he was repaying her
favors in ways she couldn't begin to understand. "I have
work to do," he informed her coldly and strode for the
door. "My guards will escort you to the kitchens for your
bath and stand at the doors while the maids assist you
behind a screen."

"I'll not stay here." She scowled. "You said I could leave when I wished. I wish to go now."

"Your safety is at stake," he grunted, refusing to reveal more.

"Why? What's the danger?" Just as he'd expected, she wouldn't trust him to protect her. "I saw no danger yesterday," she continued. "We talked to no one save that man with his retainers. Who was he?"

"No one of import."

"You don't like him," she stated. "I could tell by the way you held yourself while you talked to him, your neck and shoulders all stiff."

"Brilliant observation."

"But why? Is he the danger? He didn't seem threatening to me, an elderly gentleman, obviously of some rank."

She was too inquisitive by half, and it was on the tip of his tongue to tell her it was none of her affair, but after the message he'd received from the Scots Border warden, it might become her affair. Especially if they didn't find her brother. "He's John, Lord Maxwell, until recently the Scots West Border March warden," he relented, deciding she deserved to know at least this portion of the bad news.

"Ah, Sir Edward Kincaid's counterpart. Might he aid us?" she prompted, her eyes sparkling with hope.

"You don't understand what has happened," he said harshly, deciding he had no choice but to frighten her into obedience. "Will did more than steal a few cattle. He burned two English villages to the ground and killed nigh on twenty men, as well as a few women and children who happened to be in the way. With armed warfare ready to break out at any moment, we're in a perilous position with both Border wardens. Besides, the only aid a Maxwell would willingly offer a Graham is a walk to the gibbet."

"My stars!" She fell back a pace, her face stricken. The swift quelling of her optimism brought him a curious satisfaction. Let her understand the danger they faced. Let her know, too, that evil thrived in the world.

"But why do the Maxwells want to injure the Grahams?" She persisted just when he thought he'd frightened her into silence. Was she daft, or did she simply have the tenacity of a leech?

Whichever it was, he couldn't bring himself to tell her

the details—of how the Grahams and the Maxwells had
clashed years ago over the affair of Bonnie Mary, and how
everyone kept the story alive with their ghostly sightings,
continued raids, and ugly stories about how his wife Sarah
had died because of him, though only he knew the truth.
Both families had paid over and over for the misfortune of
Mary. It was time to let it go.

"Blood feud," he whispered hoarsely, groping for the
door latch. Feeling suddenly worn out by the tumult of the
night, as well as the emotions stirred up by this lass, he
stepped out on the landing, slammed the door and locked
it before she could react. In less than a heartbeat, her fists
crashed against the door.

"What of my brother?" her voice cracked with fear from
the other side of the wooden barrier.

"Your brother is a valued hostage. He's probably safer
than we are," he assured her, mustering the effort to keep
his voice kindly. "Yet to please you, I spent a full day
searching for him yesterday. Now I must turn to other
things. You're to stay put."

"Sir Edward will kill you if you don't let me out of here."

The door jiggled with the impact of her fists, but Graham
knew it wouldn't yield. "I'll see him today," he said evenly,
hoping she wouldn't pound until she was bruised. "He will
decide where you should stay."

"But I want to see my horses."

It seemed a reasonable wish to Graham. "Someone will
escort you to the stables and back. But you may not ride
today," he added, anticipating her next demand. "You may
groom your stallion and mare and care for the packhorse,
but you may not take them out. My men will prevent you
if you try."

"But I have no company here. There's nothing to do.
Are there no women in this inhospitable pile of rock?"

The despair in her voice tugged at his conscience, though
he resented her calling his home a pile of rock. Hadn't he
given up one of the most comfortable chambers in the castle to her? "I'll have you taken to visit my great-aunt if
you wish," he informed her shortly. "She's the lady of the
castle, though illness prevents her from performing her duties as she would wish."

Unable to tolerate more of her probing, he plunged down

the stairs. She would never know the favor he was doing her. After dealing with last night's mayhem, he had learned the English wanted a hostage to serve as a bond of surety against further raiding. And since they did, so did Sir John Carmichael, the Scots West March Border warden, who always did Maxwell's bidding.

Now he regretted giving in to Lucina's whims and letting her accompany them yesterday—because Maxwell had seen her. And knowing she had come to Scotland to claim some land, the Scot wanted her.

Chapter 6

Lucina returned to the tower, more comfortable after a hot bath and a change into clean clothing, but more worried than before. From Graham's description, the Border situation was indeed bad. He'd wanted to frighten her, and he had.

Her desire to find her brother raged within her. Graham had openly admitted he would not search again, at least not today. She must do it herself, yet how could she, locked away in this tower room?

Will Mosley. The answer lay with that cunning devil. With Graham absent, she must try again to find and question her brother's captor.

Pulling a brush from her saddlebag, she let down her hair, still damp from her bath, and worked out the tangles. Deciding to leave it loose over her shoulders, since she wouldn't be riding, Lucina sat down to the food brought her and broke her fast. The buttery sweet oatcakes and hot porridge with honey were delicious, but she couldn't stop thinking of how she might reach Will. As she finished off a withered but still sweet apple, a scratching sounded in the room.

Lucina looked around anxiously, wondering if the castle were plagued with rats, then realized the scratching came from the door. "Come in," she called, hoping Graham's guards had arrived, then realizing it couldn't be them.

"The door is locked," a high, thin voice, decidedly female, answered her invitation. "Sit ye still an' I'll nip in the other way."

The other way? Lucina jumped up, her gaze darting

around the chamber. Now she would surely learn the location of the secret entry. Her mysterious visitor, whoever it was, would give it away. Choosing the sleeping alcove as the most likely place for a secret entry, she flung back the drapery and waited for the wall to move.

"Good morrow, Mary. Ye're up early this morn."

Lucina jerked around in surprise. A wizened little lady with a thick white braid swinging over her shoulder stood in the center of the chamber, giving no clue as to how she'd arrived. A welcoming smile adorned her faded lips.

"How did you come in?" Frustrated at missing the answer to her burning question, Lucina pivoted full circle, scanning the chamber for the hidden entry but seeing nothing.

The woman touched her arm. "Mary, ma lamb," she said in sympathy. "Give us a kiss."

To Lucina's astonishment, she was enveloped in a hearty embrace. Unable to resist the free flow of affection, Lucina hugged the woman back, feeling thin flesh layering sharp shoulder bones. She smelled of rose water and linen dried in fresh air, and despite the woman's obvious frailty, she had snapping blue eyes that reminded Lucina of Lady Ashley. Except that this woman's affection was for someone named Mary.

She was obviously confused, but Lucina was loathe to correct her. Her visitor was far more likely to discuss secrets with someone she knew—or thought she knew—than with a stranger. So she returned the embrace offered and enjoyed the exchange of warmth.

As they drew apart, Lucina studied the woman who kept an affectionate grip on both her hands. Of slightly smaller stature, she wore a woolen kirtle and white apron. Meeting the woman's gaze, she realized the woman's bluebell eyes were the same color as Graham's, which meant this had to be his great-aunt.

"So, ye've bathed," the woman began congenially, declining the chair Lucina offered at the table. Instead, she pulled a stool to the hearth and stirred the embers to a blaze. "Ye're looking right brawly, ma lamb." She wrestled with a peat block, meaning to put it on the fire.

"Uh, thank you," Lucina said, guessing this was a compliment, but not sure. "The bath was pleasant, but I wish I might come and go as I like." She took the unwieldy block and placed it on the fire for the woman. Curbing her obsession with the idea of escape by the secret entry, she remembered her manners and offered one of the platters. "Would you care for an oatcake?"

The lady accepted the dainty and ate it. "Thank ye, Mary. I grieve that his lordship locked ye in again. Skelp that Angus Alexander Malcolm Graham fer a brock."

"He did lock me in," Lucina agreed after a second's hesitation, uncertain what a brock might be or how to skelp it. And this was the second time the woman had called her Mary. Was her eyesight poor, that she mistook her for someone else? And did the Graham regularly lock up someone called Mary? The idea appalled her. "My name is Lucina, not Mary," she said cautiously.

"Oh, aye, Mary." The old woman pressed a finger to her lips and nodded her silvery head with a conspiratorial smile. "I'll call ye any name ye wish, an' that helps."

Lucina gave herself a mental shake. Could the woman not be in her right mind? She certainly seemed old enough to have lost touch with reality. "And what shall I call you?" she blurted, unsure what to say next.

"Why, ye always call me Isabel," the woman said in some surprise. "Dinna change now."

Lucina sighed and resigned herself to being Mary. But was she Bonnie Mary, the ghost? Putting aside her confusion, Lucina murmured reassuring words to Isabel, not wanting to lose the company of her only social equal in the castle, regardless of the reason she'd gained it in the first place. She would be anyone necessary to keep this new friend.

Isabel accepted her excuses and rearranged her apron with busy fingers. "So, love, why is the Graham angry this time?"

"He says I'm in danger and must stay here," Lucina explained, wondering how much she dared say. "But I'm not sure that's the true reason. My brother is missing, you see."

Isabel nodded sagely and helped herself to another oatcake with a graceful hand. "He's a canny one, is the Graham. He'll ken when someane's oop to a trick."

Puzzled by this cryptic statement, Lucina decided to ask

some questions of her own. "It would help me immensely to talk to Will. Could you show me where he's lodged?"

"Is that William Lang or Jock's Will ye'll be wantin'? Or could it be Wee Willie Jack?"

Lucina blinked, baffled by these choices. "All I know is he has flaming red hair and accompanied the chief the night I arrived."

Isabel lifted sleek white eyebrows as if scandalized. "That would be the Graham's Will. Ye mun keep away from him." She squinted with concern. "He's a devil in trunk-hose, he is. He's faithered babes from here to Edinburgh."

Lucina groaned inwardly. Just what she expected of Will, though she might turn his interest in her to her advantage. "But I must ask him some questions. He knows where my brother is."

"What, Bell the Cat?" A sudden concern kindled in Isabel's blue eyes. "Is he brewing trouble again for the Grahams?"

Wondering who "Bell the Cat" might be and finding the conversation more confusing by the minute, Lucina took another chance. "My brother is in trouble. The Mosley men have hidden him, and Will won't tell us where. But if I could talk to Will, he might relent. I know he's locked in the castle, in a special room."

"Ah, I wondered who they had in there." Isabel appeared to consider, a distant look in her eyes. Suddenly she snapped back to attention. "I'll take ye if ye really wish, but the Graham will be a-punishin' us if he finds oot. He might lock ye oop for some time."

"I would rather he didn't know about it, but if he does find out, I'll take the consequences." Lucina suppressed the sudden burst of elation to think her scheme might work. Despite Isabel's apparent lack of hold on the present, she appeared entirely capable of leading her to Will.

"Nae, and I dinna approve o' half o' his doings, either. Come with me, then. Ye have a duty to help yer kin." She led the way to the wall opposite the hearth where the messy court cupboard stood. Lucina had avoided looking at it. Now, brought to face it, she stared, appalled.

"A wicked tangle, is it no'?" Isabel grinned wryly at her, confirming her suspicion. "The lad needs a woman to keep order for him. He's a slackard, otherwise."

"So were my brothers as boys, but my parents wouldn't stand for it. Nor would I." Lucina shuddered at the idea of having to reorder the slovenly kept shelf. "He should straighten his own things. And someone should scrub the floor." She indicated the brown stain before the hearth.

"Och, we dinna wan' to do that." Isabel gave her a surprised look. "Ye ken as well as I do, 'tis Thrawn Jock's blood, spilled the night o' his death."

Startled, Lucina stared at the stain with rising distaste. She disliked the idea of living in close proximity to a blood-stain. "Who was Thrawn Jock?" she asked, wondering if she could hide the offensive mark with a mat or rug, at least during her stay.

"Faither o' the present Graham," Isabel answered serenely, reaching for a wide linen panel painted with a hunting scene. "Reivin' caught oop wi' him. He had a mortal wound."

Lucina gaped at the stain, thoroughly disconcerted. Graham intentionally lived in the room where his father had died, even retaining the mark of his spilled blood?

The news told her a sad story about the man, and she struggled with regret for his obvious pain . . . until a click recaptured her attention. She turned to see the secret door swing wide.

Blast it, she'd missed the trick. Clearly a maneuver performed in a precise way was required. If she hadn't been staring at the bloodstain, worrying about the Black Graham's ghosts, she would know what it was. But her disappointment was blotted out by joy at the sight of the narrow staircase within the thick tower wall.

Into the darkness they plunged, moving down. Isabel managed the steep descent with a fluid agility that defied her age. Groping behind her, Lucina felt the eerie castle seem to close around her, holding her prisoner in its grip. She hurried after her new friend, only to bump into Isabel's back as she halted at the bottom. "Oh, your pardon," she gasped.

"Dinna be impatient," Isabel chuckled. "We'll be there soon."

"What if they check on me while we're gone?" Lucina asked. Because it was dark, she resigned herself to once more missing the critical maneuver that opened a panel.

Sure enough, they stepped into a deserted chamber directly below the tower chamber. "Hasten and they willna find ye missin'," Isabel admonished, closing the panel. "They're breaking their fast." She led the way through an outer doorway, into a tiny garden squeezed between the tower and a newer wing. A pretty iron fence with a gate looked directly into the main courtyard. As Lucina hurried after her, she wondered why the perfectly good room they had just left went unused. A huge bedstead with embroidered draperies dominated the modest space, though the room's musty smell told her it hadn't been inhabited for some time. They crossed the courtyard and entered a newer wing on the opposite wall.

"What place is this?" Lucina asked, noting the wood paneling and painted ceiling, a welcome replacement to the main castle's cold stone.

"Living quarters for high-ranking prisoners," Isabel said calmly, as if all homes had them. She guided Lucina to a metal grille set in the wall next to the chamber door. "Speak tae him whilst I sit on the bench ootside the door. If someone coomes, I'll tap twice an' dinna ye move. I'll say I'm oot fer a bit o' air, then will fetch ye when they're gone."

Lucina regarded the grille doubtfully. "Is there a way into the chamber?"

"Och, ye dinna want tae be *close* tae the monster," Isabel advised, patting her on the shoulder in motherly fashion. "Talk tae him, like, and when ye're done, we'll coom away." With that, Isabel went out the door and pulled it closed behind her.

Knowing the extent of Will's ruthlessness, Lucina allowed that her friend was right. So she tapped at the grille and was rewarded by a grunt from within. "If 'tis ye, Jasper, go away."

" 'Tisn't Jasper," Lucina called softly, hoping he wouldn't refuse to speak to her. To her relief, Will appeared at the grille, his red hair more tousled and wild than ever, his smile eager and interested. For the first time she saw his eyes were a brilliant, poison green.

"Female company at last," he burst out, dropping to his knees by the grille. "Hello, sweet. Coom to sample a kiss?"

"I thought you might be lonely." She didn't mean to be

coy, though to her own ears, Lucina sounded it. But if she asked him about her brother too quickly, she sensed it would cast a pall over the discourse. She must win his favor first.

"I canna kiss ye through the wicket," he said, clearly confident that she could hardly bear the waiting. "Ye'll have to coom in tae me."

"The door is locked," she protested. "We'll have to talk instead."

"Did Graham send ye?" He sounded suddenly suspicious, his voice so like Graham's they might have passed for twins.

"No, he would roar my head off if he knew I was here," she admitted.

"Ha!" Will chortled and slapped his knee. "He's a clever one."

From the spark in his eye, she thought he fancied himself the clever one, not Graham. "Oh?" she managed.

"Aye. He'll have ye first, just as he had Sarah."

The comment jolted her. "Sarah was his wife. He should have her first and last," she said forcefully, remembering his quarrel with his chief. *I'll have her when you're done,* he'd said.

He narrowed his gaze but didn't reply.

"She was a Maxwell," Lucina probed. "Is she kin to the man we met yesterday?"

"Ye met Bell the Cat Maxwell?" Will's good humor returned at the introduction of the new subject. "Give him a message for me when next ye meet, there's a gude lass."

"We won't meet again," she objected, noting the name that had been used by Isabel. She couldn't keep track of these folk when they had such odd nicknames.

"Tell him to send for Frank. I dinna fancy it here."

"Frank?" She puzzled over this new name. "Who is he?"

"Just tell him an' ye see him. Sarah was his youngest cousin. Wed to the present Graham tae mend the feud."

"Did she love him?" The question leaped from Lucina's mouth before she could stop it. She bit her lip, regretting her show of interest in Graham's tie with his wife.

Will chuckled slyly as he put a finger through the grille and stroked her cheek. "All the lasses love him. Sarah was like the rest," he said with a sweetness Lucina knew was deceptive. "But the bastard used her ill, just as his grand-sire beat Bonnie Mary, his bride."

Lucina swallowed hard and steadied herself to endure his caress as well as his unpleasant answer. She couldn't imagine the Black Graham hurting his wife, not after seeing him with a newborn foal. "He ill-used her?" she croaked, finding her mouth dry.

"Ugly story. Not fit for a lady's ears." He ended the subject, as if he'd suddenly grown scruples, which she knew was impossible. "Aboot that kiss," he continued blithely. "We could experiment through the wicket. Coom here."

"I would rather talk about my brother," she said firmly. Disappointed by his meager disclosure, she turned to the subject that concerned her most. "Will you tell me where he is? I won't interfere with your ransom," she assured him hastily. "I only wish to go to him and provide for his comfort so he doesn't fall ill."

Will grinned, displaying a guileless charm. "If ye get me oot o' here, I'll take ye tae him."

He was strikingly handsome, Lucina reflected, observing the friendly smile in the finely featured face and his piercing green eyes. She could imagine his attraction if one didn't know his nature. But *she* knew it all too well. "I don't believe you'll keep your word."

"I swear on ma sire's grave. Here, I'll even share a secret wi' ye. 'Twill give ye good luck." He felt in a pocket, withdrew an object, and held it up for her to see.

Lucina stared in surprise at a round, polished crystal richly bound in filigreed silver. It was obviously old, perhaps a family heirloom. The crystal spun lazily on its chain, catching the light. Mesmerized by its purity, she gazed into its depths, drawn by the seemingly magical sparkle. "It's beautiful. What is it?"

"Touch it if ye like." Will's oily smile remained. "It brings good luck."

Lucina stretched a tentative hand through the grille and balanced the crystal on her fingertips. As her flesh met the cool surface, the crystal glinted, and she felt a sudden rush of peace flow through her. *The sun has come out,* she thought, looking around for a beam. But she found none.

"It likes ye," Will said, as if understanding her bafflement.

"You speak as if it were alive."

"O' course. 'Tis the Dunlochy Charmstone. Belongs tae the Maxwells," Will said carelessly, as if he were accustomed to possessing other people's property and not feeling guilty. "It keeps away evil spirits, guards the health of the owner, and cures sickness."

"If 'tis the Maxwells', how do you come to have it?"

"I pilfered it as a lad. Maxwell thinks 'tis lost. 'Tis verra powerful, ye ken." He held the spinning stone close to his face and peered into its depths, as if communing with the stone's power. Then he snapped his gaze back to her. "I'll make a bargain with ye. If ye help me, I'll loan it to ye for a few days. Ye can take it now if ye like. 'Twill aid ye in finding yer brother an' keep him in health."

Lucina stared at the stone, acutely aware that he waited for her to agree. Will was essentially saying he would take her to her brother if she did as he asked. The urge to say yes tugged at her heart. Yet she felt like a mouse, frozen in place by the stare of the cat that meant to pounce and tear her to shreds.

Torn in her decision, she remained mute. She dared not trust Will Mosley, with his poison green eyes. He might trick her somehow.

He grinned at her. "Not willing, egh. No matter. We'll both be oot by and by." He refused to elaborate as he held the charmstone before her face, letting it swing gently. "Brings good luck to the bearer," he repeated before retreating from the grille. Their interview was at an end.

Reluctantly Lucina rose, admitting she had failed. As she and Isabel returned to the empty chamber next to the garden, voices sounded in the passage. As she froze, panicked, Isabel reached behind the wall hanging and flipped open the secret door.

"Hurry," she ordered, leading the way and opening the upper panel before Lucina could see how it was done. "They're coomin' to check on ye." Isabel hustled her through the opening and closed it firmly behind her.

Lucina sighed at having missed the secret again. But her thoughts were too taken up by her encounter with Will to trouble about it just now. Had she chosen wrong? No, she wasn't so desperate yet as to barter with mad Will. Besides, she reasoned, eventually his supporters must come to him for orders. She would watch for their arrival, for she dared not let him out of the chamber. Danger seemed to hang about Will.

Some time later, after the maid Alice had checked on her and asked if she needed aught, Lucina sat before the fire and thought how glad she was to have Isabel for an ally. Only with her help could she leave the tower chamber. Admittedly she hadn't accomplished much in her first sortie from her prison, but she hoped to try again soon. She must. Graham had troubles to settle, but hers required attention as well.

Over the last oatcake, she pondered the complexity of the Border. When her sister Rozalinde had checked, she'd been told of the violent life on the Border in years past. From her description, armed plunder had flourished, with Scots raiding English and the English raiding the Scots, or even raiding their neighbors, ignoring the Border line.

But they had been assured that all was now quiet under the firm rule of King James VI and the English-Scots Border wardens. For certes, Lucina might claim her land without a qualm.

With a heavy heart Lucina realized they had been told wrong. Impossible disputes stood between her and her cherished future, though she would not shed tears over her trouble compared to the pain of others. A pang pierced her as she remembered the widows Graham had described, and she wished she might help them. But freeing her brother was enough undertaking for now.

An hour later guards arrived to escort her to the stables. She seethed with impatience to be free of the chamber that had seemed cozy during her initial exhaustion but now oppressed her, despite its white plastered, vaulted ceiling, and broad windows. Genuine concern for her horses quickened her step as she was led by two men, one before and one after, down the tower stairs, across the courtyard, and into the welcome dimness of the stable block.

After quick greetings to Orpheus and Cygnus and the promise of longer visits later, she asked to see the packhorse. He had carried their baggage the entire time he'd roamed with the other livestock, and she suspected he had sores. Sure enough, his poor shoulders and belly were rubbed raw. Lucina called for healing salve and a hearty bran mash. As he ate, she cleansed his wounds and rubbed in the soothing ointment, worrying about her brother the entire time.

She *must* do something. She was unaccustomed to idling or to feeling helpless. And if freeing Roger was a low priority on Graham's list, it must be high on hers.

Satisfied at last that the packhorse was properly cared for, she fed him an apple and scratched his poll while he ate. Then she moved on to Orpheus's stall, gathering up currycomb and brush, ready for a long session with her friend.

"Hello, fellow. I have an apple for you. Can you guess where?" she greeted him affectionately. Orpheus swung his head around, his ears pricked forward in delight. With languid grace he nuzzled her, his breath soft on her hands.

She opened them both, palms flat, to show she wasn't holding the apple. "Which pocket is it in," she teased him.

She giggled as he snuffled at her waist, tickling her with his stubbly whiskers. He nosed her arm and wrist, then dropped lower to discover the bulge against her left hip. With a whicker of triumph he nudged her, his enthusiasm causing her to stumble back a step. "Right as always," she laughed, recovering her balance and pulling the apple from her pocket. "You win the prize."

As he crunched the apple, head lowered, she embraced him, wrapping both arms around his neck as far as she could reach, drinking in his reliable strength and warmth. How she loved this friend who would never desert her. He would give his last ounce of energy to serve her. Unlike some people she had met recently, she trusted him and knew he trusted her.

His comforting presence brought temporary relief from her worries, but even as she played with Orpheus, sorrow ate at her. Maggie Johnstone had called Castle Graham haunted, but Lucina knew the truth of it. The Black Graham carried the ghosts within.

Chapter 7

Graham rested an elbow on the stall partition and feasted his eyes on the Cavandish lassie as she groomed her stallion, unaware that he watched. After the wretched trials of the night, after hours of exhausting, depressing discussions with the two Border wardens this morning, he deserved a moment of respite.

Loose, shining hair tumbled over her shoulders, rippling with her every move. A smile adorned her rosy lips as she jested with Orpheus. She had dressed in a clean but simple kirtle skirt and bodice that clung to her curves, accentuating her supple back and graceful arms. He wouldn't mind having a prize from her, though he wouldn't settle for apples, as Orpheus did.

As he watched, she embraced Orpheus. The display disconcerted him. Effusions were pointless and embarrassing. Yet in a fit of contrariness, he suddenly wished he had brought good news for her—about either her brother or the peace negotiations—about anything if she would just turn that flood of devotion his way.

He considered Sir Edward Kincaid's demands this morning for restitution, which he'd met with his own demands, and realized the English raid had saved his miserable hide. Will's destruction would have cost him more than he had in ready coin. It would have taken everything he expected to earn from the autumn harvest and then some—now that sacrifice was not required since the English owed him in return.

He imagined what Mistress Cavandish would say, had he spoken aloud. The picture of virtue, she stood with one cheek pressed against the stallion's gleaming ebony neck, caressing his shoulder with lingering strokes. A sudden vision of those white hands on his own body created a jolt of sensation deep within him. "I have a letter for you, mistress," he said brusquely, deciding he'd seen her lavish enough affection on a damned horse.

She whirled, looking startled. "A letter? For me?"

No, for Orpheus, he almost grumbled, unaccountably irritated by what she did to him. He held out the sealed vellum. "It's from Sir Edward Kincaid."

She took the paper, eyeing him with such distrust one would think he'd arranged for the letter to announce her death sentence. He'd done no more than confer with Sir Edward about the best way to ensure her safety. Still she hesitated, obviously wishing to read her letter in private. Grudgingly he turned his back on her and studied the horse in the next stall.

He heard her break the seal. The page crackled as she unfolded it to read. Curious at the prolonged silence that followed, he glanced back.

She stood with the letter lowered, one hand gripping Orpheus's mane, her expression stunned.

"Well?" he prompted helpfully.

"You know full well what he says." Bitterness laced her voice as she shifted her gaze to connect with his. "He asks that I remain here until he finds Roger. But I dislike imposing on your hospitality. It could take weeks to find Roger, even months."

"I don't mind." He shrugged in an attempt to appear disinterested.

Her gaze was skeptical.

"I have the provisions to feed an extra guest," he said patiently, as if she had asked for an explanation. "You will be no trouble." Although she was causing trouble right now, the very sight of her fresh, innocent face holding him fast, arousing him.

As if sensing his unspoken message, she looked dismayed. "But why does Sir Edward insist I remain here? He doesn't explain, only threatens vague disaster if I don't. He says I could be ruined or murdered otherwise. But by whom? Why?"

Graham heard the quiver in her voice and had the oddest

urge to take her in his arms and reassure her. But the very thought also swamped his mind with erotic images irrelevant to her concern. He imagined placing her hands against the bare flesh of his chest, then bidding her run her palms slowly down to his waist, his hips, his thighs, lower, until . . :

He cut off the torrid daydream before it gained momentum. She wanted answers, but he had few he was willing to share. Yet he must be discreet, or she would sense his holding back. "To put it briefly, we're struggling to keep the peace," he said, reining in his insistent male interest. "I'm not sure 'twill hold. You're safest here."

"Does that mean there's war?"

He shook his head. "No, but 'tis better for you to remain in one place rather than travel to Carlisle. Sir Edward agrees."

She squared her shoulders. No tears. He liked that. Women should face things reasonably, without turning into fountains, yet a small show of feminine softness was never amiss. Her delicacy combined with courage renewed his wish to assure her that all would be well as long as she remained in his care. He wouldn't frighten her by telling of Sir Edward's plan to raid one of Will's strongholds if Roger wasn't produced in a fortnight, or of the other insanities of the night. He opened the stall door and approached her, wanting to take her in his arms.

Orpheus flattened his ears against his head and lunged, just missing Graham's arm with his teeth. "Damn," Graham muttered, retreating to a safe distance, cursing the jealously protective stallion.

"Oh, your pardon." Lucina was immediately contrite. "Orpheus, shame on you. You've eaten this man's grain. That's not a polite way to repay him."

The stallion had a better sense of it than she did, Graham thought acidly. He knew what Graham wanted of his mistress, could probably smell the male heat of his lust for the lass. Sure enough, as he watched, the stallion once more bared his strong white teeth.

"He's testy from so much confinement," she apologized again, hurriedly catching Orpheus's halter to restrain him. "I'm sure that's all it is. I know he would appreciate a run. Might I take him out briefly? Please?"

Her plea, so prettily put, aroused his protective instincts.

"Very well, I'll take you myself." He turned to fetch his horse. "But you're to keep to the paces I permit you. No racing off. You would easily become lost in these hills. Have I your word you'll obey?"

She assented demurely, seeming compliant, though he didn't quite trust her. She had too many unknown qualities for him to relax his guard. He politely offered her a saddle and bridle for her stallion, expecting her to refuse with haughty disdain. Instead, she accepted them with a downcast gaze he would have called shy. Except he knew she was no such thing.

As they trotted across the grazing land nearest the castle, he noted the way she rose in her stirrups, touching the saddle gingerly when she came down. He hid a chuckle, guessing she was sore between the legs from the day of riding bareback. He imagined the chafing of the horse's backbone against the petals of her woman's softness, then the friction of his own hardness in the same place. The idea inflamed him beyond bearing. How he longed to toss her into the straw of the stable and make her his.

Instead, he remained the picture of courtesy, restraining his base impulses by sheer willpower. He needed a good run as much as she did—to outdistance his obsession with this female and her irresistible appeal.

Outside the walls the day was mild, the signs of approaching summer everywhere. Broom flowered in profusion, and the rich scent of rainwashed earth engulfed his senses. Every spring he hoped for change and renewal, for the chance to care for his land, uninterrupted by strife.

Instead, his tenants straggled toward the castle in ragged groups, having left their plowing and sowing because of last night's events. The lassie eyed them with a questioning gaze, but he pretended to admire the scenery, unwilling to explain. Though spring brought fertility and renewal, he reaped nothing but the fruits of war.

Anger at the injustice of his world heated the blood in his veins, and every glance at Lucina made it worse. As if sensing his tumultuous mood, Red Rowan displayed an intense dislike for Orpheus. The long-legged, muscled chestnut who had sired Gellie's colt flattened his ears and threatened to bite if Orpheus came near. Graham eased him into a fast, tight trot that begged for greater speed.

Like a tightly wound spring, the living power beneath him coiled, straining for release. That same need pounded within him, each heartbeat driving his blood until he wanted to explode in rage.

At his side Lucina was a vision of sleek motion, increasing the ache in his loins, driving him to the edge of restraint. What he wouldn't do for the chance to lock his body with hers, to strain nerves and sinew in the pounding race for completion, to transcend the moment . . . the day . . . his entire life.

With a raw groan he nudged Red Rowan to a canter. Lucina and Orpheus picked up their pace. It was almost too much, having her near yet still entirely beyond his reach.

"Let's race to those trees," she challenged, tossing back her loose, shining hair and pointing to the distant woods. "We'll beat you easily."

Her taunt inflamed him like fire against tinder. "If you think to outrun me and Red Rowan, think again," he flung back.

She laughed. "You sound brave, but I think you're afraid of being beaten by a woman. And you should be. We'll leave you in the dust." With a tantalizing flick of her marvelous mane of hair, she touched her heels to Orpheus. The black stallion responded like an arrow sprung from the bow. Flattening into an all-out run, he poured on the speed and pulled ahead of Red Rowan.

Her audacity dealt a punishing blow to his pride, releasing a fury within him for all that kept him helpless on the Borders, unable to live in peace. How he hungered to fly free as the lass did, to cast off the fetters that held him back. As she raced ahead, bent over her horse's back, her mirth shimmered over her shoulder like a mantle of beauty. He longed to catch it and share her joy. All his rage at Will, his pain and sorrow for deaths and pillage, merged into a storm of emotion. Just when he could least bear it, she pushed him too far.

Faster, his mind and body cried to Red Rowan. *Fly.*

Furious with his rival, Red Rowan responded. Stretching into a gallop, he strained to catch the horse ahead.

Inch by inch the gap narrowed until Red Rowan's nose drew parallel to Lucina's right boot. She glanced back, startled to find Graham beside her, and he chuckled low in his throat. Red Rowan flew now, carrying him so swiftly the ground blurred beneath the pounding hooves. Graham's heart pounded in answer, recklessly wagering all to win. The race was what he lived for—the chance to fly, like a heedless savage, letting the purity of speed cleanse his soul.

As he watched Lucina poise in her stirrups, lips parted, breathless with excitement, Graham's torment lightened. With the breath of the gods teasing his face and tugging his hair, with the power of his steed beneath him, his spirit reached out, groping for the intangible. And in that moment he imagined that this woman might give it to him, that he might run another kind of race with her, her slim body straining for completion against his until they both found release.

"I'm going to win." Her laughter was a crescendo of joy, devastating his defenses, turning his resentment to shapeless mush. "I'm going to best you, Lord Graham."

Bending low over Red Rowan's neck, he vowed she wouldn't. "Faster, friend," he murmured. "You can do it."

Red Rowan gathered his powerful muscles in a new burst of energy. Graham shouted with elation as the chestnut stretched out and soared over the ground, bringing the two horses neck to neck once more. "You never wanted to race," he shouted smugly over the roar of wind in their faces and the thunder of hooves in their ears. "You wanted me to chase you. Well, I've chased and caught you, Lucina Cavandish, and we both know what's going to happen next. I'm going to bed you and make you mine."

Her jaw dropped at his rude prediction. Orpheus must have felt her break in concentration, for he faltered in his stride. The pair fell back by a nose, and Graham sent her a smoldering, satisfied grin as desire leaped between them, white-hot as flying sparks.

The naked desire on her face was as good or better than winning the race. He and Red Rowan shot forward as he clapped the reins against the stallion's neck and whooped in triumph.

The firebrand wanted him.

He reached the trees first. She arrived a second later, steaming with rage as her mount steamed from the exercise. Orpheus looked baffled and injured as he circled Red Rowan warily, frustrated by having lost.

Red Rowan held his head high and pranced with skittish, scornful steps. Their horses moved in an elaborate, adversarial dance, their wide chests heaving to draw air into their lungs. Graham's gaze locked with the Cavandish lass's, and the energy of their antagonism and attraction crackled between them.

"You cheated," she accused, her amethyst eyes flashing a mixture of scorn and arousal. "You didn't play fair."

"Life is rarely fair." With a tug of the reins and a nudge of his heel, he swung Red Rowan's hindquarters sideways, worked his heaving, sweating horse next to hers, and snaked one arm around her waist. As if paralyzed, she let him sweep her soft body against his. Ravenous for a taste of her lips, he kissed her full on the mouth. Hard.

Her lips thinned as she resisted his onslaught, but not for long. Skillfully he tempted her, coaxing her mouth to soften, delving with his tongue into her silky depths.

She yielded suddenly, accepting the inevitable. The heat of her beauty roared through him. Females never refused him, yet this one was a special prize, holding intangible qualities he craved—strength of will, depth of spirit and heart. Better still, she responded to his challenge, as if she'd starved for the moment that had come at last.

Their horses hated the contact as much as he reveled in it. One hand on the reins, the other on Lucina, he fought to control Red Rowan as he devoured the woman in his arms. The angry prancing of his mount, the knowledge that the moment had limits, heightened the pressure. With his hands he explored the lass's fine-boned body as he searched her lavish mouth. He felt her ribs beneath his spread fingers, her obstinate backbone against his arm. And he vowed to possess her, one way or another, longing for the strength of her spirit to invigorate his body and seep into his soul.

As if sensing his intention, Orpheus squealed in sudden rage and attacked Red Rowan with his teeth, abruptly ending the kiss. With a scream of fury Red Rowan half reared, nearly unseating them both. Releasing her quickly, Graham steadied her in her saddle. Assured she was secure, he concentrated on calming Red Rowan. "Easy, fellow. You've won the race. Let it end there."

But he didn't want it to end . . . not yet. As they sepa-

rated their horses, he consoled himself with the thought
that it wasn't over. Truth to tell, it had hardly begun.

He grinned, satisfied with the success of his first foray.

"You're so sure you're superior to women," Lucina muttered, casting him a baleful glance. "But women are superior in things you can't begin to understand."

The truth of her claim struck him. In at least one realm
she reigned supreme—in the way she had bonded with his
birthing mare, two females bringing forth new life with a
skill and affinity that rose above pain. Despite the help he
had offered, the colt had responded not to him, but to her
mysterious power. He would never forget the sight of her
competent, magical hands freeing the foal. "Why don't you
show me how superior you are," he challenged. "I invite
you to my bed." He found her answering splutter of ire
endearing.

"You took unfair advantage just now," she accused, her
eyes widening at his blatancy.

"I acted on what I read in you."

She tossed her head and refused to meet his gaze.

"Admit it," he hissed, "you're halfway in love with me
now."

"What if I am?" she cried, her ferocious admission amazing him. She looked as shocked and startled by what she'd
just said as he was, which warmed him thoroughly. What a
wondrous prize for his winning the race—she unwittingly
admitted her own awareness of him. The meaning of her
confession spread through his mind, feeling marvelous, like
rain falling gently on earth that bore painful cracks from
drought.

Her moment of shock turned quickly to chagrin and outrage. "It's no good between us," she insisted, sounding desperate to convince them both. "Despite our . . . your . . .
You know I can't tolerate you. You insist on being first at
everything. You bully me unmercifully, especially if I'm
better at something than you are, and if I displease you,
you lock me in that tower room."

He snorted in denial of her stinging words, his elation
fading. He didn't think he treated females unkindly. He
provided well for his aunt, even allowing her to pick up
after him if it pleased her. He was guarding Lucina, at great

risk to the Grahams. "You didn't object to my kissing you. If I'm not mistaken, you kissed me back."

A hand flew to her lips, and she inhaled sharply. "You shouldn't have done that."

He couldn't suppress his laughter. "Shouldn't I? But you kissed me the other night."

Lucina puzzled over this point, thoroughly confused by the discussion. She *had* kissed him after the birth of the foal. But she hadn't meant it the way he'd meant his.

Or had she? Hadn't she been attracted to him from the first, beguiled by his obvious love for his mare and foal? Hadn't she been intrigued by the fierce warrior's vulnerability when he thought the pair might die? Hadn't she wished he would kiss her all along?

The more she thought on it, the less she liked the idea. From the first, her nurturing spirit had sensed the sorrow in him and instinctively reached out, wanting to heal the scars. But that didn't make them suitable companions. Despite this, she had kissed him, thus kindling the fire between them, urging the invisible attraction to leap like a flame.

And that flame was undoubtedly dangerous. Look what he'd done—coaxed her into admitting she half loved him. From here on, she would guard against a repeat performance of what had just passed between them. The Graham was far too sure of his prowess with females.

"Yer lordship, yer presence is required in the hall."

The man called Jasper approached on horseback. The jovial satisfaction in his face showed he had seen the kiss and sensed what was taking place. And he approved.

Half relieved at his interruption and the kindly smile he offered, half sorry to lose the moment with Graham, Lucina puzzled over what was happening to her as they rode back to the castle. She had never liked the lavishly dressed courtiers Rozalinde and her sisters-in-law had introduced to her. She'd felt better understood by Orpheus.

But with Graham, she felt a kinship because of their love for horses. Add to that, his mere closeness caused her cheeks to flush and her pulse to quicken until it raced out of control. She yearned for him to kiss her again so she could kiss him back.

Perplexed by the intensity of her reaction, she stole surreptitious glances at the Borderer, wondering if he had spoken truly? Was she already half in love with a man who, according to Maggie Johnstone, was rumored to have killed his first wife? Weren't the things said about him reason enough to fear rather than care for him?

Chapter 8

Lucina didn't dwell on her feelings for Graham long, because as they approached the castle she saw a stream of people plodding through the gate. Men in shapeless, homespun tunics and muddy shoes lugged bundles of household goods on their backs, the contents ranging from cooking kettles to bags of meal. Women in plain kirtles balanced sacks on one hip, babes on the other, and shepherded before them the children old enough to walk.

No one spoke. Not a laugh or a gesture was exchanged.

Something seemed terribly wrong. Lucina looked questioningly at Graham, but he had donned the inscrutable expression she had come to know. It meant he had erected his protective wall, shutting out the rest of the world. Obviously, these people's presence concerned him deeply.

Though she hurried to stable Orpheus, Graham did not wait to escort her back to the tower. He threw Red Rowan's reins to a stable man, gestured for Jasper to attend her, and strode away without a word.

Lucina watched him go, vaguely disappointed. After their encounter, especially after her reckless admission of feelings, he left her as if she didn't exist.

Never mind, she told herself firmly, recognizing the signs of worry that wrinkled his brow. The man had overwhelming problems to solve.

Still, he might share them with her, she thought in annoyance as she stabled Orpheus, then made her way to the great hall under Jasper's escort. Now that Lucina saw him up close, the kindly old captain appeared exhausted, as if he'd been up all night.

The multitude converged in the hall surprised her, along with the cacophony of voices. Faces sagged like their owners' limp, worn clothing. A nearby infant wailed mournfully. Another stared off into space, as did his mother. Other women tried to hush young children who sat on the benches lining the wall, looking bewildered and exhausted. A pall hung over the entire chamber that had nothing to do with the smoke rising from the great hearth's fire, stinging Lucina's eyes.

Casting her gaze around the hall for a familiar face, she spied one that pleasantly surprised her. Maggie Johnstone moved among the people, stopping to talk to a woman here, wiping a child's dripping nose there. As if on cue, she looked up, spotted Lucina, and wove her way through the throng toward her charge from Carlisle.

"Mistress, when I heard ye were bid to stay here, I asked to wait on ye," she announced, drawing up before Lucina in the entry. "I wouldna coom for any reason save that."

Lucina remembered that Maggie had pronounced her former home haunted and sworn never to return. Touched, she hugged the woman, finding a semblance of stability in her stalwart presence. "I'm grateful you've come. Mayhap you can tell me what all these people are doing here?"

"Ha' ye no' heard? The Graham brought them in for protection." With a respectful nod of her head, Maggie urged Lucina into the privacy of the screens passage. "The English families attacked by Will Mosley raided Lockerbie last night," she said, her gray eyes resentful. "Burned most o' these folks' homes tae the ground."

Lucina stared at Maggie in dismay. While she had slept in safety and warmth, these good folk had endured murder and pillage? Graham, Jasper, and the other men must have spent half the night dealing with the trouble, yet Graham never mentioned it to her. Instead, he'd taken her riding, running a race with her and indulging in kisses as if they had nothing more important to do.

Troubled by his insistence on handling his problems alone, she stepped back into the entry to scan the hall, her protective instincts roused. All thoughts of Graham's secretiveness fled as the creases of weariness on people's faces took on new meaning. Not two paces away, a distraught-looking farmer jiggled an untidy bundle that mewled weakly, a piteous sound that ran up Lucina's spine until it found her heart and squeezed. With apparently no wife to help him, the man looked at his wit's end.

"Poor little one." With a sigh of pity she inched closer and craned her neck to see the swaddled child. The tiny face was red and puckered with woe. "I might be able to help," she ventured.

"I'd be grateful, mistress." The relief on the man's face cut through his dazed expression. "My wife died o' fever twa days gone. An' now this trouble coomes."

"Then, pray, allow me." Distressed to know the helpless waif was motherless, Lucina gathered the child into her arms. "Maggie, pray fetch a bowl of warm milk and a very clean, white cloth. Until we can find a woman to suckle him, he can take milk from it."

Maggie shot Lucina a doubting glance, as if questioning her decision to become involved. At Lucina's scowl she headed for the buttery at a fast clip.

Shortly after, with child and milk in hand, Lucina perched on a settle before the fire and offered the squalling babe the milk-soaked cloth. As the child latched on and sucked eagerly, Lucina smoothed back his wisps of downy hair and was reminded of her Dorset home. Growing up with so many brothers and sisters, it had always been, "Roger's crying. Someone get him. Luce, will you?" At nine, she'd enjoyed cuddling her infant brother, who would quiet when she picked him up and blow bubbles as she changed his tail clout. Much better than a doll. Almost as good as a horse. By eleven, she had charge of his bathing, his feeding, and his tucking in at night. By then she'd also had two horses, and she guarded her responsibilities jealousy from her four older siblings. Grown and with their own lives, they had lovingly overprotected her, making decisions for her, dominating her with their opinions, asking for nothing but affection in return. She'd had to find her own ways to be needed, and Roger had depended on her, as had her beloved horses.

After such involvement with people and horses, Lucina chafed at her present inactivity. If she couldn't rescue her brother this instant, she would help Graham care for these folk. Scanning the hall, she worried where they would all sleep. Clearly the castle lacked enough servants to see to

every need. Graham would be grateful for an extra pair of
efficient hands.

Refreshed by his sparring with the Cavandish lass, Graham returned his attention to the grim problem of his tenants. He spent an hour in the kitchens, conferring with the
cook about how to feed the influx of people. Huge kettles
of water were set to simmer and knives flew in preparation
of vegetables and pullens for cock o' leekie soup. His lack
of sleep the previous night was beginning to wear on him.
How he longed to lie down, despite the discomfort of the
bed in his own, seldom-used chamber. As he turned to
leave the kitchens, Jasper bumped into him at the door,
wavering on weary legs.

"Shall I tally the cattle reived on our side now,
Graham?"

Graham caught his kinsman as he stumbled, sorry he
hadn't noticed Jasper's exhaustion earlier. "You've done
more than your share since last night," he admonished. "I
suppose you returned all the animals Will stole."

"Tae the last one." Jasper straightened with an effort,
seeming determined to prove he could stand without his
chief's help. "I'd best see tae gettin' ours back."

"I've set Arthur to that task. Eat and to bed with you."
Graham squeezed Jasper's shoulder in thanks. "We'll take
it up again on the morrow."

Jasper nodded his grizzled head, too tired to argue.
"What o' the wardens?" he asked as the cook ladled out
a bowl of soup for him and placed a stool before the fire.

"At their wit's end, just as we are." Graham shook his
head, the foul memories of his day's meetings scourging
him. "Kincaid was grateful I stopped a return raid from
our side. He apologized profusely for the unruly elements
on his side and says he has them in hand now. But he
doubts the peace will last."

"And Sir John Carmichael? Did ye meet wi' him?"

Graham nodded. "At Caerlaverock Castle, Maxwell's
hold."

"Does he still want a bond of surety?"

"He wanted the Englishman that Will took, but said he'd
settle for his sister instead."

Jasper choked on the spoonful of soup he'd just taken.

"Jesus, Graham," he barked once his coughing had cleared, "what did you say?"

Graham snorted in deprecation. "Carmichael is little more than Maxwell's mouthpiece. We know she would end in his hands. And I'm as like to entrust a gently bred virgin to that den of thieves as it is to snow in Hades. So I told him, too. Maxwell loitered in the background, pretending he wasn't interested, but he heard every word."

Jasper scowled, showing a chipped front tooth. "He probably enjoyed insulting you. Did he throw you out?"

"It was just like old times when he used to help his uncle chase me away from Sarah."

Jasper stirred his soup to cool it and looked thoughtful. "Why does he want the English lass in custody, I wonder. It seems unusual."

Graham knew it was, though he didn't say as much. The strength of Carmichael's demand had betrayed Maxwell's desire to have Lucina. Having lost the warden's post of late, Maxwell had had Carmichael appointed so he could continue to dominate the West Border March. What better way to boost his waning power than by marrying the wench, thus acquiring more coveted land?

Whatever the reason they wanted her, Graham must keep Lucina safely out of sight in her tower room. He should never have taken her riding today, but the pleading in her eyes had been more eloquent than words.

As he headed for the great hall to check on his tenants, he recalled her smile of bliss as the black stallion had surged beneath her. Little wonder he'd seized the first opportunity to put his hands on her sweet body and woo her with his own.

Memory of her generous mouth, moist and silky beneath his, churned his blood awake. That kind of kiss demanded another—and another—and he'd claimed them eagerly, welcoming her response after the brutality of the night.

How he'd struggled to control his temper and appeal to his tenants' emotions as well as their reason. He'd never thought to be an orator, relying on words rather than sword or fists. The role was foreign to him, yet he'd had to convince them to trust him. Having sworn to negotiate compensation, he must not let them down.

Nor would he, though he wished they would quiet down.

He winced at the din as he approached the hall. Giving up the quiet of his household had been a grave sacrifice, though he hadn't hesitated. His people must be protected; thus, he would keep them behind stout walls until the trouble was resolved.

Even so, the noise throbbed in his ears, more annoying than when his father and his entire garrison had gathered to drink and play dice. From the screens passage, he gazed at the hubbub, then saw his great-aunt's snowy head weaving through the crowd. What the devil was she doing here?

As he drew near, he saw she was handing out oatcakes from a basket lugged by her two maids. Their task was to keep his great-aunt from endangering herself or others, though she seemed sane enough now. When she was at her worst, she thought it was fifty years in the past.

"Aunt Isabel." She ignored him as he confronted her, reaching into the basket to bring forth more cakes. Her usually pale face was flushed with exertion and concern. "Aunt Isabel," he repeated more gently, knowing he must guard her fragile strength. Left alone, she would work until she collapsed. "Allow me to escort you to your chamber. You must be tired."

She finally acknowledged him, tilting back her head to look him critically up and down. How well he knew that disdainful expression. Bracing himself, he waited for her to object.

"There's work tae be done, laddie." As expected, she tapped him briskly on the chest with one finger. "People to feed. Places found to bed them doon. This is woman's work, so out o' my way, ma puddock. Ye manage the stolen goods. I'll manage here."

He resisted the temptation to grin at her. Despite his aunt's tiny stature and frail form, her personality was as delicate as a smith's anvil.

As if aware that he found her amusing, she tossed the end of her mantle over her shoulder and glowered up at him. In his youth, when he and his brothers displeased her, she'd never hesitated to give them a tongue-lashing or to deal out discipline with something stouter and decidedly more painful. But time had turned the tables on them both. Whether she liked it or no, he was laird now. And whether he liked it or no, he must guard her health. "Aunt Isabel, the hall is drafty and you've been unwell." Firm but patient. That was the way to manage her. "And 'tis past the hour when you ordinarily rest."

"Why not let her help, your lordship. She knows what she's about, and you have other matters requiring your attention. She and I can manage here."

Graham swung around to find Lucina ensconced before the fire, her pretty face flushed with heat. A baby swaddled in clean linen nestled in her arms, basking in the warmth. Its eyes were half closed, and one tiny hand was fisted around two of Lucina's fingers. A ragtag, redheaded girl hung on her knee, gazing up at Lucina with adoration, as if she were a fairy queen.

She'd given his colt life. Now she lavished care on his tenants' children. Her first success had shocked him even as it pleased him. But how had she managed this? Border folk distrusted outsiders, so how had she formed attachments to them as easily as others donned new clothes?

Her expression, as she cuddled the baby and smoothed the girl's wild hair, radiated strength and caring. Watching her forced an odd, painful sensation into his chest.

Ruthlessly Graham quelled it. She shouldn't be here, rubbing shoulders with so many people. Not after Carmichael's recent demand.

Then there was Will. His cousin threatened to escape daily, hinting he would have help. That meant someone was helping him, possibly in Graham's own household. Until he caught the party, he wanted no reports of Mistress Cavandish bandied about.

"Mistress Cavandish, go to your chamber. At once." He addressed her formally for the benefit of the onlookers.

She pressed one finger to her lips. "Shh. The babe is almost asleep."

He would suffer argument from his great-aunt, but not from a hostage—and she was a hostage, though she didn't know it yet. "I shall ensure that its needs are met. Go now."

She rolled her eyes and gave an exaggerated sigh. "Very well. Pray be so kind as to come here." Her answer smacked of insolence. She had accused him of being a tyrant earlier. But if he was, she must live with it. In this, he would prevail. He planted himself in front of her expectantly and waited for her to rise.

"You must sit here." She patted the settle next to her.

He frowned, wondering what she meant, and refused to budge.

With a huff of exasperation, she stood. "You wish to take charge, sir? Here." She thrust the infant into his arms, spun on her heel, and strode toward the door.

The infant burst into a yowl at losing the warmth of her arms. Caught off guard, he grappled with the squirming bundle, all but dropping it. A wetness soaked through his shirt as he stared in disbelief after Lucina's retreating figure. Damn.

Chagrined at being insulted in his own hall before people who called him laird, he thrust the dripping bundle at his aunt and stalked after Lucinda. He was sure the women hid furtive smiles. The few children who grinned openly were quickly reprimanded, but his vanity wasn't soothed. Though the men looked carefully in other directions, he sensed their amusement at his expense, which singed his pride.

Mayhap he should be pleased, having afforded them an entertainment for the evening. Under the circumstances, they had nothing else to amuse them. But he wasn't pleased. The Englishwoman's pertness wore on his nerves. He'd had quite enough of her saucy ways. It was time to put her in her place.

Chapter 9

"Mistress Cavandish, I am trying to protect you, and you reward me with rudeness." Graham slammed the door to the tower chamber behind him. Lack of sleep grated on his nerves. His eyes stung with fatigue, and things were slipping too far out of his control.

He expected her to rise as he entered, but she kept her seat before the fire, her face purposely turned away. "I fail to see what your orders had to do with my safety," she said coolly. "But since you wanted to take charge, I permitted you to do so."

"You're being obtuse on purpose. Proper behavior is to obey the laird without a fuss."

"You're not my laird." She whipped around in her seat and unleashed the anger he'd known lay hidden behind her cool exterior. "I am your guest, or so you said the first night. I refuse to behave like one of those poor serfs in the hall."

Graham's jaw ached as he ground his teeth. She was correct; she wasn't a serf. She was a hostage, but he had no intention of telling her that. "They're not serfs."

"Mayhap not, but you expect them and everyone else to obey you instantly," she insisted. "And why did you not tell me about the raid last night? I could have been helping earlier. That poor babe has been robbed of his mother and needs a woman's care. The babe's father accepted my help with good grace, but you . . ." Her figure was rigid with outrage, her breathing so rapid that her chest heaved. "Is it against your code of honor to accept help from a female? You kiss me and entice me into admitting my feelings, which I regret by the by. Then you shut me out of your affairs as if I hadn't a brain in my head. Is that how you treated your wife?"

Her barb struck all too near the truth. He hadn't included Sarah in his affairs, though she'd never seemed interested . . . until that fated night. Hurt swept through him as the old wound reopened, throbbing and fresh. His face must have shown his pain, because she bent her head and pressed both hands to her temples, eyes squeezed closed.

"My stars, I am sorry. That was a terrible thing to say."

"You might as well say it. Everyone thinks I caused her death," he said tightly.

"No!" Her eyes snapped open, and she sat up straight. "I don't believe it of you. You hurt me when you showed such interest, then walked away after we returned, as if you didn't care. But I know you had weighty problems. You would never purposely hurt someone, certainly not your wife. And I had no good reason to hurt you in return. I hope you can forgive me."

"Forgiven and forgotten." He spoke without thinking, still caught up in the idea that she didn't believe him at fault for Sarah's death.

"Thank you, but I'm not quite finished." Her expression softened. "You see, I was hurt when you ignored me because . . ." She paused, as if debating whether to go on, then nodded decisively and continued, "I find myself more interested in you than I have ever been in a man."

She offered a patient smile at his dumbfounded reaction. "I'm as surprised as you are, believe me. You're not at all the sort of person my family would choose for me. Nor does this seem like the right moment in my life to become, er, attached to someone. But as you aptly pointed out, I am becoming attached, so I can't help but wonder what you meant by your kiss."

Graham felt like a stone in the path of a cattle stampede, buffeted by powerful forces. He couldn't tell her what his kiss meant. He didn't know himself. Or rather he hadn't dared think about it yet. The driving attraction he felt for her mixed confusingly with irritation at her outspoken demands to be part of his affairs. Stirred in on top came the stabbing pain left over from Sarah's death, and he felt torn in two. He could never be like this Englishwoman, willing to discuss her feelings openly, outspoken to a fault.

Thoroughly taken aback by her candor, Graham dodged the question. "How do you come to know so much about babes, an unwed woman and a virgin as well?" Her obvious comfort with utter strangers, particularly infants, also unsettled him, though he couldn't say why.

As if deciding to punish him for avoiding her question, she tilted her chin in a superior manner. "Of course I know about babes. I helped bring up my younger brother and sister. I have more nieces and nephews than I can count, and have fed, changed, and comforted every one of them. And as you can see, I've cared for newborn foals. No one was displeased by my actions in the hall save you. Even Elen liked me."

"Who the devil is Elen?"

"Why, the girl who was sitting with me. The babe's older sister, of course. There are two other siblings as well."

Her expression suggested he'd committed a faux pas by forgetting the girl's name, though Graham remembered her well enough. Who could forget the look of adoration on the waif's freckled face as she gazed up at Lucina, as if she were starved for a dream. The exotic Englishwoman, who by the child's standards was richly dressed, and by all standards was a beauty, had obviously brought hope into her shabby life.

With a pang he realized he was much like the child, starved for a dream. For six years he'd nursed painful memories and hoped for nothing more.

But then Lucina had swept in like a breath of fresh air, bringing an innocent faith in people that combined so strikingly with her maternal tenderness, he urgently wanted to seize, reap, and store her wondrous bounty the way he would lay in hay against the cold winter months.

Rising from her seat, she scolded him much as his aunt had. "I see 'tis not your way to discuss such things, but you'll find you must. My father, God rest him, always said people cannot live in peace unless they discuss differences and mend them. There were seven of us children, you see, and he had to keep order somehow." She chuckled wryly at his darkening expression. "I know, you'll say managing a household is nothing like managing peace along the Border. Still, if you share your problems, your load will be lighter. I cannot possibly idle while my brother suffers, nor can I sit and watch your people suffer. I *need* to help. Can you try to understand?" Passion swelled in her voice and lit up her eyes, testing his decision not to touch her again.

"I understand more than you think," he said, holding himself in check.

"You don't show it."

If he showed it, he would kiss her again. He strode to his court cupboard, needing to divert the torrent of feelings pouring through him, overpowering reason. As he searched for a book he didn't really want, he wondered how he would ever sort this out. "Mistress Cavandish, I'm head of my family and laird to many people," he said tentatively, searching for the explanation she deserved. "People expect their laird to be treated with deference, and I prefer to conduct myself with dignity. I don't flaunt my feelings like a giddy girl with a new gown, nor do I babble about everything I think and feel."

From the corner of his eye, he saw her flush angrily, her nimble fingers fidgeting with the laces on her skirt. "You suggest that I do?"

He rummaged among the things on the shelf. "You are overly effusive at times. It seems you want me to be like you."

"I'm not asking you to be effusive," she snapped. "I am asking you to understand my feelings and treat them with consideration."

He found the book and swung around to face her. "Most of the time, action suits me better than words." He sent her a smoldering look, and the attraction leaped between them. He stifled a smirk as she retreated behind the table, clearly unsettled by his response. Let her cower. She'd been the one to demand feelings. He'd shown her what he felt, sure enough.

"Action suits me better at times as well," she said in a more subdued manner, clearly taking his point. "Just now I would like to help your tenants. If you're uncomfortable with my going among them directly, pray choose something else I can do."

He had an army of people to care for, close to five score. If she wanted work, he could promise that. "If you insist, you may fill straw pallets for people to sleep on. In the stable. Under the protection of a guard."

She brightened at his words. "Thank you, I should like working in the stables. I can be with Orpheus and Cygnus. In fact, I can stuff pallets in one of their stalls."

He narrowed his gaze skeptically, waiting for her to worm out of the task, but she remained pleased with the idea. He doled out the most unpleasant work he could think of, and she thanked him? Did she always find the good side of things? "Come along, then," he growled, disconcerted by this new aspect of her. "I'll take you down."

"Must there be a guard?" she asked, now as meek as a newborn kitten.

"Yes." His gruff tone was meant to quell further questions. If he watched Cousin Will carefully and managed the peace negotiations, she need never know about her change from guest to hostage. And he would check on her in a few hours. After she tried the work, she might not be so glad to have taken it on.

Three hours later, after a hard sleep without dreams, Graham rose from the bed of his seldom-used chamber, feeling half human again. The unruly emotions storming through him earlier had subsided, much to his relief. He wasn't accustomed to feeling out of control. Nor was he anxious to repeat the experience soon.

He washed, donned a fresh shirt, and went to talk to his scouts, who reported that all was quiet on his land. Neither English nor Scots had disturbed them again.

His second duty was to make further provisions for his tenants—scores of extra mouths to feed was no jest. The cook pointed out he hadn't eaten since last evening, so he paused to drain a bowl of cock o' leekie. As he savored the rich broth, he considered visiting the stables to see how Mistress Cavandish fared. He wagered she would have quit her arduous work long ago and retired to her bed. Why not see if he had guessed aright?

As he passed by the great hall, he noted that the last of the folk were settled for sleep. Since it was now past ten of the clock, someone else must have stuffed the last pallets. He couldn't imagine the refined Englishwoman spending three hours at such a task. He would look in on Red Rowan before sitting down to more letters that must go off.

As Graham entered the lantern-lit stables, a merry whistle wafted to his ears, brightening the dim warmth of the stable block. The place seemed deserted, and Colin Johnstone, the man he'd posted to ensure the lassie's safety, was nowhere to be seen. She had undoubtedly retired. Nonetheless, he approached the stall where Cygnus was housed. The tune emanated from there.

"Here you are, Colin. The last of the lot." The whistling stopped, and Mistress Cavandish spoke from the depths of the stall. "I do thank you. You've been such a help."

Graham felt his gut tighten with apprehension as he realized she'd not gone to bed.

"I were nae help a-tall, Mistress Lucie," he heard Colin protest. "You did the stuffing. I merely pitched down the straw."

"But you told those wonderful stories while we were at it. I didn't know about the Norse raiders and their dragon ships. Do you really think they brought their horses with them over the sea?"

"I dinna ken for certes," Colin answered, "but 'twould make sense if they had fine ones, not wanting to part wi' them. The Borders are a fine land to breed horses."

Colin emerged from the stall, an awkward straw pallet slung in his arms and an annoying grin of bashful delight on his face. First she beguiled his horse, Graham thought grimly, then tenants' children, and now his men, who were devising familiar nicknames for her. Mistress Lucie, indeed.

Colin flinched the instant he saw his chief. Guilt chased the adoring look from his face, and he opened his mouth to stammer out an excuse for being so close to his charge. Graham cut him off with a hand slice and motioned for him to be gone. His annoyance didn't extend to Colin. Next time he would choose a guard less susceptible to a woman's charm.

As Colin retreated with the straw tick, Graham looked into the stall. Lucina was bent over, spreading the last of a straw heap around Cygnus's stall, her comely bottom angled for intimate viewing. She began to whistle. Though he'd guessed earlier she must be the whistler, the happy, spritely lilt of the tune threw him off balance. Three hours of boring labor and she could be merry? What manner of woman was she, working so hard and not seeming to mind?

"Ah, Cygnus, my back is stiff, but did you see all those pallets I stuffed? I must have done three dozen. Every one of those people has a bed." She straightened with the grace of a swan, its wings unfurling as it prepared to settle for the night. Raising both arms in the air, she stretched languidly.

By heaven, she was beautiful.

She turned to the horse and peeled off a pair of heavy gloves that Graham realized were his. "Won't Graham be surprised when he hears I did so many," she confided to Cygnus, reaching up to scratch her poll. "Though he'll probably be angry as well. He's always angry about something, the stubborn goat."

Graham's enjoyment turned to outrage. Blast it, none of his people called him rude names, nor would this vixen. "How dare you seduce my guard?" he growled.

Lucina startled and whirled, flushing hotly. "I didn't seduce him," she said defensively. "I merely asked Colin if he had a sister or cousin named Maggie, the woman who'd just returned from Carlisle. She's his cousin, so we fell to talking and have become friends."

"Border folk cling to kin, not to strangers. They don't befriend anyone who happens by."

She stiffened. "They have with me. At least Colin and Elen have, and Maggie and your great-aunt, and others as well." Her expression softened as she mentioned Elen. "Oh, Graham, I do like that girl. She reminds me of one of my nieces, so well-spoken and honest. She was clearly brought up well by her poor mother. Now that the girl's lost her, she needs a new place. Her father seems uncomfortable with an almost grown girl on his hands. Might she wait on me while I'm here?" In her usual, impulsive way, she put one hand on his arm to claim his attention. "She can sleep in my chamber and help me with any manner of things. She says she likes horses, so she could help me in the stable as well. It would be a good arrangement, don't you think?"

"She's never been around horses," he said, fighting the leap of need caused by her touch. "She can't possibly know she likes them. Choose a man if you need help."

"You're giving me free choice?" She squeezed his arm

and shot him a teasing smile that reeked of innuendo.
"Aren't you afraid of which man I'll choose?"

"*I'll* assign one," he barked. Blast the wench. Didn't she
know that the man should initiate intimacy? It was difficult
enough to resist her when she *didn't* touch him.

Yet she seemed oblivious to this fact as she favored him
with a rosebud of a pout. "Poor Angus Alexander Malcolm
Graham, chief of all the Grahams, afraid of a girl."

"That's not my name," he said, wondering how she'd
assigned it to him.

She looked puzzled. " 'Tis the name your great-aunt
called you."

" 'Twas my grandsire's name," he explained tiredly.
"Mine is John Alexander Malcolm Graham. At times Isabel loses touch with the present. 'Tis why I often insist she
stay in her chamber. And why I forbid her to help in the
hall." Lucina appeared shaken by this news. "She not only
mistakes people for those long dead," he continued, driving
the point home, "but she grows careless at such times.
Once she set her gown afire by forgetting what she was
doing. She could have been seriously burned, mayhap
even killed."

"But surely you can tell when she has her wits about her
and when she does not. She seems perfectly well to me."

"You'll have to leave that judgment to those who
know better."

She looked furious, but instead of pursuing the issue, she
doggedly returned to her original request. "I want your
agreement that Elen shall wait on me. 'Twill be for the
best. As I said, her father seems uncomfortable with her.
He's better with his son."

Because he isn't the girl's father, Graham wanted to
shout, frustrated with her meddling. He had no intention
of discussing Elen's illegitimacy with an outsider. "There
are many things you don't understand about us and never
should. They're best left alone."

Lucina regarded him, seeming to ponder the riddle he
had just posed. "I'll learn the reason one day," she said at
last with a confidence that rattled him. "Now, then, when
you speak to Elen's father, pray propose that she join me
on the morrow. But permit him to choose another time if
he prefers."

As he grudgingly granted her request, he felt sure she'd guessed half of what he wasn't telling. She had a keen intuition for people's thoughts and feelings that unsettled him completely. "Time for you to retire," he said, shooing her from Cygnus's stall.

But instead of obeying him, she moved toward the next stall. "I must first say god'den to Orpheus," she insisted, not even asking his permission.

He rolled his eyes at the new delay. Why wasn't she exhausted and eager for her chamber? Any other lass would be. "I'll put down more hay. But when I finish, I'll expect you to be done as well." Keeping one eye on her, he strode to the loft ladder. If she thought he would leave her alone in the stable, to mount and escape unobserved, she could think again.

From above, he forked down mounds of sweet-smelling hay to replenish Red Rowan's manger, then paused at the stall where Orpheus lodged. The lassie was crooning to him. Through a gap in the floor planks, he glimpsed her slim, gentle hand caressing the stallion's sleek hide. He closed his eyes. The velvet of her voice flowed over him, and he imagined those hands on *his* body, wishing he might yield as easily to what she called friendship, as Colin had.

But it wasn't his nature. They were opposites—she so free and easy with her attachments, he forced to avoid them and remain solitary.

He pictured her again as she'd been today, riding Orpheus. Ahead of him, her hair fluttered like a messenger's banner as she reached without shame for her desire. Win or lose, she threw her heart into the running, living fully for the moment. If only he could shake off the shackles that fettered him to duty and pain. If only he could know joy as she did.

But she was forbidden fruit, and the guilt he felt came of wanting what he couldn't have. Just because she brought a moment of light to the dark recesses of his soul didn't mean his night had passed. He knew what would happen should he claim the English firebrand, with her brother a captive of his own clan. Scots relations with the English would go straight to the devil. Peace on the Border would become a forgotten dream. And ultimately, the darkness within him would overwhelm her, just as it had Sarah.

Chapter 10

At seven of the clock the next morning, Graham was awakened by a painful cramp in the back of his neck. To his relief, he'd slept through the night without waking. Still, he felt drained by the tension brought by the raids.

After breaking his fast, Graham visited the quarters where his fifty men-at-arms lodged. The minute he entered, he felt their unrest and anger, as thick as haggis you cut with a knife.

"With all respect, we've endured an outrage from the Dacres and the Ridleys." Angus Johnstone, a cousin by marriage on his mother's side, stepped forward to be recognized after they had all come to attention. "Our kin ha'e been killed. Why shouldna we raid in return?"

"Because it leads to a return raid from them," Graham rapped out sternly, "which requires a counterraid from us, which urges them to raid us again, and the death continues. And because I forbid it."

"But sir, hear me out." Jamie, the one Lang who had not accompanied Will on his raid, stepped forward, his youthful face twisted with rage. "The thieving bastards dinna hold to yer tenants. Aline Mosley, my betrothed, was doon at the village visitin' her grandam. She was violated." His voice cracked with agony on the last word. Desire for revenge burned in his eyes.

Graham ached for the lad but could not permit pain to rule. "Your best place is at her side, assuring her you don't care what happened and will support her recovery. I'll see that the men in question are punished." Though he sympathized with Jamie and his betrothed, he kept his tone curt, signaling that he would brook no argument on this score.

"They'll ne'er own it," Jamie muttered in fury, falling back amid grumbling from the other men. "They'll gang free to violate our women again. Ye know well enow how that feels, when someone taints yer wife."

Scalding rage coursed through Graham at the reference to Sarah. "I do know, damn it, and that's why I order you to stay with Aline and comfort her, not go raging across the Border to be murdered and dress her in mourning before she's even wed. I'll settle this dispute, and I expect all of you to obey. I'll not have the agreements violated under any circumstance."

Sullen silence met his command.

"What o' the Graham's Will?" Jasper asked, speaking for the others. "He brought last night's raid on us. Yet he lives like a king in that chamber, with us forced to empty his slops an' wait on his every whim."

Graham winced inwardly at the use of Will's nickname. "He remains under lock and key."

"But he swears Bothwell will free him," put in Archibald Irvine, whose family had been feuding with the Grahams until Alex became the Graham and healed the breach. "We hear he's coom to Roxborough. Will's boosted o' it all day."

"Set a guard on Will," Graham ordered. "Outside, watching the window. Do any of you know of messages being smuggled out?" Men shook their heads. "If you discover or suspect anyone, I want a full report. And the Earl of Bothwell has been outlawed by King James. He will be apprehended in time." Even as he said the words, he doubted them. The earl was considered as mad as Will Mosley and even more dangerous. Having once been in royal favor, he had recently fallen from grace. Yet over the years, he had built a strong following. As the keeper of Liddesdale, he no doubt intended to take refuge on his own land.

"I thought ye were gang to punish Will," Colin Johnstone said, drawing Graham back to the present trouble. A general murmur of agreement supported his statement. The men were eager to see someone's blood flow—a public whipping would do if they couldn't take enemy lives.

"I'm beginning to doubt Will's sanity," Graham said. "If he's not in his right mind, he'll be confined permanently. No amount of punishment can heal a madman."

A general hubbub of dissent burst from the men, arguing the treatment for the insane. None agreed that confinement without physical punishment was enough in this case. Again the complaint that Will lived in luxury circulated the group.

Graham ground his teeth. Lord, would they ever understand? He was straining every ounce of will, fighting the urge to do just as they wished . . . hell, he'd like to do worse. On the night of the raid, he would have relished choking the life out of his thieving, murdering cousin. Didn't they see it was harder to control the violent impulse than to give in to it? The only thing checking him was the knowledge that it wouldn't help.

He laughed inwardly, a mirthless sneer at his own weakness. Having chosen the path of peace, he now wanted to veer off and spill them over the cliff's edge. The family's future depended on every one of them, to a man, swearing to take no lives. That included him.

He repeated his order to keep the peace, then checked the day's assignments with Jasper, whose words of solid support comforted him. But as he strode from the quarters, the distinct sense of his men's doubt followed. To them, old ways were best, and belief in them died hard.

Their reservations added to Graham's burdens as he set to the day's work. Messengers came and went hourly, crossing from Scotland into England and back again. No one was satisfied with what was offered. Everyone demanded more.

In the midst of his troubles, Mistress Cavandish appeared to badger him about searching for her brother. And now the cook was complaining that the Englishwoman had appropriated his scullery to bathe Elen and wash her clothes. Graham calmed his servant by promising the invasion was temporary, but he was secretly pleased to know Lucina had left his tower room, leaving it free for his use.

He sat at the table and composed a letter to Sir Edward. This chamber, removed from the bustle of the rest of the castle, was much preferred to his other chamber.

"Ah, since you have your quill and paper out, I would like to borrow them when you're done." She swept back into the chamber when he least expected it.

He'd been so absorbed in countering Sir Edward's latest terms, he hadn't heard her on the stair.

"I could also use a place to store my clothing besides in my saddlebag," she continued, striding around the chamber, ruining his concentration.

"You may use that coffer under the window." With only a few lines left to complete, he tried to ignore her and focus on his writing.

He heard her grunt as she tugged open the heavy coffer lid. "My stars, this is disgusting," she exclaimed. "Don't you ever throw anything away?"

"The other coffer." Graham glanced up in irritation. "That one is private. Close the lid at once."

Instead of obeying, she rummaged among the contents. "What's private about this trash? And what's the point of keeping it. This is useless." She gingerly held up a broken stirrup leather, nose wrinkled in disdain.

Graham closed his eyes and counted to ten. No one questioned his personal habits, not even his aunt, who cleared up after him but said not a word of reproach. "It's none of your affair," he snapped.

"I could sort everything," she persisted, tossing the strap back and rummaging deeper.

"You're not to touch my things," he exploded, jumping to his feet. Meddling female, wanting to rearrange him both inside and out. "I won't be able to find a thing."

She straightened, flushed from bending over. "But you can't find anything now. If I sort everything into three piles, one to throw away, one to—"

She squeaked and leaped back in alarm as he strode over to the coffer and banged down the lid. "I could find everything without trouble before Isabel swept it away when you arrived. Don't touch anything more."

She stared back at him in defiance, the look in her eyes suddenly reminding him of Sarah, of when they had argued about the very same thing one evening, and he had distracted her by luring her into his bed. By the gods!

He grabbed his papers and swept from the room. Not only did this lassie provoke him, she made him hunger for the comfort of female closeness, for the pleasure of arguing about trivial things and making up their differences in bed.

This chamber hadn't seen a woman's presence since Sarah, not even a whore.

Yet he wanted more than a bedding from this lassie. He wanted the light that radiated from her firebrand soul.

Ousted from his chamber again, Graham finished his letter in Arthur's workroom and sent it off, then saw to a number of other mundane tasks. By mid-morn, he realized he couldn't be under the same roof as the lassie without wondering what she was doing. Frustrated, he prowled the castle and found his aunt working among his tenants, undoubtedly overtaxing her strength.

"Isabel, how are you this morn?" he inquired, drawing her aside to assess her state of mind. If she dwelled in the present, she might stay for another hour or so, but under strict supervision of her maids, Marie and Margaret, though they were nowhere in sight.

She knocked his hand aside and laughed at him. "Dinna meddle wi' me, Angus. Ye think me too auld to work as hard as Mary, but I can gang as hard as she."

He grimaced, realizing the fit was upon her. No wonder her maids had slipped away. They always concocted excuses to be idle when their mistress couldn't remember who they were. "Mary's not here," he said, hoping to placate her while avoiding the fact that Mary was long dead.

"She assuredly is," Isabel announced blithely. "An' 'tis about time ye let her coom among us again. She's a sight for sare eyes, sure."

Graham stared, aghast, as his aunt pointed to Lucina Cavandish, where she stood at the hall entry, a stack of clean linen in her arms. It wasn't unusual for Isabel to think he was his grandsire, but now she thought Lucina was Mary Maxwell, his grandam.

His gaze snapped back to his aunt in time to catch the glow of love kindled in her eyes. "Ye owe her better than ye give, Angus. Ye can no' repay her fer bringin' young Jock into the world. He's a fine lad, as weel as yer heir. An' dinna forget she saved ma Helen." She placed one hand on his arm and pressed it pleadingly.

Graham strained not to be sucked into the past along with her. The pain of good memories hurt as much as the bad, these days. As a small lad, he'd heard the stories at

Isabel's knee, of how Great-Uncle Gavin had died reiving, then Cousin Helen, Isabel's last surviving child, had fallen ill. Bonnie Mary had nursed little Helen, using her knowledge of cures and herbs, and the girl had lived to wed. The miracle was one of the few good stories, but later, it had taken a turn for the worse. Helen had borne two daughters, then a lad—Will. By the time it was clear to all the lad had maggots in the head, Helen's husband had, in his turn, fallen victim to Border reiving. Bent down by the sorrow of his death, Helen had taken ill and died. Once more, reiving took its toll.

As they both watched, Lucina sought out Elen's baby brother and took him from his father. Deftly unwinding his swaddling, she cleansed him with a damp cloth and re-swaddled him in fresh linen. Then with the happily babbling babe tucked in the crook of her arm, she moved among the others, assessing their needs. Graham heard her speak to a group of women, where a lassie of nigh on ten wept. The child clung to her mother's skirts and refused to be comforted, despite the scoldings that she was too old for tears.

"What's wrong, dear?" Lucina knelt beside the girl, her sweet face tender with concern.

"My bairn was burned," the child blurted, emboldened at receiving attention from a lady of the castle.

Graham saw Lucina's brow knit with dismay.

"She means her plaything," the mother snapped with impatience, as well she might, having lost things of far more importance to the family. "She's been a-glaiverin' like this since we arrived. 'Tis not as if her wee brother were harmed." She indicated an infant in an older child's arms.

Lucina smiled on the girl and wrapped her briefly in an embrace. "Your mother is right, dear. People are more important than playthings. But I understand how you feel. Love has no law."

Graham started as Lucina spoke the familiar words he'd heard quoted since childhood. It was Bonnie Mary's favorite saying.

Rendered speechless by her use of the words, he turned to Aunt Isabel. A beatific smile gilded the old face, and he understood her contentment. For the first time in years, she believed Bonnie Mary had returned to her in the flesh.

*   *   *

At the earliest opportunity, Graham urged his great-aunt
to her chamber, extricated himself from her affectionate
clutches, found the truant maids Marie and Margaret and
reprimanded them severely for deserting their mistress,
then retreated to the stables and the company of Red
Rowan. By then his bewildered frustration had built to such
a peak, he wanted to pound his head against the rough
stable boards. Where had Lucina Cavandish learned that
saying?

Out of habit, he mechanically reached for a brush and
applied it to Red Rowan's sleek hide, using such force that
the horse jerked in surprise.

"Sorry, laddie." Graham placed both hands flat on the
stallion's sleek coat, forcing calm into his limbs. Red
Rowan swung his head around and nuzzled his master,
looking for a treat, but Graham couldn't respond. His mind
still reeled from what he'd heard. He must explain it away
without miring his emotions in the past.

Had she learned the saying in England or from someone
here? If it were here, who had said it in her presence. The
serving women? Grissel? One of his men could have used
Bonnie Mary's favorite saying, he rationalized. Most of
them had grown up in the castle. But only the very oldest
men would have been alive when Mary Maxwell lived here.
Still, Isabel had kept the saying alive. . . .

With a grimace he cut off the fantasy he was inventing.
However unlikely it seemed, Lucina Cavandish knew the
saying. Why couldn't he just accept it and put it out of
his mind?

By the noon dinner hour, Graham was so wearied by the
concerns of the reiving, he wanted to lie down and sleep
for a year. His new chamber offered little comfort. It felt
stiff and unlived in, as indeed it was. But if he returned to
the tower chamber, he would argue with Lucina. And that
was like fighting a head wind. For every step forward he
won, she pushed him back two.

Having her at Castle Graham was driving him to distraction. He imagined her untamable emotions getting her into
all kinds of trouble. She needed a firm male hand to guide
her, that was sure.

By evening, he had seen to most of his duties and relieved the guard hidden near Will's window. Suspecting that Will slipped out messages at night, he would take the next watch himself. If you wanted something done right, you often had to do it yourself.

Close to eleven of the clock, Lucina heaved a tired sigh, kissed Orpheus a last time on his velvety nose, and slipped from his stall. While it was still light outside, she had spent an hour watching the beautiful foal she'd helped give life. The still unnamed youngster had frisked and gamboled in the green pasture near the castle, looking carefree while she was ladened down with cares. Foolishly she'd hoped her guard might step away, but of course he hadn't. Which meant another day lost in the search for her brother. She despaired that he would ever be found.

Leaving Orpheus, she dragged her feet dismally as the guard followed her. This new man, Angus Mosley, was old, surly, and refused to speak to her. Just as well. In her present mood she might say something rude. The thought of the soft feather mattress in the tower tempted her to retire. She would just see who was about in the great hall before she went up. Isabel might be there, or mayhap she could settle a babe or two.

Angus waited by the hall entry as she wove her way among the tenants, crowded willy-nilly on the stone floor. She smiled in satisfaction to see her stuffed ticks warming these folks. Most were already asleep, men snoring on their backs, women and children curled around each other, recovering from their trials.

At length she spied Isabel in the gloom, attended by Marie, passing out blankets and comfort to those who couldn't sleep.

"Greetings, Mistress Cavandish. May I assist you?" Marie curtsied politely as they met, as if attempting to ingratiate herself with Lucina.

She was probably hoping to escape her present assignment, Lucina thought. From what she had seen, the girl took poor care of her mistress. One side of Isabel's hair had slipped from its neat coil, and food stains decorated her smock around the neckline. As Lucina spoke to the maid, she noted that Isabel narrowed her gaze at the pair of them.

"Why are ye usin' this Cavandish name, Mary? You're confusing me wi' so many. Settle on one an' have done."

"Lucina Cavandish is the only name I use," Lucina hurriedly assured her. Once again, her friend's lack of hold on reality disconcerted Lucina, but before she could act on her concern, a child sat up nearby and refused to lie down again.

"What's wrong? Is she ill?" Lucina knelt beside the mother.

" 'Tis naething," the woman assured her. "Lie down, Annie. 'Tis all right."

"But I'm sare afeared o' Bonnie Mary. She'll eat me in the night."

The child's mother threw Lucina an apologetic glance. "Pay the hinnie no heed."

But Lucina knew too much about night fears to pretend they didn't exist. "There's no ghost, Annie," she assured the child. "And even if there were, do you think she would come in here? She would stumble over all the people. Everyone would wake up and frighten her."

Annie grinned at the jest and lay down, appeased for the moment.

Prepared to retire, Lucina met with Isabel and they left the hall. As they entered the passage, Lucina steeled herself. This time, if she saw the "thing," she would confront it rather than running like a frightened goose.

To her relief she saw nothing. Nor did Isabel seem worried about the possibility as she stood with Lucina at the foot of the tower stairs, saying good night.

"I dinna think I'll sleep," Isabel sighed in response to Lucina's heartfelt wishes for pleasant dreams. "I'm sa tired in the morn, I feel I've walked ten leagues in ma sleep."

"Would you like me to sit with you?" Lucina offered. "I would be happy to bear you company for a time."

Back in the old lady's chamber, they sat in companionable silence once Isabel was abed. Marie, whose turn it was to sleep in her lady's chamber, dropped off as soon as she settled on her pallet. She wheezed lightly, giving full evidence that she was deep in slumber. Reminded of the times she had sat with Lady Ashley, Lucina smoothed the coverlet on Isabel's bed and patted her hand reassuringly. "You will sleep well tonight. I know you will," she said.

"I shall, wi' ye here, Mary."

Seeming soothed by her presence, Isabel eventually dropped off to sleep. After waiting a reasonable interval to ensure she wouldn't wake, Lucina tiptoed from the chamber and softly closed the door. Old Angus followed her stolidly back to the tower stairs, never uttering a word.

Back in her chamber she crept toward her bed, not wishing to wake Elen, who was now installed in the tower with her. But as she passed the pallet before the fire, she noticed the coverlet lay flat and unrumpled. Elen was gone.

Her first impulse was to race back down the stairs and wake everyone, to insist they search until the child was found.

"Angus." She tapped at the door for the old man's attention, but he didn't answer. Stars above, had he gone back down the stairs? She banged harder and called his name, then shouted for him. Still no reply. Mercy, she could die up here while he was below stairs, where she suspected he was playing at dice with a fellow, even drinking an ale or two. It had been so late when she finally retired, he had probably expected her to go straight to sleep.

How she wished she knew the secret to opening the hidden door. But the smooth wall behind the hanging revealed no key to its release. Frustrated, she considered flinging open the windows and shouting to be released, but discarded the idea. Elen would not come to harm in a castle full of people. She had probably become frightened, left alone so long in an unfamiliar chamber, and rejoined her family in the hall. Lucina hadn't meant for that to happen, but since it had, she would look the fool if she screamed out the windows and frightened the entire household. Assuring herself that Elen was well, cursing her inability to open the secret panel, Lucina prepared for bed.

But as she drifted into sleep, Lucina felt the claws of the castle's hopelessness closing around her and knew she must fight them. She didn't believe in the ghost in the passage, but the ghosts of the past haunted Graham, Isabel, and all the family living in this lonely stronghold, and none of them would be free until they were gone.

Chapter 11

Lucina awoke to darkness and the sharp sound of a click. Or had she dreamed the noise in her sleep? Twisting in bed, she spied a shadowy form closing the secret panel in the wall and knew it was no dream. "Elen, where have you been?"

The child froze to the spot.

Realizing she had frightened the girl, Lucina groped for her stockings and sat up. "Come, you can tell me," she said more gently. "When I came to bed and found you gone, I was so worried, I couldn't sleep for some time."

Elen sat down on a stool and covered her face with both hands. Sobs racked her thin body with such violence, it seemed the child's heart would break. Or perhaps it was broken already by her mother's death and the odd, unfeeling way her father looked at her, not at all the way he looked at the other children, proud and protective. Pierced with remorse, Lucina guided Elen to the bed and held her as she wept. The grief of losing her own father welled up inside her as she murmured to Elen, tears stinging her eyes.

"Everyone hates me," the child sobbed, pulling out a tattered handkerchief.

"I don't! I'm your friend." Lucina produced her own square of clean linen and insisted Elen take it. "That means you can trust me with your problems. I'll do everything I can to help."

Elen lifted a troubled face. "Ma mither always said to keep family things family."

Lucina squirmed in discomfort, searching for a way to put the child at ease. "Family matters should be private, but in a way, I'm your family now. I should have explained more thoroughly when I first asked you to wait on me . . ." She trailed off, feeling her explanation was a lame one. She had offered words of condolence to Elen when the girl first joined her in the tower chamber, but Elen had said nothing in response, so Lucina had moved on to bathing and clothes washing. Yet beneath the child's courageous exterior, tears had been waiting to break loose. Still stinging from her own unresolved sparring with Graham, Lucina ached to have her trust. But perhaps she expected too much. "Elen, would you rather stay with your family? I know you agreed to serve me when the chief asked, but you need not. If you wish to stay with your father and siblings, you've only to say so and I'll understand."

Elen continued to sob, but she shook her head vigorously at Lucina's question, mumbling something about wanting to stay with "her leddyship."

"Very well, if you choose to remain with me," Lucina said, hoping desperately she was taking the right tack, "then I become responsible for you and will help you with your troubles. You remind me of my niece Mercy, you see, and we're very close. And I grew up with six brothers and sisters. The younger ones, Roger and Angelica, were often in trouble, and I helped them all the time, so I'm quite used to such things." She tried to laugh lightly though she was near tears. "You can tell me, and I won't be angry. Who are these people you believe hate you?"

Elen shook her head, her eyes tragic. "I'm naething but a daft gaislin," she whispered. "No one could like me."

Though Lucina didn't know what a gaislin might be, Elen's response did not bode well. It reminded her all too poignantly of her siblings' self-deprecations when, as children, they'd done something they shouldn't and suffered from guilt. She concluded Elen must be in a similar circumstance. "You must feel the way Angelica and Roger did the time they stole out the window at night to visit our nephew, Christopher, who had the fever. We were forbidden to see him, for fear we should catch the sickness, so we drew lots and I lost, which meant I had to stay behind. I wrote him a letter, and the other two sneaked out and visited him for half the night. After, they were terrified they would get the fever and our parents would know what they'd done."

Elen stopped sobbing and looked up. "Did Christopher get better?"

Lucina nodded. "His fever broke while they were with him, so we knew the visit had cheered him. By morning he was on his way to recovery. But you see, I had to keep the secret that Angelica and Roger were gone, and the nurse, who was half-blind, came to check on us." Lucina paused in her recitation, hoping her trespasses would inspire Elen to confide in her. "So believe me," she finished, "you can't shock me with anything you say. Won't you tell me what's wrong?"

"I . . . I . . ." Elen couldn't seem to get past the first word.

"You've done something you're not sure about?" Lucina guessed.

"I only obeyed ma faither," Elen admitted in a small voice. " 'Tis right, is it not, to do his biddin'? No matter what he asks?"

"Yes, of course. Your father is an honest man."

Despite the reassurance, Elen's face twisted and she burst into another storm of sobs so violent, it seemed her heart would break. Hurting for the child, Lucina smoothed back her unruly red hair and held her close. "There, there," Lucina whispered as the salt of tears stung her own eyes. "I'm sorry I left you alone in the dark, but I thought you were asleep and wouldn't miss me. I was sitting with Madam Isabel, who couldn't sleep." She waited for Elen's tears to slow. "Did you go back to the hall so you wouldn't be alone?"

"I-I went to see Faither," Elen quavered. "I kent he would want me. He sent me on an errand to Lockerbie. He even gave me a-a . . ." She hesitated, as if unwilling to name what her father had given her. " 'Twas to keep me safe on the journey," she hastened on. "He said I might keep it for a while if I did well. I mun give it back later, but he trusted me. 'Tis truly an honor, his trust, and the . . . the . . ." She drew something from her pocket and held it in a tightly clenched fist.

The girl seemed so eager for approval, Lucina couldn't help but give it. Yet her thoughts whirled in puzzlement. Why would the humble tenant farmer who was uncomfortable with his daughter speak to her in secret, then send her on an errand outside the castle in the dead of night? How had Elen managed to leave the castle, an impossible feat with a guard at the gate? "A father's gift is to be treasured," she consoled, groping for appropriate words.

Elen relaxed slightly. Leaning against Lucina, she opened her fist to show the bauble. To humor her, Lucina glanced at it, but the flash of the jewel caused her to look more closely. A crystal twinkled in Elen's hand, seemingly lit from within.

It was the Dunlochy Charmstone that Will Mosley had offered Lucina as a bribe only that afternoon.

Aghast at what Elen's possession of the charm meant, Lucina shook her head. Stars above, the poor girl was Will Mosley's illegitimate daughter. No wonder her mother's husband didn't like her. She was a constant reminder of his wife's infidelity or the fact that she had come to their marriage carrying another man's babe. Yet as Lucina digested the one fact, another occurred to her. "Elen, you say you were just with Master Mosley, your father. Can you take me to him?"

Elen's green eyes widened in surprise at her request. Doubt flickered across her face.

Lucina pondered how much to tell her. Yet she clearly understood the ugly truth of her illegitimacy. Could she also bear to know that her father had kidnapped a man? "Your father is a man of much knowledge," she said, deciding against the full details. "I am hoping he can help me find my brother, who is lost somewhere on the Border."

Elen's mouth quivered and fresh tears pooled in her eyes. "Ma faither kidnapped him," she wailed, hiding her face in her hands again. "I knew 'twas the way o' things."

" 'Twas no fault of yours," Lucina assured her, dismayed that the child knew her father well enough to guess what he'd done. Pity filled her for Elen, clearly raised by an honest, loving mother who had taught her about honor, yet having to live with the dishonor of her birth. And having Will Mosley's wild ways for an adult example couldn't be good. She pressed her cheek against Elen's red hair as she hugged her. "I'm sorry you had to know, but mayhap you can help put it right."

"I would if I could, but naebody tells me naething. Not

ma mither nor ma faither." A strangled sob escaped. "But I hear what they say aboot me, ye ken? I saw Master Mosbley bring coins to ma mither and knew what it meant. I'm nae daft. I asked him straight out one day if 'twere true. He laughed and said aye."

"When was this?"

"Two springs ago."

Furious at Will's uncaring candor, Lucina searched for comforting words. "You have borne the truth bravely and are no doubt a better person for it." The minute they were said, though, she thought them too feeble to banish the hurt from Elen's eyes.

Yet the child straightened and went on valiantly. "Do I have to go back to ma faither . . . that is, to Goodman Andrews?"

"You will stay with me for now, and we shall make the arrangement permanent as soon as we can. I wish always to be responsible for you if possible," Lucina said firmly, sorry she could do no better. Though she yearned to make solid promises, she dared not when she had no idea what her own future held. What if she were forced to return home in the end? What if Graham removed the child from her care?

The possibilities lowered her spirits, and Elen, too, fell silent, as if aware that their future together might not be smooth. She disengaged herself from Lucina and stood. "I'll take you to ma faither now," she said, squaring her thin shoulders clad in the clean gown Lucina had procured for her. "I ken that is right."

She wasn't doing anything wrong to seek out Will Mosley a second time, Lucina told herself as she descended the secret stairs behind Elen. With each passing day, her fears for her brother grew stronger. She could not just sit idle and do nothing. The thought reminded Lucian that she had let Elen open the upper panel without learning its secret. "Pray show me how to work the mechanism," she whispered at the bottom of the stairs, wondering how the child even knew about it.

"Ma faither said to feel from this timber." Elen guided Lucina's hand in the dark to a metal spring. "Pull, an' it releases the latch."

"How do I open it from the outside?" Lucina asked as the panel clicked open.

"Ye thump it so the spring bounces," Elen said.

It sounded simple enough. Resolving to practice opening the panel later, Lucina followed Elen through the deserted chamber and into the garden. Will must also have taught his daughter how to escape the castle undetected, for Lucina could not guess how it would be done. Easing out the gate, she inched along the shadowed wall behind Elen, out of sight of the guard on the wall-walk. At the chapel, Elen pried open the heavy door and motioned Lucina through.

Lucina hung back. "Master Mosley is not in here. Why—"

"Shh," Elen cautioned. She glanced around the quiet courtyard, then slipped through the door and disappeared. Lucina had no choice but to follow.

Inside, massive stone walls rose straight up, disappearing into lofty darkness with no end in sight. Unsettled by the vastness of the space, Lucina stumbled down the aisle after Elen. By the time Lucina caught up, Elen stood before a small, steel bound door behind the altar. Producing a key, she opened the door, revealing the wild night outside the castle walls.

Another castle secret known by Will Mosley, Lucina thought as she crept through the door after Elen. This was undoubtedly how the child had slipped out to Lockerbie earlier, to fulfill her father's errand. Without question, Will had supplied the key.

Elen pulled her behind some shrubbery and whispered, "When I went to see ma faither earlier, I found the laird had set a guard at his door. He dinna stop me fram talkin' to ma faither, but he would stop yer leddyship. Ye'll stand a better chance talking to him at the window. Stay close to the wall. Ye'll find the window four doon once ye turn the corner. I'll wait for ye here."

Lucina squared her shoulders and ventured on alone. Turning the corner, she pushed through shrubbery that screened her view ahead.

What an odd country, she thought as she groped through the thick bushes. Here, hostages were exchanged regularly, housed in specially built chambers, and served with all the amenities save their right to go free. As she marveled at the strangeness of it, a vine caught her foot and she pitched forward, landing on hands and knees. "Ouch," she muttered, struggling to rise.

Shouting broke out in the distance. Lucina froze.

The thick bushes several paces ahead rustled. She stared at the source of the sound but saw only a shadow against the castle wall . . . until slowly her eyes focused, and she realized it was a man. He was watching her.

"Dinna move, lass," he said softly as the shouting in the distance grew louder. "If ye make a sound, ye're dead."

Graham sprinted across the meadow, intent on discovering the reason for the shouting and cursing coming from the main castle gate. For two infernal hours he'd stood in the damp grass outside Will's window, seeing and hearing nothing. This would probably be his cousin's attempt to smuggle out a message. But he found the space before the huge wooden portal deserted.

"What the devil is it?" He squinted at old Angus through the wicket.

" 'Twas a beggar asking for alms. All is well," Angus assured him. "As supper was long past, I offered him a bed for the night and bread. The fellow must be touched in the head. He had a fit like, shouting and demanding hot food."

"Did you take him in?" Graham asked.

"Aye, an' ye needna fear him," Angus insisted. "He were bent and feeble, for all his shouts. We'll bed him doon in the stable after he's had his broth."

Immediately suspicious that he'd been lured away by a decoy, Graham whirled and raced for his guard post. Sure enough, as he drew closer, he spied two figures before Will's window—one of them female.

With rage in his breast, he ran faster, damning the distance. He would wager Red Rowan that this was one of his cousin's many women and an accomplice, come to liberate him. And for that, he fully intended to have their heads as well as Will's.

Lucina struggled out of the bushes and to her feet. My stars, she'd blundered into an escape attempt. Her first instinct had been to flee the man who'd threatened her. Yet if Will escaped, she would lose her chance to find her brother. She stopped cold, knowing she must sound the alarm.

Before she could do anything, she saw the man at Will's open casement. The window was barred to prevent escape, but as she watched, he lifted one of the bars and removed it.

"Hurry oop, man," he snapped to someone inside. "We haven't all night."

"Christ, ye're impatient, Frank. I'm the one who spent three full days sawing through this damned iron bar." A head appeared at the window. Even in the dark, Lucina recognized Will. "Do ye have mounts?" he demanded of his companion.

"We will. Ha' no fear." He gestured in Lucina's direction. "We also have a female visitor. Friend o' yours?"

Will's head whipped around. As Lucina stood rooted to the spot, he squeezed through the bars and leaped at her from the sill.

Lucina whirled to run, then screamed as his weight slammed her to the ground.

" 'Tis the Englishwoman." Though dazed by her fall, Lucina knew Will's voice as he bent over her. "We mun take her with us. She has land hereabouts, and I intend to wed her for it, ye ken."

"I'll wed her mysel' if she owns land," Will's accomplice sounded jubilant at the discovery.

Though she struggled fiercely, he overpowered her easily and flipped her onto her back, straddling her as she flailed both arms and legs. With seemingly little effort, he pinned her wrists to the ground on either side of her head. Will's companion bent over her. Lucina stared up into his narrow, sharp-featured face, horrified by what she saw. The castle ghost, even Will, seemed tame in comparison to this beast. His eyes leaped with feral blood lust, and she knew this one would dare anything to gain his ends.

"Hold where you are," a fierce challenge interrupted. Though controlled, the voice burned with rage. "Let her up, Will. Bothwell, I want you off my land."

Lucina was unceremoniously hauled to her feet, but not released. Her head still spun from the crashing fall, and she wobbled as Bothwell took charge of her, pinning her arms roughly behind her back. Despite her disorientation, relief flooded through her as she recognized her savior. The Black Graham stood only yards away, his broad-shouldered form a dark silhouette against the night.

"Yer doxy was out wandering," Will sneered. "Coom tae take her back to bed?"

"Release her now."

"We're taking her hostage, as Carmichael ordered," Bothwell said. "Sir John said she should stand as surety in her brother's stead. Only you refused to obey."

The news shocked Lucina. Twisting against Bothwell, she opened her mouth to demand what he meant.

"Be still." He jerked her arms hard, forcing tears to her eyes as pain wrenched her shoulders. She swallowed back a moan.

Will's hysterical laughter rose. "Think o' the grand jest, coz," he chortled at his chief. "I could kill the verra woman ye covet and put the English on yer trail instead o' mine."

"I thought you fancied her for her land," Graham growled.

"Not as much as ye fancy her." Will laughed and strutted forward to taunt his cousin. "Cut her a mite, Frank. Let's see him beg."

The sting of metal burned Lucina's throat, and she squeezed her eyes shut, praying silently as a wet trail of warmth trickled down her neck.

"I said let her go."

Bothwell grunted suddenly and lurched forward. As his dirk slipped from her neck, Lucina twisted in the opposite direction, guessing Graham allies had attacked from behind. Curses and shouts rose around her as Will, Graham, and others joined the fight. Still Bothwell held her, his grip unflinching as he fought his attacker, dragging her with him as he moved, her arm at an awkward angle.

In the dark and the chaos, a wrenching jerk broke the link between them. Pain exploded in Lucina's right shoulder, and she fell to her knees, whimpering with anguish. Around her, men continued to struggle in a confusing clash of steel and grappling bodies as she bent to the ground, immobilized by agony. Blinding dots of blackness spun before her eyes, urging her to sink into a blessed faint. . . .

Suddenly a hand jerked at her good shoulder, snapping

her to alertness. She cried out as her fingers were pried from her bad shoulder and something pressed against it hard.

"Be still so I can stop the bleeding." Graham's voice rasped in her ear. Stars above, was she also wounded? She couldn't understand what he was saying as he tied a strip of cloth so tightly around her arm, she clenched her teeth to hold back a scream. Then he began on her shoulder, attempting to realign the bone that had clearly been pulled from its socket.

"No more," she begged piteously. He said something, but the words swam laboriously in her head, as if through thick, cold seas.

He cursed, looped her good arm around his neck, encircled her waist with one arm, and half carried her toward the castle gate. She sagged against him, vaguely aware of blood all over her kirtle. She *had* been wounded.

Her thoughts thickened, cloying in her brain, urging her into oblivion. A last coherent idea formed before she answered the summons . . . she was going to die in the arms of the Black Graham.

His face haunted Lucina's dreams, his eyes pleading with her to live. What nonsense. She wasn't dying. Or was she?

The agony in her shoulder snapped her back to consciousness. She lay flat on a bench, feeling like a fish out of water, landed on its belly. Graham knelt beside her, cursing loudly in her ear. The fear in his voice hurt almost as much as the torment sawing at her shoulder like hot knives, and she fought for control as Isabel appeared out of nowhere, ghostly in a white night shift.

Isabel's cool, firm fingers lifted and manipulated her shoulder while her arm dangled to the floor like a limp piece of meat. The pain droned like hot bees burning through her brain and body. She yielded to their evil pressure and screamed.

"Jesus, help her!" On one knee beside her, Graham ground his teeth so hard she could hear them, like millstones crushing grain. Unable to escape, she closed her eyes against the mask of anguish transforming his face. Isabel's fingers moved her shoulder in a painful, jiggling dance until suddenly, with an ugly pop, her bones clicked into place.

The pain lessened as suddenly as wind dropping from a sail. Sapped of energy, she closed her eyes, praised the stars above for her deliverance, and spun into blackness once more.

Chapter 12

Lucina awoke to Isabel's cool, dry hands on her brow, feeling she had slept forever. Darkness still wrapped its veil of silence around the tower chamber. She knew she was back in the tower, because she heard the moss-green curtain whisper on its rings as it glided aside. She also recognized the softness of the eiderdown bed.

Eyes closed, she leaned against Isabel, wanting to thank her for banishing the pain. *Ministering angel, you can't be mad.*

Isabel spooned a bitter liquid between her lips. The gnawing ache in her shoulder eased, and she drifted in and out of dreams.

Graham's face came and went, his torment wrenching her heart from her breast. Or was it the pain in her shoulder that hurt so? She thrashed her head on the pillow, unable to separate one from the other—the pain in his face from the pain within her.

Waking or dreaming? She slipped from one to the other, unable to tell the difference. Once Graham waxed angry, swearing revenge against his cousin. Another time, he took her hand and carried it to his cheek. She felt the rasp of his beard stubble against her palm as he bent near.

"Don't die. I need you." His whisper pierced the veil that muffled her consciousness, making everything distant and unreal. Tender expressions from an angry man?

What she knew of him strongly suggested she had heard wrong. Nor did she hear such a thing again. His face changed to angry and stayed that way, shifting only from grim to vengeful.

She closed her eyes to escape his rage. In those moments he was so like Will, filled with angry passions she could never accept in her proper English life. Had Isabel's brew brought her visions, that she imagined him tender and open? Or had she dreamed what she wanted to hear?

Throughout, Isabel flitted in and out of her sight, ministering to her, offering water or broth to wet her lips, then more bitter brew for pain.

Finally she lapsed into deeper sleep where the dreams took full command. The Norse dragon ships of Colin's tale were coming across the sea, the spray curling around their bowsprits and their green-painted wings unfurled in flight. She clenched her fists and awaited them onshore, welcoming their invasion, welcoming the wild pagans who came to change her life. . . .

With nothing to stop them, they shot into a clear firth of translucent blue water, where the shore gleamed with shining white sand. She felt their triumph at discovering the Scots Border, a majestic land of grassy lowlands pierced by sudden lakes and woodlands, replete with heather-clad moors broken by glens and rippling burns. A land to be proud of. A land untamed and free.

Down ramps of wood their horses charged, into the shallow firth. Spray flew from their hooves as they raced for the shore, glad to exchange the shifting vessel for solid earth. Clouds of steam shot from their nostrils as they tossed their heads. Their leader, a magnificent stallion of mighty proportions, bid her mount. Helpless in the face of his wizardry, full of joy that his command was her wish, she climbed onto his sleek, heathen back. As the stallion leaped forward, he bid her give in to her desires and fly free with him.

Together they raced across lush pastures clustered with bluebells. They crossed shining streams that flowed into deep, silent lochs, then passed tossing forests of larch, rowan, and oak. Higher they mounted into the air, and Lucina knew she rode on the back of Pegasus. The mighty steed of the gods spread his wings and carried her toward the white-capped mountain crags.

She entered a deep, dry cave lit only by the dull glow of embers. This was the lair of the mountain king, of the mysterious, powerful Black Graham. His pain drew her, and she stretched out both hands, wanting to remove it as she would hot coals from the fire. She must pluck out each burning secret and extinguish its sorrow. Only then would he be whole.

Comfort. Strength. Security. His lips promised this and more as they pressed against her hand, and she knew they were hers, if she could fight her way past his pain.

"Live, Lucina." His voice caressed her, the way it had the night he cared for Gellie, like a tangible touch. "Live, or I'll cut my throat and die at your side."

Her eyelids felt like leaden weights. She forced them open a crack and tried to speak. A croak emerged from her throat, and she squeezed his hand weakly, embarrassed that she could not respond. "Idiot," she mouthed as he put his ear close enough to hear.

"Call me an idiot. Call me anything," he whispered. "But don't die."

Had she dreamed those words or had he really said them? They merged with her dreams, spinning away into confusion.

She woke again later, feeling more alert than she had previously. Morning burned through the tower windows, hurting her eyes like the ache burning in her wounded arm and shoulder and the men's angry voices burning her ears.

No more, she pleaded silently, wishing herself safely away from the Border's fighting and chaos. Would it never end?

Isabel appeared the instant she stirred. Gratefully she sipped the broth her friend offered on a spoon, her parched lips welcoming the fluid that gave her strength.

"Does the shoulder pain ye?" Isabel asked, so tenderly that Lucina caught her hand and pressed it in thanks. "Do ye want mare o' the brew?"

She nodded mutely, feeling like a coward but welcoming the liquid that would numb her body's pain. Unfortunately, it would numb her mind as well.

"I want a full explanation of what happened," she heard Graham say beyond the curtain.

"I-I am sorry, Graham." She had never heard Jasper falter before, but she recognized his rusty voice creaking with apology. "When Mistress Cavandish screamed, we kent something were wrong and opened the gates to coom to yer aid. That beggar we'd let in rode Red Rowan oot right behind us. He meant to take Orpheus, as well," he added, "but the animal fought him. You know the rest. Will was too swift for us, mounted on Red Rowan. We couldn't catch him."

"Damn!"

Lucina squeezed her eyes shut, feeling Graham's pain at losing his stallion. All because he had been helping her. She opened one eye a slit and peered up at Isabel. The good dame put a finger to her lips. "Be still. Yer shoulder needs rest."

"What of the beggar?" Graham asked. "Do you have him in the dungeon?"

"Aye," Jasper said, waxing angry. "He's no auld man, neither. 'Twas a ruse to trick us. He's a mere lad."

Graham swore an ugly oath.

" 'Tis my fault, Graham," Lucina croaked as loudly as she could. "You could have stopped Will from taking Red Rowan save for me."

"She's conscious." The curtain was swept back, and Graham leaned over her. Concern mingled with the anger in his face.

"You let them get away because of me," she protested weakly, wanting to bear the brunt of his anger. "You've lost both Will and your horse."

"What choice did I have?" he responded grimly.

"You should have stopped them," she insisted again.

"And let you bleed to death?"

His curt reply bore no hint of caring. Without a doubt she had been delirious earlier, her muddled brain imagining his ardent plea for her to live. The words to question him hovered on her lips, but she held them back. After his tenderness, even if she had dreamed it, his indifference would hurt too much. "I . . . I am eternally in your debt," she ventured, unsure what could possibly compensate for such a loss. "Is there some way I can repay you?"

"Rest assured that I will let you know. After I question the ruffian who helped Will escape." He turned back to Jasper. "Pray prepare him. I will join you shortly."

"Graham, he's only five and ten, mayhap six and ten years of age," Jasper said.

"I was training to be chief by then," Graham said sourly.

"Lad or no, tell him he'll answer my questions or suffer my wrath."

"Graham, you must not hurt him. He's a child," Lucina insisted, unable to contain her protest. The herbal brew was working on her, urging her eyes to close, but she couldn't let Graham torture a boy. Despite his foul mood, he must listen to her.

But before he could answer, Elen shot into view and hurled herself at the Graham's feet. "I pray ye, m'lord, dinna put him to th' rack. Take me instead."

"No, no! You must not torture either one of them." Lucina added her plea to Elen's, terrified that at last she would see the true brutality of this Border laird. "Bring him here, and you and I can question him."

Graham looked from her to Elen and back again, either taken aback or disgusted by their pleas, Lucina couldn't tell which.

"Child or no, he stole a valuable horse and deserves to be punished the same as any reiver. He all but stole your stallion." Graham leveled a stern gaze at her, giving her a minute to appreciate the fact that Orpheus had been spared. Then he pulled Elen none too gently to her feet. "Stop groveling, lass. You shan't be tortured. Tell me what you know of this lad."

"I pray you, let me suffer in his place," Elen mumbled. "He's ma half brother."

Another of Will's loyal bastards, apparently sent to steal the fastest horse in the stable so his father could escape. Lucina couldn't blame Graham for his murderous frown, but she prayed he would not resort to torture. Would she feel so lenient if Orpheus had been taken as well?

"What is his name and what do you know of him?" Graham demanded coldly.

"His name is Drummond, m'lord," she said. "He lives in Annan with his mother, Elizabeth Storie, who is a weaver."

"And why are you so soft for him?"

"He brought me several ells o' cloth once. Made by his mither, it were, an' me in a tight gown that rode so high, ma shins showed. He brought me other things as well o'er the years."

"I wonder he could afford it. What else?"

Elen shrugged evasively. "He took me places where I could earn a coin or twa."

"Is that all?"

She nodded, but it seemed to Lucina she had a desperate air, as if afraid she might implicate the lad further. Little wonder. The man she had judged as heartless was at the same time farsighted. Will fully understood that the many bastards he'd sired could serve his selfish schemes as adults one day. Understanding this, she disliked Will all the more.

Apparently Graham was of like mind, for he quickly rendered judgment. "Elen, both you and Drummond must be confined until I recapture Master Mosley. 'Tis necessary, though I shall not put you in the dungeon. Nor shall he remain there."

Elen burst into tears. Lucina struggled against her own dismay. "Let her stay with me, Graham. Why should you lock her up?"

"Who do you think provided the file Will used to cut through his window bars?" He clamped one hand on Elen's shoulder and guided her from the room.

A moan of defeat escaped Lucina. Graham was right. If Elen had given her father the file, she could not be allowed to go free to help him further. And she must also have taken a message to Bothwell, given her journey to the neighboring village in the dead of night. And now there was worse to come. "I pray you, Graham, do not torture the boy," she pleaded as he returned to her bedside. "I'll do anything you ask. I'll give you Orpheus to make up for the loss of Red Rowan."

He leveled a long gaze at her, his eyes narrowed, every line of his body reflecting anger or disapproval, she wasn't sure which.

"I have no rack in Castle Graham," he finally spat out. "But I won't hesitate to take my belt to his backside if he's uncooperative. Or to yours, once you're well." Having made his point, he strode to the door, slamming it as he left.

Mortified to have misread him, yet at the same time relieved he hadn't taken her offer of Orpheus, Lucina sank back against the pillows. Stars above, what an error. That hadn't been anger on Graham's face. It had been hurt. She had believed the worst of him when it had been the farthest thing from his mind.

He had suffered enough without her adding to it. Yet now he must bear her mistrust as well. She had let him down, after the incredible sacrifice he had made to save her life.

It was all too upsetting. "Oh, Isabel"—her wail was thin and weak—"I'm always saying the wrong thing. I should have known."

"How could ye?" Isabel urged her to lie back down. "Dinna abuse yersel' for someit as is done. Be still, now. Ye're still too weak."

"But I should have—"

Without warning, Isabel cradled Lucina's head in one arm and held the spoon to her lips. More sleeping potion. As Lucina opened her lips to protest the medicine, the spoon nipped in. Too well-bred to spit back the liquid, Lucina sank against the pillows and swallowed. It was probably opium, she thought with regret. Though it would kill the pain, it would render her unable to help Elen or her brother.

Feeling too hopeless to fight further, she gave in to the potion. It was easier to hide in her weakness than to struggle and error again.

Dreams haunted her once more. Someone sang, as if to soothe her, the voice sweet and high. Isabel? she wondered drowsily.

A haunting ballad of fairy magic. A woman at midnight on the wild moor. The queen of fairies had stolen her lover, and she waited to wrest her knight back to the mortal world.

> *About the dead hour of the night,*
> *She heard the bridles ring;*
> *And Janet was as glad o' that*
> *As any earthly thing!*

> *Will o' Wisp before them went,*
> *Sent forth a twinkling light;*
> *And soon she saw the Fairy bands*
> *All riding in her sight.*

> *And first gaed by the black black steed,*
> *And then gaed by the brown;*
> *But fast she gript the milk-white steed,*
> *And pulled the rider down.*

Whether Janet won her true love or no, Lucina did not learn, for the singing stopped abruptly. A rustle of fabric swished by her ear, as if someone had called away the singer.

Don't go. You must finish the ballad and free the knight. Lucina struggled to voice the protest, but the potion lay heavily on her consciousness, rendering her mute. Like the maiden of the song, she could not wrest her love from the enchanted world where he knew no peace. She had tried to fight for her brother and failed. How could she think to rescue the Black Graham? The ballad's words circled on her mind, until she felt she was Janet, standing alone on the moor, the blackness of midnight surrounding her like the garb of despair.

Sleep threatened to carry her away once more, but the singing began again. Or was she dreaming? This time a new song wound its folds around her, haunting and painful. It was the ballad of Bonnie Mary, the story of a fair young maiden, mistreated and unhappy, bearing her chief's heir, then dying at the hands of her angry, brutal lord.

A sob gathered in her chest. So that was how Bonnie Mary had died, murdered by her husband. Tears wet her cheeks, and she wept freely, unsure whether she was waking or sleeping. All her past sorrows seemed as nothing in the face of this tragedy that had torn two families apart. If only she could find the key to their peace.

But the pain in her shoulder reminded her. She was weak in the face of their hatred. She could not heal the wounds of this man or his country with love alone.

The sharp odor of medicinal ointment filled Lucina's nostrils when next she opened her eyes. Isabel bent over her, bandaging her wounded arm. Despite its stiffness, it hardly hurt. "Was I cut deeply?" she asked.

Isabel's thin face hovered over her, tired and concerned. "Nay, ye merely bled overmuch. Yer shoulder was the worst hurt."

The tumult of the escape still weighed heavily on Lucina, but she was on the mend and feeling curiously safe in the Black Graham's chamber, guarded as long as she remained in his care. What a fool she had been to venture beyond the gates.

"Can ye eat same solid food?" Isabel asked, pushing straggling strands of gray hair under her white kertch. "Ye've slept away twa full days."

Realizing Isabel had not left her in all that time, Lucina caught her friend's hand and carried it to her cheek. Isabel patted her gently and gave an encouraging smile.

Nodding, Lucina sat up. She was hungry but otherwise feeling reasonably fit. Eagerly she took the bowl Isabel offered and ate the porridge straight down.

Isabel smiled at her show of appetite. "I believe ye're ready for someit more substantial," she laughed. Going to the chamber door, she summoned a maid and ordered a tray of food.

A short time later, as Lucina devoured roast hare and turnip greens, Isabel clucked over her, smoothing her hair, reminding her of her mother when she'd been ill as a child. A feeling of great affection washed over her, as well as gratitude for having such a friend. Isabel's skill had repaired her shoulder and eased her pain. Such a person couldn't possibly be mad, could she?

She ate everything Isabel offered, then let her friend draw back the curtain partitioning the alcove. Graham sat at his table writing. As Isabel withdrew to a place near the door, he set down his quill and stood.

Lucina felt a mixture of fear and excitement lace through her as he strode to the bed and studied her, arms folded at his chest.

"Are you assessing my state of health," she asked, suddenly remembering their earlier quarrel over Elen and her unjust accusations. But he had been tender with her before that, when her pain had been great. At least she thought he had.

"Aye, and you seem fit enough to answer a few questions," he said curtly. "What were you doing outside the castle walls, and how did you get there without being seen?" Cold displeasure radiated from him.

"I meant no harm," she began. "I was—"

"You caused a great deal of harm, whether you meant it or no," he barked. "You meant to question Will Mosley, did you not?"

Resentfully she raised her chin. "Why shouldn't I question him?"

"Because he would never tell you a thing." He stormed away to stand before the window, his profile showing the angry set of his jaw. "You're far too impetuous, Lucina Cavandish. When will you learn to let a man manage these things?"

Lucina pressed her lips together, ready to admit her error if he would admit his inability to rescue her brother. But he would never do that. "Did you find Will or Bothwell while I slept?"

A black look was her reply. Of course he hadn't. "Who is Bothwell?" she asked.

"The fifth Earl of Bothwell, Francis Stewart. A distant cousin to King James."

"He doesn't behave like an earl," she said with conviction. "He acts like a demented ruffian."

Graham shrugged, as if that were a foregone conclusion. "The Border has bred ruffians for years. He's been outlawed by King James several times. Once for murder, once when he was accused of using witchcraft against the king but escaped from the Edinburgh Tolbooth before he could be tried, and most recently for an attempt against the royal person, which he denies. As a relation to the king, he was once a trusted adviser when James was younger."

Another mad Borderer, Lucina thought dully. Did she draw them to her, or were they everywhere? "What did he mean, I was the hostage?" she asked.

Graham eyed her for a minute, as if assessing her strength to deal with the answer. "The Scots West Border warden, Sir John Carmichael, wants you for hostage in your brother's place, as a guarantee that peace will be kept."

She shook her head, baffled by this information. "Why me? Why not another Englishman?"

"Word seems to have spread about your land."

"Wasted time," she stated stoutly. "They can't have it for any price."

He cocked an eyebrow at her skeptically. "You heard

Will. He's willing to wed you for it, which is why I've decided to wed you myself. Quickly. Before he tries again."

She narrowed her gaze at him. "You're not serious, of course."

"I am. Reverend Atkinson waits below stairs."

"A churchman?" He did look serious. Lucina pushed back the blankets, preparing to rise, then stopped, seeing she wore nothing but a shift. "But you can't just . . . that is, I . . . we . . ." She stared at him helplessly, thrown into confusion. She had admitted her attraction to the man and her mad desire to assuage his pain. But marriage?

She had come to Scotland to escape her oppressive family, not to acquire a new one that was twice as oppressive, bound by rules of loyalty to kin, chief, and feud. She had especially intended to avoid a demanding husband who would control her every move. It had been one thing to dwell under the Graham's roof as a free agent, almost enjoyable to defy him as long as he'd had no legal right to control her behavior. But if she wed him, he would have every right to enforce his will.

Graham clearly intended to do just that. Opening the door, he motioned in a black-clad churchman. Her lips parted as she realized Graham wasn't even awaiting her acceptance. "Isabel, do something," she cried. "I can't be married like this. I can't be married at all."

"You're not wed already, are you?" Graham asked politely. "Not irrevocably betrothed?"

"Of course not, but I cannot—"

"Then, 'tis settled." He cut her off as the churchman stepped forward and snapped opened his prayer book, as if used to clandestine marriages at odd hours. Jasper and two other men entered the room at Graham's signal, obviously to serve as witnesses.

Lucina gaped at them, speechless. She'd heard tales of women captured by Border Scots and forced into marriage, but never had she imagined being such a prize.

" 'Tis for yer own safety, ye ken," Isabel assured Lucina as the reverend began the marriage ceremony. Her friend pressed her hand gently. "The Earl of Bothwell is said to dabble in witchcraft, an' if 'tis so, Will might turn to foul means to have ye. He's that hungry for land."

"I-I cannot believe anyone would wed me for some

land," she stammered, wondering wildly what she ought to do.

"Free land is a rare thing on the Border. Men kill for less. And since Will ne'er wed the women he coupled wi', he can well wed ye. Aye, ye'll be safest wed tae ma grandson."

Lucina stared, distracted from the churchman's reading as she puzzled over Isabel's words. Will was her grandson, not Graham. Had she gotten them mixed up again? She seemed entirely lucid to Lucina, yet she had clearly confused Graham and her grandson.

"Lucina Cavandish, do you take this man to be your lawfully wedded husband?"

The churchman's question snapped her back to the ceremony. "Graham," she burst out, "do you truly intend to make me wed you?" Despite the reviving meal, her senses reeled, and she was thoroughly baffled by his determination. "I'm so different from all of you."

"Mayhap that's why I intend to have ye." With a flick of his finger, he signaled the churchman. "She does. Pray continue."

Despite her lack of assent, the reverend intoned the final words of the ceremony that joined her to John Alexander Malcolm Graham for life.

Annulment, she thought as the churchman and the witnesses signed the necessary paper, then glared threateningly at her until she scrawled her signature on the line indicated. *Annulment,* she thought again as they took their leave and she leaned back against the cushions.

Graham knelt by the bed and kissed her lightly on the lips as if to seal their vows, but she couldn't respond, or look at him, or even think properly. Confused, she closed her eyes in weary desperation. As she sought refuge in sleep, she thought an annulment was indeed her only hope.

Chapter 13

Lucina awoke the next day, the third since Will's escape, sweating beneath the blankets from the sun slanting across her bed. She sat up and was pleasantly surprised to find the pain in her shoulder as no more than a remote dream. The bandage had even been removed, and the knife wound was a mere healing scab.

But memory of recent events did hurt, even more than her shoulder had yesterday. Will and his accomplice were still at liberty. Red Rowan was still gone. Her brother was still missing. And now she was wed.

Lucina considered her next move. She must have a sling for her arm, to keep it immobilized and avoid strain. She needed a bath as well. Smelling like this, she would drive her bridegroom away before he could even consider making her a wife in fact. Her fingers caught in tangles as she pushed her hair back, knowing she must look a fright.

Someone beyond the curtain rose as she stirred. But the face that peeped around the curtain was neither Graham's nor Isabel's. Grissel, the serving woman she'd overheard her second night at Castle Graham, curtsied and asked if there was aught she required.

"Where is Madam Isabel?" Lucina asked.

"She's lying doon, ma leddy." Grissel lowered her gaze, but not before Lucina saw the derision in her expression and knew her opinion of Isabel.

From the start, Lucina had not liked this woman's manner of treating the other servants, especially the youngster Annie. "She is entitled to lie down after nursing me unceasingly for so long," she stated. "Her wonderful skill has saved me great pain."

Grissel seemed to catch the warning in her new mistress's voice, for she tempered her reply. "She'd been sleeping here, ma leddy, so she could tend ye. But this morning she were wandering again. Thinking 'tis another year. The Graham sent her to her chamber." She paused, then added in a burst of indignation, "She calls him laddie and threatens to whip him if he displeases her. And he dinna stop her talkin' to him so."

Despite Lucina's sorrow at the news of Isabel's wandering, the image of her friend, so frail in body yet powerful in spirit, threatening to whip the mighty Black Graham, urged her to smile. "I'm thirsty, Grissel," she said, changing the subject. How she wished to be rid of the woman, with her pale blue eyes that were too intent on other people's affairs. "Would you be so good as to fetch me something cool to drink?"

Grissel shuffled away, then returned bearing a pewter mug filled with a chill of condensation. The spice of mulled barley water wafted to Lucina's nostrils as she took it and sipped, the cool liquid relieving her thirst. "How many years has Madam Isabel had this trouble?" she asked, speaking of Isabel's failing so she could learn more about it.

Grissel assisted her from the bed to a chair, handed her the mug of barley water again, then began changing the bed linen. "Ever since her sister died, ma leddy. An' Bonnie Mary's been gone mair years than I can count. I were a mere lassie when they buried her in the kirkyard."

Startled, Lucina set down the mug. "Isabel Graham is Bonnie Mary's sister?"

Grissel eyed her with surprise as she finished with the bed and moved to mend the fire. "Weel, o' course she is. She were born Isabel Maxwell, and so she is still."

"But I thought she was wed to the old chief's brother."

"Aye, tae Gavin Graham, but Border women keep the name they were born wi'. 'Tis sad that Mad Isabel thinks herself the same girl of long ago." Finished with the fire, Grissel took up the mug Lucina had emptied.

Hiding her irritation with Grissel's smug pronouncement about Isabel, Lucina asked for a bath and prepared for the journey to the warm kitchens. But all the while she puzzled over the morass of Scots family relations. Isabel had been a Maxwell, sister to the dead woman whose ghost walked Castle Graham. Why did this surprise her?

She couldn't think why. Yet she'd never imagined that Isabel and Bonnie Mary had been reared together, had shared secrets and loves and hopes for the future, then seen it all crash to ruin in the face of Mary's unhappy marriage to an abusive lord. How terrible for Isabel to bear that, as well as to see the seeds of the Graham family's instability blossom in her grandson Will.

Lucina's stomach tightened with apprehension as she realized she had wed the grandson of a man who had beat his wife to death.

The thought of annulment returned to her. She was still a virgin. The bond could be broken. But how would she seek one? She understood little of this country's laws and customs. She understood even less of John Alexander Malcolm Graham. Would he permit her to obtain an annulment? Did she truly want one?

As with all the troubles she had encountered since her arrival in Scotland, this one taxed her patience. She was expected to bide her time until the required solution presented itself. She must play the part of obedient female and wait. And in her five and twenty years of life, Lucina had learned that waiting quietly was something she wasn't willing to do.

What had he done?

A stiff wind whipped Graham's face that afternoon as he cantered across open land back to Castle Graham. He was tired, ill-tempered, and empty-handed. Jasper had accompanied him on his search for Will, but he'd remained silent, offering only a simple congratulation on acquiring a new wife. But Colin, Angus, and the six others were more vocal, and Graham pulled ahead of them, needing to avoid their bawdy jests hinting at the pleasures that would soon be his.

His head spun with the enormity of his action. Driven by his desire to possess Lucina, he'd wed again. Ironic that having done the deed, he'd left his bride to a chaste bed.

Nor had he found Will. As lads, he and Will, his brothers, and their cousins had ridden these hills and glens together, exploring, trespassing, and getting into scrapes. He'd searched a good many of those old haunts, but Will was hiding in none of them.

He was probably on the move daily, which complicated the search. One day Will might hide in some deserted croft, but move on to a mountainside cave by nightfall, then on to one of the Earl of Bothwell's castles the next day.

Will's apparent friendship with Bothwell added further difficulty to finding his cousin, Graham thought as he entered the castle. He must assume Will could take refuge with Bothwell, who was also a refugee, hiding from authority. Bothwell's family, followers, and tenants all relied on him for their daily bread and shelter, and would never tell. With the earl's help, Will could hide with Roger Cavandish anywhere along hundreds of leagues of Border.

The only spot of light in Graham's black mood was in thoughts of his new bride. He would not attempt to bed her while her shoulder and arm were healing, yet the thought of her return to health set him on fire. In seeking the different, he'd chosen a woman who stood out from the others. Her temperament, her background, and especially her attitudes, were as different from those of the Border people as day was from night.

That very difference fascinated him, distracted him, and held the ghosts at bay. At least he was counting on that happening . . . as soon as he got her in bed.

" 'Tis aboot time ye came tae see me," Aunt Isabel said curtly as Graham entered her chamber.

Whenever he had to confine her, Graham visited Isabel daily to ensure she was well. Most of the time he had to chastise the maids set to attend her. Whenever her mind wandered, they neglected their mistress. At times he thought he would do better to assign one of his men, who would at least obey orders. "You're up and about," he said.

"Nae thanks to you." She sniffed and refused to look at him, instead taking up her mending.

"I do what is best for you."

"Ye dinna do any sooch thing." She slapped the mending on a nearby table and scowled at him. "Ye said 'twas no harm in lettin' Helen and Jock's Janet visit that gypsy woman, but I'm sorry now I agreed wi' ye. Mair than ever at times like this."

"What are you talking about?" He sat down on the stool opposite, sorry she resented him. He couldn't blame her for being frustrated, but he couldn't let her roam free. Not when she was babbling nonsense again. He steeled himself for yet another story about Isabel's daughter Helen and his mother Janet.

"I told ye aboot the gypsy." She pushed back tangled hair that clearly had not been combed or arranged that day. As he made a mental note to order it done, her expression became remote. "She told Helen and Janet that Janet's bairn would be mad, puir mite, an' ye see, 'tis true." She sighed. "I wish we dinna do as she said."

She muttered more beneath her breath that he couldn't follow, but it was clear to Graham she had him and Will mixed up again. And though she'd often told the story of his and Will's birth, he'd never heard of a gypsy prophecy. "Take comfort," he said gently, hoping to bring her back to the present. "The gypsy was wrong, for I'm not mad. You may put that fear from your mind. I came to thank you for supporting my marriage," he said, to fulfill the other purpose of his visit. "You helped Lucina understand she must agree to wed me."

His great-aunt smiled faintly. "O' course I did, Alex. She's good for ye. Good for this place." She cast him a knowing glance. "Have you bedded her yet?"

"You're tired, Aunt Isabel," he soothed, rising and patting her hand. He was glad she seemed to understand who he was again, but he didn't want to discuss his bedding of Lucina. "Rest now."

She would have none of his urgings. "I asked ye a question, laddie. Have ye consummated the marriage so she won't run away?"

He quickly lowered his gaze, sure his unquenchable desire for Lucina Cavandish showed in his face. "She won't leave. Not now."

Isabel chuckled. "Dinna take for granted what she'll do and what she willna, laddie. She'll surprise ye. She's not your Sarah, weak and obedient to a fault."

The memories she roused hurt. Sarah hadn't been obedient when it most mattered, which had driven them apart in the end. "Sarah was your own kinswoman," he pointed out. "Pray don't find fault with her."

"I loved her well, so dinna gang putting words in my mouth, laddie," his aunt said crisply. "But Lucina Cavandish is no' like her, so dinna make another mistake. Ye're a good lad, but too hasty, expecting others to think the way ye do." She changed the subject. "Now, then, when are ye lettin' me oot o' this place? I want tae be helping those folk of yers. Ye mun settle them back at their crofts."

Graham nodded, too tired to think of all the details. "I'll send them back by week's end."

"Aye, they're getting restless. Best send them on the morrow."

In all the times he'd feared for her health, Graham had imagined she was only a little confused about people's names and dates, not lacking in basic judgment. But her seemingly capricious advice made hm wonder. "I can't do that. There might be another raid," he said.

"There will be," she said decisively. "Nae doubt o' it. An' ye'll need yer men, so best get these folk settled before then."

His gaze shot to her face, his suspicions roused by her cagey expression. "What do you know about it?"

"Naething," she said vaguely. "But ye're not thinking, Alex, which is no' like ye."

He examined the question of another English raid from every side. Sir Edward mentioned he might conduct a raid to rescue Roger Cavandish if he could learn where the lad was held. "Where's Maggie Johnstone?" he snapped, suddenly sure the time of the English raid had arrived.

"In the scullery, nae doubt." Isabel nodded sagely, increasing his suspicions.

Maggie Johnstone wasn't in the scullery. Nor was she anywhere in the castle. With ease Graham deduced where she had gone. Sir Edward's castle was her home now, with her sister whose husband served in the garrison. Carlisle Castle was also the center of English West Border March intelligence. Putting those two things together, along with her attachment to Lucina, and he knew what that implied.

Maggie Johnstone had gone to Carlisle to learn when and where the English would stage their raid to rescue the Cavandish lad.

Chapter 14

Graham cursed the English, the Scots, Maggie, Lucina, and everyone in general all the way up the lengthy, winding stairs to the tower room. Devil take it, his weary muscles demanded rest after a full day in the saddle. He didn't want to chase after the intractable Maggie Johnstone.

It ruffled his pride, having to fetch her back to find out what she knew. He hated seeking news from a woman because she had easier access to it than he. What he wanted was a soft feather bed and time in it with Lucina. Because if he didn't have a chance to bed his bride soon, he might be driven over the edge.

What a disgusting idea, he thought as he reached the top of the stairs. At times it seemed he was turning into Will.

Lucina jumped as Graham barged into the tower chamber without knocking, frightening her half out of her wits. Without offering her a proper greeting, he launched into a series of orders. She was to prepare to receive guests. She was to dress in suitable clothing that he would provide.

He left the chamber and returned with a beautiful kirtle skirt and bodice. Without a word, he spread them on the bed and withdrew.

Puzzled by his insistence, she examined the garments. Their cut suggested they were a good ten years old, yet the fabric was beautiful. Watered blue silk shimmered and pooled across the bed.

"Whose gown is this?" she asked Grissel, holding up the kirtle skirt, letting the silky fabric slip deliciously through her fingers.

" 'Twas Sarah Maxwell's. She wore it the day she was wed."

Lucina put it down. "Pray take it away, and tell his lordship I thank him but will wear my own clothes." She refused to move until her own best kirtle skirt and bodice were brought to her, washed and starched and pressed. After allowing Grissel to dress her, she settled before the fire, her arm in a linen sling. "Tell his lordship he may come in."

She saw at once his displeasure that she had refused the gown. "I will wear my own clothing. I am not Sarah Maxwell and do not pretend to take her place." She lifted her chin, determined to argue if she must.

"I merely wished you richly gowned to meet your people," he said quietly, taking a stance before the fireplace.

She flushed with embarrassment at having assigned him motives that didn't exist. Muttering an apology, she squared her shoulders and faced the door, wondering what would happen next.

A baffling ceremony followed that Lucina could hardly believe was real. Men entered the tower chamber, one by one, and knelt before her to swear their fealty. She had heard of such ceremonies, held for lairds or chiefs, but was it done for wives?

She guessed it wasn't, but that Graham did it to ensure everyone knew her by sight as well as by name. Whatever the reason, she admitted she enjoyed having the likes of loyal old Jasper, Colin, and even crusty, bad-tempered Angus kneel at her feet, swearing to honor and protect her.

After the brawn of the male garrison, the tenants from the hall came. The women offered humble gifts, along with whispers of appreciation. The men stolidly swore their allegiance to her and any children she bore. A mother who'd been separated from her child in the crowded hall thanked her for finding her "we'ane." A widower with two children confided that he meant to wed the widow she'd found to help care for his girls.

Even the Mosley man past whom she'd slipped in the gully the first night was brought from his dungeon cell to swear fealty. "I ha'na ever seen one ride as ye did that night, ma leddy." He fingered his cap, displaying awkward admiration. "Ask of me what ye will, I swear to serve ye."

"I only ask that you obey your chief. No more reiving," she said gently. "Do you swear?"

"On ma oath," he swore fervently, putting his cap over his heart. "I swear."

She shot Graham a glance as the man withdrew. She had won friends since she'd come and hoped he approved. Yet even if he didn't, she couldn't hold back her offerings. It was how she'd been taught, and whenever she gave friendship, her heart went with it. Most people seemed to sense the glow of satisfaction that lit her from within as each gift was given. That glow warmed her heart as the ceremony continued, the stream of people seeming never to end.

Just when Lucina felt she could take no more adulation, Graham announced it was over. He bid Grissel bring food and drink for two, then told her to withdraw.

"I'm so tired." Lucina's glow of satisfaction turned to a bonfire as she looked up and found Graham watching her. Her breath caught at the desire in his eyes. Suddenly she felt more frightened than when she'd dared to mount an untamed moor pony as a child and been bucked off.

Graham heard the intake of her breath and knew what it meant. She believed he wished to bed her now, which he certainly did. But with her hurt arm bent like the wounded wing of a bird, he knew the time was not right.

He had no intention of taking an unaroused girl, but she didn't seem to know that. "You're hungry," he soothed. "Food will revive you." He placed a stool with a cushioned seat before her and drew up another for himself.

"There," he instructed, pointing at the stool. "Put up your feet."

She regarded him warily, as if she sensed his raging need for her and didn't trust him so close.

Slowly, he cautioned, willing his male interest into abeyance as he placed the tray of food on her lap with a flourish. "What takes your fancy? The trout in butter looks good." It steamed as he boned it, deftly handling the sharp knife. He cut the first piece of fish and mopped it in melted butter. "Open," he commanded.

She accepted it between her lips. The sight of their silky softness, within easy reach, set him aching. He wanted to claim this female who was now his wife. Her woman's scent, mingled with flowers from the bath soap, stoked his desire.

Quickly he cut more fish, surprised that his hands weren't shaking. He was shaking within, afraid she would freeze up and shut him out. He was, after all, the Black Graham—the savage Borderer, cold and rejecting. He'd kidnapped her and forced her into marriage, and now he was about to steal her virginity and claim her for his own.

But as he fed her the next piece of trout, she seemed to relax and savor it, lulled into temporary security by his attention to her meal. As if convinced he wouldn't bed her, at least not immediately, she sighed and closed her eyes.

"I've never tasted fish quite this delicious." She melted against the cushions.

"It was caught only an hour ago." He cut another piece. "Try it with the herbed sauce."

She did as he bid her, accepting the tidbit docilely. "Heavenly!" She closed her eyes again, the flutter of dark lashes enticing. But then she leaned forward. "You must be hungry, too." She held out a piece of fish to him.

With his gaze locked to hers, he caught her wrist, guiding the morsel of fish until it passed between his lips. Then he pressed her fingertips against his mouth. She didn't move as he licked away melted butter, slow and sensuous, his flesh against hers.

A tremor shook her. He felt as well as saw it race through her body, betraying her response to him. His need roared like an inferno. As if scorched by its intensity, she blushed and averted her face. Unable to resist the temptation, Graham leaned forward, caught her chin with one hand, and covered her mouth with his.

Her lips remained closed and chaste. Disappointed, he drew back, noting she was wide-eyed and nervous, as if intimidated by the force of his male heat.

Damn. She wasn't ready. She must be filled with her own heat before they could join. Not meek and passive in the face of his. That wasn't like her, nor would it yield a satisfactory coupling. "More?" He indicated the fish.

She nodded weakly, as if relieved to be spared his further attention.

"Would you like to visit your horses after you dine?"

He had not permitted her out of the chamber since her accident, except for a bath.

She leaned forward eagerly. "Yes, I would. I miss my horses terribly. You will take me to them? You promise? As soon as we're done?"

Soon, he promised silently, enthralled by the glow his offer had kindled in her eyes. Despite his vow to wait until her arm healed, the need within him had built to a raging crescendo. But he didn't want her helpless in the face of his craving. He wanted her swept away by her own desire.

Hope flickered through him as Lucina licked a last bit of sweet pudding from one finger, then smiled at him.

Soon she would respond as eagerly to him as to a suggestion she visit her steeds.

Wrapping her in a cloak, he swept her to the stable, letting her enter Orpheus's stall while he gave Jasper and Colin instructions for their journey. He would bring Mistress Johnstone safely back by morning. They would ride in a few hours.

'Twas already nigh on sunset, he reasoned as he dismissed the men to make preparations. An hour delay would do no harm. He would claim this time with Lucina, and they would see . . .

He found Lucina grooming Orpheus with her good arm, sweeping a soft brush over his broad, glossy back. Orpheus stood with his head lowered and eyes closed. Graham imagined a foolish grin on the beast's face, he was so clearly in horse heaven, enjoying his mistress's attention and touch.

"Fortunate creature. What did he do to deserve such care?" Graham broke the silence, unable to bear any more.

"He loves me," she said serenely, glancing over her shoulder as if she'd known he was there all along. "Take a lesson."

At his sour expression, she tossed her head in a saucy gesture. "I want to ride."

"Not with your shoulder."

"You can boost me up," she insisted. "I'm feeling much better. Say yes."

He noted the feverish excitement that sparkled in her eyes. Wasn't this how he'd wanted her—full of an urgency that refused to be denied? If he could just shift that urgency from wanting to ride Orpheus to wanting him. "I agree only if you go slowly and mind your arm. Would you like a saddle?" he offered. " 'Twill aid your balance."

She agreed, once more surprising him. Usually she disagreed, if only to be contrary. As he boosted her into the saddle, she settled without a wince or grimace, but he wasn't reassured. "Let me check your sling," he insisted, lifting her down again. Feeling as protective as Gellie with her foal, he tightened the knot. "We will walk during the ride," he ordered sternly. "No trotting or cantering. And I expect you to remain close to me."

She obeyed him as they rode from the castle into the early evening, and at her request, they paused to watch Gellie and her foal being led in from pasture for the night.

"Have you named the little one?" she asked, the faintest hint of accusation in her tone.

She had broached the subject several times of late, but he had refused to discuss it. "I won't name him until your brother is safely returned," he said.

A smile lit her face. "I'm glad to know you haven't given up the search for my brother. Do you know where he is?"

"Of course I haven't given up." Her assumption that he had soured his mood. Or did she say it to provoke him into telling her more? "I know how to discover where he is, but his rescue may not be easy," he warned as her smile widened. "I advise you not to raise your hopes too high."

She tempered the smile. "I'm merely glad to know you're making progress."

"I've been working on it all along." It felt odd to explain himself to another. Still, he *was* making progress in finding her brother. All he needed was Maggie to provide details of the forthcoming English raid, and the picture would be complete.

Lucina appeared satisfied with his efforts. "Let's race," she proposed, seeming to grow more invigorated the longer she was in the saddle. Leaning forward, she spoke to Orpheus. "You're set for a run, aren't you, fellow? You've been idle for several days."

The stallion's ears twitched with pleasure at her lively tone. He tugged at the bit and pranced, indicating that he would indeed enjoy the run. She turned back to Graham. "What do you say? To the trees like last time?"

"No racing," he admonished, concerned for her safety.

"Not until you can hold the reins comfortably with both hands. Until then, you'll ride at the gait I tell you or not at all."

She shot him an impish grin. "If you're too much of an old stick to race me, I'll run it alone. Your choice." With a saucy flick of her hair, she nudged Orpheus with her heels. Eager for the treat of vigorous exercise, the stallion leaped forward, propelling them to a canter in a trice.

Appalled at the risk she took so soon after her injury, irate that he had to chase her, Graham urged his gelding to a canter. Blast the wench, give her a length of rein and she grabbed the bit in her teeth, charging off as if to a fire. But hadn't Isabel said she needed the chance to make choices of her own? And didn't he want her inflamed by her own passions? She was that right now, in a way that might be dangerous. And he was powerless to stop her without Red Rowan. He wouldn't catch her until she agreed to stop.

A pang went through him as he thought of his horse in Will's keeping. The idiot would butcher his steed's sensitive mouth and cut his sleek sides with spurs, just as Lucina had said was his wont. The need to recover Rowan scourged him in the midst of his pleasure.

At the same time, his competitive male pride hated losing, especially to a one-armed female. That rankled, but he assured himself he had more to gain by doing so. If letting her feel superior would deliver his desire, she was welcome to reach the trees first.

He grimaced as his gelding loped after Lucina. Imagine. The Black Graham, choosing to lose a race. Hoping to reap benefits by doing so.

Keeping his gaze locked on Lucina, he savored the sight of her body swaying to Orpheus's smooth gait. She balanced lightly in the stirrups, her seat firm despite one arm in a sling. With her hair fluttering in the wind, she kept her gaze homed on her goal, never once looking back. Torn between concern and pleasure, Graham paced his gelding so she remained ahead of him no more than a few lengths.

The glow of the day's last light was heartening. The sinking sun warmed the air, turning it to gold. The moment itself was golden. By the heavens, how he needed her.

She reached the woods before him. Pretending chagrin, he took his time about joining her.

"You are an impudent scoundrel, John Alexander Malcolm Graham." Her acid statement greeted him as he entered the shadows. She had dismounted without assistance and now stood, one fist planted on her hip, her entire body radiating injured pride.

"What? I did nothing." He held out both hands, the picture of innocence. "You won the race. I lost."

"You didn't even try," she accused. "It was no contest from the start."

"Did you want me to best you like last time?"

"Your gelding could never have beaten Orpheus, but you could at least have tried." She was trembling all over. His gaze riveted on her tapering hands, and he pictured them again on Orpheus, caressing and grooming him. How he longed to feel her hands on him, lulling him in a similar manner.

He tethered his gelding to a tree, feeling her presence behind him. The reins slipped from his fingers as he turned to her.

Her tangled hair lifted on the evening breeze to float about her face, giving her the delicate air of a fairy as she stared at him, seeming transfixed.

He felt weightless, suspended in uncertainty, unable to draw breath as he waited for her to make the first move.

"Black Magic Graham," she whispered, using a name he'd never heard. "Alex, you do things to me I've never . . ."

"Yes, call me Alex." He caught her wrist as she reached out to touch him, much as he had when she fed him the fish. But this time he brushed her palm with a kiss, then tenderly placed her hand to his cheek. From there he drew her palm down his jawline, reveling in their contact, settling her fingers at the base of his throat. The thundering of his heart roared in his ears. Could she feel it, too?

She stepped toward him, her hand firmly held to his flesh. A tremor of need ran through him. Her touch felt every bit as good as he'd imagined, making him burn for more.

Her breathing quickened. Taking that as a good sign, he slipped the first buttons of his shirt and moved her hand down.

Her eyes widened with innocent wonder as she moved her hand lower, exploring his upper chest. Could she be caught in the same snare of madness as he?

Touch me, he willed her in silence. *More.*

As if she heard his unspoken plea, she tugged at his shirt, attempting to draw it away. Delighted to oblige her, he stripped off the garment. She looped her good arm around his bare torso and nestled against him, pressing her lips to his neck, his shoulder, his arm.

Shocks of sensation vibrated through him. Hungrily he captured her mouth. She learned the art of kissing quickly, offering lush, openmouthed caresses as she leaned against him, making it impossible to think clearly. He couldn't think at all. Only touch and feel. The scent and feel of her petal-soft skin invaded his senses. Feminine curves sparked his desire.

He wanted to part her clothing and release her from the layers of fabric. A growing excitement mounted within him, as if he were riding Red Rowan, racing toward salvation on a magical steed.

Life flowed through him as she twined her good arm around his neck, playing with the hair at the nape of his neck. She seemed so eager, as if she wanted him as much as he wanted her. For the first time in years, an alien feeling suffused him. Did he dare name it, having lived without it? As she smiled up at him and invited his kiss again, he felt he stood on the brink of rediscovery. Could this possibly be . . . joy?

What madness drove her that night, Lucina wasn't certain. But suddenly she'd needed to race, to throw away caution and fly like the wind. For three full days Graham had treated her like an invalid, saying she needed to rest and heal. He'd wed her without her agreement, then acted overly possessive, then denied her her horses until *he* decided she was well. Even mounted, he insisted she go slowly. He pushed her beyond endurance, fueling her need to fly free.

But once on Orpheus's back, her strength had returned. Throwing temperance to the winds, she'd urged Orpheus forward, eager to escape Graham, to race him and best him, to prove herself once and for all.

But when the race had ended, she had needed to touch

him, to absorb his essence—his fierce sense of justice and
his warrior proud ways. True, he was possessive and domineering. Yet he desired peace against all odds, proving he
was sensitive, that tenderness lay behind his tough outer
mask. And though he'd demanded she wed him, in truth,
she'd invited him first. On the night of Gellie's travail, she
had offered him more than aid. She had offered him intimacy—not physical but emotional.

What had made her do it without really knowing him?

His expression as he'd bent over the mare returned to
her.

*Who would have thought it? The Black Graham, a fierce
warrior with a reputation for violence and coldness, his face
tender and full of an ardent, honest love.*

She'd seen his love and yearned for it, for him to love
her as much or more than he loved the mare. Her own
strong feelings could sway him—strong feelings she bore
for him alone.

Now as he kissed her, those feelings urged her to experience him in every way. His hope for the future, his willing-
ness to struggle for it, was her hope as well.

Driven by her decision, she untied her sling, wanting to
escape her confining clothes. With barriers between them,
she couldn't experience him, nor could she reach her con-
founded bodice, which laced in back.

"Alex, do you suppose you could . . ." She pointed at
the laces, and he understood, continuing to kiss her as his
deft fingers worked. His hands and lips performed magic,
the first exposing her body as the second explored her need.
The laces were unlaced, buttons unbuttoned. His gaze became hungrier as her body emerged. He drew her against
him, his fingers moving lightly against her bare breasts.

His touch evoked a tingling that delighted and confused
her. Eagerly she pressed against his fingers, demanding
more.

"Like that, do you?" He laughed softly, sounding happy.

Above all else, she wanted him to be happy, to know the
happiness he'd never had. And if releasing her passions
made him happy, she was more than willing to comply.

He bent over, as if to examine her more closely. "If you
liked that, let us try this." To her surprise, he covered her
breast with his mouth.

His lips pulled strongly. Tongue wet and warm. Fireworks of feeling exploded in her core.

Heat surged through her, pooling deep in her belly, coaxing wetness between her legs. She cried out in pleasure, hardly daring to believe such sensation could be real. His caresses made her feel strong and beautiful, and full of the power to bring him the same bliss. If his life had been sorrow and he couldn't feel love, she swore to give him the next best thing.

Wanting him to know it, she raised his head, and on tiptoe, urged him to meet her kiss.

His lips devoured, his tongue demanded. His hunger spoke like an audible voice. She was his bride, and nothing would stop her from bonding with his fascinating male heat.

Vaguely she was aware that he spread his cloak, then lowered her to it and sat at her side. His tongue teased hers, his hands stroked her body, filling her with the urge to please him as well.

But she couldn't think clearly how she ought to do it. Her mind spun as if she'd drunk flagons of wine. That same intoxication urged her to bite him at delicate intervals along his muscled neck. Not too gentle. Not too hard. "Husband, I want you." *Husband*. The word was heady magic, giving her pleasure of another kind.

He stilled, as if stunned by her declaration, then tightened his arms around her waist.

She nuzzled his ear, glad to surprise him, wanting to do it again and again.

It seemed that she had, for he shuddered with desire as she explored the lobe of his ear with her tongue.

"I don't want to hurt you," he rasped.

"You won't hurt me," she insisted. "I'm not made of glass."

He frowned. "It will cause you pain when I breach your maidenhead. And you have a bad arm." He sighed with disappointment. "We must wait, Lucina, until you're healed."

The offer obviously cost him much effort.

"You don't want to wait. Nor do I." With a grin she eyed the bulge in his trunkhose.

He looked away. "I can be too rough when I'm out of control."

Out of control. She liked the sound of that. She would like them both to break past their barriers, to race out of control, searching for fulfillment in each other's arms.

She felt certain he would like it as well, for as he turned back, his gaze locked with hers, need glittering in his eyes. If the breaching of her maidenhead troubled him so greatly . . .

"Then, don't hurt me," she proposed. "Let me do it."

"How?" He looked wary, as if he didn't trust her proposal.

His doubt fueled her decision. "I may be a virgin, but not an ignorant one, and I want you for my husband. Now. Tonight." She captured his hand, put it between her legs, and rubbed his fingers against her womanhood.

"God, you're wet. So ready for me." He seemed to choke on his own breath, her touch apparently pushing him over the edge. With a mutter he leaned over and yanked off his boots.

Fascinated, she watched him strip off his clothing, revealing firm, tight hips and lean, hard thighs. Most amazing was the sight of his manhood, rampant with desire for her. The moon sculpted his body, defining his muscled chest and arms in silver. He paused for a moment, hands on hips, legs planted wide, obviously at ease with his nakedness.

She became acutely aware of her half-clothed state. More so than she had been with him clothed. "Here," she whispered, patting the cloak beside her. She couldn't wait to feel his body against hers. As he sat, she struggled out of her remaining clothes.

More heady feelings as their bodies merged, his fingers exploring her sensitive flesh. His hands roamed everywhere, hot and possessive, discovering the nape of her neck, her back, her ribs. His breath quickened as her hand brushed his manhood; she touched him again, and he seemed to swell. *Love me now,* she wanted to cry. But she had promised to spare him the guilt of hurting her, and she was nothing if not a woman of her word.

Without breaking their kiss, she eased onto his lap and wrapped her legs around his waist.

"Isn't your shoulder hurting?" He was all consideration, thinking of her first, though he sighed as she touched him, pressing her feminine softness against his engorged flesh.

"Only a little. I swear I'll be careful." She pressed his hand to the small of her back. He responded eagerly, hold-

ing her against him, his body saying he wanted more. *She*
wanted more, wanted to breach all barriers, wanted them
to be as one in their mutual need.

*Down with the barricades. Reveal yourself. Let me know
who you really are. Loving and tender. Kind and caring.
Let us race together on the wings of the wind.* Inspiration
swept through her, and raising her hips, she grasped Graham's arousal and guided him in.

"Ah, Lucina." He groaned, his hands tightening on her
waist as she settled over him. She pressed down, taking
him deeper, until the barrier of her maidenhead stopped
her descent.

"Will this do for a start?" she gasped.

"God, yes." He rocked against her, holding and petting,
his lips on her throat, in her hair, on her cheeks. His hands
found her bottom, clenching and unclenching. His breath
came faster as she nibbled his neck.

Friction but not conflict. Heat but not pain. Her need to
triumph drove her on.

Away with the barriers. She wanted past them. With
nothing between them but their own raw desire. "Now,"
she whispered, seized with urgency. It swept her along, refusing to be denied.

He tensed as she pushed harder, cradling her against him
as she allowed his maleness to penetrate her core. "Gently," he cautioned.

But she didn't want gentle. The heat in their bodies demanded they race. She wanted to be part of him, and him
part of her. She sank onto him a little more. More friction.
She pressed harder. Pressure but not pain. Need, not force.

"Kiss me," he ordered, his breath ragged. "Kiss me, Lucina. Don't ever stop."

Their mouths met, sweeping words away, the kiss bruising, but she didn't care. She kissed him back and pressed
lower still.

Her flesh yielded when she least expected it. She sank
down, his body encased within her own. She felt no pain,
only joy at their joining. This barrier between them was
broken at last.

He had gone completely still, as if waiting for her reaction. "Are you all right, Lucina?" He touched her cheek
lightly, as if looking for tears.

But she had no tears, only great happiness. She arched her back and laughed in reply. She soared on his heat, on her ability to please him, on their unusual marriage bed— a cloak on the ground.

Tenderly he cupped her chin with two fingers, brushed hair from her eyes, and kissed both her cheeks. "You're so beautiful, Lucina. So brave. So good." He shifted her to her back and lay over her, remaining joined with her the entire time.

She gazed up at him, clutching his shoulder. Stars twinkled between the shifting leaves above his head. New sensations and emotions grew inside her, building as his face hovered above hers. He withdrew slowly, then thrust in again slowly.

"Faster," she cried as she arched up to meet him, wanting him to move and fulfill her need. The heat of his maleness seemed to swell inside her. Fire built within her, the passion of the race. His tempo quickened, and she kept pace with him. "Let us both fly."

He lowered against her, his excitement growing, his breath ragged gasps against her neck.

Pressure building. Need reaching. Their breath mingled as they raced with the wind. Their rhythm meshed, and her heart contracted as she realized heaven was within her grasp.

"Oh, Alex, I love you," she moaned against his throat, wanting to race with him forever at this incredible speed.

Then their joining took her soaring, as if she had left her flesh and flew on the wind. Her body strained toward the ultimate moment, and as she gained the finish line, she heard his cry. His hot seed spurted deep within her. It was a victory greater than any race.

Graham collapsed beside her, holding her carefully to avoid hurting her bad arm. The night breeze was like the breath of heaven cooling her hot cheeks. Stars above twinkled their approval as she again said she loved him.

"And I need you." He kissed her forehead gently.

She sighed with contentment, knowing she'd done it. She had given him a happiness he'd never possessed.

As the haze of pleasure receded, memory of her plans for an annulment resurfaced, but only for an instant. She didn't want an annulment. She wanted the Black Graham.

Chapter 15

The trouble was, Lucina decided as she returned to the castle at Graham's side, if she had him, she must accept his horrid, impossible family as well, complete with kidnappers, lunatics, meddling, unsavory servitors, and ghosts.

She was less than pleased with the extras who came with him. Nor was she confident she could live in harmony with the Graham. He had been reared in a warrior-dominated household that lived continually on the brink of war. As the head of his family, he was expected by custom to make all decisions. He wouldn't change that habit solely at her request.

Still, the uncomfortable thoughts gave way to pleasure. She felt as light and buoyant as when she had raced across the meadow on Orpheus's back. For their lovemaking had banished the black thundercloud from Graham's face.

Glancing down at her kirtle skirt, she realized that every castle inhabitant would guess what had transpired in the woods. A telltale trace of her virgin's blood clung to her hem. But in truth, she didn't care. She was drunk on the heady power of their mutual joy.

Love knows no law. Her dear friend Lady Ashley had been wise to appreciate that saying. Never had Lucina suspected she would find a lover among the savage Scots Borderers after failing to find one in her own land, but the saying had proved apt. And although Graham hadn't spoken words of love in return, his body had betrayed his caring. In that moment, except for the trouble over her brother and her wish to claim her land, she couldn't have been happier. She couldn't wait for the chance to retire with her husband to the tower chamber alone.

As they entered the castle courtyard, she looked to him expectantly, hoping any tasks he must first perform would be brief.

"You will go up to bed in the tower, Lucina." He dismounted and lifted her down from Orpheus, being very cautious of her arm. "I'll sleep in my own chamber tonight."

Words of disagreement sprang to her lips, but he apparently saw them coming. Sweeping her into the castle, he sought the tower stair and pulled her into a hard embrace. She leaned against him, her excitement revived by the caress of his lips on hers.

But something had changed. She couldn't quite name it, but he didn't respond the way he had in the woods.

At length he calmly detached his lips from hers, confirming her suspicion that he'd meant to block her protest.

"The bed above stairs is too narrow for us both," he said. "I might hurt your arm."

The cheat, she thought in helpless annoyance, struggling to still her pounding heart. He immobilized her defenses while remaining unaffected. What a sharp contrast to their earlier joining. He hadn't been cool and detached then. Now he acted as if something more important claimed his thoughts.

His uncompromising expression convinced her no pleading would change his decision. That, coupled with his lame explanation, roused her suspicions that he was planning something.

Hours later, she lay in the narrow bed, wide awake and frustrated, gazing at the point where white-plaster ceiling met stone wall. Graham's manner in the woods proved he *could* be tender and considerate, but that didn't stop him from issuing orders without giving reasons. Or from hiding his intentions. He was indeed a complex man.

The image of the Dunlochy Charmstone returned to her, swinging from Will Mosley's hand, glittering with its own special light. The stone's reputation was well established— it could heal and bring good luck. Graham's reputation for coldness was equally well-known. Yet like the stone, Graham had unexplained depths that were not obvious at first glance. He hid his thoughts and doings from her with ease.

That should be no surprise. Foolishly she had wed him after knowing him only a handful of days.

Yet her own need had driven her, as it had driven her to be the assertive one in the woods. But she knew why she had been so eager. Within a few strides of where she lay, old bloodstains marred the wood floor, reminders of the sorrows that haunted Castle Graham. The more they pressed in on her, the more she wanted to fight back with optimism and hope.

With Lady Ashley, she'd fought the devils of a loveless life and won. She'd taught her friend to trust again. Instinctively she longed to repeat the success with Graham.

Yet loving him and being loved in return was a far more formidable challenge. For years he had killed others and stolen their property. No matter that he seemed intent on change. The habit of taking what he wanted was thoroughly ingrained. Look how he'd married her, answering for her and not caring whether she protested.

Yet he had pledged to be her husband, and as such, she expected him to begin life anew. She would eventually cover the bloodstained planks of the floor, pull them up, or do whatever was required in order to make her point.

And she needed affection in return for what she offered. Even irascible Lady Ashley had softened and learned to show she cared—by a pat on the hand or a word of thanks. Lucina had known that those small gestures equaled a hundred caresses from someone more demonstrative. Coming from a woman unaccustomed to family closeness, they'd been a major coup.

In the woods Graham had shown he could be demonstrative, though he didn't speak of love. She supposed she should consider herself fortunate to have any display of affection from him. It might be all she could expect.

At that last uncomfortable thought, she pushed aside the blankets and sat up. She wanted to go to him and sleep at his side. Erotic passion wasn't necessary all the time. She must teach him the comfort of companionship.

But she suspected he hadn't retired to his bedchamber. And if not, where had he gone? Wherever it was, she guessed it was linked to her brother, and she intended to find out.

"Ma leddy, is there ought you need?" Alerted by her stirring, Grissel clambered from her pallet and pulled back the curtain.

Irritating Grissel, always there when she wasn't wanted. What was Lucina to say? That she lusted for her husband and intended to seek his bed? "I, ah, cannot sleep, Grissel. I think I'll visit Orpheus and Cygnus. You needn't come. Pray go to sleep."

"Ma leddy, ye canna wander aboot in the dead o' night."

Grissel's carping annoyed Lucina further. The woman understood nothing about attachment to horses. "I do it often. The guard will come along." With a resolute motion she pushed past Grissel and caught up her clothes.

The dim, lantern-lit scents of the stable greeted Lucina, along with Robbie, who emerged from the equipment room, rubbing bleary eyes. Both he and the odor of grain were heartily welcome after the annoyance of Grissel, who trailed at her heels.

Choosing an apple from the barrel, Lucina entered Orpheus's stall. The stallion sleepily nuzzled her pockets, never too tired to play their game. As he found the apple and crunched it happily, she climbed the slats of the manger and slipped onto his back. The vantage point allowed her to survey the stable. True to her suspicions, several horses were absent from their stalls.

"Robbie, where's the Graham's gelding?" she asked casually some minutes later as she bolted the door to Orpheus's stall and moved toward Cygnus's.

"Ah . . . oot to pasture, I believe."

"No, he was in his stall earlier. Graham put him there after our ride."

"I, er, I . . ."

Lucina entered Cygnus's stall, leaving the boy to stammer. 'Twas obvious Graham and his men had left on a sortie. He'd probably planned it all along.

It took all the willpower she possessed to keep from demanding answers, and as she greeted Cygnus and offered her an apple, Lucina's mind whirled with worry. What was Graham doing? Might someone be killed?

Her concern increased as she left the stable. Reluctant

to reenter her prison, she lingered in the screens passage, peering at the sleeping folk whose pallets crisscrossed the hall.

"M'leddy, I, er . . ." Her guard, young Willie Johnstone, shuffled his feet.

"Yes, Willie, what is it?" she said gently.

"I dinna ha' much supper tonight. Would ye permit me to nip into the kitchen for a bite?"

"Of course. Go at once. Grissel and I will wait at the stair." Lucina moved on toward the tower as Willie disappeared into the kitchens. If she could only be rid of Grissel as well.

"Ma leddy, ye mun return to yer chamber and lie doon," Grissel nagged as they entered the darkened passage. " 'Tis bad for yer shoulder to be up and aboot."

Illogical, Lucina thought with exasperation, adjusting her candle.

"In truth, ma leddy, ye mun keep tae yer chamber at all times, except when ye're aboot yer duties. 'Tis mair fittin' to yer new rank. When Leddy Janet were the—" Grissel's annoying lecture changed abruptly into a shriek as she clamped onto Lucina's bad shoulder.

Agony shot through Lucina's arm, and she dropped her candle. The light fizzled out. "Grissel, you're hurting me. What is the—"

Grissel shrieked again, her hysteria uncontrollable, her grip on Lucina's arm crushing. " 'Tis the . . . 'tis the . . . g-g-g-ghost!"

Dizzy with pain, Lucina pried off Grissel's hand and turned in the direction she pointed with one skinny, shaking hand.

The diaphanous form of the castle ghost wavered at the end of the black passage, a tormented reminder of past pain.

A chill shot up Lucina's spine. "This is ridiculous." Furious with Grissel for hurting her, furious with her own fear, she headed down the passage, despite the dark. "I'm going to find out what this is about."

Grissel's sharp cry called her back, and Lucina turned in time to see the woman slump to the floor in a faint.

"Such a half-wit," Lucina muttered, turning back to find

the diaphanous form gone, no doubt frightened away by
the serving woman's screams.

It seemed half the castle had been aroused by Grissel's
hysteria. The place was in an uproar in no time. Frightened
gossip moved as swiftly as a stick on the flood, and in vain
Lucina labored to calm everyone. It was nothing, she assured old Angus, who was head of the night guard.

"Ye saw it as well as me," Grissel cried, still shaking
from her trauma. " 'Twas bloody Bonnie Mary hersel'."

"There was nothing bloody about her," Lucina argued,
then realized she'd admitted to seeing something. The faces
of the Graham men who had come to their aid were ashen.
Not a sound came from the great hall, where the tenants
cringed, afraid to move now that the ghost had appeared
to more than one person. The cook, who had come running
from his little chamber off the kitchens, gaped at her,
clearly unnerved.

" 'Tis a sign, ma leddy," said old Angus solemnly, "that
the Grahams' ills agin the Maxwells be remembered still.
Revenge shall be wreaked on us once more."

"It's not a sign," Lucina insisted. "There was nothing to
suggest it. No one was hurt." She stalked down the passage
and back again with her candle to show it was safe. "You
see, there's nothing here. I am not afraid. Nor should you
be."

They dispersed with reluctance, as if afraid to retire, for
that meant lying awake in the dark, and in the dark, the
ghost might appear again.

These people were impossible, Lucina thought wearily as
she mounted the tower stairs, Grissel trailing behind her,
whimpering. They seemed determined to believe in their
ghost and curse their own future. She had no power to
make them see otherwise.

Grissel added to her burdens. Once safely back in the
tower and tucked in her pallet beneath warm blankets, the
frightened serving woman continued to tremble and moan.
Lucina's chances of sleep fled, yet most irritating of all was
that she still didn't know where Graham had gone.

In a defiant mood, she built up the fire and stared at the
bloodstain on the floor. The people of Castle Graham
seemed shackled to chilling superstitions and past pain.
Well, she refused to have any part of it.

Long after Grissel slept and the castle was quiet, Lucina heard the rumbling of pounding hooves. She ran to the window in time to see Graham and a cavalcade of men enter the courtyard. By the light of torches, she spied a lone female riding pillion behind one of the men. She was lifted down and smacked on the bottom in a friendly, chastening gesture.

Lucina immediately recognized Maggie Johnstone by her stocky figure and the way she shook her fist at the man who had swatted her.

Where had the woman gone and why? She hadn't seen Maggie since the night of Will's escape, but she'd assumed that while she lay abed healing, Maggie had been somewhere below stairs. Now she knew that wasn't the case, but she wouldn't know where Maggie had really been until the morrow. And with Graham safely home, she might as well go to bed.

Worry plagued her as she burrowed among the blankets. Had Maggie tried to go home to Carlisle, and had Graham forced her back to Scotland against her will? As a Johnstone, she was part of his family. He might resent her choosing to live elsewhere.

To Lucina's dismay, her usual optimism seemed to have deserted her. She suspected unkind motives of her husband, even when she lacked clear evidence. It seemed the ghosts of Castle Graham were closing in on her, and she didn't know if she could fight them off alone.

How she managed to sleep after Graham's return, Lucina was uncertain. Sheer determination to conserve her strength, she supposed as she woke to find the day fully dawned. At least her courage had returned, and despite Grissel's attack last night, her shoulder seemed much improved. Satisfied with her progress, she scrambled from the bed and broke her fast. She must take breakfast to poor Elen, who had been locked in the chamber formerly confining her father. The sawed-through bar had been replaced so she could not escape.

Lucina descended the stairs with Grissel clinging to her heels, along with her morning's guard. To her dismay, as she reached the bottom and turned into the screens passage, she spied Graham talking to a group of men, blocking the way to the kitchens.

She didn't want to meet him in front of others this morning. She wanted to see him alone. To demand explanations. To coax him into kissing her again, as he had last night . . .

Stars above, she must think of other things. She would visit Isabel first in order to avoid Graham. "Grissel, pray carry a message to our chief," she instructed, stepping back into the passage out of sight. "Say I beg an audience with him in my chamber an hour from now."

Relieved to be quit of Grissel, Lucina hurried down the passage toward Isabel's chamber. Burly Tam Mosley leaned against the wall, guarding the door, which stood ajar.

"Good morrow. 'Tis glad I am to see ye, Lucina." Isabel greeted her tap at the door and gave her a conspiratorial wink as she entered. Isabel seemed to know her, but by morning's light, she looked tired. Despite the number of servants present, her hair had not been dressed for the day, and she still wore her white night shift.

"How are you today, Isabel?" Lucina embraced her as she eyed the others. Alice, Annie, Marie, Margaret, and two tenants' wives huddled together, chattering like a flock of magpies.

"I'm fit, as always," Isabel said, hugging her back. "Daft lad, keeping me here."

But she didn't look fit. The paper-thin flesh of her face was strained taut over her fine bones, and dark smudges had gathered beneath her eyes.

"Did you not sleep well?" Lucina shifted from the hug to take Isabel's hand.

"I sleep, but 'tis no' restful," Isabel admitted, gesturing for Marie to bring Lucina a stool. "Some mornings, I feel I've been a-runnin' a race."

Lucina squeezed her hand in sympathy, then nodded toward the women. "Why are you not dressed? Have you broken your fast?"

"My linen's being washed, and they're too excited to bring food. Maggie's back from Carlisle."

Indignant that the servants were so distracted they couldn't feed or clothe their mistress, Lucina pushed in among the women. Maggie Johnstone sat at their center, clearly in the midst of telling the tale of her adventures.

"Here, here, enough gossiping," Lucina interrupted. "Marie, pray fetch Madam Isabel's clean linens. Annie, fetch her morning porridge and some of those newly picked cherries. Margaret, fetch one of the lads with hot and cold water for madam to wash. You may help her, Alice. And you ladies"—she paused to indicate the tenants' wives— "Master Tam will see you back to the hall. You may visit with Mistress Johnstone at the dinner hour."

The tenants' wives leaped to their feet, appearing astonished to be interrupted so imperiously but pleased to be referred to as ladies. Marie and Margaret departed more slowly, clearly resenting the newcomer who set them to work. But Lucina was outraged. How dare they neglect the woman who had been their chatelaine long before Lucina had arrived?

She would see they cared for Isabel or else, Lucina thought angrily as she turned to greet Maggie with a hearty kiss on the cheek. "Don't curtsy, Maggie," she insisted as the stout woman attempted to rise. "I didn't know you were gone until I saw you return last night. I'm sorry if you came against your will, but I'm glad to have you here."

"Aye, she's back," Isabel chuckled before Maggie could answer. "I sent our chief after her."

The women leaving the chamber stilled. Lucina glimpsed scorn in their faces as they scuttled from the room and heard their derisive laugher echo in the passage. She had to admit she, too, was surprised. If Maggie had wanted to go home to Carlisle, why would Isabel send Graham to fetch her back against her will? Such an oddity only reinforced the belief that Isabel was daft. But she managed to question Isabel with outward calm once the others had left.

"Why did I do it? So she could return with adequate escort." Isabel grinned with satisfaction. "She went tae Carlisle tae bring back news o' yer brother."

"Is that why you went?" Lucina turned to Maggie in surprise.

Maggie smiled with gap-toothed affection. "O' course, love. Ma sister's man is part o' the garrison. I kent she would ha' all the gossip, so I went to learn what it was."

"Oh, Maggie, I am fortunate to call you friend." Lucina hugged the maid, her heart warming as she realized the obvious risks and trouble Maggie had taken. "How did you manage to travel safely all the way to Carlisle?"

Maggie grinned with an air of pride. "I still ha' kin here who are willin' tae help me. There's ma wee cousin Colin, fer one."

"Oh, dear, if he accompanied you, Graham is no doubt furious." Lucina kneaded her hands in concern. "He's never gotten over your leaving Castle Graham. Now that you're back, he expects you to obey him implicitly, like the rest." Even as Lucina thanked Maggie, she cursed her misjudgment of Isabel. She was beginning to think like the others, assuming the worst when Isabel had actually done the right thing. "Did Graham rant at you all the way back?"

"His temper were right hot," Maggie admitted, planting both hands on her wide hips with an indignant air. "He demanded I stay on one side o' the Border or t-other, nae runnin' back and forth, draggin' ma cousin wi' me. So I told him I wanted to coom back. Then he called me fickle, unable to make up ma mind." She rolled her eyes and snorted. "He knows why I went."

"What did you learn?" Lucina asked, eager to hear the news.

" 'Tis ill news, I fear. Sir Edward plans to raid Hermitage Castle." Maggie's mouth thinned into a grim line. "His Border patrol learned yer brither's there. I told Graham so."

"Hermitage Castle? Does it belong to Will?"

"Nae, 'tis the Earl of Bothwell's, so he'll be there as well. He'll counter the raid, tae be sure."

The frightening possibility set Lucina to pondering the problem of rescuing her brother from a stronghold. "I thought the earl had been outlawed," she said at last.

"So he has, but he lives like a king in his own lands, ye ken. He's keeper of Liddesdale and owns houses and castles all alang the Border. His people depend on him, and he cares for them weel. If they deserted him, King Jamie wouldna feed nor clothe them."

Lucina sank onto a stool, now thoroughly worried. "How soon do you think this raid will take place?"

"No' for another sennight," Maggie said. "They're still gatherin' weapons, horses, an' men. The Graham warned me no' to tell ye," she added. "But I didn't promise him a thing."

Lucina sighed, sure that Graham was even now making plans to travel to Hermitage. This sounded very bad indeed. She was about to say more, but Marie returned with Isabel's morning meal, trailed by a kitchen lad and Annie, each bearing dripping buckets of water. Forced to make trivial talk with Maggie while Isabel washed and was dressed, Lucina could scarcely contain herself until Isabel was seated in her chair, her porridge set before her, and the others had retired. "Isabel, Graham cannot side with either Will or Sir Edward," she burst out the instant the door closed. "If he supports his cousin, 'twill mean battling the English. If he joins Sir Edward, he could kill his own kin."

"Ye ha' the right o' it," Isabel agreed with equal concern.

"Stars above." Lucina rose in agitation and, looking for something to do with her hands, took up Isabel's hairbrush. The maids had done the bare minimum in serving Isabel, even to leaving her hair undressed. Lucina unbraided the abundant gray tresses and plied the brush while thinking aloud. "The only solution is to find Roger before the English arrive at Hermitage Castle. That way, we might avoid battle. With Roger free, there would be no reason to fight. The question is, can Graham do it in time?"

"Mmm." Isabel tilted back her head and closed her eyes, clearly appreciating the luxury of the attention. "I canna think either Will or Bothwell will lead him to yer brither. He'll have to search fer him, which will take time. An' mark ye, dinna let the Graham ken ye wish to travel to Hermitage. He'll expect ye to stay here."

Lucina lost her hold on the braids she had coiled around Isabel's head. One snaked loose, destroying her work, and she suddenly felt her hope of rescuing Roger had even less chance of success. "Oh, dear," she sighed, despairing. "You're correct. And what would be the use of going unless I knew where Roger was kept."

"Ye mun ask one who's close in blood to the Graham's Will," Isabel advised.

Lucina reflected on this idea. "Do you mean Elen?"

Isabel shook her head in the negative.

Lucina wrinkled her brow. "You mean Drummond, then. He probably does know where Roger is, but he hates Graham. Will told him so many lies about the family, he'll refuse to help."

Isabel twisted on her stool to face Lucina. "He'll lead *ye* tae yer brother if the price is right."

"True, he wouldn't lead Graham, nor would Graham consider for an instant asking him. But I cannot think Drummond can be bought with money." Lucina knew Borderers were fiercely loyal once they chose a cause.

"Not bought wi' money, but wi' a promise," Isabel said. "Drummond hates the Grahams because he's been barred from a life wi' the family, where he rightfully belongs. The irony is, his ain faither caused it by setting his bastards to work at cross-purposes to the family. But Drummond and Elen are kin to the Grahams, nae matter from which side o' the blanket. See how Elen has taken to ye. Drummond wants a place in his family, mark ma word."

As Lucina successfully pinned Isabel's plaits in place, she puzzled over this advice. The first step would be to win the lad's trust before she even considered the possibility of going to Hermitage. But how could that be done? From what little she'd seen of Drummond, he trusted none but Will. Clasping the hairbrush, she scarce noticed that Isabel had gotten up and was putting on her favorite white kertch. "Oh, Isabel, I can do that for you." Lucina arranged the headdress, tucking Isabel's hair beneath its white wings.

"I dinna ken why I bother. I canna leave this cursed chamber today, else I would help ye mysel'. But Graham ordered them to keep me close." Isabel dropped onto her stool, looking ready to weep. "I hate sitting here like a rotting log when I mun help."

"Oh, Isabel, you're not rotting." Lucina was deeply touched by the woman's desire to assist her. "You do help me," she insisted, dropping to one knee. "You cared for me when I hurt my shoulder. You've been my best friend since I've come to Castle Graham. I often feel so alone here, I couldn't manage without you."

Isabel embraced her in return, seeming buoyed by Lucina's affection. "There, now, run alang to see Elen. She'll help ye wi' the lad." A look of peace settled on her face, and she patted her kertch. "I've been blessed wi' a fine husband. 'Tis no' fair that fate dinna do as well by ye. I love ye, Mary, an' I'll see ye happy yet."

Chapter 16

Isabel thought she was Mary again.

Disappointed to find her friend's memory had slipped once more, Lucina kissed Isabel on the cheek and left for the kitchens. As she traversed the passage, she mourned the irony of fate. Isabel had given her such good advice about how to find her brother, yet she couldn't remember who Lucina was. Why must this be? It simply wasn't fair.

Though still troubled by the problem, she shifted her thoughts to Elen and Drummond as she entered the kitchens. She must plan how to get Drummond to help her. Isabel had told her the lad desired a place with the Grahams. Yet a mere invitation wouldn't be enough to sway him from his father. She needed a convincing approach, and Elen might know what that should be.

Knowing the child would only have bread and water to break her fast, Lucina ordered hot porridge, a pot of honey, and fresh milk. With a kitchen lad carrying the tray before her and her guard trailing behind, Lucina crossed to the wing she called the "prison block," though she never said it aloud. Borderers thought of their captives as guarantees of their relatives' good behavior, though she couldn't imagine Will improving his behavior for anyone, let alone his relatives.

"M'leddy, ye dinna forget me." Elen fell into her arms the instant Lucina was allowed to enter the locked chamber. Lucina's guard remained on the other side of the door.

Lucina hugged Elen in return, feeling the child's ribs through her rough homespun gown. "Of course I didn't, Elen. I promised to visit you every day, and I shall." With a pang she noted the grimy streaks left by tears on Elen's face. The poor child was drooping from her confinement, like a sickly little bird forbidden to fly. "Come, let us wash your face and hands," she proposed.

Elen's eyes clouded, and she began to sniffle. "Please, m'leddy, ask the chief to let me oot. I'll be ever so gude, if he will. I swear."

Lucina searched in vain for a suitable answer, knowing Graham would refuse. "I'll speak to him, but until then, I'll find something for you to do. Can you sew?"

Elen looked at her as if she'd suggested something evil. "A little, m'leddy, but I'm far better at fetchin' water and watchin' the goats."

Lucina racked her brain for another choice. Small wonder that confinement upset Elen, after an active life outdoors. "Have you ever woven rush mats for the floors?"

Elen hadn't, but the idea seemed to appeal to her.

"It's a useful skill," Lucina said. "I used to make them as a girl and enjoyed weaving the rushes in and out. Now, dry your tears, because I've brought you a dainty to eat." Relieved to have found a temporary solution to the problem, Lucina helped Elen wash her face and hands, then seated her at the table and arranged the crockery. "This will give you strength so you'll be alert for your first weaving lesson. I'll find someone to teach you today. And while you learn, you can pretend you're a princess awaiting liberation by a knight."

Elen gazed toward the prison chamber next to hers, a wistful expression on her face. "I would ha' Drummond for my knight. He's verra clever, and kind. He once gave me a top I loved so."

Lucina was skeptical as to why Drummond, who was undoubtedly poor, brought things to Elen. From her experience, older brothers didn't seek the company of younger sisters unless they needed someone to aid them in their wild schemes, which usually got them all in trouble. She realized Will had probably given the boy numerous tasks while teaching him to coach the girl. Yet despite the unsavory nature of the tasks, one good had come from them. Will had unconsciously nurtured love between his two offspring. The thought reminded her of how fortunate she was to have a loving family, which brought her back to Roger's plight.

"Elen, have you ever been to Hermitage Castle?" She drizzled honey on the porridge and waited eagerly for the reply.

Elen's eyes grew big with excitement as the sweet ribbon twirled from the spoon. "Not I. Drummond has." She was so intent on the honey, she hardly noticed the question. "Is that for me?"

Lucina added more honey, then milk to the bowl. "Of course 'tis for you. Try it." As Elen eagerly shoveled a large spoonful into her mouth and her face lit with pleasure, Lucina asked another question as casually as she could. "Does Drummond know Hermitage well?"

"Och, I should guess he does." Elen spoke between hearty spoonfuls. "He were born there and goes back tae work for the earl. Our faither arranges it, ye ken. He and the earl are great friends, and ma faither met Drummond's mither there."

Lucina nodded. "Do you suppose Drummond would guide me to Hermitage?"

Elen looked up from the tantalizing honey pot. "Why would ye be a-goin' there, m'leddy? 'Tis some distance away."

"My brother is there. Since you love Drummond, I'm sure you understand that I must find him. Can you convince Drummond to serve as my guide?"

"Oh, yes. There's many things I canna do, but I can do that." Elen pulled the Dunlochy Charmstone from her pocket and held it out to Lucina. "Give him this an' he'll ride through hell for ye. But you mun say 'tis from me, an' that we mun return it tae Faither later. But he'll do anything ye say for the favor of holding it. I ken he will."

Lucina took the stone, wondering why the Borderers put such store in it. True, it was a fascinating bauble, and it glittered beautifully. But she couldn't think it was magic. Still, if it would help her brother, she would give it to Drummond.

Thanking Elen and promising to visit her again later, she returned to her chamber, pleased with her plan. She was also ready to confront Graham. He had a good deal of explaining to do.

*   *   *

By the time Graham entered her chamber well over three hours later, Lucina fretted with impatience. For the first time that day, she was alone with him in a bedchamber. But instead of having an opportunity for closeness, they had unpleasant business to discuss.

"Good morrow, sweet." He greeted her with a kiss on the cheek.

She clung to him for a moment, then forced herself to speak her piece. "You'll not cosset me into your schemes today."

He spread his hands, palms up, in a placating gesture. "I, cosset you?"

"Don't pretend to be innocent. I know why you sent me up here alone last night."

"I did that?"

She wanted to wipe the teasing grin from his face. "I speak of life and death, and you mock me."

"Whose life and death?"

"My brother's. Mayhap yours. Why won't you tell me what you're doing? I know you're planning something, and I'm afraid for you. Afraid for my brother. Please." She caught his arm and buried her face in his sleeve, over-wrought by fear.

His arms encircled her, bringing welcome warmth. "I will come home safely to you. You've only to wait here, where you belong."

She grimaced as she burrowed against his doublet. He, too, was worried. She could tell by the tension in his shoulders, but he wouldn't share his troubles. Instead, he would ride out, mayhap to his death, leaving her shut up here.

"What if I don't remain at home," she asked, looking up at him.

His expression radiated disapproval as his hands tightened around her. "Your place is here, not rampaging about the countryside. Why can't you for once trust me?"

She pushed away, unable to bear his embrace when he became domineering. "For the same reason you don't listen to my suggestions or tell me what you plan." She retreated behind his worktable, needing a barrier to protect her from his touch that lulled her into acceptance. "I see armed men gathering at the castle gates and what can I think? 'Tis clear you're taking them to Hermitage. The result can only be armed conflict."

"You have it all wrong." He negated her words with a slash of his hand. "You can't think to understand our ways after such a short time. In this land, a man needs a show of arms, even if he only wants to be heard. Without it, he stands no chance."

His argument sounded suspiciously like something he had learned from his father and grandfather. To her, it meant he was falling back into old ways, at the very moment when he should be exploring new. "If you went alone and spirited Roger away before the English arrived, you wouldn't risk a fight."

"That plan has serious flaws, Lucina." His look was pitying, as if she were too young to comprehend all aspects of her idea. "I don't expect you to understand, but I do expect you to accept my decisions and obey me."

"Your plan has flaws as well," she said tightly. "We need someone who knows exactly where Roger is. If Drummond came with us to Hermitage, he might be able to—"

"Drummond?" he interrupted, looking as if he thought her demented. "The lad freed his father from confinement only days ago. He helped steal my favorite horse. 'Tis out of the question for reasons I would expect you to comprehend."

Lucina winced at his assumption that she didn't understand them. She might not be familiar with Borderer ways, but she understood the testing of loyalty. "Drummond will have to make his choice someday. Why not now, when he may be the key to finding my brother quickly? He could well save many men from death. We could—"

"Lucina, you're *not* coming with me." He propped both hands on the worktable and leaned toward her. "You are to stay here, and I shall take steps to ensure you do."

"Is that always your solution, to lock up those who oppose you?"

"It serves its purpose at times."

Resentment and rebellion boiled together, stirring her temper. He was withdrawing from her, putting emotional distance between them. Deliberately she selected another battle front.

"I've been to see Elen, and she's miserable. There's no

reason to keep the child in custody. I ask you to release her. Please."

He shook his head vehemently. "You've forgotten about the file. And she was the one who carried Will's message to summon Bothwell. She finally confessed after I threatened to beat her bottom to blisters, so don't defend her. She's guilty, and there's an end."

Lucina winced, pained to know the details of Elen's complicity but relieved to know Graham hadn't beaten the girl. "I'm sure she's learned her lesson," she pleaded. "I've explained that she must obey you from here on. She has sworn she will."

"Good. She'll stay under lock and key until I'm sure of her."

Frustrated, Lucina turned to the subject of Isabel. "Your great-aunt should be allowed free movement about the castle. I believe confining her weakens her health. She needs fresh air and the chance to walk out daily. And I am not pleased with her maids. They didn't even bring her a morning meal today until I ordered them to."

"She's not your responsibility. I'll see to her."

"At least tell me this," she demanded in frustration, wanting to put Isabel's life to rights, "do you truly believe her mind is addled from age?"

The hard mask he usually kept in place slipped, and she glimpsed pain in his eyes. "I don't know what to think. At times she seems healthy and in her right mind. But at others, she clearly thinks herself in the past. She calls people by the wrong names."

Lucina sighed, knowing he was right. "Can you not at least let her out and about when she appears well, as she is today?"

"You haven't seen her at her worst." He retreated from the battleground at the table and sank onto the bed, as if exhausted by the effort it took to clash with her.

She, too, felt weary and drained. She collapsed into a chair, propping both elbows on the worktable, her temples cupped in her hands. "I haven't even thought of my land since this trouble began. I wonder if I'll ever see it. Mayhap it's all a foolish dream."

"I'm having the deed checked by several authorities,"

Graham said in a low voice. "We'll determine if it's a valid deed or no."

Puzzled, Lucina pushed out of her chair and went to the bedside. "How can you do that? I have it here." She pulled the saddlebag from beneath the bed and flipped it open. But her rummaging turned up nothing. "You took it," she said, aghast at his audacity. "You didn't ask permission first."

"Why should I do that? What's yours is mine."

She straightened to face him. "That may be so, but I still insist you ask first when you want something. I expect that much courtesy, now we're wed."

"And if you don't agree," he said with exaggerated politeness bordering on mockery, "what then? Do I ignore your wishes over your protests, so you can accuse me of cruelty, as you suggest I am with Elen? Though I never hurt the girl."

"I didn't accuse you of cruelty," she countered hotly, then looked at him more closely and realized something else was on his mind. "What is it?" she asked, dismayed that her stomach fluttered like a flight of butterflies in response to his intense gaze.

"Pray sit beside me." He caught her wrist and guided her to the bed. His fingers burned like a brand, imparting a rising excitement to her flesh. She liked him to touch her, wanted to finish this argument so they could enjoy each other. But it seemed he was about to demand something of her, something she wouldn't like. Or was he about to give her bad news?

She sat primly on the edge of the bed, anxious to know what he wanted. But before she could say a word, his arm wound around her waist and his mouth descended to hers.

She reared back, startled. "Don't try to cajole me. Say what you want straight out."

"What I want," he echoed, rubbing her back in an enticing motion. "Isn't it clear?"

His meaning cut slowly through her confusion. He was trying to say he wanted her. She stared at him, speechless, then melted into helpless laughter. "My stars, you thought I expected you to ask permission for *that*? You need not." Flinging both arms around him, she kissed him exuberantly.

"I thought you were going to demand something I wouldn't like."

"And you like this?" His fingers sought the laces of her bodice, loosening them until the garment hung open in front.

"With you, I do." She closed her eyes and sighed in contentment as he slipped a hand inside the bodice to capture her breast. His thumb caressed her nipple, and she leaned against him. "I love it when you touch me. I can never get enough."

Her candor swept away any remaining inhibition. Eagerly he removed her bodice as she unbuttoned his shirt. "Away!" she cried, seeming to relish undressing him. Tugging off his doublet, she tossed it to the floor. "I want everything that stands between us gone."

She meant the words in many ways, and he seemed to understand her. His fingers flew, loosening and removing her clothing as she removed his. He, too, must wish that nothing stood between them—no conflicts, no secrets. Yet for now they could only bare their bodies to one another, not their souls . . . not in all things.

Still, she craved whatever he was capable of giving at this time of his life, and his caring for her was all too evident as he lowered her to the bed. Holding her in his arms, flesh against flesh, legs intertwined, he kissed her forehead with infinite tenderness, then her cheeks and her lips.

She felt a rush of belonging in his embrace. This was what she'd waited for these many years. Desire sparked in his gaze, igniting a pleasure that pulsed through her veins. She had been right to accept the marriage, despite how it had been thrust on her.

Graham took full advantage of Lucina's change in mood and exuberant kisses. But as he stroked her inviting flesh and arousal flamed, he thought that women were maddening creatures. She expected him to ask first about taking something like her deed, but not about coupling. He would have thought the one unimportant compared to the other. Would he ever understand her?

Damn it, he was trying. He'd never bothered before. Sarah hadn't demanded it of him, only prior warning when he wanted her, and ample kisses and lovemaking once he had. He'd taken for granted the tacit understanding between them . . . until he'd lost her.

Never had he thought to find another woman who fit him so comfortably. After the first agonizing year of mourning, he'd had Will hire an expensive courtesan in Edinburgh, desperate for relief from the agony of body and mind. No use. He'd hated every moment of it and left the woman to Will, his despair blacker than ever.

Eager to drown his grim thoughts in Lucina's sweetness, he groped for her thighs and thrust them apart.

"Graham, don't hurry." She laughed and sat up, gripping his forearms. "I want to see you. I want to touch you all over. Why not lie still and let me pleasure you?"

How like her to sense his difficulty, yet to offer a solution rather than accusing him. And such a solution! "What do you know about pleasuring a man?" he rasped, surprised that his mouth had gone dry with anticipation.

She grinned her impish selkie's smile. "I've had instruction from my sister."

"Only in theory."

"Of course. But even theory can be useful. Now, I want you to be still."

How like her to tell him what to do. At a time when most women lay passive and waited, she reached out and gave to him.

With a quick motion she traced his mouth with a fingertip, then drew the line from his jaw down. He pressed her hand to his throat, his pulse thundering so hard, he could scarcely breathe.

With eyes closed he slid her palm downward, her warmth on his chest, his stomach, his hips. The harsh world receded as he savored the pressure . . . the welcome spikes of feeling as she encircled his aroused flesh.

He groaned with appreciation and hardened further.

She rubbed him tentatively. "It's soft, like velvet."

On the contrary, he was as hard as a stone. But he wouldn't stop her as she eagerly explored him, measure by measure, a little smile of rapture twitching at her lips.

Could he go beyond old habits? He must. Forget the pressing need to ride for Hermitage within a sennight, he told himself. Forget Will. Forget everything except the drive to touch, to feel, to possess this exotic creature so like a fine mare, sensitive and responsive, tempting him with the ride of his life.

With both hands he explored her tantalizing breasts. He traced her jutting nipples, and she moaned, igniting a ripple of fire in his groin.

Fear came with it. Was he out of control? Out of his head as well as his depth? During their first mating he'd been buoyed by their closeness, by her virginal wish to offer him escape. But wishes couldn't heal him. Escape was only momentary, a chance to hide from impending war.

And he still felt vulnerable . . . too vulnerable. At the mercy of his emotions, going beyond sex.

Yet she was his now, and however wrong he'd been to wed her, he wouldn't let her go. Gazing up at her, he was rewarded with the sparkle of love that glowed in her eyes. Coherent thought melted. Worry ebbed. Nothing remained in the world but her. Her rich woman's scent hinted of passion, and the promise she offered him like a gift . . .

As if sensing his need, she prepared to mount. Like the rider straddling a favorite steed, she guided him into her newly initiated depths.

They raced together, reaching for completion. Or was it only for escape from pain? *Try to outrun it. You can . . . you can do it . . .* As if he whispered it in his stallion's ear.

But it wasn't Red Rowan whose name he called.

Lucina. Lucina. He bit back the urge to shout to the heavens as the pleasure she brought him shot through his veins. Her long hair fluttered as she rode him swiftly, his firebrand bride bringing him trouble and hope.

The sharp bite of her nails swept him to the edge. She arched her back and writhed against him. "Oh, Alex, I love you." At that moment he cracked.

Her sweet flesh tightened, and he swelled within her. As he culminated, a burst of light flooded his brain. A sudden vision of tranquility flashed in his mind—of a night flower, white and gleaming, enfolding him in pure flame, lighting up his world.

He floated on a cloud of contentment afterward. What heaven he found in Lucina's love. He closed his eyes and slipped into a welcome doze, his arms linked around his wife, praising heaven that she had come into his life.

Chapter 17

Eventually Graham had to open his eyes and face the world again. No amount of loving woman flesh could spare him that trial. Yet as he sat up and tried to judge the time, Lucina's contented smile, her touch as she smoothed back his tangled hair, went a long way toward salving his wounds. The world around him might be dismal, but the light of her love made it somewhat easier to bear.

Unwilling to burden her with his many concerns, Graham rose and dressed. No use dragging her down with him, or getting sentimental and sloppy about the distasteful truths of life. Red Rowan had been stolen. The English would raid Hermitage Castle. His cousin would kill again. And the Border wars would never end.

In sharp contrast to his black mood, Lucina whistled as she slipped into her clothes, seeming to retain the joy of their coupling. She bustled around tidying the chamber, appearing to savor rearranging the cup and pitcher by the bedside and straightening the hanging on the wall. She did, however, stay clear of his untidy court cupboard and work-table. Praise heaven for that.

He might tackle the papers one day. They ought to be protected in storage boxes to keep them clean and dry. But he wasn't ready for drastic change yet. It felt odd enough to share his space with her. He needed more time.

"I see you like your new domain," he observed.

"I like the people, not the place." She stopped in the midst of pulling the green curtain closed and grinned at him, softening the harshness of her words.

She had called his castle a heap of stones. He still resented that. "What don't you like about it?"

"Oh, this and that." She shrugged noncommittally. "May I change a few things?"

"Within reason."

"How will I know what's 'within reason'?"

"I'll tell you." He stiffened, worried about what she meant to do.

"Hmm, I don't doubt you will." Seeming oblivious to the idea that she might change the very things that gave him comfort, she settled in a chair before the cold hearth. "I wish everyone at Castle Graham to dine together in the great hall, beginning tonight."

Everyone? Tonight? He didn't know why her proposal unsettled him, but they hadn't all dined in the hall since his father died. "The tenants are still here."

"But you intended to serve something special tonight, did you not? I heard talk of barley broth, various meats, and ginger cake." She lifted her eyebrows questioningly.

"They're returning to their homes on the morrow," he admitted gruffly, embarrassed to be caught in a kindness, though he wasn't sure why.

"All the more reason to make an occasion of it. 'Twill give them pleasant memories to take with them."

"The hall is filthy," he disagreed. "It needs a thorough cleaning before it's fit for dining again."

"They can help with the cleaning. The promise of an evening's entertainment will give them reason to do it with a will."

Entertainment? What scheme did she have in mind now. "Do you think I have bottomless money coffers?"

She sprang from her chair and crossed the room to him. Guiding his hands to her waist, she held them in place with her own. "Alex, let me be a partner with you, not merely the female who shares your bed and board. Tell me the truth. Can you afford the food and one or two musicians? If not, pray say so and I'll give up the idea."

He didn't know why he objected to her plans, except that he wasn't accustomed to sharing decisions. "I can afford it," he conceded, the feel of her waist beneath his hands soothing away his discomfort. "But we haven't any entertainers. We'll have to make do with the food."

"What of singing?" She rubbed his forearm in a pleasing, intimate gesture as she considered. "Have you a harper or a fiddler? Someone who can offer a few ballads? Though he's not to play the 'Ballad of Bonnie Mary.' Talk to him beforehand and choose songs that will put everyone in a pleasant mood."

As he said he would do that for certes, he realized he had again conceded to her wishes after initially saying no. What had gotten into him? Yet discussing plans with her for a celebration was strangely calming. He had a brief, unexpected vision of them twenty years from now, well accustomed to each other, fitting as comfortably as a favorite pair of riding gloves.

"I also want Elen," she went on, slipping from his grasp and sitting down with a regal, satisfied air, as if she were a queen who issued orders and expected to be obeyed.

The calm he felt ebbed. "No." Why must she always push him too far?

"Only for the evening. She can't do any harm. You can watch her yourself."

"I said no."

She smiled up at him and nodded congenially. "As I said, 'tis only for the evening. Oh, and I would like Drummond there as well. He can—"

"Lucina, I haven't agreed to Elen's being there." She never failed to amaze him with her audacity. "Don't press me. My temper will not tolerate it."

She wrinkled her nose at him. "Your temper will have to learn a good deal of tolerance if we're to survive together. It *was* your idea we wed, as I recall. Come, now, humor me, and I'll do something for you in return. What would you like?"

She knew damned well what he would like. A repeat performance of what they had just done in bed. The male part of his body came alert at the mere mention, but he wasn't willing to admit it. The idea of giving her what she wanted in exchange for bed sport was distasteful, so he glared, hoping to frighten her into submission.

At her smile he realized he would never succeed with that approach. "What I would like in return for this favor, and understand it is a favor," he said testily, "is for you to obey me for once. I want to give an order and have you do exactly as I say. Without question or argument."

"Now?"

"Ideally, all the time," he snapped, wanting to banish the pert grin from her face by tumbling her once more in the bed. "But since that seems impossible for you to manage, then at a specific moment I will name. I want you to swear. I may need it in a crisis sometime." He wanted to point out that since her arrival, they'd had far more crises than usual. In fact, if she agreed, it might do to have such a bargain with her regularly, a handy way to subdue her each time another crisis cropped up. But he wisely kept his mouth closed as she hesitated, seeming undecided whether she would agree to his terms.

At last she nodded with a show of reluctance. "I will obey if 'tis not something illegal or immoral. But you must give me warning that you're calling in the debt so I don't misunderstand."

Lord, but she was provoking, to suggest he would involve his wife in anything dangerous or immoral. But he agreed to her request for a warning. Without it, she might well misunderstand him. That happened often enough as it was. For instance, he wanted Drummond locked up, where he belonged, not at the family board for a meal. "Why do you want the lad there tonight?"

"Because he's a Graham," she answered easily, as if aware that she provoked him.

"On the wrong side of the sheets."

"What difference does that make? I want him to see there is a place for him here."

"I never said there wasn't a place for him here. There is if his father would allow him, and if he would stop doing vicious things at Will's urging."

Lucina smiled in triumph. "Ah, but that's the trouble, isn't it? Will doesn't want him here, learning loyalty to you or the family instead of to him. And how could Will bring his bastards here? You don't bring yours, do you?"

"You're assuming I have some to bring," he said, feeling odd at the change of subject.

"I thought most chiefs did. Do you?" she persisted, her violet eyes guileless.

"Not that I know of," he admitted, feeling odder still.

She nodded, as if satisfied to hear it, a little smile curving her lips.

He restrained the impulse to laugh. "I believe you just wormed that information from me rather cleverly. But I warn you, Lucina, if Drummond Storie agrees to attend tonight's feast, I hold you responsible for his good behavior."

She propped one hand under her chin, a finger tapping her lips. "Yes, I believe I can do that." She sprang up in excitement. "Alex, I want you to see Will wed to Drummond's mother tonight. Then you can make Drummond legitimate and bring him and his mother here to live."

Graham's mind reeled at her incredible proposal. "Will's not here. Even if he were here, what makes you think he would agree?"

"You're his chief," she said matter-of-factly, brushing aside the difficulty. "He must obey or suffer the consequences. And rest assured, I'll think of some splendid ones if he refuses. As for tonight, we'll have a marriage by proxy between Drummond's mother and a relative to stand in Will's place. Then Drummond can be declared legitimate and swear an oath to the Grahams. We'll let Will know of it later. He'll most like hear of it from other sources anyway. He seems to have informants everywhere."

Graham saw a million holes in her scheme. "And what of Will's agreement? It is required, you know," he pointed out.

She wrinkled her brow and pondered the problem. Suddenly, her face lit up. "If he refuses to accept the marriage, his wife will be given control of his property and funds until he does. He has land and income, does he not?" She put the question so innocently, Graham could scarcely believe she understood the severity of the consequences she'd chosen. Yet it became obvious, moments later, that she did. "Once Will's wife and heir reap the benefits of being accepted, you will win Drummond's allegiance to the family," she stated with conviction. "There are too many outsiders fighting the Grahams. We don't need fighting from within."

Why she had gotten this scheme into her head, he didn't know, but her logic made perfect sense. Will was indeed a thorn in his side, but for years he had tried to ignore the problem, hoping it would go away. He had no desire to feud within his own family. He had shirked his duty in dealing with Will for that very reason. Now, at Lucina's prodding, he would force Will to do the honorable thing by one of his many families. With Drummond undoubtedly his eldest child, sired when his cousin was no more than fifteen, it was high time he wed the boy's dam.

Despite the disquieting fact that the entire scheme was of Lucina's making, he accepted it, won by the rightness of the thing.

She seemed to sense his disquiet, for she was beside him in an instant, as if hearing his silent call. Her soothing hands on his shoulders anchored him in the present, a stabilizing presence blocking out the past. Odd feelings of vulnerability and pleasure tangled through him as her hand slid around his neck, pulling him down. But once their lips met, vulnerability evaporated, leaving only pleasure, escalating into desire.

Whatever fate had in store for him at Hermitage Castle, he put it aside. He would live in the present, knowing once more the release brought by his bride.

Later, Graham felt strangely at peace as he sat at the high table following the ceremony, Lucina to his right, Isabel on his left, the din of one hundred celebrating Grahams, Langs, Mosleys, and tenants ringing in his ears. At first he had felt like a sham, pretending to be his father and failing dismally. Jock Graham had been a great Border chief, a warrior prince ready to lead his men into battle at any moment, whereas he, Alex, wanted only to plow his fields and breed his horses.

But he had brought peace to at least one person this night. Glancing over at Elizabeth Storie, he grinned at the dazed expression on her face. Clearly she couldn't believe her good fortune, becoming both a wife and the mother of a legitimate son in one night. Even Drummond had seemed more pleased for his mother than for himself. He'd looked skeptical at first when Arthur, as the Graham bailie, had explained the ceremony to him and his new place in the household. But the lad could no longer doubt it once the Graham chief had overseen the marriage ceremony of his mother, then announced the boy's legitimacy to the assembly, and had Drummond kneel and swear his oath to uphold the family's honor. Jasper, Arthur, and the other Graham men had made a point of welcoming him to the family, thus reinforcing the promise. Time would help him adjust and see the ways he must change in order to belong.

Throughout it all, Lucina had beamed, pressed his hand, and called him Alex until he'd had to turn away. The intensity of her happiness was too much for him. How a person could be so joyous and not split in two with the force of it was beyond him.

Alex. He hadn't thought of himself as that person for years. He was no longer the boy who had excelled at war to win his father's praise. That lad had risen eagerly to his fierce grandsire's baiting, reiving more cattle than the others, taking greater risks and still not being caught.

But now Lucina revived the name, and on her lips, it sounded like a different person. Someone he didn't know.

But he wanted to know this new Alex she seemed to have created, this man of benevolence and peace. His heart expanded as he watched his tenants enjoy the food and drink he had provided, even the music of a fiddler Lucina had unearthed. As they clapped and tapped their feet to the merry tune of "The Wark o' the Weaver," he felt a kinship with them. They all wanted the same thing—a good plot of land, the right weather to ensure their crops, fine pasturing for cattle and sheep. The only difference was that he wanted to breed long-legged English horses as well.

His problems weren't over yet, but tonight gave him hope. Will had added impetus to return to Castle Graham and behave honorably, and Graham intended he should know of both his marriage and the commitment of his funds and land. Will had amends to make, and to Graham's way of thinking, this was a fine way to start.

"Ma leddy, I'm right glad ye've done this for Drummond."

Lucina tore her gaze from the fiddler and the dancers to find Elen at her elbow, her green eyes shining with happiness. "The Graham did it, not I," she protested.

Elen smiled and bobbed her head. "So ye say, but I know ye well enough tae ken the truth. My thanks."

Lucina sighed, wishing she could make Elen legitimate, too. But Will could only have one wife, and anyway Elen's

mother was dead. The thought was depressing, and she put
an arm around the thin shoulders, hugging the girl to her.
"Eat your ginger cake, dear," she murmured, smoothing
the child's flaming hair that bristled from the plaits into
which she had woven it earlier. Elen needed no further
urging. She attacked the remainder of her cake with a will.

Lucina cast her gaze around the great hall and wished
she felt as contented as Graham looked, sitting at the head
of the table, drinking wine and trading tales with Jasper,
who sat at his elbow. Grinning men-at-arms danced with
blushing tenants' daughters. Children skipped to the music,
along with their elders, enjoying the belly cheer of full
stomachs and gay tunes. Lucina wondered how long the
mood would last, then caught herself. How unlike her to
be melancholy.

She glanced furtively toward Drummond's place beyond
his mother, wondering how he felt about his new status,
but the lad wasn't there. Bess Storie sat next to Isabel, the
pair of them chatting away as if they'd been friends all their
lives. The sight cheered her, but only a little. Lucina's own
pleasure had deserted her after the announcement of
Drummond's legitimacy, for she longed to talk to the lad,
to ask him if he would guide her to Hermitage. Events
were rushing toward her with alarming speed. Her belief
that she must find her brother before the English raid put
her in a frenzy of concern.

Reason told her she must wait a decent interval before
she talked to Drummond. She must not fall on him with
demands all at once, but let him grow accustomed to his
new place. Yet the English would not stay their attack on
Hermitage to suit anyone's needs. Time was running out.

Wanting to be alone to think, she decided to retire for
the night. As she told Graham her intention and bid the
others goodnight, Elen rose, expecting to accompany her.

"You must stay and watch the dancing. And pray watch
over Madam Isabel," she whispered to the child, realizing
Marie and Margaret had deserted their posts long ago.
"You might also eat the rest of my ginger cake, for I cannot, and we would not wish it to go to waste."

Elen's eyes glowed with gratitude as Lucina said goodnight to Isabel and Bess. She took some pleasure in her
exchange with Bess, who squeezed her hand and murmured

a fervent thanks, as if she sensed Lucina's part in her good fortune.

She couldn't know the truth, Lucina thought as she crossed the crowded hall, looking for Drummond but failing to find him. But as she reached the screens passage, she saw him slouched morosely against the doorjamb, arms crossed at his chest.

The lad, almost as tall as Graham, towered over her as she paused before him, yet his slouch conveyed a touch of uncertainty, hinting that he was uncomfortable with his height, having perhaps acquired it too fast. Something of the boy still remained.

"I wish you joy, Drummond Mosley," she said, looking into his green eyes. They were stormy, like the English Channel whipped by wind and rain, yet she felt none of the malevolence that emanated from Will. Drummond's gaze reflected a proud wariness, as if he mistrusted those who had given him and his mother such unexpected gifts. Without question he worried about what would come next. But Lucina had grown up beside the Channel and knew its many moods. It could turn from stormy to calm. So, too, could Drummond, at least she hoped he could.

"Elen tells me this was yer idea," he said bluntly, "no' the Graham's."

Lucina winced, sorry that Elen's pride in her mistress had lead her to say the wrong thing. "Not entirely," she hedged. "I believe it was actually the Graham's idea, but I was the one to tell Elen of it. She must have thought it mine."

"Why do ye want it?" he demanded.

"Because you deserve it. I'm glad for you."

"People dinna do things for gladness. What's in it fer ye?"

Feeling sorry that he believed all motives were purely selfish, as well as a little guilty because she did want something, she touched his arm, directing him into the screens passage where they could speak privately. "I played but a small part in what happened tonight," she explained, "and 'twas not done for my sake."

"Why, then?"

His terse demand showed his mistrust ran deep. "'Tis not a simple answer." She cast about for words. "The Grahams are pulled apart by many enemies. It makes no sense for the family to be pulled apart from within."

"But you think naething of pulling me apart," he accused. "Of making me choose between ma faither and ma chief. Did you no' consider that?"

She had considered it, but until now, she hadn't fully understood how it would hurt him. "Then, why did you agree?" she asked. Did he really not want to belong?

"How could I not," he sneered, derision showing in his eyes. "Do ye think me a complete loonie? Look at ma mither, how happy she is, a decent woman at last after years o' being called a whore. I'd be heartless to deny her that."

Lucina's gaze locked on Bess, sitting at the far-off table, her slim weaver's hands gesturing gracefully as she answered a question put by Isabel. "You didn't agree only for her sake, did you?" she asked haltingly. "I hope you take your oath to the Graham seriously."

"I do," he snapped. "But there's the trouble, in case ye dinna ken. I expect to have opposite orders from ma faither and the Graham one day. What then?"

Lucina knew this was the very problem from which Graham wished to protect Drummond. "You might have to choose one day," she began. " 'Tis easy to put that burden on you, since I don't have to—"

"Ye said that a-right," he scoffed. "Ye dinna ha' to decide. I do. Did anyone tell ye, ye think tae mooch for a woman? Ye should obey yer chief. We're nae tae think. 'Tis better that way."

"But you *are* thinking," Lucina protested. "You're saying you'll have to choose, and it won't be easy. Which side would you support, for instance, in this dispute between your father and the Graham?"

A shadow darkened his face. "Are ye speakin' o' yer braither?"

"Yes, of my brother," she agreed. "As long as your father holds him hostage, the entire family is endangered. Neither the English nor the Scots Border warden can let this go unpunished. But if my brother were freed, the trouble would end. Graham knows this, but because he makes decisions by the book, not by his heart, he refuses to use the one tool that could prevent bloodshed. You."

Drummond snorted. "Ye dinna care aboot me. Ye see me as a tool."

His accusation hurt. Even if helping him was only part of the means to a greater good, she had still improved his life. "Do you feel 'tis right to hold a man hostage for money?" she challenged. "Am I selfish and self-serving if, in the process of freeing my brother and saving the Grahams from further conflict, I help you as well?"

He shifted from one foot to the other, clearly undecided how to answer.

His hesitation brought Lucina hope. Upon meeting Bess Storie, she judged the woman to be another like Elen's mother, an honest woman seduced by Will in her youth. It seemed to Lucina that Bess had bestowed much love on her child and worked hard to care for him, despite the hardship of living unwed. "I see you don't wish to answer the question, so I presume you do not entirely approve of ransoms."

Drummond continued to shift and avoid her gaze.

"Let me tell you something. I do want your help in freeing my brother." She felt sure this was the moment to confide in Drummond. "We can help the family, and you can receive compensation." She pulled out the Dunlochy Charmstone and held it cupped in her hand so only he could see it. The crystal glinted temptingly, and Drummond's eyes widened in amazement to see it in her possession.

"I didn't steal it, if that's what you're thinking," she said. "Elen gave it to me, to give to you."

"To me?" He stretched one hand toward the bauble in a yearning gesture.

Lucina whisked it away. "Elen said you might have it only if you agreed to guide me to Hermitage Castle and help me find my brother before the English raid it."

His expression turned wary again. "Why shouldn't I tell the Graham ye're plannin' someit, instead? He wouldna approve, and ye're to obey him, same as me."

"He wouldn't approve," she agreed, knowing she must be honest with him. "Even though he agrees that finding my brother before the raid would be best, he's, er . . ." She stammered, realizing she shouldn't say Graham didn't trust him. "He's too proud to call on you for help."

"He doesna trust me. I ken that well enow."

Lucina heard the pain of rejection in the lad's tone and felt a rush of affection for him. He reminded her of Roger, young and full of life, his feelings showing so clearly in his voice and eyes. "But I trust you," she said simply. "I believe if you agree to accompany me, you will help me to the best of your ability and not betray my trust. I trust you, too, to take the charmstone for a set period of time and reap the benefits." *If there are any,* she added silently.

He stared at her, wide-eyed with surprise, as if unsure whether to take this as a compliment or foolishness. "Ye dinna think I'm a good-fer-nothin' ruffian?" he muttered. "Everyone else here does, an' they ken far more aboot me than you."

"I don't think it because your mother trusts you," Lucina insisted. "And Elen loves you so, she gave up the charmstone to you, though she considers it most precious. But if you tell Graham about it, you know what he'll do." She watched dismay creep over his features as he understood her meaning. "That's right," she nodded. "The Graham would return it to its rightful owners, the Maxwells. I don't approve of their having it, since they refused to share it, but I suppose 'twill have to go back to them some time. If you want a chance with it, you'd best take it now."

She watched the emotions play across his finely cut features—desire for the stone, hope that he might find a place with the Grahams, fear that he faced hard choices if he took the stone and did as she asked. Yet she also sensed he was sensitive and intelligent enough to choose aright.

"Pray consider what I've said, Drummond," she said, drawing back to indicate their discourse was ended. She held the charmstone over the pouch at her waist, let it glitter one last time, then tucked it out of sight. "When you're ready to help me, say the word and the stone shall be yours for a time. Until then, pray watch me and decide if what I do is driven by selfishness or no."

Chapter 18

Lucina enlisted Bess's help the next day in supplying the tenant families who would be returning home. There was far too much work for her and Isabel alone. Now that Bess ranked in the household, it only made sense to Lucina that she should help.

To her gratification, Bess proved eager to help, her ordering of the work efficient, probably due to her years of managing a frugal household. As they counted bags of oats for the families, Lucina guessed Will had added to Bess's meager income from weaving but forgot her the rest of the time. Will enjoyed seducing females too much to stay with the first conquest of his youth.

"M'leddy, I pray ye look here." Bess had been systematically checking each sack of grain, not just counting them. "This sack has gone moldy. We dinna want to give it to a family. And we mun be sure that others aren't ruined as well."

As they tugged the sack toward the storeroom door, Lucina was pleased that Bess's scruples matched her own. She was also glad to see Drummond watching them from the kitchen. She hoped he was learning to trust her, because in a few days, he must make his decision. And if he decided against helping her, she wasn't sure what she would do.

The Graham tenants returned to their homes after the noon dinner, escorted by a dozen of the Graham men-at-arms and led by the Graham himself. Lucina, Isabel, and Bess saw them off at the castle gates, after hours of ensuring that each family had a decent store of food. Lucina had also learned that Graham had posted regular scouts to ensure they were not attacked again. Their returned cattle were separated from the Graham animals by their brands and sent with them.

That day and the next two tried Lucina's nerves. As a distraction, she exercised her new duties as lady of the castle, pleased that Graham conceded a bit more responsibility to her each day. On the second day, as she checked the wine stores with Arthur, she decided Graham was learning to appreciate having a partner to manage his affairs. He hadn't turned over his keys to her, but he had let her take command of the kitchens. That alone was a major sign of trust.

But he hadn't agreed to let her roam without a guard. One of the men dogged her footsteps each day, even if she was with Arthur. She had privacy only in the tower chamber, where she was frequently joined by Graham.

There, she alternately made love with him and tried to wangle from him his plans to rescue her brother. A small army of men had camped outside the walls of the castle. Yet he steadfastly refused to discuss the matter with her. Every time she detailed her concerns, he listened politely but did not comment. His only response, when she pointed out that Drummond would know where to find his father, was to insist that Drummond could not yet be trusted.

"Men don't change allegiances overnight," he insisted. "I won't take the chance."

Lucina grimaced and left the subject alone after that. Graham believed that life's choices were black or white. Either you did or you didn't. There was no in between.

Yet to her way of thinking, Drummond could support his father and still refuse to help with his illicit schemes. If Will couldn't control his base impulses, the family would have to help him. It was their only hope for the future, if he wasn't to ruin them all.

But she was meddling in other people's lives again, Lucina reminded herself, which, according to her sister, was wrong. So she tried to make the most of her time with her husband instead.

On the afternoon of Graham's departure, they lay in bed, savoring the aftermath of a last coupling before he left. Though she had sworn to avoid the subject, Lucina couldn't resist several oblique hints about freeing her brother, but each time she was rebuffed. At last she could bear it no longer. Terrified that Graham might be killed in a battle, she tackled the topic head on.

"Alex, how can you possibly avoid fighting either Will or the English? You're preparing for battle, yet it would be folly to fight either one."

He sat up and groped for his shirt. "I must go. I shouldn't have lingered."

"Take me with you." She didn't mean to do it, but she used her body to tempt him, rubbing against him, adding to her plea.

He stared at her as if she'd gone mad. "This isn't a pleasure journey."

Of course it wasn't. Lucina suppressed an answering frown as she saw the thunderclouds rising, portents of one of Graham's black moods. "You needn't go yet," she coaxed. "A few more minutes." She rose and poured him mulled barley water from a corked jug. As she padded back to the bed, bare feet against the cool wood floor, she avoided looking at the bloodstain before the hearth. She pulled the curtain closed to hide it from view. "Which parent do you favor most, father or mother?" she asked conversationally, putting the cup in his hand.

He drank, seeming willing to be appeased with idle chat. "I have my father's dark hair and blue eyes, so I suppose I look like him, though many Graham men had dark hair and blue eyes."

"Why was your father called Thrawn Jock?" She perched at the end of the bed to watch him, conscious of his lean, bare body so close to hers, of her own nakedness and his awareness of her.

"Thrawn means to have a mind of your own. Unwilling to do as others wish if you don't choose. He bore the nickname most of his life."

"So he was stubborn?"

"Yes, like you. You would have been a pair."

She grinned and toyed with a lock of her hair, glad she had distracted him from departure, at least for a while. "What of your mother? Did she have dark hair as well?"

"Nay, she was red haired—Janet Lang—as were my brothers. Truth is, I had more mothering from Aunt Isabel than from my mother. Isabel had time on her hands, and Bonnie Mary, my own grandam was dead, as you know."

Wanting nothing to spoil this rare moment of intimacy, she chose another subject. "Were you close to your brothers?" she asked.

"Close?" he repeated, squinting as if the question puzzled him. "We never thought or spoke of closeness. We just did everything together—rode, practiced fighting skills, went on raids."

He shrugged and drank again from the cup, but she could see the journey into the past affected him. She didn't want to uncover too much pain, but she wanted to know more of him from the time before tragedy struck. "Did you have a favorite horse when you were a lad?" Surely horses could only be associated with pleasant things.

A ghost of a grin softened his mouth. "I liked them all, and they liked me, so I had my choice. I was one of the few who could ride my father's big English stallion. He was a godsend when we went reiving, able to run for hours without tiring. He never failed me on a raid, and several times saved my skin. But he was also wicked, biting chunks out of anyone who grew careless around him. I told him from the start he had naught to fear from me."

"Did he believe you?" she asked, giggling at the image of Graham having a heart-to-heart discussion with a great horse.

"He did after he bit me, and I didn't bang him across the nose with a whip, the way my father did. I grabbed him by the muzzle and held his mouth shut. Had a stern talk with him. He never did it again. But then, I never turned my back on him again, either."

Lucina nodded slowly, understanding the wisdom of his remark. Some horses, if badly treated when young, could never be trusted fully. In a sense, she and Graham were like the pair he described, willing to give their all for each other even as mutual distrust held them apart.

It was as if Graham read her thoughts. "Look at me, Lucina," he said softly. "I told that animal he could trust me, and he did. There are others who might do the same."

He raised his eyebrows meaningfully, and Lucina looked away, embarrassed. She trusted him in many things, but not in all. She knew he would sacrifice his life for her, if necessary, but that was just the trouble. His loyalty, his reliance on old ways, could get him killed. She struggled to find acceptable words to tell him her fears.

"Did you have a horse as a child?" he asked before she could speak.

She was both relieved and sorry that he changed the subject. "I stole my first horse," she confided, his interest in her past pleasing her greatly. "The local squire's oldest nag. I was five, and to me, he seemed a splendid steed."

He laughed lightly, without a trace of mockery. "I can imagine you doing it, too—a young fairy, seducing the old fellow away from his pasture."

She lowered her head to hide her grin of triumph. She'd made him laugh, even on this day of woe. "I had to give him back as soon as my father found out," she said ruefully. "Then I shoveled manure until my back and arms ached. My father often punished us with offal disposal, as he called it. Sometimes I thought he looked for faults in us because the stable needed cleaning. My brothers Matthew and Charles did nothing but shovel some days, but then they were terrible rascals." She shook back her long hair, which was tickling her breasts. As his gaze fastened on them, heat pooled between her thighs. "You told me of your father's horse," she hurried on, "but not of your own. Didn't you have at least one?"

He toyed with the creamy wool blanket, then glanced at her slyly. "I told you I had my choice of them. All the fillies and mares liked me." He winked. "Still do."

"Oh, you." Lucina chucked a cushion at him, pleased to have him tease her. How right and easy it was to talk and jest with him. She felt as comfortable as if it were Roger. But Graham wasn't her brother, and a shiver of anticipation ran through her as he caught the cushion and lobbed it back at her. It hit her in the chest, and another wave of awareness tingled through her as she sat on it, removing it from play. "Naturally, they like you," she teased in return, shaking a finger at him. "But you'd best have a care. You're a married man now."

"And?" he taunted, setting the cup on the floor so it wouldn't spill. He poked her thigh lightly with one toe and smirked, as if it pleased him to hear her sound jealous. "What would you do?"

"I would do . . . this!" She pounced on his foot and tickled it.

He roared with surprise and laughter, trying to jerk his foot away, but she held on with dogged determination, her fingernails dancing lightly over his arch.

"Stop!" he shouted, shaking with mirth.

She stopped as suddenly as she'd started. Still holding his foot, she grinned at him. "*You* are ticklish, my lord," she announced. "Did you know that?"

He slumped in a show of mock defeat, holding up both hands. "I confess I never engaged in rough play of *that* sort. I had no idea."

"Not with your brothers?"

"No."

Nor with his other female bed partners, he seemed to say. She stared at him, in love with the way his dark hair parted on one side and swept across his forehead, with the way years of frown wrinkles bracketed his startlingly blue eyes, with the way he looked at her now, his desire evident between his legs and in his gaze.

"Now that you know my weakness, will you have mercy on me?" he asked gravely.

Her throat tightened, and she had to will back tears. "I doubt it," she promised saucily, unable to match his tone for fear she would weep. She did know his weakness—he was afraid of tender emotions, and at this moment, so was she. Because in another hour or so, he would ride away from her, perhaps forever. And if she felt too much, loss would hurt all the more. Yet so much was unresolved between them, and she couldn't bear for their last moments to be bitter.

This first brush with intimacy, of confidences exchanged behind the moss-green curtain that shut out the rest of the world, was all too brief. Why must the treasured moments be so fleeting? She wanted to capture each one and lock it away forever in her heart.

He must have felt something of the same sorrow, for he held out one arm and pulled her to his side. She nestled in the crook of his arm, praying this intimate moment would not be their last.

"Don't tease me anymore, Alex," she murmured, nuzzling his neck, wanting to relish their last moments together. "Tell me a story of a horse that was your very own."

"There was a little dappled filly," he said, rubbing one hand up and down her arm as he spoke. "She belonged to my older brother Edmund, but she performed best for me no matter how many carrots or apples he brought her. Once I visited Sarah, and Edmund came along to keep watch and give the alarm so I wouldn't be caught. Of course her cousins learned I was there. Edmund and I raced away, but my gelding outstripped his filly easily, even though the exact opposite had happened just the other day when we raced and I rode the filly. But you see both horses were fast for me. Just not for him. He blackened my eye when he finally got home. Sarah's cousins had caught him and threatened to cut off his . . ." With a chuckle, he gestured broadly instead of finishing the sentence. "You understand."

She understood all too well and thought the entire affair appalling. "He escapèd safely, did he not?" she asked in concern.

"Aye, he was a lusty fighter. But he gave me the filly, saying he never wanted to ride her again."

"So Sarah's family didn't approve of your visits." She was astonished to hear him mention Sarah and laugh in the same breath. She might as well take advantage of the moment and learn more. "If your families were on unfriendly terms, how did you come to wed her?"

"To please me, my father demanded her as part of a settlement after a Maxwell raid on the Grahams." His expression darkened. "He did many things to please me, as I did for him."

The intensity of his words broke over her, and she sensed the love that had been between father and son. Graham had upheld a way of life he ultimately hated, probably even believing he liked it at first, merely to please his sire. "If her family didn't approve of your visits," she hurried on, determined to keep the confidences flowing, "how did you manage to see her? How did you meet her in the first place?"

"I saw her with her sisters at a fair and thought her bonnie. Our eldest brother Archibald said I couldn't climb to her chamber window, and I said I could. I said I wouldn't

be turned away, either, when I got there. And I wasn't."
No smile surfaced this time to accompany the memory.
"Once I'd been with her, I knew she had to be mine."

Stars above, she'd touched on a gold mine of intimacy
tonight. Never had she thought he would trust her enough.
Though he was far from telling all, this was a beginning.
At the same time her own guilt increased, for she conspired
to disobey his wishes, though only because she feared for
his life. "Did she return your feeling?" she asked. "From
the very start, I mean."

He didn't answer, but his grim expression became tender,
and she knew Sarah had. Having touched a nerve in him,
she probed for more. "What of children? You were wed
several years."

The tender look in his eyes turned to sorrow. "She didn't
conceive, though 'twas not for lack of our trying. She also
took every potion known under the sun to quicken a child."

"But I thought she was with child when—" She brought
herself up short as the reference to Sarah's death slipped
out.

His sadness deepened, and she wanted to weep for him.
"She was with child," he said quietly, "but the child wasn't
mine. I never blamed her, though." His eyes suddenly
blazed with anger as he gripped her by the shoulders. "Say
you believe me. No one else does. They say she died because of me. That I drove her to her death."

"I believe you, Graham." She knelt on the bed to embrace him, wondering if he would push her away. But the
pain of his past so distressed her, she would take the risk.
In this matter, at least, she could and did trust him . . . and
oh, dear heaven, how badly she wanted to trust him in all
things, to have him trust her as well.

Her arms closed around him, and he sat rigid and unmov-
ing, neither accepting nor rejecting the comfort she offered,
only staring straight ahead.

Lucina lay her cheek against his hair. The woman he had
loved was dead, and he could never love fully or freely
until the ghost that haunted him was laid to rest. Clearly
he carried a terrible guilt over Sarah's death. Yet if she
had conceived another man's child, why hadn't he blamed
her? How had it happened? And why had Sarah then died?

Mixed with these questions was the issue of Graham's

virility. They had tried so hard to get a child but failed. Yet another man had succeeded. What a terrible burden to bear. And again, his secrets and pain from the past extended into the present. Was he unable to sire children? Might she and he never know the joy of seeing their offspring inherit a wealth of love?

Not for the first time did it occur to Lucina that the many secrets lurking in Castle Graham held danger for her . . . secrets whose answers, once exposed, could unlock old pain that even she, with her optimism and love, might not be able to heal. In accepting marriage to the Graham chief, had she taken on too weighty a burden? Might the pain merely extend to her?

This, she realized, was the source of her fear, why she felt such a desperate need to give him what she could, even as she remained unwilling to lose all of herself in their joining. Mayhap it was another reason she could not completely trust him with her brother's future . . . or her own.

Painful thoughts mingled with bittersweet pleasure as she and Graham lay in one another's arms on the narrow bed, twining their bodies together in the intimate pattern they had come to love. She knew they could not hide forever from the world beyond the moss-green curtain. And she may well have gotten in too deep this time.

Chapter 19

From the tower chamber, Lucina watched Graham prepare to ride for Hermitage. The hilt of his huge claymore glinted in the last daylight. Dirks bristled at his belt, as sharp as porcupine quills. She still marveled that he had idled away time with her before rallying his men. By rights, he should have set out hours ago.

Recognizing the clear sign of his desire to be with her, she felt more vulnerable than ever. Her stomach tightened as she considered how love was no more than opening oneself to pain. She would be torn apart if he died.

But he wouldn't die, she told herself as she changed into warm clothes for riding. She would find her brother before the men could clash, thus staving off the menacing specter of death.

Still, she grieved as Graham and his men clattered out of the castle gate. If only he had agreed to call on Drummond for assistance. But he had steadfastly refused to involve the lad, nor did he reveal that he had a better way of finding Roger quickly. He left her no choice.

Once the war party was well away, she gathered a change of clothes and donned her cloak. Just now she needed Isabel's advice. She couldn't possibly escape the castle undetected without help. Nor did she know how she would free Drummond, even if he agreed to go with her, which he had not yet. After five of the clock, the lad was usually locked in the prison wing. Graham felt it was too soon to trust him. Was she mad to put her faith in him?

She didn't think so. Several times since that day in the storeroom, she had caught Drummond watching her. She

knew he was assessing her, trying to decide whether her
motives were unselfish and whether he should guide her to
Hermitage. But he'd not given an answer, and she still
might have to convince him of the urgent need for his
support.

The tasks before her seemed monumental. Yet her father
had taught her to solve difficult problems by taking them
one step at a time. Her first step now was to coax Colin,
her current guard, to let her visit Isabel.

"Colin, are you there?" she called at the door.

Silence met her call. Blast the man, had he gone down
the wheeling stair to sit at the bottom, as Angus had
often done?

"Colin! Your mistress wants you!" she shouted, and was
greeted by more annoying silence.

Irate with him, she went to the wainscoted wall and
jerked back the hanging. She would have to escape the
secret way. But as minutes ticked by, her thumping failed
to spring the door.

Devil take it, why must she endure being locked in her
chamber like a naughty child? Angry with Graham, frustrated by her failure to open the panel, she pounded on
the wall with vigor, accidentally knocking into the court
cupboard. An avalanche of Graham's trash dumped on
her head.

"Blast the scoundrel and his untidy ways." She flailed
with her good arm to deflect the flying items. "And to think
I married the slovenly, miserable . . ." One fist hit the wall
with a smart crack. A click sounded, and with ghostly silence, the hidden door opened, emitting a breath of cold
air.

Too pressed for time to analyze the exact thump required
to spring the latch, Lucina scrambled for a piece of vellum,
folded it small, and used it to jam the panel open a crack.
Arranging the wall hanging to conceal the opening, she felt
her way down the dark stairs.

"Ah, ma lambkin," Isabel greeted her a short time later,
as if it were perfectly normal for Lucina to enter her chamber by the window. "Ye're gang to leave tonight, then,
are ye?"

Lucina leaned into Isabel's embrace, panting from haste,
afraid she'd been seen. "Oh, Isabel, yes, I must go after

all. Graham has been impossible and refuses to listen to
me. But I don't think I can manage my plan without
some help."

"Of course I'm here tae help ye." Her friend's frail body
radiated strength. Isabel eased her onto a stool and sat
opposite, leaning forward with clasped hands. "Tell Isabel
what ye need."

"Well, to start, how can I take Orpheus without anyone
noticing?" She studied her friend's encouraging expression.
"And since I've thought on it, why do you agree I should
go. Do you really approve of my taking matters into my
own hands?"

Isabel steepled her fingers and propped them beneath
her chin as she considered. " 'Tis indeed a great step ye're
taking. There's nae turnin' back once 'tis done."

"True," Lucina agreed, still searching for a clue to Isabel's motives. "I am determined to go, but why are you
willing to help me?"

Isabel leaned forward and grasped Lucina's hand, pressing it warmly. " 'Tis simple, lassie. Ye've no' been happy
here, and I mun see ye happy."

This seemed an odd reason to Lucina. Interfering with
Alex's plan for handling the crisis wouldn't necessarily help
her find happiness, yet Isabel stated the truth. She hadn't
been happy since her arrival in Scotland. Despite her love
for Alex, how could she be happy with her brother kidnapped and her land unclaimed? And knowing that Isabel
wanted her happy gladdened her heart. "Isabel, I do thank
you for your kindness. Sometimes I think I could be happy,
but this trouble over my brother gets in the way. And although I've made progress with Graham, he still locks me
in my chamber at night."

"At least he dinna beat ye this time," Isabel said with
feeling.

Lucina winced inwardly at the words. They hinted too
strongly that once more, Isabel had her confused with Bonnie Mary. Hating the probability, she concentrated instead
on Isabel's affectionate concern. "He won't beat me," she
assured her.

"He has struck ye afore and will again," Isabel said with
conviction. "There's nae denying it. Ye've thought long on
this trouble and made yer decision. 'Tis time tae go."

Lucina shook her head in confusion. Isabel wasn't making sense at all now. Too pressed for time to sort through it, Lucina jumped to the problem at hand. "Isabel, Graham has left the castle with his men. Now I must take my leave as well, but how can I manage? The castle gates are locked, and men-at-arms are everywhere. I was hoping you could advise me."

Isabel smiled wanly. " 'Twill be simple. We shall wait until everyone is at supper. Unless we're under attack, Master Arthur allows all boot one guard to leave their posts and sup in the hall. I shall join them as well this even, but you must remain in your chamber. When all are assembled, I'll have a fit."

Lucina grimaced, appalled by the proposal. "If you have a fit, 'twill convince them you are truly mad. They'll treat you worse than before."

"They dinna treat me badly."

"I consider it very bad indeed when Marie and Margaret don't wait on you properly," Lucina insisted with indignation. "So does Graham. But every time he isn't looking, they do it again."

Isabel shrugged. "Nae matter."

"It does matter," Lucina insisted, wishing she could dismiss the two women.

Isabel's jaw tightened in sudden sternness. "You will do as I say, now that all is arranged. I'm not so feeble I willna survive. When ye hear me scream, gang to the gates and tell the guard Master Arthur requires all hands. Here are the keys. Ye can let yersel' oot."

Lucina's eyes widened to see the ring of keys Graham always carried except when he left the castle. "How did you get them?" She knew well enough that Graham would have entrusted the keys to Arthur, who wore them on his belt.

"I told ye, I'm no' so decrepit as ye think." Isabel seemed to enjoy her secret. "Ye'll find Drummond's cell key here as well." She pointed to the appropriate one. "Now take our Bible and gang wi' God." She lifted her mending to reveal a book that she placed in Lucina's hands.

Lucina reached for the pouch at her waist, meaning to put it away, but something about the little book made her pause. Could it be . . . her own Bible? Baffled, she riffled the pages and saw it was indeed the little book given her by Lady Ashley. How had Isabel gotten it?

The question clamored to be asked, but Lucina pressed it back. They lacked the time for a complicated discussion that Isabel's confusion might muddle further. Seven of the clock—the supper hour—approached. She must return to the tower in all haste.

"Isabel, you've done so much for me." Lucina rose from her stool and hugged her friend. "I thank you. And I love you."

Isabel's lips curved into her warmest smile, and Lucina knew that despite her confusion about the year, her friend's love was genuine. "Go wi' God," she said, "and let time heal yer pain."

Lucina blinked in surprise at this suggestion. "My pain? I have no pain."

"Dinna ye not?"

The sharp eyes inspected her, and Lucina couldn't help but remember her frustration with the oppressive affection heaped on her by her elders as a girl. She hadn't been allowed to manage her own life until she finally broke away and went to live with Lady Ashley. "I was loved as I grew up," she began.

"But they squeezed the will out o' ye, doin' for ye, making the decisions when ye wanted to make them yersel'. I was the last o' the ten. I know."

"I suppose they did," Lucina admitted, reluctant to blame her loved ones for their good intentions. Yet hard on the tail of her uncharitable thoughts came guilt, for her family had loved her well.

Isabel stood up and patted her hand. "I ken how ye feel, ma lamb. 'Twasn't Faither only who told me what to do. Everyone had orders for Isabel, whilst Isabel had no one to order but hersel'. My greatest happiness was becoming Gavin Graham's bride. He was no' hard to please, and I loved him so, but he had to get killed reivin'." Her eyes misted, and Lucina reached for her hand.

They stood in silence a moment, then Isabel roused herself. "Dinna be loitering here, lassie. 'Tis time tae be off!" She shooed Lucina back through the window.

As Lucina slipped to the ground and hurried back to the tower, the question about the Bible returned to her. Clearly

Isabel had gone to the tower chamber and taken it. But why? And once she'd had it, why in heaven had she so lovingly given it back?

True to her promise, Isabel feigned a fit loud enough to wake the dead. She made such a noise, Lucina heard her all the way up in the tower. Without a doubt she would rally every able body at Castle Graham to her side.

At the signal, Lucina jumped to her feet and hastened through the secret door, this time closing it behind her. Once in the empty chamber below, she slipped into the garden and surveyed the deserted courtyard. As Isabel had predicted, all the men were at supper in the great hall.

She crossed to the stable and chose two bridles from their pegs. Again checking the courtyard, she spied a lone guard at the gate, his back turned to her as he paced to stay alert.

Slipping through the early evening shadows, Lucina crossed to the prison wing. Drummond lounged at his table, staring morosely at the remains of his supper.

He started at her entrance, a mixture of surprise and disdain on his face. "What do you want?"

"I am leaving for Hermitage Castle, Drummond Mosley. Are you coming with me?" Before he could answer, she leaned across the table and dangled the charmstone before him. "Don't forget the crystal will be yours for a time if you help me."

His green eyes widened, and he leaned forward but did not reach for the stone.

Realizing he was debating his decision, Lucina stepped back, still dangling the sparkling stone. "Yours for a full sennight," she repeated firmly to encourage him.

For several moments the inward struggle showed openly on his face. He stared hard at the charmstone, as if seeking a sign from it. Glancing down, Lucina saw it glitter in the light of a single candle, the one light becoming many in the stone's clear depths.

"It is beautiful," she said softly, feeling some of the attraction it must have for others. Holding it in her palm, she tilted it to better catch the last light of day.

"It likes you," he breathed, his gaze riveted on the stone as it winked brightly.

She glanced up, surprised by the sudden approval in his voice. "What makes you think that?"

Drummond gazed intently at the stone. " 'Tis said to shine only in the hands of those with honest hearts. I mun agree to what ye ask." He held out his hand for the charm-stone, but she recovered her wits quickly enough to hold back. "First swear that you will help me as best you can, Drummond. Swear and the stone is yours."

"I swear by the blood of ma faither to help ye." Drummond never removed his gaze from the glittering crystal as he spoke.

Had some invisible power in the stone driven him to agree? Lucina wondered as she let him take the crystal. The instant it left her, she felt an odd sense of loss. How absurd. The crystal meant nothing to her. But it obviously meant a great deal to Drummond. He cradled it in his palm, a protective gesture that also hid it from her view, as if he were jealous of every glimpse others might steal of the precious thing.

"It belongs to ma faither," he murmured more to himself than to her. "I mun give it back."

Though he wasn't asking Lucina's opinion on the matter, she chose to pretend he had. "I would recommend you keep it for a time, Drummond. Your father isn't in a position to collect it from Elen just now. And I understand it brings the bearer good fortune."

"That's so," he breathed, admiring the stone.

Despite the lack of bright light in the chamber, despite the way he shielded it in his hand, Lucina still caught the characteristic glint of the charm as he shifted on his feet. Did that mean he, too, had an honest heart, as he'd said of her?

The idea that the crystal might predict personality was an eerie one that Lucina didn't wish to ponder. "May we depart now?"

He glanced up, looking as if he'd forgotten she was there. "Oh, aye." He hung the chain around his neck and tucked the crystal down the front of his shirt, then caught up his hat and leather jack and moved toward the door.

"You wait here and join me as soon as I've sent the guard from the gate. Bring these when you come." Lucina indicated the two bridles she'd left in the outer passage. As she prepared to slip out the door, she heard Elen's whisper through the grille of her chamber.

Glad that Elen would further convince Drummond he had made the right choice, she moved toward the main gate. "Oh, Tam," she cried to the guard, letting all the fear and desperation that had built within her show in her voice. "Madam Isabel has taken ill in the great hall. Master Arthur requires everyone's aid at once."

He sped for the great hall, and she followed several paces behind, letting him enter the tower house before she'd so much as crossed the courtyard. As he disappeared, she hurried to the gate and fitted the largest key on the ring into the lock. She struggled to turn it, then Drummond materialized at her side. He opened the gate, pulled her through with him, and closed it.

Lucina took the keys and hung them on a nail protruding from the door. It would be some time before those inside discovered them in such an unexpected place. That done, she surveyed the pasture just outside the castle. A whicker signaled that Orpheus had heard her voice. He loped toward her as quickly as his hobbles allowed, Cygnus close behind.

"Conceal yourself," she ordered Drummond, taking the bridles from him. He slipped behind the recess of one pillar ornamenting the gate as she ran to meet Orpheus and Cygnus. Two men who had been guarding the four grazing horses headed her way. "Madam Isabel is ill," she called. "Master Arthur requires you to seek a physician at Annan. I'll take my horses in for the night. You take the other two and go."

The two men nodded immediate agreement and took the bridles she offered without protesting the lack of saddles. Borderers were accustomed to emergencies, and if Master Arthur ordered them to fetch a physician, they would do so in all haste.

Within minutes the men were galloping southward on their sturdy hobbies. Lucina removed Orpheus's hobbles and beckoned to Drummond. "You may ride Cygnus, but first, I pray you, give me a leg up."

"Women dinna ride stallions," he said. "Men do." He reached for the stallion as if to mount.

"Stop! Are you mad?" Lucina pushed Drummond away

as Orpheus laid back his ears and bared his teeth. "He could kill you. You must do as I say and ride the mare."

Drummond retreated, eyeing Orpheus warily. As he mounted Cygnus, Lucina thought she detected a new respect for her in his eyes, but it was still mingled with resentment.

"What is your plan once we reach Hermitage Castle, if I may be so bold, m'leddy?" he asked with a meekness she didn't trust.

"The English mean to raid the castle to free my brother," she said. "I must stop them and your father from fighting a battle over him."

His subservient manner dissolved. "If ye think to do that, yer the ane who's mad. A female canna . . ." He paused, then corrected himself. "A leddy canna do that."

"But I will do it, and I gave you the charmstone in exchange for your help." She was thoroughly tired of being doubted and contradicted. "I expect you to comply with all that I ask. If you don't, I'll order Cygnus to buck you off."

Her announcement that her horse would obey such an order seemed to amaze him. He said no more, instead staring at the dirt track ahead.

"You do want a place at Castle Graham, do you not, Drummond?" Lucina ventured once they were well beyond sight of the castle.

"I want ma mither to keep hers." His response was noncommittal, his gaze fixed on the road.

"Do you believe your father requires your service more than your chief? Is that it?" she probed, drawing her cloak closer against the chill evening air.

"I know what's required o' me to keep ma mither in her place."

"You think your chieftain doesn't really accept you?" she persisted. "He's given you a place in the family, Drummond. Later, he'll give you one in his heart. Give him time."

"He won't ever accept me," he burst out, as if frustrated with her questions. "Because of who ma faither is. Ye've nae power to change that. The Graham loathes him. Has done for years."

His voice burned with hatred, which bewildered Lucina. "I know they disagree over the things your father's done,"

she protested. "But I'm sure the Graham doesn't hate him.
He only wants him to keep the peace."

"Ye dinna ken a thing aboot it."

His cryptic words hinted at old secrets that reared their
menacing heads whenever she hoped to win Graham's
trust. Lucina rubbed Orpheus's neck, seeking comfort from
the sting of Drummond's declaration. It was frightening to
think that Will Mosley, despite his lack of sanity, had the
strength of character to win faithful followers who cared
for him as Drummond did.

"Do you intend to try to please them both," she asked,
knowing it was none of her business.

"I'll ha' tae." He sounded glum, as if he knew it was
impossible.

The idea of being squeezed between two such obligations
chilled Lucina, and as they rode onward by moonlight, she
hoped fervently that for everyone's sake, Will would not
make it harder than necessary for his son to honor his new
ties. But from what she knew of Will, it seemed a prayer
said in vain.

Chapter 20

In the hazy light of morning, Graham halted his one hundred men and squinted east toward where Hermitage Castle reared its centuries-old head, guarding the Scots side of the Border. He had ridden all night, passing Langholm, then heading deep into the roadless forest of Liddesdale.

Graham frowned at the stark castle walls with their high-set arrow slits. There would be no cracking this stronghold without stealth and a good plan. Yet he would learn where Roger Cavandish was being held. He had his ways, and he would discover what he needed to know.

"We'll camp in the curve of the hill," he said to Jasper, pointing out the glen that stretched upward behind the castle. Jasper passed the word quietly along the line of men that they were to circle the castle undetected. Above, they would be invisible from the castle yet still have the vantage point. No one could approach or leave Hermitage without being seen by the Black Graham.

A little later Graham leaned against a tree at the lookout point he'd chosen, waiting impatiently while the others cared for the horses and ate cold food. He couldn't eat.

As always, a circle of ice settled in his gut before battle. Coming so close on the heels of his interlude with Lucina, it hit doubly hard. He'd lingered with her, wasting time because she represented his wish to be done with battles such as this.

Memory spun a soft cocoon, reminding him of when he'd held Lucina in his arms, feeling her eager response to his raw desire. As she'd reached completion, her tight, sweet depths had convulsed around him, driving him to the pinnacle. For that instant he'd felt free, as if the future he'd hoped for lay just within reach . . .

Time to shut out feeling. Death to everything but the task ahead. Find Roger Cavandish. Alert the English. Be ruthless and succeed.

How could he dare to hope, knowing that within hours, he, the English, his lunatic cousin, and one of the most powerful Border earls in Scotland might well clash? He would do everything in his power to avoid it, but he sensed disaster ahead.

As soon as Jasper had eaten, they formed a plan. They would scout the area on foot, covering all the land around the castle. Then they would post lookouts along the eastern side of the castle close enough to warn them when the English arrived.

"Let's get at it." He turned to seek the other scouts.

Jasper started to speak, but Graham cut him off. He knew exactly what his captain intended to say. *"Why not take a rest? Let others do the work."*

Jasper was ever considerate of him, but Graham wouldn't leave the important work of scouting to others. He would know firsthand how the land lay.

Near dawn, Lucina halted Orpheus at the edge of a tiny village deep in the roadless forest. She hoped to find water and grazing space for the horses here so they could recoup their strength. She hoped to have a rest. And Drummond, although he'd not complained once the entire night, must want one as well.

She wiped her face to remove the dust, regretting her lack of foresight in not bringing some grain. Her horses had carried them all night without flagging, but now they must have sustenance or they could not proceed much farther. Patting Orpheus's neck, she praised first him, then Cygnus, who had halted just ahead. "Not much farther, my friends," she said, hoping this was true.

Her tired muscles throbbed with fatigue, but it was nothing compared to her growling belly. She had some silver coins with her, but since they had turned off the main track, the woodland folk to whom she'd spoken had stared at her blankly when she requested food and offered to pay.

Now they had come upon another gathering of huts deep

in the forest and, frustrated, she bid Drummond try. They were too hungry to turn away empty-handed again.

Drummond cast Lucina a derogatory glance, dismounted, and sauntered over to a hut. A rapid exchange with someone followed. To Lucina's mortification, almost every word was unintelligible. No wonder none of the folk had responded to her previous requests. They hadn't understood a word she'd said. Drummond had probably thought her ridiculous the entire time.

Despite embarrassment at her failure, Lucina rejoiced as Drummond quit the hut carrying two bowls of breakfast soup. She even overlooked his superior air as she chose a silver piece and offered it to the old man who had followed. He gave her oatcakes and a hunk of yellow cheese, then snapped the coin from her palm, understanding the language of money readily enough.

Once Drummond had requested permission for Orpheus and Cygnus to drink at the village trough and graze on the green, Lucina settled on a stone by the village well to eat.

Drummond stood nearby, too busy wolfing his food to find a seat. As she dipped her hard oatcake in the bland soup, she considered his obvious skill in befriending people. He had established an instant rapport, and now the small population appeared enthralled by him. Lucina spied two lassies peeping at him from their hut until an older woman hustled them away.

He did look appealing, she thought. The red shock of hair and slant of sandy brows added an alert, questioning note to his face. Like Elen, he had a pale dusting of freckles flying across the bridge of his nose, and his unusual green eyes were sharp and inquisitive.

Thoughtfully, she bit into her oatcake, remembering the collection of dirks he'd worn that first night Graham captured him. Will had clearly taught him much about how to handle weapons and win supporters. The lad showed promise if he avoided his father's thieving ways.

"I've been wonderin' why ye think yer brother's at Hermitage," Drummond said.

"I don't think it. I know it." Finished with her food, she shook crumbs from her skirts, then went to Orpheus and patted his sleek neck.

"Who tol' ye?" Drummond persisted, though he kept his distance from the stallion, going instead to Cygnus.

"Someone who knows." Her evasive answer did nothing to allay Drummond's rising interest. He knew his father held Roger for ransom. He was probably considering what he should do for his father once he'd fulfilled his promise to her.

"If your father visited Hermitage Castle, where might he lodge?" She put the question casually, her attention ostensibly on their path ahead.

"He dinna stay in the castle proper. He stays where ma mither lodged when I was born."

"Where were you born?" she asked.

"In a cave up the nearby glen. It werena a hole," he snarled in response to her look of surprise. " 'Tis warmer in winter than the huts by the castle. Ma faither and I lodge there when we work for the earl." Knowing she could guess what sort of work the earl wanted, he turned surly after that, riding ahead and refusing to look back.

Lucina studied him, wondering his exact age. He might be as old as Roger going by looks, but he was more hardened than her brother. Being a bastard had shown him the unpleasant ways of the world early, which saddened her. But she buried her pity, knowing he resented it.

Why should she try to change him? Yet the urge to mold a loved one was part of nurturing, wasn't it? Was it permissible if it were called guidance? Perhaps, but she must not attempt to change Drummond simply because she thought another way of life better for him. She must offer alternatives and let him choose.

The same was true of Alex. She might know what she wanted for him, but only he could reach for it. She must concentrate on her own needs instead of meddling in those of others. But Alex was one of her needs now, and she couldn't let the man she loved go about killing people. The dilemma held. Should she leave him be? If she did, he would make all decisions without her. Not that hers were superior, but decisions should be made together. She had wed him and pledged him her future. Was it wrong to want a part in how that future played out?

In fact, she had pledged him more than her future. She had let him touch her heart, never knowing if she could

touch his in return. Her choice was based either on great
trust or great foolishness. Some days she didn't know
which.

Somewhere ahead in this deep, roadless forest lay Hermitage Castle and her two loves—her brother *and* her husband. The haze of the Border obscured most movement
and, it seemed, clarity of thought. She prayed that if the
Dunlochy Charmstone were truly magic, it would help free
her brother and bring her husband through the conflict
unscathed.

An hour later the sun had risen, but its rays scarcely
trickled through the fog. The air was sodden with moisture,
and the ground had turned marshy. The odor of rotting
bracken added to the sense of gloom and decay.

Ahead of her Drummond halted, and she murmured to
Orpheus to do likewise.

"Hermitage Castle is just beyond," he announced.

Lucina peered through the fog, wondering how he knew.
Yet he must have identified landmarks that told him where
he was. "I prefer to go to my brother straight away."

He removed his hat and pushed back his tousled red hair.
"The horses canna make the climb past a certain point."

She nodded briskly. "We'll leave them to graze. Pray
take us to a grassy spot not often traveled by those coming
to and from Hermitage."

Drummond led her to the back of the castle. Lucina
slipped from Orpheus's back and guided him to a stream
to drink. She embraced the stallion, then went to Cygnus.

"You'll leave them untethered?" Drummond asked,
clearly doubting her choice.

"Yes," she said firmly. "They will wait for me." With
her keen hearing and sense of smell, Cygnus would note
her mistress's location and come when summoned, only
fleeing if someone tried to catch her. For strength and brav-
ery, Lucina relied on Orpheus, but Cygnus was the elder
and the wiser. The young stallion would follow his dam's
lead.

"I'm ready," she announced, giving Cygnus a last caress.
Prepared for the climb, she faced the glen behind the castle,
trusting Drummond to know the way.

Half an hour later, hot and puffing from the climb, they

reached the place where the glen curved. Drummond stopped short, and she bumped into his back. "Are we—"

He clapped a hand over her mouth.

She froze and stared until gradually she made out the outline of horses tethered among the trees. In the mist she saw only that they were hobbies. She could not tell if they were Alex's.

Drummond backed them away stealthily and gave the area wide berth. The stone ledge to which he guided her after more climbing formed a narrow shelf set into the hillside. She wasn't at all fond of heights, but Drummond seemed unruffled by the precarious perch as he pulled a coiled rope from beneath a pile of rocks and checked the knot that held it to a nearby tree. Then he paid out the rope over the side of the ledge.

"Would ye care to gang first, m'leddy?" he offered, rising and gallantly sweeping off his hat.

"Where to, exactly?" She hung back, watching him from the safety of solid ground.

He grinned at her with a touch of derision. "Tae see yer brother. He's in the cave below." As if pleased to see her blanch, he nodded, then slithered down the rope.

Unnerved, she sidled onto the ledge and peered over the edge. The view of the rocky glen below was dizzying. And Drummond was nowhere in sight.

She hesitated, disliking the idea of putting one shifting rope between her and a terrible fall.

"Ho, Luce. You up there?"

"Roger?" Lucina tensed. "Is it really you?"

"No, 'tis Orpheus," he said with a snort. " 'Course 'tis me. Who'd you think?"

It was Roger, sure enough. She could tell by his teasing as well as his voice. "Can you not come up here?" She wished to avoid the descent.

"Nay," barked Drummond. "Ye're to coom down if ye want to see him."

Her heart pounding, Lucina took the rope and eyed it miserably. "Catch me, will you, Roger?" she called, lying full length on the ground and swinging her legs over the edge.

The descent wasn't bad as long as solid rock and crumbly earth remained beneath her legs, stomach, and chest, supporting both her and the rope. But suddenly the support disappeared.

In terror she gripped the rope tighter but couldn't check her descent. She slid faster, the rope burning her hands, her feet thrashing to gain purchase but failing. "Roger," she cried, "help."

"Stop kicking, and I'll catch you," Roger calmly ordered. His reassuring hands gripped her calves, then grappled with her skirts, and clasped her around the hips.

A heartbeat later she stood at the mouth of the cave, clasped in her brother's arms. "Roger," she whispered, hugging him hard. "I was so frightened for you. I thought you would be starving and cold."

"I'm reasonably fed and dry, but you seem a bit unsteady. Come away from the edge."

The darkness of the cave pulsed before her eyes after the comparative brightness of the day, and she hugged him tighter, thinking she might never let go.

"I must say, I'm surprised to see you." Roger gently patted her on the back. "You came here with this limmer?" He jerked his head to the right, and Lucina saw Drummond over his shoulder. Out of courtesy, Will's son was looking the other way, allowing them a moment of privacy.

She hugged Roger one last time, then let him go. "I couldn't rest until I found you. Every time I sat down to eat, I worried what they were feeding you."

Roger chuckled. "The food's a disgrace." As her face fell, he hastened to reassure her. "Healthy enough, just not my preference. The Scots are no cooks."

Lucina grinned as tears misted her eyes. Trust Roger to think first of his belly and the quality of the cooking before the safety of his own skin.

He pulled her braid affectionately. "I worried about you, too, Luce, though I felt sure Sir Edward would keep you out of mischief. He has done that, hasn't he?"

She felt her color rise and ducked her head. "I fear not. I'm wed."

"The devil you are. Who did you marry?" He jerked his head in Drummond's direction again. "Not that limmer, I hope."

"No, not him." She paused a moment, baffled. "What's a limmer?"

"A Scots rascal."

"Pfft, you're starting to talk like them," she accused, relieved to know he was well enough to jest. "Next thing, you'll be having an accent."

"They can be amusing at times, but I really am a prisoner," he said more soberly. "Now, answer my question. Who did you wed?"

"The Black Graham." She smiled as she said her beloved's name.

"I see you're in the mood to tease me." He turned and walked deeper into the cave, leaving her no choice but to follow. It curved, then broadened into a low-ceilinged room. By the light of a lamp on a rough-hewn table, she saw the walls and floor were hard-packed clay, swept clean. Rush mats covered the living area. A bench stood before an iron stove that vented through the ceiling. At the table sat a red-haired ruffian in a greasy leather jack, fingering a pair of dice.

Roger pulled out a chair and invited her to sit, and for the first time she noticed his wrists were bound by a short length of rope, leading her to wonder how he had managed to catch her when she'd slithered into the cave. Suddenly more moisture clouded her vision, and she sat down abruptly. "You've been here this entire time?" she murmured, furtively brushing away tears.

He patted her back again kindly. "You know me, Luce. I take care of myself. I even had a companion to while away the time. Meet Andrew Mosley, my erstwhile partner at the bones. Andrew, may I present my sister, Mistress Cavandish. Actually," he smiled cajolingly, "Andrew and I have had a game going since I arrived. I was winning for a while, but at the moment, I owe him a few shillings. You wouldn't happen to . . ."

He trailed off, looking at Lucina with the begging expression she knew so well, and she smiled, despite her tears. It was just like old times in Dorset when he would come down from Oxford for the holidays and implore her for help with his gaming debts.

Just as she had done then, she dug in her pouch and offered him several coins. He chose two, which he flipped to Andrew. Leave it to Roger. When held a prisoner, he would gallantly introduce her to his jailer, then pay the man for entertaining him.

"I wasn't jesting before," she said, wishing they could be alone so she could speak openly.

"About what?" Roger poured himself a drink from a jug. "Care for some ale?"

"No, thank you, Roger. I wasn't jesting about marrying the Black Graham."

He put down the cup. "You've gone mad." His brow creased with concern. "You can't know the man well enough to wed him. It isn't binding, is it?"

"I wanted to wed him," she said with conviction. "You'll understand when you meet him." She glanced at Andrew, not sure she should say more about Graham and the English, then decided it was no use trying to be secretive. Drummond, though he pretended to kindle the fire, was listening as well. "The English are coming," she said.

Roger gave her an odd look. "I assumed they were here already and I was to be ransomed. No?"

Lucina shifted uncomfortably. "Er, yes. I mean not exactly. Sir Edward isn't here yet. But he will be," she added hastily.

Drummond clearly thought this news valuable, for without a word, he turned and left the cave. With a twinge of concern, she wondered if Will was nearby.

"Oh, this is wonderful." Roger heaved a sigh of disgust, evidently thinking the same thing. "Now Will Mosley will demand a ransom for you as well as for me."

Lucina sighed, too. She had thought to locate Roger, then slip away to meet Sir Edward as he arrived, but now, with departure from this cave so difficult, she wasn't sure what to do. "Sorry," she muttered, wishing she'd refused to come down the rope.

Her worst fears came true when she heard an angry voice from the mouth of the cave. Minutes later Will strode in, Drummond at his heels.

"I pray ye, Faither, let us depart quickly and there'll be nae blood shed," the lad pleaded.

"Shut yer muckle mou," Will snapped at his son. He grinned widely upon seeing Lucina. "Canna stay away from me, egh, lassie? That pleases me well."

She seethed in silence, cursing the jaded coxcomb who thought the world centered on him.

"Faither." Drummond plucked at his father's sleeve, ardent concern written on his face. "If we leave now, 'twill be nae reason for the English to attack. Master Cavandish can walk oot to meet them an' all will be weel."

Will rounded on his son and smacked him across the mouth. "I tol' ye to shut yer mou," he growled, turning away. "Pack up, Red Andrew," he ordered his kinsman, who pulled out a saddlebag and began to fill it with foodstuffs.

Lucina was appalled at Will's crass treatment of his son, especially since the lad was trying to help. "That was an unkind thing for a father to do, to strike his son when he was only offering helpful advice," she said. "You should talk to him, not hit him."

Will didn't smile. "Keep yer counsel 'til ye have lads o' yer own, wench. They're a plague worse than red ants."

His lack of repentance infuriated Lucina. "Well, you're going to have to improve your dealings with him in the future, because he's your true son now, and Elizabeth Storie is your wife. You're not to hit them, else you'll be punished yourself."

"Egh?" He stared at her, his poison green eyes suspicious. "What are ye sayin'?"

Lucina tightened her hold on her temper. "I said, you're wed now. The Graham joined you by proxy to Elizabeth Storie, and if you fail to honor her and Drummond, who is now your legitimate heir, she will control your lands and income until you do."

As the words left her mouth and Will spun to face Drummond, Lucina realized her error.

"Did you swear the oath to the Graham?" he snarled. "By the de'il, if ye did . . ."

"I swore for Mither's sake," Drummond said staunchly, though he shifted on his feet, clearly afraid of his father's fury. Sweat gleamed on his forehead. "There's naught harm in it."

"Yer mither's a whore and ye're her bastard. That's the harm." Will's expression was murderous. "Nae wonder ye're tellin' me to run like a whipped pup, tail between its legs. Ye've sworn to uphold the Graham over me."

Drummond shook visibly now, yet Will had apparently angered him in return. " 'Tis not for the Graham I gave the oath. I did it to give Mither her due. 'Tis the least I can offer," he said bitterly. "Ye've never cared aboot what happened to her."

A growl of fury broke from Will. His fist shot out and connected with Drummond's face. Lucina gasped, horrified, as blood spurted. Drummond stumbled back, banged against the wall, and slumped to the floor.

Appalled that she had brought on the blow, Lucina hurried to kneel by the boy. "Stars above, I cannot believe this. Drummond, lad, what's bleeding? Let me look."

"I think 'tis his nose." Roger knelt beside her, looking equally concerned as he offered his handkerchief.

A swift assessment suggested Roger was correct. Lucina wadded her handkerchief with Roger's and gently pressed it against Drummond's bleeding nose, hoping it wasn't broken. The lad closed his eyes and submitted to her ministrations. Once the blood stopped flowing, Lucina rose to confront Will, who was unconcernedly tucking goods into the bag. "You're making a terrible mistake, treating Drummond this way," she insisted. "He's always been loyal to you, but if you strike him and call his mother names, he may be forced to change his mind."

Will glanced up from his packing. "I do the thinkin' for the family. No' him."

"But what kind of family do you have if you call him and his mother horrible names?" Her rage built as he continued his task, obviously more angry at her interference than he was concerned about the issue. "You'll end with no one to support you if you go on this way. You have about as much feeling as a codfish, and I'm beginning to think as much brain."

Will's murderous fist shot out, aimed straight for her face, but Lucina was prepared. She dodged, and Will's blow glanced off her shoulder.

"Here, now, you can't hit a lady." Roger leaped to intervene.

"I can indeed." Will pushed Roger hard, sending him careening against the table.

"Stop! There's something wrong outside!" Lucina waved

her arms frantically at Will, frightened by what she had just heard.

At the alarm in her voice, everyone froze. The whinny of frightened horses drifted to them from the mouth of the cave.

Will swore. "Someane's after ma mounts." Will herded them toward the cave entry, including Drummond. "Red Andrew," Will commanded, "up wi' ye first."

Lucina's legs shook, and she clutched Roger for support as she watched Andrew shinny up the rope. Stars above, but this was horrible. Will was demented, his son was still bleeding, and she might not be able to reach Sir Edward before he met with Graham. Bothwell could be nearby, too. If he was, all three forces might clash.

Her mind churned through alternative plans of action as she impatiently awaited her turn to leave the cave. She couldn't wait to be in the open air, where she and Roger might escape Will. The rope she had feared previously became a welcome alternative to staying another second in close confines with the deranged man.

Once Andrew disappeared over the top, Will ordered Drummond up the rope. He obeyed in silence, his gaze averted from his father's. Then it was Roger's turn.

Lucina watched him climb, heart in her throat, afraid he would fall. Will had refused to unbind his hands, but he climbed skillfully despite the handicap, disappearing over the ledge.

Lucina breathed in relief to see him safe, then realized she was alone with Will. Before she could dodge, he hustled her roughly to the rope, then squeezed her breast and planted a probing kiss squarely on her mouth as she struggled to pull away.

"Eager for it, egh, lassie," he chortled as he broke off the kiss.

"It's my turn to go up." Hiding her gag of disgust, she grasped the rope.

He boosted her up, pinching her bottom at the same time. Repelled, she clawed her way upward, moving faster than she had thought possible. Anything to escape Will's wandering hands. Once they were all assembled on the rock ledge, she stayed as far from him as she could.

"Tie her to her braither," Will ordered Andrew.

To Lucina's dismay, Andrew bound her wrist to Roger's and marched them down the glen. As they reached level ground to the east of Hermitage, Lucina sensed horses before she saw them. She counted five sturdy hobbies as their party emerged from the woods. One for Will, one for Drummond, and one for Andrew. Two other men were mounted on the remaining horses, which left her and Roger on foot. She and Roger were herded ahead toward the northeast.

"Roger," she whispered without turning her head. "Let us slip away first chance."

"Right," he whispered back. "I hope Bothwell isn't looking for a fight when the English arrive."

Lucina's heart sank. "I had hoped he wasn't here." She slogged through a puddle.

"He is, though." Roger tripped on a branch buried in old leaves as he answered. He pitched forward into the mud, dragging Lucina with him.

She broke her fall with both hands, ending up wrist deep in muddy water. Struggling to rise, she realized Roger was like a lead weight, holding her down.

"Delay," he whispered to her. " 'Twill give us time."

"No talking." From horseback, Will prodded Roger with the point of his sword. "Move on."

"You can't expect us to walk to wherever we're going while you ride," Lucina protested.

"Ye'll ride," Will said cheerfully. "I ken ye dinna coom here on foot, so lead us to yer mounts."

Lucina grimaced. The last thing she wanted was to put her horses in Will's clutches.

"Halt where you are," a deep voice boomed just as she and Roger managed to stand.

Lucina turned, her heart pounding so hard it hurt.

Chapter 21

It was Alex Graham with his company of men at his back.

Lucina had never been so glad to see him. But her joy faded as Will turned, the nasty smirk on his face suggesting he looked forward to a confrontation with his cousin.

"Will, the English are at hand," Graham said in a steady voice, as if pacifying a maddened horse. "Let the Cavandish lad go, and they'll not attack."

"What of her?" With a wicked glint in his eye, Will poked Lucina with his sword point, forcing her into view.

The dawning horror on Graham's face showed he hadn't realized Lucina was there. She swallowed hard, knowing his anger with her would be great.

His face settled into a mask of steely calm. "You're too late," he said to Will, his voice betraying nothing. "You cannot wed her for her land. She's already taken vows."

"Wi' ye?" Will shrugged. "Makes nae difference to me. I'll have her anyway. I've been biding ma time, ye ken, an' I'll have ma chance. I did with Sarah."

Fury replaced the mask of calm on Graham's face. "What are you saying?"

"I'm a-sayin' that I were the one to have Sarah the night o' the raid. She never dared tell ye."

"You raped her on purpose that night?" Graham snarled, tight-lipped.

Will nodded insolently. "Took ye five years to guess. Ye're slow, man."

"You bastard." Graham kicked his horse forward and smashed his fist into Will's face. Lucina screamed as Will locked his hands around Graham's throat. Instead of intervening, Will's men edged away. Jasper broke from the Graham ranks and attempted to separate them, but the rest of Graham's men stood stock-still, as if paralyzed by Will's ugly news.

Lucina was sickened by what she'd heard. Although she didn't understand the circumstances, clearly Will had raped Sarah all those years ago, then purposely lied to them all. It was too much for anyone to bear. "Roger, there's a knife in my pouch. Can you get it?"

As Roger fumbled for the knife and cut their bindings, she saw Graham pummel Will, apparently oblivious to Will's hands clenched around his throat or to Jasper trying to break his cousin's grip. "Roger, Will's killing Alex," she said in dismay.

The ropes parted at last. "I'll help Jasper. You get the horses." Roger raced to Jasper's aid.

Lucina blew a piercing whistle. Cygnus burst from the swirling mist, Orpheus at her heels. The pair snorted and tossed their heads as they approached, skittish and unsettled.

"What's wrong, Cygnus?" She caught the mare's head in her hands and stroked her, but she sidestepped, rolling her eyes. Orpheus backed away, stamping. A second later Lucina heard the jingle of harness and thudding of hooves. A mounted company approached.

"Here, Orpheus," she called. As she clambered hastily onto the stallion's back, she noted that the Graham's force had all, to a man, readied their weapons. Lances and swords bristled.

"No, no!" She waved both arms frantically. "Put your weapons away. Whoever's coming will attack the instant they see you're ready to fight."

They ignored her, and she felt as useless as a flea, trying to get their attention with tiny bites. Yet they would be attacked unless they put down their weapons. "Will Mosley, the English are coming and mean to hang you!" she shouted.

Will released his hold on Graham. Startled, Graham stopped bruising Will with his fists. They both stared toward the east.

A force of mounted men burst into the clearing. Their steel morions with combs glinted dully in the morning light.

They carried lowered lances, and the leaders wore the red cross of St. George. It was the English Border warden's party.

"Sir Edward!" Lucina shouted to be heard over the din. "My brother is here, safe . . ."

Another force sprang from the opposite direction, roaring the Scots battle cry, "A Bothwell! A Bothwell."

The Englishmen recognized their attacking enemy and charged. Lucina wheeled Orpheus to dash for cover but was unable to escape. The two companies met around her with a mighty clash.

Confusion reigned in the frenzy of fighting. Caught at the edge of the chaos, Lucina gestured furiously for Roger to mount Cygnus. As he vaulted onto the mare's back, she searched for Graham in the melee. The world around her blurred as men hacked, fought, and bellowed. To her right, Roger stared at the spectacle, seeming as shocked as she.

"Away!" She turned Orpheus, smacking Cygnus on the rump as they moved. The mare squealed and sprang into the wood, all too glad to escape. Praying Cygnus would carry Roger to safety, Lucina turned back to search for Graham.

"Head north, Lucina!" He appeared suddenly, blocking an attacker who came at her.

"You must come with me." She focused on the man who fought her husband. With a gasp she recognized John, Lord Maxwell. The man's eyes burned with savage satisfaction as he wielded his sword. He had found the perfect chance to spill blood in the name of the old Maxwell-Graham feud.

Despite being weaponless, Lucina urged Orpheus forward, trying to reach Graham's side, but fighting men on foot and horseback blocked the way, forcing her back. Orpheus snorted and plunged, maddened by the smell of human blood. A Scotsman suddenly grasped her around the waist and half dragged her from Orpheus's back.

Panicked, she flailed both arms and kicked out with one leg, fighting to break his grip. He released her abruptly. As she thumped back in the saddle, she saw Drummond grappling with the man. Mounted and wielding a knife, the lad had come to her rescue.

She drummed Orpheus's ribs with both heels, and they sprinted to safety, then wheeled around. Drummond still fought her attacker, who slashed at the lad's face with his knife.

"Not his eyes!" She saw blood spurt and Drummond toppled from his horse, shouting for his father. Some paces beyond, Will ignored his son as he battled two Englishmen.

Against all better judgment Lucina fought her way to Drummond using Orpheus as her weapon. The stallion reared and flayed with his deadly shod hooves, scattering men and horses from his path.

"Mount behind me," she shouted as she drew near. Drummond clambered up behind her, Lucina tugging his shirt to help. Her gaze flew to Graham who was mere yards away, fighting off Scots attackers. Maxwells or Bothwells? In the chaos she couldn't tell. She could barely guide Orpheus from the conflict with Drummond clinging to her waist, blood from his wounded face dripping down her back. As they neared the edge of the fighting, his hands tightened on her.

Whipping around, she saw Will wave his sword and charge his horse straight at a sword-wielding man on foot. The Englishman raced forward, and Will decapitated him in a single stroke even as the man's sword sank into the horse's chest. The horse shrieked and crashed to its knees, throwing Will from the saddle.

"God, no." Drummond slumped against her, clearly devastated.

Will raced toward them, pursued by another Englishman with a poleax. "Give me that horse," he demanded. With a savage push, he tried to dislodge Drummond and Lucina. As Drummond stared and clung to her in silence, Orpheus caught Will's scent. With a hatred born of instinct, the stallion attacked.

"Will, behind you!" Lucina warned, restraining Orpheus.

Just in time Will spun and thrust his sword through the man with the poleax.

Lucina urged Orpheus away from the battle. As he moved beyond the fighting, she glimpsed Will grabbing the reins of a riderless English horse. He leaped astride and charged back into battle with a shout of relish.

Lucina bent over Orpheus's neck, struggling not to be ill. She was outraged that Will had sacrificed his horse, then demanded hers. Without a qualm he would have left her and his son on foot in the thick of battle, perhaps even sacrificed Orpheus if the horse had obeyed.

Drummond moaned at intervals, a tormented, animal sound that frightened her.

"Are your eyes unscathed?" She twisted around to examine him, reassured to see the knife had missed his eyes, passing through one eyebrow and across his forehead. He was bleeding copiously. "Are you in pain? Can I help?" she asked.

Drummond pushed away her tentative hand. Hiding his face, he shook with silent sobs.

Knowing he was shamed to weep in her presence, Lucina pressed Orpheus on, putting distance between them and the insanity. The battle had driven pain into her mind like nails through flesh. Over and over she relived the horrifying shriek of Will's horse as it died.

Dazed, she allowed Orpheus to slow as she drew a shaky breath. The unexpected appearance of Bothwell's force, with Maxwell among them, had fueled the clash. And if the English hadn't fought them, Graham would have had to, for Will had meant to keep her and Roger prisoners.

What troubled her most was that Sir Edward would not know Graham had meant to resolve the dispute peaceably. She should not have left the conflict. Yet what could she have done, had she stayed?

Tears tracked down her cheeks as she rode, paying no heed to where they were going. As they crashed through the bracken, she felt Drummond's grip on her waist slacken. For him, the painful encounter with his father, Will's boast of raping Sarah Maxwell, added to his conduct in battle, were all too ugly. His fair skin had whitened with shock.

With one fist she rubbed away her tears, then hugged him. "There, there," she murmured. "I know it hurts. My father died when I was smaller than you. I—"

He recoiled violently from her. His hands fell from his face to reveal anger laced with pain. "But *ma* faither isna dead. Ye ha' nae idea what 'tis like."

No, she admitted, she had no inkling how it felt to be betrayed by the father he'd loved, who went on to prove himself unworthy of respect and loyalty by any standard.

With a grunt, Drummond slid off Orpheus and stumbled away into the woods.

"Drummond, come back." Orpheus halted, but Drummond blundered on, paying her no heed. As he disappeared, swallowed by the green depths, waves of emotion overwhelmed her. Fear for her husband and brother. The terror of the battle and men dying before her eyes as she watched, helpless to intercede. Blinded by a fresh deluge of agony, she bent over Orpheus's neck, clinging to him as if he were the only stable thing left, and sobbed out her heart.

"Dinna move. Ye're ma prisoner, lassie. And yer bonnie horse as weel."

Lucina stiffened at the sound of a male voice. Too frightened to go on crying, she sat up cautiously, rubbed her eyes with her sleeve, and struggled to see, hoping against hope that the voice belonged to an Englishman.

But his accent had been Scots. Her swift assessment proved the dismal fact—he brandished a short ax with curved blade, a weapon preferred by the Scots. She didn't recognize him as one of Graham's men, which meant he belonged either to Bothwell or Maxwell.

Through her own lack of attention, she had ridden east, not north as Graham had told her. And blundered directly into the hands of her husband's sworn foes.

Graham pulled off his steel bonnet in disgust and surveyed the tail of the retreating Scots force. Bothwell must not have liked the way the battle was going to sound the retreat so soon. Hermitage's huge portcullis had creaked open, and the gateway swallowed the last of the Scots, including Will.

Graham searched the clearing, noting that only two of his men were dead. He also wanted reassurance that Lucina had gotten away. Seeing no trace of her, he could only assume she had. The instant he'd seen her with Drummond, he'd understood that the young beast had guided Lucina here, bringing her straight into his father's clutches. Oh, he'd seen Drummond defend Lucina when a Scot tried to grab her. He'd been too far away to help her and was grateful to the lad. But if Drummond had refused to show her the way, she would still be safely at home.

As for his cousin, he was going to capture Will, lock him up, try him for murdering his wife, and see him hung. At last everyone knew who had raped Sarah. It hurt so, he wanted to hide somewhere to lick his wounds in private, but he couldn't.

Pushing aside his pain, he picked out the English Border warden and waved his bonnet to catch his attention. Jasper thrust his sword back in its scabbard and joined him.

"What's the meaning of your presence here, Lord Graham?" Sir Edward Kincaid halted his long-legged courser and saluted in return.

Graham explained his peaceable intention and how it had been foiled, apparently because someone had warned Bothwell of the coming English raid.

Sir Edward's eyes narrowed as he listened. "I noted that the Maxwell chief attacked you," he said grimly. "He had no place here. I might have expected Sir John Carmichael, as the official Scots Border warden, but not Maxwell."

Graham agreed but refrained from saying so. He still seethed at the treachery of the attack. Clearly Maxwell had joined Bothwell solely for the chance to murder Graham, his chief rival for power in the West March. "In any event, Master Cavandish fled north when the fighting started. I would hope he awaits us somewhere in the woods." He hoped Lucina was with Roger as well.

Sir Edward issued brief instructions to his captain, then turned back to Graham. "Let us find him," he said. Wheeling their horses, they found the trail made by a single horse through the woods and followed it north, tracking it to a shady glen.

Cygnus cropped grass on a sunny slope. Nearby, a male figure knelt by a rushing burn. As they drew closer, the man wrung out his handkerchief and applied it to the forehead of another man, propped with his face turned away. The thud of their horses' hooves on the packed earth alerted him to their approach. He rose and ran to greet them.

"Sir Edward, I am most heartily glad to see you!" the lad said.

Graham knew at once he must be Roger Cavandish. From his thick brown hair to his stubborn, jutting jaw, his strong resemblance to Lucina was enough to give him away.

Sir Edward dismounted, and he and Roger embraced as if
they were long-lost friends.

Graham glimpsed the man Roger had been nursing. It
was Drummond Mosley, who gazed up at him apprehen-
sively.

Rage swept through Graham. He ought to be apprehen-
sive, having endangered his wife. Grasping the lad by the
collar, he jerked him to his feet. But as he started to deliver
a blistering reprimand, Roger's kerchief fell aside. A
bloody wound arched to Drummond's temple, dividing his
eyebrow and narrowly missing his eye. Appalled at how
close the lad had come to losing his sight for Lucina, Graham touched the gash. Drummond winced as the wound
bled afresh.

"You need proper bandaging." Diverted from his anger,
he pressed the boy back to his resting place. Then he rummaged in his saddlebags and unearthed a package of ban-
dages and healing salve that Lucina had insisted he bring.

"Permit me, Lord Graham," Roger offered, kneeling by
Drummond. "I'm rather handy with caring for wounds if I
have the supplies."

"What the devil did you think you were doing, guiding
my wife to Hermitage?" Graham demanded as Roger
worked.

Drummond was abject with regret. "Forgive me, Graham. I argued again' her coomin', but she swore we would
save yer life or that of our kin. I told her she shouldna go,
but she gave me a hundred reason she should. I confess"—
he looked embarrassed—"I believed her in the end."

Graham understood exactly what had transpired. The
lassie could badger a shepherd into buying wool. "Never
mind," he said impatiently, hating to let the boy off but
knowing Lucina was to blame. "I want to know how Bothwell heard the English were on their way."

Drummond looked miserable. "Her leddyship wad ha'
managed to deliver Master Cavandish to Sir Edward, save
ma faither wouldna listen to me. Instead of leaving Hermitage when I warned him, he . . ." The lad hesitated and
bent his head. "He told the earl, who called his men to
arms. I tried tae do ma duty by both of ye an' tae her
leddyship, but I failed. I understand if ye wish me tae leave
Castle Graham."

Finished with the bandaging, Roger stood back, and Drummond struggled to his feet, his head bowed in humility, awaiting his sentence.

"I was there," Roger said in a low voice. "He tried to convince Will to leave Hermitage but Will refused. Will also struck him for swearing loyalty to you, Lord Graham. I thought he'd broken his nose, he bled so. I can't respect a man like that."

Graham felt a surge of sympathy for the boy. In all justness, he couldn't condemn Drummond, but this was exactly why he'd meant the lad to remain under lock and key, so he wouldn't have to choose between loyalties. Lucina had refused to listen, which maddened him. Yet he had to admit Lucina's scheme would have succeeded if it hadn't been for Will. "I don't wish you to leave the family," he said gruffly. "I want your help finding her ladyship. Do you know where she is?"

But although Drummond tried his best to help track Lucina and Orpheus after they had parted company, and although Sir Edward and his men helped, they found no trace of her. Lucina had vanished as cleanly as mist before the sun.

Chapter 22

"The English firebrand." John, the eighth Lord Maxwell, hefted his bulk from the chair before the great hall fire and took a slow circuit around Lucina. "We meet again."

Lucina gripped her cloak and tried to hide a shiver. His inspection made her skin crawl. The gloomy hall did nothing to improve her spirits, smelling of rancid meat and smoke. They had ridden a long way after the battle at Hermitage, so this must be Caerlaverock Castle, the Maxwell stronghold in the West Border March. After so long without sleep, she was fainting on her feet. "Why have you brought me here?" she managed to ask.

Maxwell stopped before her and scratched his chin thoughtfully. "Ye're to serve a caution, to guarantee the peace, ye ken."

"You've no need of a hostage. The Grahams will certainly keep the peace now that my brother is free."

"Ye're sure he's free?"

"I assume he . . ." She stopped, realizing Maxwell might have taken Roger prisoner.

"Never assume," he said in the tone of a schoolmaster, scrutinizing her from beneath bushy black brows flecked with white. " 'Tis a dangerous practice. Ye shouldna ha'e been at that battle, either. But Graham women seem tae go where they dinna belong. Sarah did the same."

"You mean Graham's first wife?" She swallowed hard, realizing word had traveled fast. He had apparently heard of Will Mosley's public boasting and was about to regale her with the tale of how it had all come about.

"Sarah thought to stop a Maxwell raid on the Grahams,"

he said, his face twisting with anger as he took a turn around the end of the hall. "Naturally, she learned of it because she was a Maxwell, so she set off in the middle o' the night. When the raid came, she ran oot into the middle o' it and were raped in the dark and the mayhem. Ma innocent cousin. No one ever kent that Will Mosley did it until now. All these years, he an' your bloody Black Graham kept the secret."

"Graham didn't know until Will told him at Hermitage," Lucina protested. "Sarah must have been too shamed to tell him. When Graham found out, he almost killed Will."

Maxwell shook his head. "I'm no' sure I believe yer bloody Black Graham dinna ken, but he finished off my cousin by hating her for what happened. She carried another man's bairn."

Sorrow rushed through Lucina as she fit this new piece into the puzzle of Graham's pain. "Did Sarah die giving birth to the child?" she asked.

"She died a few days after 'twas born. The child, too."

"She may well have died of milk fever," she said gently, feeling a twinge of sympathy for him. "Sadly, many women do. I know Graham loved her and did all he could to care for her."

"He killed her!" Maxwell said with an unexpected vehemence. "The Graham an' nae other. An' I'll have his death in revenge." His shout rose in the great chamber, illuminating another side of the Maxwell-Graham feud—these Borderers, whom she had imagined were so strong, sought revenge because they couldn't bear the pain of an unfortunate but inevitable death.

Suddenly she pitied the aging Maxwell, another man who hurt for those he'd lost, a man without love in his life. Yet that didn't excuse him for joining forces with Bothwell in retaliation. Nor could she understand why he had, since Bothwell was friends with Mosley, who had raped Sarah. It was impossible to understand the morass of confusing relations on the Border and the tangles of hate built over the years.

She could scarce meet Maxwell's gaze, but she knew he was studying her. As if his own family's hurt would lessen if he found ways to pierce her heart.

"So," he said. "Now ye ken what sort o' monster ye've

wed. An' it seems tae me the Black Graham has taken hi'sel' another wife who meddles in men's affairs. Ye'll go the way of Sarah."

"He's not a monster," she snapped. "He's most kind to me, as I believe he was to Sarah. And if you loved your cousin so, why didn't you help her in her time of trouble? You could have seen she had special care to lessen the chance of milk fever."

"Ye dinna ken what ye're sayin'," he exploded. "Any child she bore would ha' been as daft as its sire. Begotten in violence by a lunatic."

"But you didn't know Will was the father until now," she declared. "You're trying to excuse your own bad choices by blaming the trouble on others. Nor am I Sarah, even if I've done something similar to what she once did. I'm different. Do you understand?" It was suddenly of vital importance to her that she be recognized as a different person from Graham's first wife. She would not be known as "the second wife, who went the same way as the first."

"I wonder." He stepped forward, so close, she could smell the foul odor of his breath. "How would ye behave to yer husband if ye'd been ravished by another man and carried his child?"

He pulled her roughly to him and fastened his big, wet mouth on hers. His breath nauseated her as he held her body against his bloated frame.

Lucina jerked her knee toward his crotch in an attempt to break free, but he released her quickly, stepping beyond her reach.

"Bitch o' the de'il," he cursed her with a hatred that curdled her blood. "Wait in the chamber ye're assigned, an' dinna remind me ye're here, else I decide to return Will's favor to Sarah."

Exhausted, Lucina stood, shoulders drooping, quite ready to go wherever directed. If she didn't sleep soon, she felt sure she would splinter like a shell hit by a falling rock.

Two men-at-arms guided her up winding stairs to a bed-chamber and locked her inside. As she collapsed on the bed, her last thought was of Orpheus and the devil who had forced her to leave him in the stable. She had refused to be separated from her stallion until, at his wit's end, one of her captors had threatened to blow off her horse's head with a caliver.

She had capitulated, hating the man for using her love against her.

As she drifted toward sleep, she understood how the Grahams and the Maxwells could hate one another, because they were doing everything in their power to teach her to hate as well.

One day and a hard ride later, Graham stood among ancient trees and stared up at the leafy canopy arching overhead. These same trees had sheltered him of old when he had studied the stronghold of Caerlaverock, imagining the pure, forbidden beauty of Sarah Maxwell, devising a plan to woo her into his arms.

Now, years later, Lucina had been placed in that same chamber, as a lure to draw him in. Maxwell had insisted he wanted Lucina as a caution the day he'd first laid eyes on her. But what he really wanted was her land.

With a shrug Graham acknowledged the irony of life. He'd lost his first wife to Border strife. It only remained for him to lose his second as well.

The ghost of Sarah, her smiling face as she greeted him at the window of Caerlaverock, formed in his mind, forcing moisture to his eyes. Lucina would be waiting in Sarah's former chamber. A trap, pure and simple. And because he had no choice, he would walk into it, but not with eyes closed. He would use stealth and cunning. He'd sent his main force back to Castle Graham and the neighboring environs. If he could avoid endangering men, he would.

He thought of his own risks at Hermitage, then of the risks he was prepared to take here, and didn't care. Death was inevitable, but at least he had a cause he believed in. He must rescue the woman who gave purpose to his life.

Lucina warily opened her eyes to the light of morning, uncertain where she was. She felt sore all over, as if someone had been pummeling her. Her spirit felt equally bruised as she sat up.

Stars above, she'd hoped yesterday had been a bad dream, but the events of the past day were all too real. The pleasure had come during her feverish sleep of exhaustion; she'd dreamed of the russet colt born to Gellie. Grown to adulthood, muscular in proportion, he had taken her soaring across a waving sea of green. The fresh air, tangy from sea salt, had teased her nostrils. This was her land. Hers! The purple-brown hills of this ancient land welcomed her. Her destiny lay here.

But at last she turned back, knowing she had to. The Black Graham awaited her at the paddock, a man who made her a prisoner. Using her emotion, he wrapped it like a rope around one hand, reeling her in, drawing her body to his.

His kisses sent hope shooting through her blood, like gem-sparks sprayed from iron-shod hooves striking stone. The friction of their mating heated her love for him. Curve against hard muscle. Ivory flesh against bronze. She mounted to fulfillment, as if riding Pegasus, soaring above earth into the spiritual realm. And lying in his arms, she knew she loved him, would lay down her life for him or all she held dear.

Would he do the same for her? Despite his inability to speak of love, she knew he would. He would risk his life to free her from this place.

She pushed off the bed and went to the window. The water of the moat shimmered two levels below, standing between her and freedom. She wrestled with the window latch and jerked it open, then leaned as far out the window as she dared. Sitting on Solway Firth, Caerlaverock possessed thick curtain walls. There would be no easy escape from this place.

Discouraged, she went to see if the washbasin pitcher contained water. With time on her hands, she might as well wash.

"Ye're not gang up there, are ye?" Jasper asked.

Graham studied the forbidding red stone of the triangular keep. As a lad of eighteen, full of the devil's own brashness, he'd climbed to Sarah's window, succeeding out of sheer bravado. But he doubted his body was as adept at finding footholds in vertical rock walls as it had once been. Little about him was the same as it had been over ten years ago.

"They'll be waiting for ye," Jasper worried aloud. "Ye know that. 'Twould be disaster to go."

"I promised not to go until Maxwell departs," he said aloud.

"I'm to be content with that?" Jasper groused. "At least let me distract 'em."

Graham grinned at him wolfishly. "You have something in mind?"

Jasper swatted a fly on his shoulder. "How much sil'er did ye bring?"

Graham frowned at him. "Why would you be wanting my silver?"

A smile split Jasper's face. "Tae buy a few tuns o' good French wine."

Graham smiled slowly. "You're going to get the garrison drunk."

"As lords," Jasper agreed. "Save I ha'ena decided how to get it in to them."

"Wenches," Graham said promptly. "Know any hereabouts?"

"Ane or more," Jasper admitted modestly.

Graham rubbed his unshaven cheeks thoughtfully. "I like your plan. Tell the women to present the wine as a gift from Bothwell. And Jasper, send in a churchman around midnight. He can marry all the couples who are still conscious. Mayhappen even a few who are not. Maxwell will be furious to find half his fighting men wed. Lucina's escape won't be noticed at once."

Jasper chortled, pleased with the plan.

With the scheme settled, a lengthy pause stretched between them, which Graham broke at last. "Did you speak to Arthur, as I asked?"

Jasper rubbed his nose, tugged his gray whiskers, and frowned. "I follow my orders."

"How soon will he show her ladyship's deed to the lawyer. When will we know?"

"In a sennight," Jasper muttered, unable to meet Graham's gaze. "Mayhap less." He hesitated, looking as if words struggled within him for release.

"What?" Graham snapped, then regretted his harshness. This one follower had never questioned him since he'd become laird and chief, had stood behind him, offering the

gift of his simple faith. "What is it, Jasper?" he asked
more gently.

Jasper looked embarrassed. " 'Twill break her leddyship's heart if you do this, Graham."

"If the deed is false, she needs to know it, as do I,"
Graham said testily. "It seems to me that you, Arthur,
Colin, and I don't know how many others, have become
remarkably concerned about her ladyship's feelings since I
wed her."

"So we have." Jasper sounded defensive. " 'Tis right
comfortin' to have a leddy bringing cheer to the castle
again."

Graham squared his shoulders. "Then, you might credit
me for bringing her in the first place, Jasper. And she
mustn't languish in Maxwell's hands. So stop whining and
do your part." He rummaged in his pouch and produced
several pieces of silver.

Jasper took the money but refused to take the hint to
leave. "I'm nae complainin' for mesel'. But she has her
dreams. Ye wouldna want tae destroy those."

Graham shot him a sharp glance. "I had mine as well
once. I had to learn the hard ways of the world."

Jasper mounted his hobby and shook his head mournfully. "Ye had yer dreams. So ye know how it feels when
an innocent heart full of faith breaks."

The noonday sun shone wanly between spates of rain
outside the window of Lucina's prison. Time crawled forward like a slug. Lucina shivered as she imagined Maxwell
playing the slug, a trail of slime following wherever he slithered. She managed a sip of sour beer, then, vowing to keep
up her strength, forced a cold bannock cake down her
throat.

She had discarded the idea of jumping out the window
into the moat, for she couldn't tell how deep the water was.
What other choices were left?

She knelt on the polished wood floor and, using her hairpin, probed the door's lock. Finding the mechanism, she
pressed hard and felt it give. She pressed harder, and the
hairpin snapped.

She cursed with frustration. Stars above. Some locks
could be picked easily but not this one. Discarding the bro-

ken hairpin, she glanced around the chamber, deciding it must have been unoccupied before she arrived. No personal belongings lay about, nor were there any signs that the place was lived in.

Whose room had this been? The beauty of the bed and window hangings suggested a woman's chamber, but the bed hangings had yellowed, hinting that they were old. Even its pattern of embroidered bluebells was faded.

Closing her eyes, Lucina remembered the field of bluebells near Castle Graham, the flowers nodding their bonnie heads in the sunlight. A fierce love of the land had welled up within her during those first days as she'd ridden the hills and moors. She'd loved Scotland at first sight. But the land was fraught with strife that led to battles. Would she ever be able to claim her property?

Discouraged by the unlikelihood of that dream, she forced her eyes open and once more searched the room for a tool to pick the lock. A portrait on the wall caught her eye. A beautiful young woman with eyes the color of the bluebells gazed at her from the painting. Who was she? Bonnie Mary? Graham's Sarah?

The portrait offered no clue to the answer. It wasn't signed or dated. Little of the subject's gown and no jewels showed. The soft curls clustered across her forehead and coronet of braids hinted at no particular year. But for some reason, Lucina imagined she must be Bonnie Mary Maxwell.

A sadness fell over Lucina as she gazed at the girl. She was dead now, and had not, from the gossip, died under happy circumstances.

Lucina caught herself and returned to her search. Best get on with her task rather than feed fear. She opened a coffer and removed a blanket to find a pair of brass candleholders. Next to them lay a book bound in leather, no title on its spine. Its brittle, yellowed pages were covered with the delicate tracery of handwriting, as fine as a spiderweb. Someone's personal diary.

My end is near. I ken it. On the morrow I am forced to wed Angus Graham, and I'm sare afraid. I went tae the smithy, pretending tae need a new shoe for Sheltie, but Duncan had been sent away. Faither has guessed

*my interest in the smith's lad and removed the tempta-
tion from my reach. I can only pray my beloved friend
has not died for his part in teaching my heart to reject
Angus Graham. Yet knowing Faither, chances that
Duncan is well are few. As God is my witness, I never
meant to injure Duncan, but I have . . . My weakness,
my foolish yearning for love, has destroyed us both.*

Page by page, Lucina glided through the progression of
passion between the girl and her forbidden lover—the initial pleasure of hands touching in the dark during a night-
time search for a lost scarf, the first tentative exploration
of lips, the wild ecstasies of stolen kisses melted into the
tragic exchange of words of love. Yet needs remained un-
fulfilled as the brave lad refused to deflower his laird's
daughter.

Tears slipped from Lucina's eyes as the story continued
to its heartrending, inevitable end. The writer had wed the
chief of the Grahams, a man known for his violent temper
and cruel hand with enemies and kin alike. The writing
broke off just before the wedding, leaving the rest of the
pages blank. With suddenly impatient fingers, Lucina
turned to the front of the book. Surely there would be a
name. She found it, as expected, the beautiful script washing across the page.

Mary Katherine Maxwell.

Feeling Mary's pain, Lucina collapsed into a chair and
sobbed openly. Here, in the girl's chamber, she felt the
sorrow, as if a ghostly presence begged her to understand.

Though the rest of the story was unwritten, Lucina knew
it by heart. She had pieced together its fragments. Angus's
claiming of Mary as a peace prize to terminate war. Her
bearing of the Graham heir, her death some years later,
reportedly by her husband's hand. What irony that Mary
had unwillingly perpetuated hate between the families
when she'd been meant to heal a breech.

Lucina raised her gaze to the portrait and met the blue
eyes of Bonnie Mary. She imagined how Angus Graham
must have coveted that beautiful face with the stunning
sea-colored eyes. Had he really killed her in one of his
famous fits of rage?

Lucina put down the book, unable to avoid the likelihood. Her heart felt as wrung out as an old shirt, boiled and twisted in so many washings, it could never again be pure.

Picking up the book again, she flipped to the back pages. All blank. She turned them more slowly, hoping for something. A stray word or mark that would illuminate the truth of how she had died.

But even as she searched, she recognized the futility of it. Disaster in life befell some and not others, with no explanation as to why.

She found nothing more until the inside back cover. A saying had been penned in the same, neat hand. Eagerly she focused on it, hoping she had found the key to her questions.

Love has nae law.

Chapter 23

How could Lady Ashley's favorite saying also be Mary Maxwell's favorite, even to the point that she wrote it in her diary? This question led Lucina to consider in a new light many pieces of information that before had seemed separate and random. But suddenly she wondered if they didn't all add up. Key in her mind were the odd things Isabel had said since Lucina's arrival at Castle Graham. Although Isabel's grasp on the present was often tenuous, might her memory of the past be intact?

From the first, Isabel had mistaken Lucina for her sister Mary. At their first meeting, Isabel had referred to the chief's locking her in her chamber again. Lucina had since learned that Angus Graham had locked his wife Mary in the tower chamber often. Another time, Isabel had insisted the chief would beat her again, an obvious reference to Angus's abusive behavior. And on the night Lucina had prepared for her escape from Castle Graham, Isabel had said she supported her leaving because she had never been happy. What if she had been referring to Mary's happiness, not Lucina's?

Isabel had also removed Lady Ashley's Bible from Lucina's chamber, then returned it to her at her departure, calling it "our" Bible. Had she taken the Bible from the tower chamber, mistaking it for the one she and Mary had shared many years ago? What if she was not mistaken. What if it was indeed the same book?

If it was . . . Lucina stared into space, stunned by where her conclusions took her. Might Mary Maxwell have run away with Isabel's aid?

One night in the great hall, a maid had called her Mistress Cavandish, and Isabel had taken her aside and told her to "settle on one name and be done." At their first meeting in the tower, Isabel had called her Mary, but when Lucina had corrected her, Isabel had agreed to "call her any name she wished and keep her secret." Could Mary have changed her name when she ran away?

Lucina scrambled for the Bible, tucked away in her pouch. She produced the palm-size book with brown leather flaking from the spine and opened it. The name Lady Katherine Ashley was inscribed on the thick paper of the first page.

Opening Mary's diary, she held the two side by side and compared the signatures. The loops in the *K* of Katherine appeared fairly similar. Yet the slant of each set of writing differed, and Lady Ashley's was shaky, a product of her friend's age and unsteady hands.

Frustrated by the lack of a clear answer, Lucina returned to the portrait. Were those Katherine Ashley's blue eyes gazing out at her, so serene and calm? Was that her determined chin and curling hair? Lady Ashley had been seventy years old at her death. Even if they were the same person, few physical features would linger in the older woman to link her to the younger.

Lucina struggled with the idea and found more reasons to reject than accept it. Bonnie Mary had died. Her body lay buried in the kirkyard.

She had to be imagining things. It wasn't unusual. Her mother and elder sister often said she was given to peccadilloes of the most outrageous sort. She closed the Bible and put it away with a sigh, knowing she must get on with her escape plans. But instead of replacing Mary's book in the coffer, she placed it tenderly in her pouch. She would treasure it and say prayers for Mary. Maxwell would never know it was gone.

As she continued her search of the coffer, she found some thin metal strips, apparently from a dismantled corset. Lucina took up one shiny strip eagerly. It might be just the thing.

Kneeling at the door, she inserted the strip into the keyhole and probed for the locking mechanism. As she worked, she heard footfalls in the passage beyond. A key thrust into the lock, clashing with her strip. She yanked it back and stumbled to her feet.

With a lunge, she thrust the strip beneath the counterpane on the bed just as the door opened.

A guard studied her from the doorway, his little eyes thinned to suspicious slits. He took her elbow and guided her down the corridor to Lord Maxwell's private cabinet. Lucina felt as if she gazed into a bottomless abyss as she faced John, Lord Maxwell, who had threatened to ravish her mere hours ago.

Graham knelt behind a screen of briars, watching Caerlaverock Castle. Seagulls sought their nests as the dense fog of evening floated inland. He glanced at the man kneeling beside him. Of the dozen who had volunteered to accompany him on this mission, the one who surprised him most was Roger Cavandish. A free man once more, he had insisted on joining them to rescue his sister. Graham admired him for that, but he admired him just as much for riding all day yesterday from Hermitage in the gray drizzle without complaining. Despite having endured long days as a prisoner, he exhibited a plucky spirit that inspired the others. If Graham had been in a similar situation, he wasn't sure he'd be nearly so game.

A rider emerged from the trees, leading several scores of men. They crossed the flat sea plain leading to the castle and approached the gate.

"Who would that be at this time of day?" Roger asked.

"The Earl of Bothwell. He's easily recognizable by his red hair, if not by his coat of arms."

Roger studied the castle intently, his open, honest face reminding Graham of Lucina. Like his sister's, Roger's eyes were lit with laughter in all but the worst moments. This was such a moment. Roger's concern for his sister was clearly etched on his youthful brow.

"You don't suppose he followed us here, do you?" he asked.

Graham watched as Bothwell summoned the castle guard and the drawbridge was lowered to admit him. "I doubt it. He has other things on his mind. He's been outlawed for treason, as has John Maxwell. And when men have a thing in common, they generally join forces to plan."

"Who proclaims a man outlawed?" Roger shifted from one knee to the other, ignoring his soiled netherstocks.

"King James."

"Are they planning a revolution?"

"I wouldn't call it that, but I'd venture he's planning some measure to convince the king to forgive his trespasses and bring him back to favor. He's tried such measures before, but they came to naught."

"The king hasn't punished him for this 'treason,' if it was treason?"

"You understand he used to be Jamie's friend and one of his chief advisers. I believe that because of their past friendship, the king is hoping he'll lie low and cause no more trouble, but that's not Bothwell's way."

"And you say Luce is in that chamber?"

"Likely so. Look, the window is open." Sure enough, the window was ajar, suggesting that someone was in residence. "We'll climb up and look in on her come nightfall. But first we'll wait to see what Maxwell and Bothwell do next. Frankly, I'm hoping they'll leave soon."

Roger nodded, looking as eager as Graham felt to get on with the rescue.

The dim chamber to which the guard guided Lucina reeked of small beer. It contrasted unpleasantly to Graham's tower chamber at Castle Graham, which smelled of saddle leather and fresh air from the windows thrown wide. She regretted her complaints of his untidiness now.

The florid-faced chief rose and lumbered to greet her. Anxiety ground in her belly as she wondered what was to come.

"You ate the food I sent up this morning." He smiled broadly, displaying darkened teeth. "I am pleased my humble hospitality suits you. I trust you slept well."

Baffled by his congeniality, Lucina narrowed her gaze, unable to find an apt reply. Though his threats of yesterday had frightened her, at least she'd known where she stood. She had no idea how to respond to his polite inquiries about her sleep.

He appeared unruffled by her silence. "Now that you have rested and dined, I wish your assistance, lovely Lucie," he said affably. "Pray have a seat."

She didn't like being called Lucie. Nor did she like the dangerous-looking antlers bristling from the chimneypiece. Casting them a nervous glance, she stepped reluctantly toward the seat indicated. "What could I possibly do to—"

"Hold yer tongue an' sit." He thrust her toward the chair with little gentleness.

Shaken by his sudden force, Lucina slid into the leather chair, heart in her throat.

He swept away some papers and set a clean sheet of vellum before her. "Ye're gang to prepare a legal document, Lucie. I'll tell ye what to write. Choose a quill."

As she studied the array of pens laid out beside an ink pot and considered how to avoid following his orders, someone tapped at the chamber door.

A male servant entered at Maxwell's order and announced the Earl of Bothwell had arrived.

Lucina shrank in her chair. Bothwell was the last person she wanted to see.

"Francis." Maxwell boomed a hearty greeting as the earl strode into the chamber.

Lucina held her breath, hoping the earl wouldn't notice her as the pair exchanged news with a respect and civility she could hardly believe possible of two rogues.

Bothwell stripped off his gloves and planted himself before the fire to warm his backside. "I'm for the Falklands," he announced. "Ye coomin'?"

Maxwell nodded, his expression speculative. "How many men ha'e ye put in the saddle?"

"Several hundred. Will is raising the Border."

"I'm coomin'," he said. "But I ha' a piece o' business first." He jerked his head toward Lucina.

Bothwell's face lit up as if he had just met a favorite acquaintance at a revel. "The fair Lucie," he crowed. "How is it ye happen here?" To Maxwell he added, "She's a landed heiress, ye ken."

"So you said at Hermitage. And I intend to have that land," Maxwell announced.

"Ye gang to make her a widow?" Bothwell asked, lifting his eyebrows. At Maxwell's surprised expression, he rapped himself on the head. "Och, how absentminded I am. The Graham wed her since I saw ye last."

"He wed her? After ma cousin?" Maxwell's incredulous

expression said fathoms to Lucina. Clearly he had thought her the Black Graham's mistress, not his wife. But Maxwell rallied quickly. "If she's wed, she mun write this paper fer me. Fair Lucie, pick up that quill and write, 'I do hereby solemnly swear, in the presence of two witnesses . . .' You may be one of them," he said magnanimously to Bothwell, "to sell to John Archibald, Lord Maxwell—"

"I don't agree to sell my land," she interrupted sullenly, now clear on his intent.

"Consider the alternative," he said merrily. "Ye could be widowed and wed to me."

"You've wished my husband dead for years, but he isn't."

"He will be." He narrowed his gaze, his eyes crafty and cunning. Offering no further explanation, he began dictating again. "To sell to John Archibald, Lord Maxwell, a total of . . ." He paused. "How much land is there?"

She didn't want to tell him anything about her deed from Lady Ashley, but talk delayed the writing. "Two hundred hectares. But I don't know where it is. I've never seen it." She turned to Bothwell. "Your lordship, I pray you tell me what became of my brother at Hermitage."

"I haven't the least idea," Bothwell said without a shred of concern.

She frowned. "Is he your"—she struggled for a suitable term—"guest?"

Bothwell swung back to Maxwell and engaged him in discourse, as if determined to torture her. She concluded that if Bothwell had triumphed at Hermitage and made Roger his prisoner, he would have boasted of it. The chances were good that Roger had escaped with Graham.

She celebrated in silence as the pair speculated about her land. But a moment later they were discussing their journey again.

"Are you leaving Caerlaverock," she interrupted.

Maxwell fastened his gaze on her once more. "Aye, but I'm leavin' plenty o' men to guard ye, so dinna try anything. When you're widowed, I'll wed ye for yer widow's jointure and yer land."

"Aren't you wed already?" she asked, ignoring his threat.

His face saddened. "I miss ma wife. She died o' fever some years ago."

Genuine pain radiated from him, and Lucina thought she caught a glimpse of the man he might have been—gentle with a loving heart—but he quickly recovered his hardened stance. "I am a respectable widower, as well as a laird and chief. More than suitable for a merchant-class female. Yer land would join well wi' mine."

Lucina caught the gleam of desire in his eyes and suddenly she remembered the nickname Isabel had used. John Archibald "Bell the Cat" Maxwell had undoubtedly been so dubbed due to the pleasure he took in toying with his prey.

She must try a new tack. "Tell me, my lord, if you learned that Mary Maxwell had never been murdered by the Graham chief but had died a natural death, would the feud end?"

His calculating expression never altered. "O' course, but she was murdered, sure."

"But I believe she wasn't," Lucina protested.

Maxwell snorted in disbelief.

"Truly. I've discovered evidence that suggests she left Scotland and went to live in England." Eagerly she pulled out Mary's diary and the Bible. If she could only convince him it was true. He might even know some details that would validate the story. "Pray examine these two signatures. You will see certain similarities."

With a show of reluctance, Maxwell squinted at the pages. "This was my great-aunt's Bible," he said, "and this was her diary. They're not for you to carry away, as you please."

"I brought the Bible with me from England," Lucina insisted. "It was given to me by—"

He smiled indulgently. "Such a tale you spin."

"Truly. The Bible was given to me by Lady Katherine Ashley, and since you recognize it, 'tis possible she was Mary Maxwell. If we knew for certain, wouldn't that end the feud?"

" 'Twould settle a major difficulty," he said begrudgingly, "but 'tis nae more than a wild idea." With that, he snatched the two books from her and placed them in a wooden casket on his desk.

She stared at the casket. She'd tried to prove something but instead lost her evidence.

Clearly Lord Maxwell didn't want it proven that Mary Maxwell and Katherine Ashley were the same person. He preferred his hateful feud.

"How much longer do we have to wait?" Roger Cavandish demanded of Graham. The lad paced the small clearing from which they were watching Caerlaverock. He stopped periodically to stare at the fortress, then resumed his pacing.

"Sit down," Graham said impassively, never taking his gaze from the fortress. "Everyone will know we've been here if you wear a path in the ground."

"You'd be pacing, too, if it were your sister in there."

"It's my wife in there," Graham snapped. "I have a higher stake in this than you."

Roger grimaced. "Sorry. I can't quite get used to the idea of Luce married. She turned down so many offers . . . Oh, sorry. Shouldn't say that."

Graham's curiosity overcame his good judgment. "Didn't she ever fancy anyone?"

Roger grinned at him. "Horses, yes. Men, never. Oh, she had male friends. She played with the lads and me in Dorset when we were growing up. You should have seen her, running barefoot at the cove and the marsh, riding her horse bareback without even a bridle."

Graham imagined Lucina, young and rambunctious, galloping free like a young filly. "I can well believe she did those things as a girl, but what of when she was older?"

"She was always with her horses." Roger waxed nostalgic. "She stole her first one. Did she tell you?"

Graham nodded.

"That's Luce for you. She'd do it again if she thought she had a good reason." Roger grinned and rolled his eyes. "Did she tell you about the trick we played on the local squire's wife? Nasty, stuck-up thing, she was. Well, Madam Smythson thought she was too good for the rest of us. Always hinting at some important family connections. Turns out she was the daughter of an earl, but handsome is as handsome does, and she was most unkind to many of the families of our town. So at one of our family revels, Luce put an ass in the ladies' tiring room, dressed in a hat and cloak. Took care to take Madam Smythson there early in the evening, telling her there was someone she ought to see as she thought they were related. Madam Smythson went in alone, all eager, hoping to meet one of her noble relatives.''

Graham's unaccustomed grin was so wide, it hurt his mouth.

Roger chucked as he expanded on the details. ''Charles and I, that's my older brother, were hiding under a table, watching. Madam saw the ass and shrieked, then pretended to faint, but as there was no one to impress with her vapors or to come to her rescue, she had to get up again or lie there all night. When she did, the ass brayed like the very devil and let loose the mightiest pile of manure you've ever seen.''

Graham laughed aloud. How he enjoyed these Cavandishes, with their sense of humor and perpetual optimism. ''How old was Lucina at the time of this marvelous escapade?''

''Twelve, I'd guess. I was six and laughed so hard, I wet myself. The old witch heard me chortling, of course, and dragged me out from under the table by one ear. Charles slipped away, but Luce rescued me. She always did—''

''Shhhh. Look.'' Graham pointed out the movement at Lucina's window. As they watched, a man leaned out the window, surveying the wall below. Then he turned to study the overhang of the wall above.

''What's he doing?'' Roger whispered.

''Checking to see if I've arrived yet.''

''They're expecting you?''

''Of course. They've put Lucina in that chamber on purpose. It's where I first courted Sarah.''

There was no escaping Maxwell's evil plan.

Lucina wrote the words he dictated. Slowly. Sloppily. Delaying by pretending she couldn't spell the words.

He shouted at her, cuffed her, and made her start again.

When she finally finished, he dried the ink with sand from the caster, then snatched the paper from the desk. ''Excellent.'' He surveyed the words a final time, then favoring her with a grin, slipped the paper into a pouch at his waist.

Lucina waited in silence for the man who would guide her back to Mary's chamber as Bothwell and Maxwell settled by the window, their tones heating in anger at someone called Jamie who lived at the Falklands. She caught references to "havin' our own again else see him dead."

"Who owns the Falklands?" she asked the man who marched her back to her chamber. "And where is it?"

"Falklands Palace belongs to King Jamie," he said readily as he opened her door. " 'Tis north o' Edinburgh, across the Forth."

Lucina added the information to the other things she knew about Maxwell and Bothwell. Both had once been in positions of power under the king before being outlawed for treason. Unable to reclaim their former power, the men were clearly seeking revenge. Mayhap they even intended to take the throne for themselves, she realized. Either way, she couldn't do anything about it, locked in this chamber under strict guard.

Some hours later, drunken songs and laughter from Maxwell's men below stairs rang in Lucina's head as she worked at the lock with her metal strip.

The castle lacked its leaders. Earlier, she had seen Bothwell and Maxwell ride east, followed by so many men she couldn't count them all. Since then she had worked at the lock with unflagging patience. A peep through the keyhole had told her no one remained posted outside her door. If the mice had decided to play in the cat's absence, her guard must have joined them.

Suddenly the lock clicked. The handle turned. Too nervous to be joyful yet, Lucina opened the door, slipped to the stairwell, and peered down. No one down there, either. Nothing but the infernal din from below. Slowly, pausing often to listen, she descended the spiral stairs.

On top of the crenellated roof of Caerlaverock, Graham tied his rope to one of the upright stone protrusions of the parapet and pitched it out down the side of the castle, checking the big knots placed for grips.

"You're going down on that?" Roger asked, eyeing it dubiously.

"Certainly." Graham cast him an amused glance. "But you needn't climb down if Lucina is awaiting us in the chamber. I'll just bring her up."

Roger eyed the moat below. "It doesn't trouble me, but Luce hates heights."

"She'll have to manage."

Graham grasped the rope and prepared to descend. He suddenly felt eighteen again as he slipped over the projection, satisfied to know he was still spry enough to make the descent. He found one foothold, then another until he reached the open window, shoved it wide with one foot, and swung into the room.

He'd done it. Now for his reward—an embrace from his beautiful wife.

Except the chamber was empty.

Dumbfounded, he scanned it. She had to be here. She'd been locked in.

But the door stood open, looking out into an empty stairwell. The chamber contained nothing but Bonnie Mary's portrait on the wall. She looked so like his Sarah, his heart ached. The chamber was just as he remembered it. Full of the pain of memories. Overwhelming loss filled him once more.

And now Lucina was missing. Loss and more loss.

Chapter 24

Lucina crept down the stairs, feeling as jittery as a filly wearing a saddle for the first time. As she inched into the deserted passage at the bottom, sounds of revelry poured from what she assumed must be the great hall. If only she could reach Maxwell's chamber without being seen.

A man-at-arms staggered into view from the hall, entwined with a woman who wobbled on her legs like a top. His eyes bugged in surprise to see Lucina, and she dodged back into the stairwell. Her heart wedged in her throat, she flattened against the wall and waited to be caught.

A door slammed. Had the man decided to forget he'd seen her, choosing time with his doxy instead? Stars above, she hoped so, though she wondered who was in charge at Caerlaverock to allow such a thing. The entire garrison must be besotted with drink.

Peering around the corner, she tried to decide which door the man had taken. The one to Maxwell's chamber? Or the one she guessed led to the courtyard?

Every nerve in her body jangled like bells in a tower gone mad. Mayhap she had gone mad, putting such store in a Bible and diary. But she simply must retrieve them before she attempted an escape.

Convinced the man and his doxy were gone, she tiptoed down the passage. A tremendous crash from the great hall froze her to the spot. The rattle of falling metal followed, like a rain of steel bonnets upset on a stone floor. Shouts of disapproval rose above the din. Realizing that no one could hear her with the noise, Lucina pushed open the door to Maxwell's chamber and looked in. Fortune was with her. It was deserted.

Dodging inside, she closed the door and scrambled for the casket on Maxwell's worktable, where he'd put the Bible and diary. The lid refused to budge.

Anguished, she clawed at the metal latch. It couldn't be locked. But the lid stubbornly refused to open, and the box was too large and unwieldy to carry with her. She must find the key.

Urgently she yanked out the small drawer in the table and riffled through its contents. The drawer refused to divulge the object of her desire. She slammed it shut and scanned the chamber, her gaze alighting on another box resting on the worktable. Quills, ink bottles, and the sand caster sat inside. No key. Stars above, she must find it in the next few minutes or be caught.

Inside Sarah's chamber, Graham crept from the window to the door and looked into the stairwell. As no guard was posted outside the chamber, he guessed the man had yielded to the temptation of wine and women. If so, had he taken Lucina with him below stairs?

He swore beneath his breath at the thought of the besotted brutes touching Lucina. He'd purposely gotten them drunk, but he hadn't meant Lucina to be included in their debauchery.

The thought reminded him of when Sarah had been caught in Will's night of debauchery. The old agony returned. Once he'd known Sarah was missing, he'd ridden like the devil, chased by the nightmare of not knowing where she'd gone. The instant he heard of the Maxwell raid, he'd known instinctively she had hoped to stop it. When he'd reached the raided village, he had learned the worst.

Since then, the worst always haunted him. Now it returned, taking him into its heartless grip. Death had robbed him of Sarah. It must not do the same to Lucina.

Graham returned to the window to instruct Roger, then pounded down the stairs, not caring who heard him. No sign of Lucina. Loud snatches of song came from the great hall.

Given the choice, he knew Lucina would go to Orpheus.

He should check the stable. Flinging open the door leading to the courtyard, he charged out, determined to find her if it meant fighting every man in the Maxwell garrison to the death.

Lucina pulled Maxwell's books from their shelves, searching for the missing key. Nothing. She searched the drawers of two more small tables. Still no key.

Her time was running out, and instead of escaping with Orpheus, she was searching for a miserable little key she might never find. But the Bible was hers.

She searched every pocket of the garments in a clothes-press. Still no key. She pulled up every cushion in the chamber and felt under it. Only crumbs and balls of lint. As she replaced the last cushion on a footstool and straightened, she bumped her head on the chimneypiece.

She rubbed the sore spot on her head, thinking the mantel edge was certainly sharp. Turning to look, she found a tiny hook driven into the wood. Dangling from the hook was a key.

Grasping it, Lucina dived for the box and unlocked it. Relief swept through her as she secured the two little books in her pouch, then moved to the window.

Unlatching the glass pane, she swung open the window. The courtyard appeared empty. Praying the stables would also be empty, she climbed onto the sill and made the easy jump.

Graham stood in the stables, dirk drawn, expecting opposition, but the place was deserted. As he moved deeper into the gloom, a horse nickered, then thrust its head over the low door of a stall and shoved him hard.

Even as he stumbled, he recognized the horse. "Red Rowan, you're here!" He embraced the stallion, who nuzzled him roughly, clearly overjoyed to see him. Relieved but also frustrated, Graham leaned back and scolded his friend. "Why did you behave for that ruffian cousin of mine? Just because you've known him since you were a colt, you weren't to trust him." He rubbed Rowan's poll where he especially liked it. "I should have taught you to bite off his arm." Slipping into the stall, he ran his hands over the sleek coat and found partially healed spur gashes marring Rowan's sides. Will had no doubt enjoyed leaving his mark on Graham's horse.

Just as bad, Red Rowan's presence meant Will had left the horse after running him to exhaustion, taken a fresh animal, and raced off on another insane errand. Could he have taken Lucina with him?

The answer lay in whether Orpheus was here or not. A swift search revealed the huge black stallion, several stalls down. Lucina must still be here, for she wouldn't leave without Orpheus.

Graham slammed one fist against the wall, damning the Maxwell garrison all to hell if they had her in the great hall. It meant he must confront them and do battle. But first he would have Orpheus ready and waiting for her at the gate.

Filled with a renewed urgency, Graham led Red Rowan and Orpheus from their stalls. For once, the two stallions tolerated each other, as if they understood the dire need. Keeping an eye on the pair, Graham edged to the tack room and nabbed a bridle. He slipped the bridle on Red Rowan, adjusted the straps to fit, then returned to the tack room for a saddle. No wild, bareback rides for him. He intended to ride Red Rowan straight into the great hall, find Lucina, pull her up behind him, and spring for the gate.

With Red Rowan saddled and a lead clipped to Orpheus, Graham mounted and headed for the triangular courtyard. As they quit the stable, Graham spied a gowned figure at the gatehouse crouched over the winch that worked the drawbridge. The portcullis was up, the drawbridge halfway down. Upon hearing the commotion, the woman leaped to her feet.

Lucina! The rush of relief at seeing her left Graham breathless. Orpheus whinnied with joy and lunged toward his mistress. Graham followed.

"Alex!" A welcoming smile lit Lucina's face.

"Don't stop." He gestured at the winch. "Let the bridge down."

As if suddenly remembering the task, she fell to cranking with a will.

The drawbridge slowly lowered. They were going to make it, Graham thought.

A soft scrape accompanied by a muffled giggle behind him announced company.

Swinging around, he discovered a Maxwell man-at-arms weaving drunkenly in the stable entry. A female leaned against him, her eyes glazed from drink.

" 'Tis the prisoner. To arms!" The drunk staggered toward the great hall, shouting the alarm.

Panic clawed at Graham as he urged Red Rowan closer to the gate. Lucina cranked furiously. Orpheus stood at her shoulder, blowing anxiously through his nostrils.

Faster, Graham prayed. *Faster.*

As the drawbridge hit solid ground, the door to the hall burst open. Men poured out and milled in confusion, fumbling for swords and battle-axes. Some made for the stable to find mounts, but most were too dazed with drink to decide what to do.

Without hiking up her skirts, Lucina vaulted onto Orpheus. She landed on her stomach, legs swinging on one side, head on the other. "Go!" She prodded Orpheus into action as she twisted and clambered to gain her seat.

Graham slapped his reins against Red Rowan's neck, and they bounded over the drawbridge. Orpheus followed at a rapid trot, with Lucina still hanging like a sausage longwise over her horse.

To Graham's relief, Lucina sat upright when he looked again. He nudged Red Rowan to a faster pace, confident that Orpheus would be right behind.

"Split up," he shouted the instant he saw Roger and Jasper waiting behind a copse of beech trees. "They don't know you're here and will follow us. We'll outrun them easily. We'll meet you and those who wish to join us tonight at Devil's Gully."

As Jasper and the others plunged into the woods to the east, Graham and Lucina turned north. The pack would snarl at their heels for some leagues, but in the end, Orpheus and Red Rowan would outrun the game little hobbies ridden by the Maxwell men.

"You can do it," Graham whispered to Red Rowan, bent over his horse's neck, bonding with him as if they were one. "Carry us both to freedom, and I'll see you never fall into Will Mosley's hands again."

Glancing at Lucina and Orpheus, where they flew beside

him, he realized his old need to prove he was superior had
died when she first said she loved him. He had no wish to
outpace her, only the desire to live and love as fully as she
did. If only his heart were free to reach out, to take all he
needed and give in return.

Despite the danger, Lucina was soaring. With the wind
in her hair and her love at her side, she played with their
pursuers, the elusive game of chase she would always win.
She and Orpheus. Alex and Red Rowan. Together they
reached for a beautiful future, if only they could stop the
wars and the feuds. If only she could trust Graham to find
his solutions without falling back on old ways.

Gradually the distance between them and their pursuers
widened. At length, Lucina no longer saw Maxwells behind
them. It was time to rest.

Graham slowed Red Rowan, bringing him to a walk. The
horse was blowing, but he wasn't lathered from his
breakneck run, nor was Orpheus. Though she had to fight
to catch her breath, Lucina patted Orpheus's neck with
pride, still thrilled by their feat of outrunning the Maxwells.

"Here, we must part." Graham halted and turned to her,
his expression grave.

"Why? We've left them in the dust." Lucina imagined
the angry Maxwells and chuckled.

"I'll not argue over this," Graham said more severely.
"I want you to follow this trail up the hillside and hide in
the cave you'll find on the east face. You're to stay there
until I return."

"Why should we split up now?" Lucina was bewildered
by his insistence.

He shook his head. "They're slower, but they won't give
up. When they catch up and see me, I'll head for the pass
above, calling out as if you're ahead of me. The pass is
blocked by a fallen tree that Red Rowan can jump. The
hobbies can't get over it no matter how they try, and a
man on foot can't catch me, for I'll be long gone. Now, go
and I'll cover your tracks."

"I don't want to leave you, Alex." Lucina shifted in the
saddle, disliking the plan. "They may have calivers. If
they're close enough, they may well shoot you."

"Correct, madam, which is the reason you're staying

here. I'll not take the chance of your being shot. The best thing is for me to go where they cannot."

"Let me go with you," she pleaded, growing more uneasy by the minute. "If Red Rowan can jump the barrier, so can Orpheus."

"Orpheus hasn't jumped it before," he insisted. "Red Rowan has. It's tricky." He glanced at the sky. " 'Twill be dusk by the time they're here." He fastened his gaze on her again, entreaty in his eyes. "Lucina, I'm calling in your promise. You swore to do as I asked. I'm asking now."

He had never before asked for what he wanted. In the past, he had simply taken it. The gesture touched her deeply, and she reached for his hand.

He pulled her into an embrace that spanned more than the space between their mounts. "Dear God, I thought you'd been ravished by the garrison." His lips touched hers briefly before anointing her cheeks and temples. "I was going to kill every one of them, especially Maxwell. He didn't touch you, did he?"

She could scarce think straight, she was still so overcome by his earlier question, followed by his caresses and concern for her well-being. For the first time he did not fall into old ways. If only he would stay this way, if only he would not revert to rule by the sword. . . .

She cut off the fearful thought as Alex caught her face between his two palms, his voice urgent. "Did he hurt you?"

His need for reassurance compelled her attention. "He threatened to ravish me but decided he had more urgent business." She was glad to relieve his fears on that score, but she knew she must again destroy his peace of mind with her next words. "Unfortunately, his urgent business gives *us* urgent business. We must ride to Falklands Palace, Alex. Where is it from here?"

"We have Maxwells on our tail, Lucina. I cannot think about the Falklands now."

"But we may not have much time. Bothwell is—"

"Hush, Lucina." He stopped her mouth with a kiss, gentling her fear. "Whatever Bothwell is planning, he'll take his time about it after botching his last raid. We've time. When we've shaken off Maxwell's men, you can tell me about the Falklands."

"But what will the Maxwell men do when they cannot follow you?" Lucina protested, deeply concerned. "They might look about and find me."

"They'll be hotfooting it to the other trail that leads around the pass," he informed her decisively. "I've played this game with them many times before. We know our parts well." With a last kiss he dismissed her, refusing to say another word.

Her final view of Alex and Red Rowan showed them standing stalwart on the trail, leaving her with naught to do but hide and pray and hope they would indeed discuss the Falklands when he returned. If he returned.

Chapter 25

The wait was a trial for Lucina. At Hermitage she'd been busy with her own tasks, but here she had given her oath to remain helpless.

Love truly knows no law, she thought, praying with all her strength for Alex's safety.

Now she understood how he had felt each time he'd believed her in danger. Her imagination leaped from one ugly image of his death to another, despite her efforts to stop it. Time passed, but she couldn't tell how much. Why didn't he come back for her? Had he been hurt? Should she try to find him or had she not waited long enough?

The torment of being helpless taught her new things about herself. She *was* too reckless. For the first time she understood why Alex had locked her in the tower. Given the opportunity just now, she would have done the same to him.

Leaning against Orpheus for comfort, she tried to curb her anxiety, but it careened out of control. Alex was at the mercy of luck, his judgment in the growing dark, and Red Rowan's ability to leap a barrier that stood between him and the murderous Maxwells.

After what seemed like hours, she finally heard hoofbeats on the stone path. Quickly, she moved toward the cave's entrance.

"Are you well, Alex?" She all but tugged him from Red Rowan's back, knowing her distress was obvious and not caring. If he saw she was worried, he might be more reassuring, as she should have been with him after Caerlaverock.

As if seeking revenge for her previous reticence, he offered only a few terse words and a brief embrace before
insisting they ride.

Feeling forlorn, wanting more reassurance, she mounted
and coaxed Orpheus up the rocky trail until she stood face-
to-face with the formidable barrier they must jump. As she
studied the dangerous, jutting branches of the tree blocking
the pass, she realized Alex wasn't being inconsiderate of
her feelings. He was distracted with concern.

Little wonder. Loose rock scattered on the trail threatened a horse's footing. The tree trunk was wide. Too wide.

"Come. You can do it." Alex spoke with confidence as
he showed her and Orpheus the tree up close, pointing out
the best approach to the jump. "If you take it this way
instead of straight on, you have a clearer landing on the
other side."

A mere word and a look from him was all it took to
restore her confidence. As he coached her, demonstrated
the jump over the barrier, then waited patiently on the
other side, she made a vow. Next time she would consider
his feelings first. The infernal waiting had taught her new
respect for his needs.

But Lucina's resolution didn't lessen her concern for the
coming raid. From the tension in Alex, she knew one was
coming. They skirted a village in the dark, then found Devil's Gully, and descended into the cleft in the land. If she
had been able to see into the future that first night when
Orpheus was stolen, might she have done things
differently?

She couldn't say, nor could she see into the future this
time as mist swirled and she and Orpheus sank deeper into
the earth. Like the mythical Orpheus who traveled to the
netherworld to find his beloved, she, too, must descend into
darkness before she saw light. This journey was not just
about rescuing King James. It would set the tone for her
life with her husband from this day forward. She must risk
all for the ultimate reward.

Graham could tell Lucina had something on her mind,
something that would tie him in mental knots just when he
wanted to hold her in his arms. Devil take it, he had rescued her from Caerlaverock and outwitted their pursuers.
His blood was up. He wanted to peel off her clothes and

savor the feel of her body against his. Instead, it seemed
he would have to listen to her talk.

"Alex," she began with urgency as soon as they were
settled in their blankets a discreet distance from the others.
"We must speak of the Falklands."

"Not now, Lucina," he groaned. "I don't want to discuss
strategy. I want to . . ." Catching her hand, he placed her
palm over his bare chest to show her, closed his eyes, and
took a deep breath. Would she put aside her planning and
meet his needs?

To his relief, she seemed to understand. Though he
sensed it cost her an effort, she nestled against him. "Yes,"
she whispered. "Talk can come later." Her breath was a
soft explosion of heat against his shoulder, igniting his
senses. "I love you, John Alexander Malcolm Graham."

She loved him. He would never tire of hearing her say
the words. He kissed her lips, her jaw, his mouth sliding
over to explore the soft shape of her ear.

In her arms, no strife or feud could reach him. With her,
peace reigned. Grateful for the respite, he put away his
cares as chief. As they helped one another from their clothing, he prepared to indulge in the race for completion, to
subsume his worry in the glories of the flesh.

The beauty of her body awoke his passion. The hard
buds of her breasts against his chest. Her slender hips
molded to his. Excitement rocked him as they broke from
the starting point and Lucina guided him between her legs.

"Yes, Alex. Love me." She breathed in his ear, urging
him on. In answer to his probing, she drew him deep into
her heat.

Shards of sensation rained through his consciousness.
God, she was beautiful. Tight and hot. He withdrew slowly,
savoring the pleasure as her grasping hands and legs begged
him to return.

"Don't rush," he whispered. "Make it last a long time."
With teasing slowness he filled her, savoring the descent,
inch by inch. She arched her hips and moaned with enjoyment, spurring his pulse to greater speed.

Rise and descend. He fed on the feelings. She was wet
and slippery, so beautifully his. Her head thrashed from
side to side as they mated, her glorious hair like a burst of

silk. She was his to enjoy, his to savor. And he wanted her forever, passion without end.

Lucina wasn't sure she could last a long time. With each slow descent, Alex teased her, driving her toward a pinnacle of need. "More!" she cried, thrusting her hips against him. "Now, Alex! Please." The love she bore him swept through her as he poised above her, braced on both arms. Smiling up at him, she ran her fingers down his chest, tracing the path they both loved.

Within this mortal shell lies the spirit I love. The ridged muscles of his abdomen, the tight line of his tapering waist and hips—to touch him was to speak with the language of the flesh.

And the flesh spoke of destiny as two souls merged. Dark, consuming destiny. As the Black Graham descended with a long, deep thrust, his passion possessed her, dark like the night. He was full of need, grasping to fulfill it. Which meant he reached for life, whether he knew it or no.

This was her love. She had traveled the length of England, thinking to find love in her land. Instead, she'd found disaster. Yet out of disaster had sprung new beginnings, leading her to an all-consuming love for this man.

Alex's lean body moved against her, and she clutched his sweating back as he strained for fulfillment, sweeping both of them to the edge. With a cry, she felt her muscles convulse. Waves of pleasure spiraled through her body, pleasure that carried her to new heights. Even as she soared, his cry of pleasure meshed with hers, and she clasped him tightly to her.

In that moment she knew she would risk anything, do anything to help him love her in return. She would confront Bothwell, Maxwell, Will, anyone she had to, to bring Alex peace. For in the midst of peace, love could flourish, and then he could return her gifts with treasures of his own.

They settled to sleep, and Graham drifted off almost immediately. Lucina floated in a world between waking and sleeping, lost in the mists of Devil's Gully, where her love for Alex had begun. And as she floated, she realized that she *must* succeed in stopping Bothwell. For if she failed, she had no chance for happiness at the side of the Black Graham. She might not even have a husband if he were forced to join a bloody civil war.

＊　　＊　　＊

Morning came too soon. Lucina squeezed her eyelids tightly, wanting to shut out the sun as it peered over the edge of the world. If only she could drift in a dream awhile longer, in a place where life was perfect and death far away.

Alas, she couldn't hide there long. For all the satisfaction brought by her blossoming love for Alex, it could not shield her from what lay ahead.

Seeing he was awake, aware that they might quarrel over her attempts to counsel him, she plunged in anyway. "I know you would rather I didn't mention it, but we—"

"How do you know what I would rather?" he said sharply. "You put thoughts and feelings in me that aren't there."

She *had* done that in the past, she admitted. And he was testy this morning, quick to point out her faults. "We must go to Falklands, Alex," she tried again. "I overheard—"

"Lucina, why not begin by telling me what you know," he interrupted. " 'Tis powerfully irritating to be told what to do before I hear why." He ran one hand the wrong way through his hair, frustrated. "I would prefer to talk it through."

His reprimand reminded her of her embarrassing impatience. "I-I'm sorry, Alex. You are right." The apology came hard to her, but having made it, she took a deep breath and started again. "I overheard the Earl of Bothwell and Lord Maxwell discussing a plan to kill someone they called Jamie at Falklands Palace."

"A straightforward delivery of information. *That* is a great improvement." He nodded his approval. "Pray go on."

His condescension rankled, but she admitted she deserved it. "I saw them both leave not long after. Bothwell said Will was raising the Border."

Alex remained silent, as if absorbing this information.

"Well, is King James at Falklands?" She was unable to conceal her need to know.

"Parliament should be dissolved by now, and the king does generally go to Falklands for the hunting after he's done in Edinburgh," he said. "But you don't know King Jamie. Why are you so protective of him?"

"Aren't you?" she demanded. "I'm protective of our queen."

He laughed wryly. "Your queen has been on the throne since before you were born. People love her, especially since your country is at peace. Ours has been in turmoil for centuries. If someone isn't fighting to control our sovereign, then someone is knifing someone else in the back for their power or land."

She thought of how right this appeared to be, yet how confusing. "Why doesn't the king make Bothwell respect him? Doesn't he have power?"

"Power? Our king?" He snorted with regretful disdain. "James is intelligent, but he's also penniless. The royal treasury is so empty, he can scarce meet court expenses. He has no standing army and only a small bodyguard, which leaves him vulnerable to attack. So he pits noble against noble, or nobles against the kirk. He doesn't want them to join together and turn on him."

"And what would happen if Bothwell murdered him and took the throne?" she asked.

Alex frowned. "Bothwell is unpredictable. We don't know what he'll do. The important thing is, whichever path he chooses, he'll be challenged by the nobility."

"As well he should be," Lucina agreed. "James has no heirs yet. There would be civil war."

Alex shuddered visibly. "There would be utter chaos."

Gooseflesh crept across Lucina's arms, and she burrowed against him for comfort, pulling the blanket higher around her shoulders. "You would be forced to choose sides, wouldn't you. And where would that leave me?"

Alex pressed her to him in a protective gesture. "I wouldn't let you come to harm."

"I'm sure you wouldn't, but fighting would be bad for the country, Alex, especially the people who grow crops and raise cattle, sheep, and horses." She clung to him, wishing their world were peaceful, but she would have to work to achieve that dream. "King James must stay on his throne," she said with resolve. "At least until he has children and they reach adulthood. Otherwise, you and I can never breed horses. And I mean that we should, Alex. I truly do."

Despite the seriousness of the discussion, he chuckled.

"So King Jamie must keep his throne so you can breed horses. I'll see he's told."

"Very amusing." She pulled a face at him. "Alex, all jesting aside, do you agree we should warn His Majesty of Bothwell's coming?"

Graham was as surprised as Lucina to be discussing plans as if they were partners in the scheme. Yet they were, and he would damn well get used to it, because clearly it wouldn't be their last time.

"There is no need to assemble a force this time, do you agree?" she said.

He shouldn't have been so surprised that he did. "If we took the time to do that, we'd be racing against Bothwell, who is doing the same. We'll travel light, arrive first, and warn the king before they're even sighted. We'll need Jasper. He knows the way like the back of his hand."

"Very well, and I would like Roger along. I hate to be separated from him again."

A reasonable request, he supposed. "I agree."

"And Drummond should come, too."

"Whoa," he objected. Did they have to struggle with this again? "Not Drummond. The lad's had enough problems of late."

"But his father is about to commit treason," she insisted. "Drummond will wish to stop him."

He had too long a day before him to deal with more intense emotions. "We'll let him decide if he wants to come or no," he proposed. Feeling wrung out, he sank back. "Lucina, 'tis barely dawn. I would like a few more moments of quiet before we start out."

They settled into a favorite position, snuggled against each other. But Lucina seemed restless, unable to stay still.

"What if you knew Bonnie Mary hadn't been killed by your grandsire?" she asked after a lengthy silence.

He sighed. All he wanted was a last stolen moment in her arms, but this seemed important to her. Besides, she fidgeted in her concern, twice poking him in the ribs with her elbow as she sought a more comfortable position. "I've never completely believed she was. I heard she took to her bed and died. The question is, had she been injured by my grandsire, or was she ill? If she were ill, she might have died through no fault of his."

She seemed surprised, perhaps even irritated by this answer. "Do you mean to say there's doubt over why and how she died, yet the feud goes on?"

"I have my doubts, but the Maxwells have always been convinced he killed her."

"But what if she didn't die? What if she merely went to live elsewhere?"

He shook his head. What she proposed was one way to explain how Lucina knew Mary's favorite saying, but it was so unlikely as to be ridiculous. "How could she have done that? Everybody sees a body when it's laid out after death. And she is buried in the kirkyard."

"But did everyone know for certain the body was hers?"

Her persistence was wearying, yet he had sworn to be patient with her, so he answered as steadily as he could. " 'Tis customary for the family and retainers to gather around the bier and pray for the departed. Really, Lucina, why are you asking this?"

"Never mind. 'Tis not important."

After her intense probing, her sudden abandoning of the subject surprised him. But he had no strength left to question it. He had too many arrangements to make for their journey north.

Lucina lay as still as possible so as not to disturb Alex, but the discussion about Mary had depressed her. Alex's response proved Mary was dead and Lucina was inventing nonsense again.

Then there was Maxwell. He didn't want to believe that Mary had run away. He was an embittered old man who took out his pain on his neighbors. He had lost his wife, probably the only person he'd ever cherished, and his power in southwest Scotland. He had nothing left.

Her cause seemed hopeless. She could not mend the feud over Bonnie Mary's death. There might never be peace along the Border or in Graham's life.

The journey to Falklands Palace was one of mixed emotions for Graham as the leagues melted away beneath their horses' hooves. Their destination lay north of the Firth of Forth. To reach it, they must travel the breadth of Scotland, crossing the mid-region and passing Edinburgh. As they rode through green valleys and cool verdant forests, he watched with pleasure as Lucina drank in the beauty of the land.

When he had pointed out the snowcapped crags of White Coomb, she had gasped with awe. She smiled with excitement at the Falls of Clyde, thrilled with the rainbows hovering in the mist. She shouted with pleasure at the sight of her first loch, shining like a jewel in the sun. Beyond a doubt, they shared a love for Scotland's plentitude.

His personal misery was that she didn't trust him fully, aside from the larger misery of their journey's purpose. But the misery was subsumed as he found he liked planning strategy with Lucina. It had felt odd talking to her, holding little back. Yet it felt comfortable, too, like putting on an old but favorite garment he hadn't worn in years.

The only person he'd shared with before was his father. They'd been partners long before Archibald and Edmund died, sharing a bond of knowledge about how to strategize, how to execute plans or alter them in the heat of the moment as required.

How unusual to rediscover such a bond with a woman. He and Sarah had never planned anything beyond what to eat for dinner. Yet Lucina had a single-minded way of choosing a goal and planning toward it that reminded him of his father. It warmed his heart.

Perhaps he accepted her as she was because mutual need bound them together—her need to love him, his need to be loved. His part of the offering seemed lame in return for what she gave, but at least he appreciated her. His respect for her intelligence was growing. He took pleasure in her skill. Yet appreciation, pleasure, and need still weren't love.

Which brought him to the old quandary. He knew what Lucina wanted of him. She didn't demand his love. Nor did she whine because he failed to give it. But she wanted it, nonetheless.

He wasn't sure he could, but he would try. God knew, he wanted to escape the old ways of thinking and feeling. But even now he wanted to fall back on old ways, to assemble a huge force of men and descend on Falklands Palace, overrunning it with guards to protect the king and fight off Bothwell when he struck. At a time when their lives, their very future, hung in the balance, final decisions should belong to him alone.

Yet his unspoken agreement with Lucina to plan and proceed together took precedence. He must fight to stay on his chosen course.

Then there was his trouble with Drummond.

On the third night, they camped beside a rushing burn. After a supper of roast hare, Graham sat by their small fire, acutely aware of Lucina sitting nearby. He wanted to find a private spot away from the others, where he could coax her into coupling. The passionate race to climax would wear off the edge of his anxiety and lull him into sleep.

But Lucina seemed oblivious to him tonight. Taking a lantern, she announced her intention to wash at the burn. Only then did he notice Drummond had left the group by the fire. Immediately he concluded that the pair intended to meet.

And why shouldn't they talk if they wished? Lucina wasn't interested in Drummond. He was a mere youth, raw and unpolished. Besides, she'd declared her love for him, her husband and chief. Yet the idea of their discussing certain subjects in private made him distinctly uneasy.

Damn it, she trusted Drummond, and that bothered him. She trusted the lad more than she trusted him.

Of course she did, he reasoned. She expected less from Drummond. She hadn't entrusted her future happiness to the lad. Far easier to trust a guide than to hope someone would change his entire way of thinking for your sake. Still . . .

With a studied effort to appear casual, which Graham knew didn't fool Jasper, he moved through the trees toward the burn. At the sound of voices, he paused behind some boulders and foliage that screened him from view.

Lucina sat on a rock, looking like an elfin queen, her bare feet dangling in the rushing water as she laughed at something Drummond had said. She shook back her mane of hair, her green-clad figure washed by tendrils of mists that ebbed and flowed. Even her voice, both urgent and earnest, seemed touched by magic as she spoke, though Graham couldn't make out the words.

That she should talk to Drummond in such an intimate manner instead of to him irked Graham.

He watched the lad kneel by the water's edge, roll his sleeves high, and splash his face. Something swinging from his neck by a chain caught Graham's eye. The clear round stone shone against his leather jack like a small moon.

Lucina slipped from her seat and, holding the lantern in one hand, her skirts in the other, swished through the water to Drummond. She must be speaking of the stone, for she tapped it with the hand that also held her skirt. Drummond held up the stone by its chain, which gave Graham a clear view.

It was the Dunlochy Charmstone.

He'd never seen it. But the tales of the stone's uncanny powers were legendary on the Border, as was the Maxwell family's wrath over its disappearance when Bonnie Mary died. As a small lad, he'd heard of its being sighted from time to time. It would appear mysteriously to cure some gravely ill or wounded Borderer, then disappear again. Nor was there any sure proof of its presence when the Maxwells investigated, which had added to their rage.

Lucina and Drummond seemed engrossed in the stone, their heads so close together that Drummond's flaming locks mingled with Lucina's golden brown. The expression of shared confidence on their faces pained him. No wonder Lucina trusted Drummond. The lad trusted her. The sullen, suspicious boy he'd known at Castle Graham had changed since he'd gone to Hermitage. His allegiance had shifted to Lucina.

Graham was consumed with jealousy. Childish, he told himself. Unreasonable. But he wanted Lucina to trust him the way she trusted Drummond.

Suddenly he was furious. "That stone is stolen property." He stepped forward from among the trees into full view. "It must be returned to the Maxwells."

Lucina jerked around. Drummond lifted his head, a guilty expression on his face.

"Give it to me." Graham moved to the edge of the burn and stood, feet planted firmly on the wet bank. "I'll see it's given back."

"I pray you, Alex, not yet." Lucina dropped her skirt in the water and reached out her hand, a pleading expression on her face. "It's not possible to return it to Maxwell just now. Let Drummond keep it. When we next meet Maxwell, if he isn't trying to murder us, you can return it then."

"Nay, ma leddy. I have a better plan," Drummond said. "I would like our chief tae wear it."

"You would? Why?" Graham was so surprised, he blurted the question.

Drummond leaped from rock to rock across the stream to join him on the bank. "I've been thinkin' since Hermitage." He removed the chain from around his neck and offered the stone to Graham in a deferential gesture. "Ye ken the stone brought her leddyship to rescue me. I would ha' been killed otherwise." As Graham took the crystal, Drummond gave it a last, seemingly affectionate pat. "I pray you wear it, Graham."

Graham stared at the stone suspended from its chain. It was pristine clear in its silver setting. He'd never seen anything like it.

"Do you believe in the stone's power, Alex?" Lucina waded through the shallows and stepped onto the bank.

He shook his head slowly, unable to tear his gaze from the stone's fascinating depths. "I couldn't say for sure, but I would have to ask if the stone actually caused good things to happen, or if they were coincidence."

"No one knows for certes." Lucina touched the stone with one finger. It swayed on its chain, glittering by the light of the lantern like a living thing.

"Where did you come by the stone, Drummond?" Graham asked.

"Ma Faither lent it to her leddyship. He had it for years." Humiliation laced Drummond's voice as he once more acknowledged his father for a thief.

Graham cursed the revelation. As always, Will created chaos while pretending innocence, which threw another ugly problem into his lap. How would he return the stone to Maxwell without telling him Will stole it? And where had it been before Will got his claws on it? The stone had disappeared long before he'd been born. "Why did Will give it to you, Lucina?" he asked.

"Will loaned it to Elen, who gave it to me," she said readily. "I promised Drummond he could wear it in return for guiding me to Hermitage."

"You promised him? What gave you the right?"

"The stone gave her the right," Drummond put in eagerly. "It favors her. Touch it, m'leddy. Show him."

"A stone can't have thoughts or feelings," Lucina said skeptically. But she took the stone, as if to please him, and balanced it in her palm.

As they all watched, the light reflected by the crystal seemed to intensify, and deep within, a star sparkled, as if *it* were the source of light.

"You see," Drummond insisted in awed tones. " 'Tis said to shine only in the hands o' the pure o' heart."

Lucina shook her head, as if embarrassed. She handed the lantern to Drummond and slipped the chain over Graham's head. "You must wear the stone. Whether 'tis magic or no, it cannot hurt." She slid the stone down the front of his leather jack and shirt. "You must also hide it. Otherwise, 'twill cause talk." Standing on tiptoe, she kissed his cheek. "God-den, my husband. I pray you sleep well."

Graham accepted her kiss without returning it, too baffled by the entire phenomena of the crystal. How could the stone reflect more light when held by one person than by another? Could it be a trick played on the eyes?

But instead of finding answers, as he moved through the forest back toward camp, he noticed the beauty of the night—the tranquil rush of water in the darkness, the sigh of the breeze stirring the branches overhead. An owl called, voicing the ancient mysteries of the primeval woods. He felt the charmstone, lying warm and comforting against his bare chest, as if it held its own inner heat.

To trust or not to trust. Could Lucina ever trust him? Could he trust her not to die and desert him, as Sarah had?

The questions flitted through his mind, then dissolved. *Just accept,* a voice seemed to say as a deep serenity settled over him. Absorbed by the feeling, he moved slowly toward their camp. Behind him, he heard Lucina praise Drummond, calling him noble for giving up the charmstone.

Even that didn't bother him. He wondered who had had the charmstone before Will. How many stories had he heard of its healing power? Dozens. And the good had been offered to many families, not just Maxwells. When he returned the stone, he would propose it be shared once more.

Without a word to Jasper and Roger at the camp, Graham removed his boots and rolled up in his blanket. Although he'd meant to think about the stone's healing powers, he'd no sooner pillowed his head on his folded cloak than he fell into a peaceful state of mind he hadn't known for years.

It was temporary, he thought drowsily. On the morrow the familiar tension would return.

But for now he accepted the respite. He felt too light, too buoyant, to reject the stolen tranquility as he drifted into sleep.

Chapter 26

The tranquility of the night was indeed temporary, Graham thought ruefully the next day as he examined the left foreleg of Jasper's gelding.

"He's lame, sure enough," Graham confirmed to his captain. "We must wait until he recovers or find you another mount."

But they couldn't find one, at least not the quality they required. Their fifth day on the road passed as they searched nearby farms and villages. Graham took advantage of the delay to outfit each man with weapons, ropes, and steel helmets, but he didn't feel better for it. Lucina fretted, and Roger stopped telling amusing stories about her mischievous girlhood, a sure sign that he was depressed. Jasper complained about his rheumatism, Drummond was mute, and Graham's temper was on a short fuse. They all feared Bothwell would arrive at the Falklands ahead of them.

They arrived at the Firth of Forth at dusk on the seventh day. Graham had asked Jasper to guide them to the west of Edinburgh. At the town of Bo'ness, they found a ferryman to take them across the Forth. On their journey Graham discovered the old codger enjoyed a good gossip. Obligingly, he regaled him with ribald stories from the Border, then asked in exchange for news since Parliament broke up.

"Nae news, boot word's flyin' that his lordship o' Bothwell's right sare with His Majesty," the ferryman said, winking to suggest the weight of undisclosed details. "I hear there's extra work for ferrymen to the east. I were thinkin' o' help oot, but I dinna like the man in charge."

Graham grimaced. It sounded as if the earl was ferrying his army across the Forth as they spoke. Once they disembarked, Graham hurriedly assembled his party.

"They've probably already attacked the palace," Jasper groaned.

"We don't know that," Roger said reasonably. "They might be on their way, same as we are."

"We will continue." Graham tested Red Rowan's girth before mounting. "With only five of us, we can get there faster than they can."

They approached Falklands from the south, which gave them a clear view of the broad open landscape leading to the palace. They saw no hint of an army anywhere.

"Would we see them in the dark?" Roger asked.

Jasper snorted. "Several hundred men'd be carryin' torches an' make a de'il o' noise. O' course we'd see them."

"Then, where are they?" Lucina asked uneasily.

"We must assume we're ahead of them," Graham said decisively. "Here's the plan. I'll request an audience with His Majesty, convince him to depart with me, and bring him out to the stables to the north. Jasper, Roger, and Drummond, if you would wait at the gatehouse, you can give the alarm if you see Bothwell coming. If you see nothing, join us at the stables and we'll all ride north. Lucina . . ." He hesitated, not knowing what task she would consider acceptable.

"I'll wait with the others," she said, removing the difficulty for him.

Graham surveyed his companions a last time in the fading light. The tension among them was palpable as anxious faces looked to him for strength. He felt a sudden appreciation for each of them—for his loving Lucina, for her jolly brother, for his friend Jasper, who had stood beside him so many years, and for Drummond—he admitted he liked the lad, won by his cheerful obedience no matter what he was asked.

Now they were about to take an irrevocable step that could lead to a resounding victory or a crushing defeat. He had one, solitary chance to save the king. If indeed it wasn't already too late.

With a final nod to his friends, Graham led the way toward the twin towers of the Falklands Palace gatehouse.

Graham sat in a favored seat in King James's bedchamber, unable to eat the food his sovereign kept pressing on him. He wanted to shout and tear his hair.

"More wine, Lord Graham?" King Jamie waved his wine steward forward to top off his guest's scarcely touched flagon. "You're not eating. The roast bird is excellent. Or mayhap you prefer the carved beef."

"Your Grace, I prefer that you mount and ride with me. Bring guards to protect you, bring anyone you wish, but let us go at once."

"Patience, sir." The youthful James pushed back his gilded chair and took a turn around the room, quaffing his wine as he walked, seeming intent on showing off his new suit of paned brocade. "I've sent my guard to check the environs, but the last word I had of Bothwell, he was at the Border. Even if he's on his way north, he won't come within shooting range without my first hearing of it. We'll have ample time to depart. And if he doesn't have too many followers, I might capture him and give him the justice he so richly deserves."

Unable to listen any longer, Graham lurched to his feet to check the window for the dozenth time. His sovereign was an intelligent man, but his stubborn desire to make all the decisions just might get him killed.

Outside the twin-towered gatehouse, Lucina fretted aloud to Roger about the delay. "He's having trouble convincing His Majesty to leave. I know he is. Please."

"Lucina, there's nothing I can do." On foot, Roger tugged at Cygnus's reins, leading her away from the gatehouse.

Lucina ran after him, leaving Orpheus to graze. "The king isn't listening to Alex because he's older and seems threatening, like the regents he hated in his youth. But he'll agree to ride with you because you're younger and more like a friend."

Roger snorted gracelessly. "Lucina, you said this was a matter of life or death, but I fail to see the urgency."

"It is life or death," she insisted. "And to prove how

dire the circumstances are, you may ride Orpheus to lead His Majesty to safety." Roger had always wanted to ride Orpheus.

He looked excited by the idea. "Well, if you're that desperate, I'll do my best to be convincing, but I can't think he'll listen to me, either."

Relieved, Lucina hurried to tell Drummond and Jasper they were going in to see the king. "Do you wish to accompany us?" she asked the pair, who nervously watched the road.

"I wouldna turn doon the chance to bow to ma king," Drummond said eagerly.

"I'll stay here, m'leddy. Someane mun keep watch," Jasper said.

"Thank you, Jasper," she said gratefully. "Let us know the instant you hear or see even a hint of approaching men. And meet us at the stables so we can leave together. We don't want you endangered as well."

Graham looked up as a manservant in livery entered the king's chamber and bowed. "Your Majesty, a gentlewoman sayin' she be Leddy Graham is here. Shall I show her in?"

James, in the midst of showing Graham a new chess set of carved ivory, shot him a glance. "Who is this lady, sir?"

"It would appear to be my wife, Your Grace." Graham grimaced with annoyance and stood. Lucina clearly hadn't come to give the alarm, so why was she here?

James put down the white queen, apparently intrigued that one of his fiercest Borderers had taken a wife. "Tsk, tsk, Graham, you didn't mention you brought your wife with you. Let's see her." The king waved the servant to show her in.

Graham waited, not knowing what to expect. Devil take it, he hoped Lucina wasn't going to do anything odd or rash. His concern heightened as Lucina rushed into the chamber and fell at King James's feet. Breathless, she smiled up at him, her eyes sparkling with excitement. Or was it hysteria. "Your Majesty, I have so longed to meet you," she said with enthusiasm. "Forgive me for choosing this late hour, but I am so honored. Allow me to kiss your hand."

The few bites of food Graham had taken threatened to

reappear at her speech, but he swallowed hard and bared his teeth in a semblance of a smile as he followed her lead. " 'Tis true, Your Grace, she has traveled the breadth of Scotland to meet you."

James looked inordinately pleased by the compliment. "Lady Graham, pray rise." He took her hand and assisted her. "Your accent tells me you are an Englishwoman."

Lucina nodded. "Yes, Your Majesty, I've come to Scotland to breed horses. You must allow me to give you a fine colt once I am settled and have begun the work."

Graham noted a flicker of increased interest in James's gaze as he stared past Lucina to someone standing in the doorway.

Lucina hurried to take Roger's hand and led him forward. "Your Majesty, allow me to present my brother, Roger Cavandish." Despite a nervous tick in his cheek, Roger executed an elegant bow. As he straightened and Lucina smiled brilliantly at the king, Graham saw her reach out stealthily and thump Roger's ankle with her toe. What was she up to now?

"Your Majesty, my sister and I have brought a fine pair of horses with us," Roger said hurriedly. "Will you ride the mare Cygnus, who will carry you as smoothly as a swan racing on the wind? She's saddled and ready for you."

James raised his eyebrows. " 'Tis ten of the clock, sir. I appreciate your enthusiasm, but—"

A feverish look shone in Roger's eyes as he went down on one knee. " 'Tis a wondrous night, Your Majesty. The air is mild, and Cygnus is faster than any steed you've ever ridden. You will think yourself in heaven. I'll come with you. We all will."

Good Lord, he's gone too far, Graham thought, holding his breath as Roger waxed poetic. James would blast him in a fit of temper and toss him out on his ear.

To his surprise, the king's gaze slid from Lucina's eager face to Roger's, to Graham's poor attempt at a jolly expression, then back to Roger. "I must change into something suitable for riding first," he said, moving with languid grace toward the door.

Graham sighed in relief. Lucina had concocted what seemed to him a harebrained scheme, but she'd made it work.

Lucina was jubilant as King James VI opened the door to the presence chamber and called for his body servant. They would leave the Falklands and all would be well.

The sound of shouts reached them. Shots rang out.

Lucina tensed, her smile fading. Graham pulled the king back into the chamber and closed the door all but a crack. Feet pounded toward them across the presence chamber.

"What is it?" Graham demanded through the crack.

"Hundreds o' men, Your Majesty," a guard panted. "Armed and attacking the palace. They're already in the guard hall and will be in your presence chamber any second now. All is lost!"

"Hold them off as long as you can." Graham slammed the door, locked it, and pocketed the key.

James stared at him, his face ashen. "Bothwell *is* here. What do you recommend, my lord?"

They all looked to Graham expectantly. The guard hall led directly to the presence chamber, which led to the king's bedchamber. They were trapped.

Graham nodded briskly toward the chamber's other door. "We must leave by another route, Your Majesty. Where does that go?"

"To a stair leading to the queen's chamber above." The king looked increasingly frightened, though he retained his composure. "And to the guardroom and postern door below, where Bothwell will have stationed men."

A banging was heard below, proving Bothwell had not just stationed men at the door below; he had bid them break it down.

Graham strode to the north window and flung it open. "This way onto the gallery roof. I'll go first and secure a rope to the roof of the wing. If we're quiet, Bothwell's men won't know we're above them." He unhooked the length of rope from his belt and climbed through the window.

"Stars above," Lucina muttered at the thought of another climb. She'd had enough of heights at the Hermitage cave. Whatever escape she had hoped Graham would manufacture, it hadn't been this. Closing her eyes, she composed herself for the ordeal. Outside, the shouts of their attackers were augmented by the explosions of gunfire.

Graham swept back into the chamber. "Drummond," he

ordered, indicating the lad should go first. "Then Your Majesty."

Drummond disappeared out the window. A second later Lucina heard the rasp of his feet against stone as he shinnied up the rope as easily as if he were going up stairs. The king stripped off his ornate doublet that would impede his movement and, in shirtsleeves, vaulted out the window after Drummond.

The instant he had disappeared from view, Lucina motioned to her brother. "Roger. Go!"

Graham followed Roger onto the gallery roof and held the rope to the roof steady for him. "Bothwell's men are everywhere," he muttered. "I hope they don't look up."

Lucina peered out the window. In the garden below the king's cross-house, cries of rage and agony rolled upward as the king's guards fought with Bothwell's men. Would they notice them climbing the wall high above their heads? She imagined dangling on a rope, the entire world unstable as attackers shot at her with arrows and calivers from below.

In the midst of her fear, Graham's hands closed around hers, warm and comforting. "You can do it, Lucina. Listen to me."

"I'm brave on horseback, but not in the air." She clung to him a moment, giving in to her weakness, if only for a second. Then she pushed away from him and straightened. "I shall be fine. I'll climb quickly. They won't notice me."

Graham pulled her back into his embrace and gazed into her eyes. "Your strength impressed me the night you raced into my life, Lucina. I knew your love would be as powerful as your riding skill. You've been the answer to my prayers."

What was it she saw in his gaze? Was it faith in her strength? Or was it really love? Lucina wound both arms around his torso and held him, hearing his heart race beneath her ear. Whatever it was, this man was her life.

A pounding at the door to the bedchamber interrupted their embrace. Graham cursed. "Hurry, Lucina."

She nodded mutely and let him help her onto the gallery roof as she grasped the rope. Tilting her head back, she gazed at the crenellated parapet above, telling herself it was only one level away. But with King James's guard and

Bothwell's reivers fighting it out at her very feet, it looked
a thousand leagues away.

Forget them. Climb! her mind insisted. Boosted by anxiety and Graham's arms, she stretched for the first knot
above her head. With feet clamped around the rope, she
inched her way upward. Just as she reached the second
knot, a sharp insect-like buzz streaked past her ear.

She turned her head to look down. Another buzz grazed
her left ear, stinging her cheek.

Bothwell's men were shooting at her. She would die if
she didn't climb faster.

"Come, Lucina. You can do it," Graham encouraged her
from below. "You're too strong to give in to fear."

Did he really believe that? Or was it a convenient lie?

"This is the hardest part," he urged in a harsh whisper.
"Once we're down, you've only to ride like the wind, and
we both know you can outrace anyone who challenges
you."

Suddenly she believed him with all her heart. He believed in her strength, and she loved him for it. Emboldened by his encouragement and trust, she climbed, striving
for the next knot, then the next. Roger's face loomed above
her, backlit by the moon. He grasped her wrist and pulled
her onto the slanted roof of the east wing. All would be
well.

Except it was now Alex's turn.

Hand over hand, he advanced. *Come, my love,* she silently urged, wishing she could bring him to her side with
willpower alone.

"Damn." Graham stopped climbing.

"What's wrong?" she called softly.

His answer was drowned by the shooting and chaos
below. Had he been shot? Her heart thudded with fear as
she turned to Roger. "Help me pull him up."

Roger leaned over the parapet, grasped the rope, and
began to haul it up.

"Stop!" Graham commanded. "The rope is breaking."

"We'll let down Roger's rope." Lucina gestured wildly
to her brother. A bullet must have partially severed Graham's rope. One false move, one wrong shift of weight, and
it could snap, plunging him to the gallery roof below. The

noise would make him a certain target of archers, who were less likely to miss than the gunners.

Lucina scrambled to help Roger unhook his rope, loop the end around the crenellation, and pay it out to Graham. The new rope drew taut as he released his weight from the first.

"Pull, Roger," she urged her brother. Summoning all her strength, she hauled hard on the rope. Alex had to make it. He must.

The fighting below escalated, the sharp smell of gunpowder burning Lucina's nostrils. But between Graham's climbing and their hauling, they brought him over the roof edge. He sat on the slanted leads, breathing hard.

"Were you shot?" she whispered, running her hands over his chest, suppressing the cold fear that threatened to numb her insides.

"Only the rope."

He wasn't hurt, Lucina repeated. He was here beside her, in one piece. But they weren't to safety yet.

"The king said he and Drummond would cross to the north wing and go in a far window," Roger said, pointing. "They will descend the turnpike stair to be found there and come out on the north side of the palace where the stables are."

"Let's move, but stay low," Graham said. "We still make good targets from below." He rose to his feet and led the way.

The drop to the next window wasn't nearly as difficult as the climb to the roof. Lucina slid down Drummond's rope and clambered in the window with ease. Bothwell's men had not yet reached this side of the palace. Noise of the fighting had diminished. It seemed far away, like a bad dream, as they found the turnpike stair and exited into the cool night. The welcome scent of stables reached Lucina as they entered the torchlit yard. There was Orpheus, thank the stars, snorting and sidestepping, clearly disliking the strange groom holding his reins.

Leaving Graham and Roger, Lucina bolted across the yard. "Here I am, Orpheus. It's all right." She held out a hand to the groom. "He's my horse. You may give me the reins."

As she embraced the stallion, she noticed Drummond and the king nearby, both mounted, the king on Cygnus.

"How do you like my mare," she called. "Is she not everything we said?"

"She's indeed a beauty." James patted Cygnus's silky neck, and the mare pranced daintily, as if aware that she bore royalty. "But come, Lady Graham, we'd best be off." The king eyed the far end of the palace wing uneasily, as if fighting men would pour around its corner at any moment.

They might indeed, Lucina thought, motioning to her brother. "Roger is going to ride you, my friend," she told Orpheus, stroking his nose.

"You ride him, Luce. I've changed my mind." Roger headed toward the other long-legged English steed held by a groom. The horse should run almost as swiftly as Cygnus.

"You've changed your mind?" Lucina asked.

"Just let us be off," Graham snapped from Red Rowan's back. "We've no time to bicker over who will ride which animal." He slapped the reins against Red Rowan's neck and moved off.

Lucina hurriedly mounted Orpheus. A shout halted her. "Graham!"

A man raced toward them around the far end of the wing. As he drew closer, she realized someone pursued him. Someone armed.

"Graham, wait. Is that Jasper?" she cried. Why was he on foot?

"Go!" She heard Graham shout at the king, waving him away. "Roger, Drummond, accompany him. Go at once to Dunfermline."

The king wheeled Cygnus and raced for the woods to the north, Roger at his heels.

As Lucina turned back, Graham flashed past her on Red Rowan, heading for Jasper. Drummond, who had been closer, already raced toward the pair, angling to cut off the pursuer, whose flaming red hair gleamed in the torchlight.

Will! He brandished two silver dags as he ran.

Reaching his father before Graham, Drummond dove for him but caught empty air. Curling into a ball, he rolled and gained his feet, but by then the pair were within Graham's range.

Will raised one of the dags and leveled it at his chief.

"No!" Lucina shrieked as the gun's crash deafened her. The shot lifted and hurled Graham backward, slamming him to the ground. His head banged hard, and he lay still, the cloud of smoke dissipating in the night air.

With a growl of fury, Jasper leaped on Will. The two grappled and went down.

Lucina struggled down from Orpheus, who whinnied shrilly, frightened by the noise and the scent of blood. As she reached Alex, she saw Drummond, dirk drawn, hovering over Jasper and Will as they struggled on the ground. "Faither," the lad pleaded as they fought, "let him go. Please."

She couldn't listen. Her entire world fastened on Graham as she touched his shoulder, looking for signs of life. No movement. Nothing.

Frantic, she pulled at his limp body, turned him over, and felt for a pulse in his neck. Was he breathing? In her panic, she couldn't tell.

"Alex, please don't die. I love you. Please."

He groaned.

Could her prayers be answered? Tears poured down her face as she struggled to unhook the front of his jack but couldn't manage it, her hands shook so hard. Running her palms over his chest, she searched for the wound and found a hole in his jack the size of her thumb.

Frantic to see the wound, she fought the uncooperative hooks. The blood must be hidden by the thick jack.

She fought the hooks with all her strength. The jack opened, but she found no blood.

Puzzled, she yanked up his shirt and found the charmstone, lying on his unscathed chest, the ball from Will's dag buried in its depths.

Lucina's vision wavered with tears as she shook Graham by the shoulders. He was only stunned from his fall. He opened his eyes and stared at her, bewildered. "Lucina?"

She sobbed incoherently.

"Don't cry, sweet." He still sounded baffled. "I love you. Does that help?"

"Oh, yes. It helps," she wept into his shoulder. "I love you, Alex."

It took several minutes for him to stagger to his feet.

Once upright, he pulled her into his arms. "I thought I was a dead man."

"So did I," she wept. "So did I, but the charmstone . . . it is magic." She touched it, but he wasn't listening. He was looking at Drummond. Following his gaze, she saw the lad kneeling several feet away.

Supporting one another, they went to him. Blood was everywhere. Jasper and Will lay on the ground, locked in one another's embrace. A numbing misery spread through Lucina. "Are they both . . ."

Drummond buried his face in one hand. "Aye," he choked.

More tears filled Lucina's eyes and ran down her face as she saw the raw, gaping wound in Jasper's chest made by Will's dag at close range. Even as he had died, Jasper had managed to return Will's assault, his still hand gripping his dirk even in death. Will sprawled on his back, his throat cleanly cut from ear to ear.

Graham sank slowly to his knees, his fingers plucking at Jasper's clothes in a helpless gesture of denial. "This cannot be," he whispered.

"Alex, we must go." Aware that more attackers could pour around the corner at any moment, Lucina pulled at his arm to gain his attention. "Let us carry Jasper into the stables. We don't want him to lie here."

Alex beckoned to a groom who peered fearfully from the stable. Even in sorrow, the Graham was still the chief, Lucina thought as he took charge.

He and the groom lifted Jasper by the feet and shoulders and carried him into the building. Graham returned, took one look at Drummond, still kneeling by his father, shoulders shaking as he wept, and gestured to the groom. "This man as well. We'll be back for them both."

They rode to Dunfermline in total silence. Despite their day of travel, Orpheus, Cygnus, Red Rowan, and Drummond's mount carried them swiftly and surely by the light of the moon.

The citizenry of the town welcomed their sovereign and barricaded the gates against intruders. They were safe. They had rescued King James.

But the triumph brought Lucina no sleep that night.

Filled with pain, she sat at her chamber's window. Unable to bear it any longer, she rose and pulled a cloak around her shoulders.

"Lucina," Graham whispered in the dark. "Where are you going?"

"To the stables. Pray go back to sleep."

He caught up with her as she reached Orpheus's stall. Gripping her arm, he whirled her around. "I can't sleep any more than you can, damn it. Don't run from me."

"I'm not running."

"The hell you're not." He yanked her against him and kissed her roughly, brutalizing her lips with his own. "You're afraid," he muttered, breathing hard into her ear as he nipped her earlobe, her neck. "I've finally said the words you wanted to hear, and you're terrified. You're going to tell me why."

She turned her face away, her heart a swollen pain within her breast. "There's nothing to tell."

"There is. You know there is." He sounded savage. His hands pulled away her clothes as if he couldn't have her soon enough.

"In here, there's a fresh bed of straw." He half carried her into a nearby stall and closed the door behind them. Eagerly she reached for his shirt, suddenly mad for his loving. Only their passion could blot out the pain.

They spent little time on preliminaries. He pulled her on top of his thighs, and Lucina slid down on him, sheathing his passion. She couldn't get enough of him. She wanted to fly.

Save me, my love. Carry me with you, run like the wind and outdistance the pain. She rocked against him, seeking escape. With unflagging urgency they played the game of chase. Together they reached completion, sensation after sensation storming through Lucina as their mutual victory was achieved. But after the last shudders subsided and she had collapsed in his arms, tears choked her, and Alex held her to him, full of his own pain.

She had taught him to love her, but she couldn't stop the dying. How naive she had been, to think she could triumph. Instead she learned all too well that she had no power over life's greatest sorrow.

She had entered the netherworld and not found the light again. She wasn't sure she ever would.

Chapter 27

Sorrow followed Lucina as she accompanied Graham the next day to order the bodies of Jasper and Will embalmed, then select caskets. Throughout their tasks, Alex seemed sad but resigned. She couldn't think why he wasn't devastated by despair, but perhaps he only hid it well.

Whatever his feelings, he didn't share them with her as they prepared for their return journey and set off for Castle Graham. The bodies, he told her, would follow at a slower pace with suitable escort. They would hold the funerals at Lockerbie.

Lucina's homecoming to Castle Graham contained equal parts of joy and grief. Despite her exhaustion upon their arrival late in the day, she first visited Isabel. Shortly after, she marched from Isabel's chamber in a temper and sought Graham, who had retired to their tower room.

"I hear you're taking over the brass bath," Alex teased from behind a pile of papers at his worktable. He selected a stack of vellum and placed it in a wooden storage box on the floor.

Lucina would have remarked on his amazing decision to clear the clutter from his life, but she was too irate. "The bath is not for me. 'Tis for your aunt. Alex, we must dismiss Marie and Margaret at once." She slammed the chamber door and scowled. "Grissel must go as well. Since we left, your aunt has not had a bath, nor has she been permitted to wash. When I wanted to see her, Grissel tried to prevent me, saying madam was resting. Resting, indeed!" She shook her fist at an imaginary Grissel. "She kept me from Isabel because the poor woman was still in her night shift. Isabel told me she hadn't been out of it for two solid days. Nor had she been brought supper, and 'tis well past the supper hour. She looks too thin, Alex. I'm sure they didn't bring half her meals while we were gone."

Graham frowned as he sorted more papers into the wooden boxes. "I didn't tell you before, but Grissel lost her first and only bairn and so served as Will's wet nurse when he was born. We kept her on out of appreciation for her devotion. I have tried not to undermine her position in the castle, but you see how it has turned out. She selected Margaret and Marie."

"Well, they will be unselected," Lucina raged, swept away by her anger. "They're going, and you're to tell them of it, for they refuse to listen to me. To them, I am a lowly merchant's daughter, unworthy of their attention. Maggie Johnstone said she will gladly attend your aunt, and I know she'll be devoted. Bess, Elen, and I will spell her as required."

Graham nodded his approval, and Lucina calmed at having her decisions reinforced. "I don't mean we should turn Marie and Margaret out to starve. We'll find them other positions, or husbands if they prefer. Though what working-man would want them, I cannot think, they're so lazy. But they must go."

Alex nodded again, and Lucina sighed with relief. Of course Alex agreed with her. She had been foolish to think he would not. The poor man was probably glad to have her assume these duties. He'd had enough to see to with his men, his land, tenants, disagreement with neighbors, and raids. Little wonder he hadn't resolved the trouble. If he'd dismissed the women, he would have had to find others, and he hadn't had the time. "As for Grissel," she continued, "does she not have family she can live with?"

Graham squinted at some papers and shook his head. "We're her relations. She's been at Castle Graham since she was a child."

"Then, I will have to speak to her." Lucina folded her arms and imagined the sour-faced woman. And to think she'd been Will's wet nurse. Perhaps that was why he'd been impossible. "If she wants to stay here, she must answer to me from now on. When I tell her that, she may decide to live elsewhere."

Graham chuckled. "She may indeed."

Gratified to have his support, Lucina produced a rag rug and arranged it over the bloodstain before the hearth. Graham glanced at it, nodded, and continued to sort papers.

Exalted to know that the stain had lost its hold on her beloved, Lucina broached another delicate subject. "Alex, that chamber below us—'tis a perfectly good chamber. Might we not put it to use rather than leaving it empty all the time."

He looked up from his papers, his face grave. "Do you want it for yourself?"

She tried to guess if he disapproved of her plan but couldn't tell. "No, I would like it for a nursery, if I may. Elen can sleep there, and when our children are born—not that any are on the way yet," she added hastily, seeing his expression change, "but when we do have some, they can sleep there as well. I can leave the hidden panel open and hear them during the night. Do you approve?"

"That chamber has always belonged to the lady of the castle. It was used by Bonnie Mary, my mother, and my wife, in turn."

Lucina had suspected as much. "I understand. You would rather I didn't disturb the chamber. 'Tis no matter, I—"

"I didn't say that," he interrupted. "Disturb it all you wish. I'm tired of the cobwebs and the gloom."

Lucina wasn't sure he understood her intentions. "Are you sure? It won't be the same chamber at all when I'm done."

"I'm very sure," he said firmly. "Move out the furniture and have new made. Do anything you like and spare no expense. From the day you first came to Castle Graham, Lucina, I learned that your breed of disturbance is good for me. I believe some people call it change."

Not sure she'd heard right, she smiled tentatively, and he beckoned imperiously for her to come for a brief kiss.

Heartened by the progress they were making, she flew back below stairs, located Roger, and took him to Isabel's chamber. The old lady sat by the open window enjoying the breeze, dressed in a clean kirtle, smelling of sweet herb soap. Maggie was completing the arrangement of her

kertch. Upon seeing Lucina, Isabel rose, a welcoming smile
on her lips.

"Now that I'm fed and clean, I can greet ye in a more
fittin' manner. Bless ye, ma lamb." Isabel embraced her
warmly, kissing her on each cheek. "Ye've had yer trial
by fire an' coom through it unscathed. 'Tis good to have
ye back."

Lucina didn't feel unscathed, but she kissed Isabel, grateful for her love.

"An' our Alex fares well," Isabel continued, beaming.

"He's been to see you already? He didn't tell me," Lucina puzzled.

"Aye, he has." Isabel nodded vigorously. "An' he told
me he loved me. Ye've worked a miracle wi' ma sweet
gran'son. I canna thank ye enow."

Lucina was glad to hear this news but sorry Isabel was
calling Alex her grandson again. She had so hoped Isabel's
memory would be improved upon their return. Foolish
wish. Old age would claim them all in the end. Putting the
trouble aside, she brought Roger forward. "Isabel, I would
like you to meet my brother Roger. He came with me all
the way to Scotland and has endured great hardship for my
sake, but now he'll be staying with us for several
sennights."

Isabel smiled graciously at Roger and held out her hand.
" 'Tis charmed I am to call ye friend, Master Cavandish.
Ye ha' been through much since coomin' to our country.
We shall give ye the very best of care in the time ye choose
to remain wi' us."

As Roger took Isabel's hand and kissed her fingertips in
his most courtly manner, Lucina had a fleeting glimpse of
the stately hostess Isabel had been in her youth, welcoming
visitors to Castle Graham in her sister's absence. The pair
smiled at each other, and Lucina felt a glow of genuine
pleasure. Isabel and her brother would be friends.

But she felt no glow after Roger left and she prepared
to ask Isabel some probing questions.

"Isabel, do you remember this book?" Lucina showed
her Mary Maxwell's little diary.

Isabel inspected it. "Oh, aye. Ma sister were a scribbler
as a girl. She wrote doon everything she thought and did
in this little book."

Full of hope that she could prove her theory, Lucina took Lady Ashley's Bible from her pouch. "Do you remember this Bible?" Isabel nodded and patted the little book as if she were fond of it. "Why did you call it 'ours'?" Lucina asked.

"Did I do that?"

Lucina squinted at Isabel in frustration. "But you do remember it, do you not?"

"O' course I remember it. Ye brought it wi' ye tae Scotland."

Was Isabel playing games with her or was she really confused? If Isabel couldn't verify that the Bible had belonged to her sister Mary, she had no solid proof. "Isabel, please," Lucina pleaded, "tell me what really happened to your sister. Did she die?"

"Aye, she did. You said so yoursel'."

Lucina had to curb a shout. She was getting nowhere. Isabel was either wandering again or had sworn to keep the secret forever. Discouraged, Lucina moved to the next topic, one that would distress Isabel but had to be addressed.

"Isabel, I'm sorry to bear bad news, but Will Mosley and Jasper Graham are both dead. They were killed at Falklands Palace during an attempt on King James's life by the Earl of Bothwell." She would let Isabel decide which side Will had fought on, Lucina thought. She would not accuse the woman's grandson.

Isabel's face contorted with pain, her shoulders slumped. "I canna believe it. Jasper Graham was lang ma friend."

" 'Tis terrible but true. Their bodies are being brought from Dunfermline." Lucina moved her stool closer and embraced Isabel. "Alex intends to have a fine funeral befitting their places in the family and the love we bore them."

Tears rolled down Isabel's wrinkled cheeks and dropped onto her white smock. Lucina's eyes clouded. They wept for some time together, mourning Jasper's passing. "He died defending Alex," Lucina whispered, her throat tight with pain.

Isabel sobbed openly at this, but after a few minutes, she wiped her face on her handkerchief and tried to straighten on her stool. She couldn't quite manage it. Back bent with sorrow, she reached for Lucina's hand once more. "The foretelling has come true, ye ken."

Lucina carried Isabel's hand to her lips and kissed it. "What foretelling is that?"

"Years ago, by the gypsy woman." A sob burst from Isabel's lips, but she fought for control and mastered the impulse to break down again. "She told Jock's Janet and ma daughter Helen that one of their babes would be chief, the other would be mad an' die in shame."

So it had been foretold, Lucina thought. Sadly, she pulled the Dunlochy Charmstone from the pouch at her waist and hung it around Isabel's neck, hoping if it was so powerful, it would help her friend's memory and health. Isabel said nothing upon seeing it, but she did mutter something over and over that made no sense.

"I didna want to do it, but we did right. We did right in the end."

Lucina's reunion with Elen was as glad yet as heartrending as that with Isabel. The child flew into her arms, clearly relieved to see her mistress well and whole.

"Ye were no' hurt, m'leddy? Ye're sure ye're well?" the child asked anxiously.

"I've been through danger, but I'm well," Lucina assured her, smoothing Elen's wild red hair.

"I'm glad ye're back, because I have a secret to tell ye."

"I like secrets if they're pleasant."

"Well, ye'll like this ane." Elen seemed ready to burst with excitement. "The wee colt has befriended me, m'leddy. He coomes to me in the pasture and nuzzles me wi' his soft nose. I laugh because it tickles-like, and he does it more."

"That's an excellent surprise." Lucina smiled at Elen's pleasure. "But does Gellie mind you getting so close to her foal?"

"She dinna let any close save me." Elen threw back her shoulders with pride. "I've named the wee ane Red Hawk, because he's fierce with the stable men and lads, nipping them an' all. Do ye think the Graham will mind? Me namin' him, I mean?"

Mind? Lucina thought with a grin, he'll be furious to have his prize colt named by a mere slip of a female child.

But he would have to adjust. "I'm sure the name will stick, whatever the Graham thinks," she said aloud as she steeled herself for the next part of their discourse. Though she hated to extinguish the light of pleasure in Elen's eyes, she must tell her of her father's death. At the news, Elen paled and began to cry.

"He was a bad man, m-m'leddy," she stammered through her tears. "I dinna ken why I weep for him."

"You have a loyal heart, and he was your father," Lucina offered. The loss of both mother and father in so short a time was too painful to be borne by any child. Yet once again, death took the reins from her hands, leaving her helpless. " 'Tis your right to mourn him, as will Drummond and Madam Bess. All the Grahams will mourn with you."

"May I walk wi' Drummond and Madam Bess as one o' the chief mourners in the funeral?" Elen blurted as Lucina produced a handkerchief.

It was a mature idea for a child, Lucina realized with pride, to offer to honor her father in this way. "I will speak to the Graham," she assured Elen. " 'Tis right that you should have a place with your father's family."

Graham knew Lucina was telling Isabel and Elen the sad news. He had similarly sad duties to perform. He'd felt a burning need to start life afresh upon his return, to reorganize his belongings in keeping with the change in his heart. The papers had proved a good place to start.

The small measure of satisfaction brought by his half-clear worktable consoled him as he waited outside Bess Storie's chamber. Drummond was within, having gone to her the instant they arrived. Graham had purposely lingered in the tower, giving the lad time to tell of his father's fate however he wished. No aspersions would be cast on Will's name in death.

Deciding he had waited a decent interval, he tapped at the door. Bess Storie opened it, the red rims of her eyes and the handkerchief balled in one hand telling him how she'd taken the news. Pretending not to notice, he took the seat Bess offered across from Drummond.

"Despite the lack of my cousin's signature on the marriage documents," he explained to them, "the union is valid in the eyes of the church. You will both have an honored place here as long as the castle is held by Grahams."

Bess pressed the handkerchief to her mouth, trying to hold back sobs. But as Drummond encircled her shoulders with one arm, she buried her face in his shoulder and poured out her grief.

Graham felt for her. Though Will had never been good to Bess, she was apparently suffering because he was gone.

Drummond, on the other hand, gazed at his chief with stoic calm. As Graham met his gaze, as he gripped Drummond's hand in the handshake of peace, he sensed a new maturity in Drummond. The lad had suffered the torment of seeing his father kill and be killed. He had spent his tears at the Falklands, the last he would shed as a youth. Now his eyes were dry, and Graham knew Drummond was a different person than he'd been upon setting out. He was a man and would prove an asset to the Grahams.

Graham's next task was a talk with Arthur, though he'd hoped this one would be less painful. "Well, friend," he greeted his bailie in his workroom, "what did you learn?"

"The deed is as false as sham sil'er." Arthur held up Lucina's deed and slapped it with one hand. "This description of the location is the trouble—it dinna exist. 'Nae sooch place,' the lawyer told me."

Graham paced to the window, not uttering a word. He'd suspected this all along.

"What are ye gang to tell her?" Arthur looked anxious. "I dinna wish . . . that is, none o' us wish tae see her hurt. Ye ken Jasper had a soft spot in his heart for her. In the name o' his memory, would ye consider—"

Graham shot him an indignant glance, and Arthur snapped his mouth shut. "I am not going to tell her the deed is false," Graham said tightly. "You have no reason to think that I would be so hard-hearted that you must plead in Jasper's name." His voice caught, and he stopped as his throat tightened. The mere mention of Jasper's name took him to the edge of tears.

Arthur looked vastly relieved to hear of Graham's decision. He fanned himself with the deed. "I'm verra pleased to hear it, Graham. But what, might I ask, will you tell her leddyship aboot her land if ye dinna tell her the deed is false?"

"I'll give her that piece of land I own to the northwest. The large pasture with the upland meadow will be her gift from Lady Katherine Ashley." It would really be his marriage gift to Lucina, but she would never know, and he didn't want her to. He would never hurt her with the knowledge that she had been sent to Scotland for nothing.

Arthur's mouth spread in a grin of delight. "A fine idea, that. But, Graham, do ye think . . ."

"Go on, man. Speak," Graham growled, wondering what Arthur would plague him with next.

"Do you think 'tis possible, this woman, Lady Katherine Ashley, were really our Bonnie Mary Maxwell?"

"Good God, has her ladyship told everyone in the castle her insane idea?"

"I suppose that means you dinna believe it." Arthur seemed unaffected by his chief's indignation. "But it could be true, ye ken. The handwriting looks similar."

"But we have no more than that to go on," Graham pointed out. It was no use getting your hopes up unless you had proof.

Lucina still didn't know for certain if Mary Katherine Maxwell and Katherine Ashley were the same person, but she intended to find out. The next day, after seeing Marie and Margaret on their way to Lockerbie, she began preparations for a celebration feast. Sitting at Graham's now meticulously clean worktable, she carefully penned invitations to numerous neighbors. Among them was John, Lord Maxwell.

"Lucina, what earthly excuse can you conjure for inviting that man here?" Graham complained as she wrote. "Have you forgotten? We have a blood feud."

"Had a feud." She dipped her quill and continued writing. "Based on misinformation. 'Tis time for it to end."

"He won't accept," he warned.

"I think he will when he reads my letter." With studied effort, she avoided glancing at the Dunlochy Charmstone, which lay in a black velvet box at the corner of his worktable. But she knew he'd guessed her plan. She would lure Maxwell to them with hints that the long-lost stone had been found.

"Lucina."

Graham's voice, husky with emotion, interrupted Lucina's daydreams of mending breaches between feuding families. She met his gaze, which roved over her body as tangible as a physical touch. His message was clear. She closed her eyes, but the tingling in her breasts spiraled down to her belly, settling between her legs. Sensation shot through her in response—need, desire . . . mixed with guilt. She didn't deserve to enjoy passion with him. She had opened him up to feelings, and now he would be hurt again and again.

"I have invitations to write." She knew it was a lame excuse.

"The devil with the invitations." He stepped to the table, took away her quill, and pulled her to her feet. "I want you to come here."

"Oh, Alex." Miserable, she leaned against him, her ardor quelled.

"What is it, Lucina? You wouldn't tell me at Dunfermline, but I insist you explain." He seemed genuinely hurt. "You want me to make love to you, but you won't allow it. Why?"

She felt her face crumple and hid it against his chest. "I'm sorry you've wed such a fool."

"You're not a fool. If you were, 'twould speak poorly of my taste," he teased gently. But he didn't press her to explain, only held her, rubbing her back in firm, calming strokes until she chose to speak.

"I-I thought I could make our lives perfect," she said, humiliated to admit it. "I was wrong."

"I don't expect perfection. Nor should you. I am content as we are." The pleasant pressure of his hand on her back continued, but she sensed his puzzlement.

The painful knowledge that death would always haunt them pressed in on her. She didn't know if she could explain without breaking into more embarrassing tears, but she must try. One word might tell him. "Jasper," she whispered very low.

He seemed to understand at once. "You believe you failed me because he died?"

She nodded, expecting him to deny it though they both knew it was true. She *had* failed.

"You forget that if Jasper hadn't died, I would have," he said.

She lifted her head. "You're wrong. The charmstone would have saved you."

"Would it? Will had another dag with a second charge. What were the chances of the charmstone taking two shots in a row?" The pointed look in his blue eyes tempted her to believe. "Jasper chose to stop Will to spare me," he continued, "as I would have done for him, given the chance. The charmstone had nothing to do with it."

His explanation was eminently sensible, yet Lucina doubted it. "You might be correct about the charmstone," she admitted, "but how can you possibly be happy as long as there is . . . death." There. She had said it. It would stand between them and perhaps part them while they were still young. She could live with it. When she accepted him as her husband and the Border as her home, she had accepted the possibility that she, he, or others she loved might die before they reached old age. Though she would never stop fighting for peace.

"Lucina." He seemed to know just what she was thinking, for his voice was husky with loving reproach. "We're all going to die one day. But before I met you, I thought of nothing else. Those I had lost and those I was about to lose haunted me every moment of the day. You've changed that. You've given me strength and wonderful things to live for. Together we'll raise horses and work for peace on the Border. And someday, please God, our children or our grandchildren will live without fearing death by a reiver's hand."

His words stunned her so, she couldn't quite believe them. "Do you truly mean that? You're sure? You don't hate me for making you . . . feel things again?"

He laughed softly. "I don't hate you. I love you, Lady Selkie, with your violet eyes and your midnight birth. Get that into your head and keep it there."

His words sent exhilaration roaring through her mind. He loved her. He finally recognized the feeling and said the words. She could scarcely believe her good fortune. People seldom changed when you wanted them to, or if they did, not necessarily in the way you had hoped. Yet he said his love for her helped him bear anything. Slipping her arms around his middle, she hugged him hard, then drew back to gaze into his eyes. "Alex, you make me happier than I can say. I love you with all my heart."

He stroked her cheek with his thumb. "As I love you. And to show my love, we're going to see your land on the morrow."

"You know where it is?" she asked in delight.

"I do indeed." Graham grinned at the pressure of her breasts against his chest and was glad as well. At last they could satisfy the needs of the flesh without the troublesome worries of the mind to interfere. And he wanted no interference when he showed Lucina how he loved her. Not from clothing, intruding servants, or missing land. He'd almost died before he'd realized he had to risk everything and feel again. And he was infinitely grateful she'd inspired him to take the chance.

Even now his selkie was inspiring him by pulling off her shift and tossing it aside. Standing before him, proudly naked, she reached for the button on his trunkhose. Which moved him to strip off his own clothes and lead her to the bed.

Her beauty inspired him to touch her everywhere, with his mouth, with his hands. Her firm young breasts and erect nipples begged to be stroked with fingers and tongue. The slick, welcoming place between her legs was ready for him as well. With a breath of wonder, he gave in to the joy he had discovered with his firebrand bride.

Friction. Feeling. Body and soul made one. As they raced together toward fulfillment, toward the ultimate moment that celebrated feeling, he made a vow. He would keep their love alive for all time.

Chapter 28

Lucina waited impatiently for the night of her feast to arrive. She wanted to end the Maxwell-Graham feud once and for all. But on the appointed night, as she sat at the high table to Graham's right, before the picture tapestries worked by his mother and grandmothers with bright red and yellow silks and wool, she had to contain her disappointment. Maxwell had not come.

She tried to be cheerful for the others' sake. Soon enough they would don their black for the double funeral. They might as well enjoy the celebration welcoming their chief home.

Isabel had especially seemed to enjoy the gaiety, smiling and chatting with friends and tenants all around. It was as if a blight had lifted from her life now that Marie and Margaret were gone.

Maggie was the perfect companion, watching her mistress attentively, always there when required. As the evening had worn on and Isabel had wilted like a tired flower, Maggie had seen her to bed, returning later to say that madam had fallen asleep. Now Maggie might dance with her cousin Colin, as Isabel had said she should.

Lucina watched the dancing, fed Elen too many sweetmeats, and tried not to brood on the charmstone sitting in its black velvet box near her left hand. She wished Maxwell hadn't been so stubborn, refusing to come, but it was his decision. Now how would they return the stone? As she considered the problem, a stir at the entry captured her attention.

Arthur bolted to the dais and stopped before Graham,

looking flustered. "John, Lord Maxwell, is come to join the feast."

"Show him in at once," Graham ordered with more heartiness than Lucina guessed he felt. Sitting down to sup with a man who'd tried to kill him couldn't be pleasant.

Just another sign of how much Alex had changed, she thought. Relieved to know Maxwell had come, she stood too quickly and bumped her calves on the bench. But the bruise meant nothing if Maxwell's arrival signified that he wasn't so stubborn after all. Perhaps she could persuade him to agree to share the charmstone.

The multitude parted in stunned silence as Maxwell entered the hall and strode toward the dais. He was dressed all in black and looked grim, but Lucina noted he'd chosen velvet and satin, probably some of the very garments she'd searched that day for the key. He went directly to Graham and saluted him.

"Graham. M'leddy." His face was florid, as if the ride over had been too much exertion. "I will no' interrupt yer feastin' for mare than a moment. I have but twa things to say."

"That's a good deal to say on an empty stomach, Lord Maxwell." Lucina stepped around Graham to show Maxwell the empty seat saved for him. "Pray be seated first. We are pleased to have you as our guest." She would show him she held no grudge for his holding her captive, or for trying to kill her husband, since he'd failed. She also needed to work on his sympathies before she showed him the charmstone.

"I canna stay." He cast Graham a wary glance as he refused, but then seemed to think better of refusing so abruptly. "I thank ye, Leddy Graham, for your courtesy o' invitin' me an' ma kin to yer home." He spoke so stiffly, it seemed certain he chaffed at the idea of thanking a Graham for anything. "But I'm told Will Mosley was killed by a Graham. Now that we ken 'twas Mosley as despoiled ma cousin, that's one wrong revenged." He locked his gaze on Lucina. "Ye write o' settling the score over Bonnie Mary an' endin' the feud. Tell me, Leddy Graham, how do ye propose to do that?"

Lucina reached for the velvet box, dread running through her. This wasn't going the way she'd hoped. Without a

proper chance to ply him with wine and charm him into a
good humor, she couldn't just show him the stolen gem.
He would be furious.

The hall was dead silent, and Lucina imagined the servants, men-at-arms, tenants, Grahams, Langs, Mosleys, and
Stories all holding their breaths, waiting to see how she
would accomplish the impossible. And she wasn't sure she
could. Not like this.

The only one moving was Grissel, with whom Lucina had
had a most unpleasant set-to earlier. Lucina had demoted
her to taking orders the same as the other serving women.
As a result, Grissel had freely voiced her doubt that her
ladyship's plan would succeed. As Lucina swallowed and
tried to think of what to say to Maxwell, she saw Grissel
leave the hall, showing a rebellious lack of interest in their
guest. Turning in the direction of the tower, she disappeared. Probably going to check on Isabel, though it wasn't
her duty anymore.

Maxwell cleared his throat impatiently. "I am waiting,
Leddy Graham. Kindly—"

A piercing scream interrupted him. Grissel raced into the
hall, her face ashen and contorted with terror. " 'Tis the
ghost o' Bonnie Mary! She's oot in the passage. I tell ye,
she's there."

A child wailed. A woman fainted, and others screamed.
Several urged their menfolk to look, but no one moved
toward the screens passage. Rolling his eyes in what Lucina
took to be disgust, Graham stepped off the dais, clearly
intending to investigate.

"There is no ghost." Lucina was infuriated that the imaginary ghost once more intruded into her life. She'd wanted
her confrontation with Maxwell interrupted, but not this
way. "Someone calm Grissel," she ordered, stalking after
Graham. "I'm going to prove to you all that the ghost
doesn't exist."

As she swept across the hall, skirts churning, Lucina
sensed Bess Storie at her heels. Good, she would have Graham and Bess as witnesses when she proved nothing was
there. At the entrance to the tower passage, she dodged
quickly around Graham, wanting to be the first to confront
the ghost.

Just as Grissel had said, at the far end of the pitch-black

passage, a snatch of white showed. Lucina's stomach fluttered in response, but she refused to give in to it. She stalked determinedly down the passage. "Bring lights, please," she ordered over her shoulder to Graham and Bess.

Lucina had expected the fluttering white to disappear once confronted. Oddly enough, as she drew closer, it appeared more solid. In fact, it looked so solid, she would swear it was . . .

Stretching out one hand, Lucina grasped the ghost. Her fingers closed on warm flesh.

"Isabel?" she asked in disbelief. "Are you not well? What are you doing in the passage?"

Isabel stared at her blankly, then down at her white night smock with its long, wide sleeves that fluttered in the draft of the passage. "I-I dinna ken. I dreamed there was a fire and I had to leave ma chamber." Isabel blinked in confusion as lights flared.

Graham and Bess approached bearing candles. Behind them, men and women crowded into the passage, as eager as if they were going to the theater, Lucina thought in annoyance. Though none of them had dared to confront the specter themselves, they were happy to let her take the risk.

But her first concern was for Isabel. "Pray fetch a stool for madam." She motioned to Drummond, who had edged in behind Graham.

Drummond obeyed, pushing open Isabel's chamber door and retrieving a stool. Isabel sank onto it, looking dazed.

" 'Tis all right now. You're going to be fine," Lucina soothed her before facing the crowd. "*This* is the ghost of Castle Graham," she said in indignation. If they wanted a drama, they were going to get one, along with a stern reprimand. "You've terrified children and adults alike with the story of a ghost, as well as fueled a feud, and the three or four times it was seen, 'twas no more than Isabel Maxwell, walking in her sleep. If she'd been better attended, this would never have happened."

Everyone babbled in excitement at her pronouncement. No, they hadn't known Isabel walked in her sleep. But she and her white night smock could well have been what a lone, frightened servant without a light had seen in three or four different parts of the castle over the years.

Maxwell elbowed his way through the throng. "Where is ma great-aunt?" he demanded. "I wish to question her mysel'." He stopped before Isabel and examined her skeptically. "Was it really ye, a-walkin' in yer sleep, an' not yer sister's ghost?"

Isabel blinked up at him, as if trying to decide who he was, so Lucina answered for her. "Of course it was. Everyone here knows Madam Isabel often doesn't sleep well. By morning, she looks as if she's been up half the night. Now we know that at times she was."

Maxwell snorted. "That doesna bring back Bonnie Mary. We still have the feud."

"Would you like to end it?" Lucina demanded. Before all these witnesses, she would have him say he would.

He hesitated, as if suspecting a trick. "I'm an auld man," he said at last. "I'd like to see ma grandchildren grow up in peace."

Now was her moment. Lucina retrieved the Bible from her pouch, along with Mary's diary. "I have reason to believe that Mary Katherine Maxwell did not die, but ran away from Castle Graham. She crossed the Border and there met and wed an English knight named Oliver Ashley, who took her to his home in Dorset. She lived out her life a happily married woman, calling herself Katherine Ashley. I met her after she'd been widowed and was her companion until her death. Here's proof of what I say." She opened the little Bible. "This book was given to me by Lady Ashley before her death. I brought it with me to Scotland. This other book"—she opened the diary—"I found in Mary's old chamber at Caerlaverock. The diary contains a saying, 'Love has no law.' Lady Ashley taught me that saying because it was her favorite. And if you examine the signatures, you'll see the formation of the letters is similar."

Maxwell bent over the two books, rubbing his chin. "Similar, boot no' identical. 'Tis hardly proof."

"But you recognized the Bible," Lucina pointed out eagerly. "When I showed it to you at Caerlaverock, you said it was your great-aunt's. You must have seen it as a lad."

"Many books look alike."

"There is proof, though, Johnnie Maxwell," Isabel said in a low voice.

"Where?" He rounded on her, looking angry at being contradicted.

"Let her explain what she means," Graham interrupted, stepping forward to support his kinswoman. "Pray continue, Aunt Isabel," he urged.

"If ye look at the first page o' the Bible, ye'll see 'tis thicker than the others," Isabel said in a stronger voice. "They've been glued together around the edge. Cut them apart."

Lucina turned to the page, knowing it had always felt thicker than the others. Closer examination verified that it could conceivably be two pages, stuck together. She fiddled with the gilt edges, trying to separate them.

"Let me use my dirk," Graham offered. As Lucina held the tiny book, he slipped the sharp blade between the pages and sliced them neatly at the top. He repeated the process at the bottom of the pages.

Lucina peeled the two apart. Two neatly flowing signatures were scrawled across the inside, right-hand page. *Mary Katherine Maxwell* and *Isabel Margaret Maxwell.* Thrilled with the find, Lucina held up the Bible for all to see.

"So the Bible belonged to the Maxwells," Maxwell blustered above the excited babble of voices. "How would Mary ha'e left Castle Graham. Someane would ha' known if she dinna die."

"I knew, Johnnie Maxwell," Isabel interrupted. "An' I'll tell ye how she left, if someone will help me tae stand."

Everyone hushed at Isabel's unexpected speech. Graham assisted his great-aunt to her feet. Maxwell stared at her skeptically.

"Great-Aunt Isabel, ye dinna ken who people are half the time," he said in a condescending tone. "And we mun listen to ye?"

Isabel plainly didn't like his tone, for she rallied, giving him a haughty stare. "No' completely mad, Johnnie, ma lad, and I'll put ye over ma knee, same as I did when you were a bairn, do ye contradict me."

Her sudden, fierce outbreak, so unlike her previous man-

ner, quelled Maxwell. He shrank back, as if he were a bairn
again, in danger of a whipping at his great-aunt's hands.

Lucina wanted to laugh aloud at the cowed expression
on the man's face but managed to suppressed the urge.
"Aunt Isabel, pray tell us what happened." This was clearly
one of Isabel's more lucid moments, for which Lucina
praised the stars above.

"Weel, mad Angus Graham beat ma sister so," Isabel
began, "she couldna rise from her bed for two solid days.
'Twas then I decide 'twas enow. I urged Mary, nay, I
begged her to leave. So one night she dressed as a servin'
lassie and slipped away to England wi' a load o' corn to
be sold. I told everyone she'd died o' contagious fever so
she werena shown. Aye, an' I kept silent all these years so
she could live in peace once she found a new husband, an'
nae be beaten to death by that monster." As she finished
the speech, she clung to Graham for support, her expression defiant and her head up, as if daring them to say she
lied.

The crowd in the passage gasped at her confession. A
buzz of speculation broke out. But Maxwell alone seemed
unwilling to accept Isabel's claim. "Silence," he shouted.
"There's more to hear, I trow." The crowd quieted. "Who's
that a-lying in the kirkyard, then," he demanded, "if 'tis
not ma Great-Aunt Mary?"

Isabel's pale lips raised in a ghost of a smile. "A poor
milkmaid from Lockerbie who died o' the pox. It took a
deal o' doin' to smuggle her body into the castle, but I
managed. As she werena shown in the casket, no one knew
save her poor auld mither and faither, who died not long
after." As she finished, she swayed on her feet, as if telling
the story had been too much for her. "Lucina," she murmured as Graham supported her, "tell him aboot the
stone."

Lucina felt every eye riveted on her. She puzzled over
why Isabel hadn't seemed to notice the stone when she'd
brought it to her daily, hoping it would strengthen her.
Nevertheless, she was right. Now was the moment. Opening
the velvet box, she held the charmstone aloft for all to see.

Maxwell's dark eyes bulged with fury as he saw it. Others
gasped as the crystal swung, catching and reflecting the light
like a star.

"The Dunlochy Charmstone," Grissel cried, pushing through the press. "Where did ye find it? Give it tae me."

" 'Twas never yers, Grissel. Ye're the thief who took it from Mary while she lay a-bed, too weak tae move." Isabel held Grissel away from the stone with a firmness that amazed Lucina. "Ye kept it 'til I learnt ye had it an' I claimed it from ye so 'twould be used for good works."

Grissel scowled fiercely at Isabel but did not contradict her, confirming the truth of the accusation.

Maxwell looked fit to have a seizure, his face had grown so red. "Whatever happened, the charmstone is stolen Maxwell property," he hissed, gesturing for Lucina to give it to him. "An' ye stole Mary's diary as well, after I locked it up, Leddy Graham."

"You are correct about the diary. You may have it back." Lucina extended it to him with a gracious smile. Though her head spun with the rapid revelation of past events, she wouldn't give him the stone. "In exchange, I want my letter back, the one you forced me to write saying I would sell you my land."

Instead of accepting the book, Maxwell suddenly lunged at her and grabbed the stone, shoving her against the wall. Lucina stumbled to her knees as Maxwell prepared to shoulder his way through the gathering.

Graham, Arthur, and Drummond sprang to block his passage, dirks drawn.

Maxwell whipped out his own dirk and crouched, prepared to fight.

"You must not fight over the charmstone." Lucina's worst nightmare was coming true. The feud would continue under her own roof, before her very eyes.

"Hold, Johnnie Archibald Bell-the-Cat Maxwell." For the third time that night, Isabel spoke, her voice ringing with authority. Standing alone now, she drew herself up imperiously. "Ye're gang nowhere wi' that stone, and ye ken why, so stop playin' wi' us like the cat wi' a mouse."

Maxwell rose from his crouch and stared at her in surprise. Graham took a protective stance beside his great-aunt. "Speak, Isabel," he bid her.

"The stone mun be used for the good of all, Johnnie," Isabel said. "Ye ken our Mary used it in her healing. Any Borderer wi' a need had only to ask."

"Mary is dead. The stone reverts to the Maxwell family." He stood immobile, unwilling to give in.

"I'm a Maxwell, laddie. *I* claim it, for I was the one who wielded its healing power all those years when 'twas thought to be lost. Aye, I kept it secret"—she flashed at Maxwell as he started to protest—"because I knew when yer father became chief, he would keep it locked oop, doin' no good to anyone. I kent how to use it, and now 'tis found, I will again." She gazed into his face and took a step closer. "Who do ye think healed yer wife, Johnnie, when she had the milk fever after the birth o' yer heir?"

"You?" His eyes glittered with what looked like sudden tears as he gazed at her. "You were the crone she babbled of, who came in secret and healed her with a magic spell?"

"Aye, an' she lived. I would ha' saved her in her last illness as well, for I loved her as ye did, boot the stone had disappeared again. Now I know 'twas taken by Will Mosley."

Lucina looked at the collected faces and saw astonishment on every one. They were all as amazed as she by Isabel's revelations.

Maxwell seemed not only amazed but deeply touched by the news that Isabel was the one who had healed his wife. "Ye gave me those years wi' ma Anna. For that, ye mun ha'e the stone." With ponderous movements he sorted out the chain and placed the charmstone around her neck.

The crystal seemed to grow brighter. Isabel straightened her back, and as it gleamed against her breast, she looked as regal as a queen. The stone was strengthening her friend. Lucina felt a happiness so powerful, she wanted to weep. She slipped over to Graham and nestled in his arms.

Maxwell's mouth twisted in an odd, half smile. "Ye're no longer young, Isabel," he said. "Who's to gang aboot healin' if I let ye keep the stone?"

"I'll teach another to do it," Isabel said with confidence. "Elizabeth Storie." She held out a hand to Bess, who stepped forward to take it, looking stunned.

"Boot she's no' a Maxwell," Maxwell protested, "nor even descended o' one."

"She wed the man who was Bonnie Mary's grandson," Isabel corrected. "The man who would ha' been chief o' the Grahams."

"What are ye talking aboot?" Maxwell barked, ruffled again.

"I'm a-talkin' aboot how John Alexander Malcolm Graham and Will Mosley were changed at birth, on account o' the madness o' the one we called Will," Isabel explained, fingering the charmstone with one hand. "The gypsy fortune-teller told Jock's Janet and ma daughter Helen that they dared no' let Will grow up to be chief. Grissel, do I speak the truth?"

" 'Tis true," Grissel said sullenly, as if angry to have to confirm anything Isabel said.

Isabel laughed lightly. "Dinna sulk, Grissel. If ye can find yer former lightness o' heart, there will soon be many Graham bairns at Castle Graham needin' yer care."

Grissel brightened visibly and fell back among the others.

Graham stepped forward to take her place before Isabel, looking as if he'd just been moonstruck. "Do you mean to say that Helen Mosley was my mother? That I'm not even entitled to be the Graham chief?"

"O' course yer chief," Isabel said. "The strong lead on the Border, and who do ye ken would ha' had the place once Will died?" She nodded with satisfaction, giving all present a minute to realize that once the direct line of Angus Graham failed, it would be carried on by the children of his younger brother Gavin, who had married Isabel. "O' course, I dinna count on ye making Drummond legitimate," she added. "Though I'm glad ye did, ye mun work oot that little detail wi' him. Boot since ye were the one who gave him his place . . ."

"I would never expect to take your place, Graham." Drummond stepped from the crowd and knelt before Graham. "Ye're ma chief first and last, and I'll swear the oath to serve ye again if ye like, for ye gave me a place in the family when ye had nae reason to care if I lived or died."

"I do care, Drummond, as if you were my own son." Graham touched the lad's shoulder to indicate he should rise. The two embraced.

Then Graham turned to take Isabel in his arms. "Then you are my grandmother by blood and always have been. No wonder you were more mother to me than Jock's Janet. No wonder you took me under your wing as a lad after Aunt Helen—that is, my mother—died."

"I dinna want to change ye with Will as a bairn," Isabel said tearfully, "boot I kent 'twas for the best." Looking over Graham's shoulder, she stretched out a hand to Lucina. "Coom, Lucina, mend the feud, as yer friend Katherine Ashley, born Mary Katherine Maxwell, meant ye to do."

Lucina took her hand hesitantly, puzzled by her words. "I don't understand. Lady Ashley, that is, Mary, willed me a piece of land because she knew it was my heart's desire. I came to Scotland for that reason alone."

"There is no land, ma lamb," Isabel said gently, drawing Lucina into the embrace she shared with Graham. "In forsaking the person she'd been in her past life, ma sister couldna legally take a piece o' land wi' her. Trust me, she thought so weel o' yer brave heart, she sent ye tae mend the feud."

Speechless, Lucina stared at Isabel, then turned to Graham. "But my land, my beautiful piece of land . . . Alex . . . does that mean it's . . ."

"My bride gift to you," he said quietly. "I never meant you to know, but intended to make your ownership legal as soon as I could."

Lucina flung both arms around him and half smothered him with kisses. Then she took his hand and, capturing Maxwell's, joined them before all present.

"Ma grandson an' ma great-nephew, descended o' ma brither," Isabel pronounced. "Mend the feud, ye two, in the name o' Bonnie Mary, who couldna rest in her grave in peace, but sent us our lovely Lucina to right the wrong."

The men shook solemnly, both clearly moved, and a cheer burst from the crowd. Then Arthur stepped forward to shake hands with Maxwell, followed by Colin Johnstone, followed by one after another of the Graham family, all exultant to know the feud was at an end. Old Maxwell's face was redder than ever, but now it was from excitement. His rage was spent.

Lucina took advantage of the hubbub to pull Alex into a quiet corner and kiss him. "Alex, were you truly going to keep it secret that my deed was false, because you knew it would break my heart?" she asked.

"I had meant to keep it quiet to the death," he swore

with feeling in his voice, "because I love you, Lucina Cavandish, my firebrand bride."

"And I love you," she whispered, looking deeply into his bonnie blue eyes that were the color of the Scots bluebell. And her heart filled with happiness as she realized that her hope for peace in Alex's future really was coming true, beginning with a new understanding between the Grahams and the Maxwells. That mayhap death by reiving and feud would no longer haunt them, and that they would live in peace along the Border, raising their children and their magical steeds bred from Cygnus and Orpheus, and building a legacy of love. In truth, Isabel had spoken rightly. Her journey to Scotland had been no fool's errand, but a journey to find the love of her life.

Historical Note

The history books tell us that the Earl of Bothwell raided the Palace of Falklands in 1592, but whether he meant to take King James prisoner or assassinate him, we'll never know. The official guide to the palace, prepared for the National Trust for Scotland, says the flanking towers of the gatehouse are still peppered with holes, probably left by the Bothwell force's bullets. They distracted the main guard while Bothwell tried to force the postern door in the east wing cross-house to reach his royal cousin in his bedchamber above. It was also from this guide to the palace that I learned of the now nonexistent gallery walks along the east wing onto which my Graham chief leads his friends in their escape. King James is said to have been warned of Bothwell's coming in time to leave the palace in safety. As in the first three books of my Cavandish family adventure series, I augmented history by assigning a woman to bring James the news of the coming attack. I call my stories "history with a woman's touch," since the details surrounding the attempt on King James are every bit as historically accurate as I could make them.

With regard to the family systems on the Scots Border in 1592, John, eighth Lord Maxwell, really was the chief of a major family power in the Scots West Border March, although I borrowed the nickname Bell the Cat from another man and another year. Maxwell was in power for years as the Border warden until he was outlawed. One of the Border families with whom he battled for power was the Johnstones. I assigned the name Graham to the hero's family, however, since the Black Graham is a more romantic sounding hero than the Black Johnstone. Devil's Gully, where Graham first sees Lucina, was inspired by a real gully called the Devil's Beef Tub.

My depiction of the Dunlochy Charmstone was also inspired by history. I learned about crystal charmstones and the Scots' belief in their healing powers from a wonderful book called *The Art of Jewellery in Scotland,* put out by the Scottish National Portrait Gallery. In this book, edited by Rosalind K. Marshall and George R. Dalgleish, you can see a photograph of the round, silver-bound crystal I used as a model for the Dunlochy Charmstone. It was this brief narrative and the pictures of existing stones that inspired me to have Isabel use the charmstone to cure others and, in turn, to be strengthened by it in her advancing years.

Finally, *Firebrand Bride* addresses the social issue of elder abuse, as depicted in the poor treatment received by Isabel from the servants assigned to her. Today, we hear so often that the ancients of our culture are misused as they advance in age. For this reason, in each of my stories, I give my hero or heroine a well-loved and respected older mentor. Granted, we don't all have the ready access to servants to assist us in caring for our aging relatives, as Lucina did in *Firebrand Bride,* nor do we have "miracle charms" that can magically restore lost strength or lucidity, as the Dunlochy Charmstone did for Isabel. My purpose was primarily to remind us to stop abuse where we can and to treasure our elders, who hold the wisdom of the years in their hearts and minds.

If you enjoyed *Firebrand Bride,* do write to me at PO Box 21904, Columbus, Ohio 43221 to let me know. I love to hear from readers and will send you a free newsletter in return. Self-addressed, stamped envelopes (SASEs) are always appreciated.

Glossary

aboot=about
ain=own
alang=along
ane=one
auld=old
bairn=baby
boot=but
brawly=comely, attractive
brither=brother
brock=badger (a bad person)
canna=cannot
coom/coomes=come(s)
coz=cousin
dag=a heavy pistol
dinna=didn't
doon=down
enow=enough
faither=father
for certes=for certain
fram=from
gaisling=gosling
gang=go/going
glaiver=babble foolishly
god'den=good evening
gude=good
hasna=hasn't
ken/kent=know/knew
kertch=kerchief
mare or mair=more

ma=my
mither=mother
mooch=much
muckle mou=big mouth
mun=must
nae=no
naething=nothing
ne'er=never
no'=not
oop=up
oot=out
puir=poor
sen'night=seven night
someane=someone
sa=so
sare=sore
selkie=fairy
skelp=to whip or beat
sooch=such
someit=something
tae=to
twa=two
verra=very
weel=well
wouldna=wouldn't

TOPAZ

□LAIRD OF THE WIND   0-451-40768-7/$5.99

In medieval Scotland, the warrior known as Border Hawk seizes the castle belonging to the father of the beautiful Isabel Scott, famous throughout the Lowlands for her gift of prophecy. During the battle, Isabel is injured while fighting alongside her men and placed under Border Hawk's protection. As the border wars rage on, the warrior and prophetess engage in a more intimate conflict, discovering their love for the Scottish borderlands is surpassed only by their love for each other.

Also available:
□THE ANGEL KNIGHT   0-451-40662-1/$5.50
□LADY MIRACLE   0-451-40766-0/$5.99
□THE RAVEN'S MOON   0-451-18868-3/$5.99
□THE RAVEN'S WISH   0-451-40545-5/$4.99

Coming in April 1999 THE HEATHER MOON
□0-451-40774-1/$6.99

Prices slightly higher in Canada